FLASHPOINT

Other titles by Suzanne Brockmann

HEARTTHROB
BODYGUARD
THE UNSUNG HERO   Tom + Kelly
THE DEFIANT HERO   mej + John
OVER THE EDGE   Teri + Stan
OUT OF CONTROL   savannah + Wild Kard
INTO THE NIGHT   Joan + mike
GONE TOO FAR   sam + Alyssa   FR
HOT TARGET   Cosmo + Jane
BREAKING POINT   max + Gina
INTO THE STORM   Jenkins + Lindsey
FORCE OF NATURE   Ric + Annie
ALL THROUGH THE NIGHT   Jules + Robin
INTO THE FIRE - murphy + Hannah
DARK OF NIGHT - Decker?

SUZANNE BROCKMANN

FLASHPOINT

BALLANTINE BOOKS • NEW YORK

For Ed and Eric
and all the laughter that's yet to come

A Ballantine Book
Published by The Random House Publishing Group

Published in the United States by Ballantine Books, an imprint of The Random House Publishing Group, a division of Random House, Inc., New York, and simultaneously in Canada by Random House of Canada Limited, Toronto.

www.ballantinebooks.com

ISBN 0-345-45694-7

Manufactured in the United States of America

First Hardcover Edition: April 2004
First Mass Market Edition: November 2004

OPM   9   8   7

ACKNOWLEDGMENTS

THANK YOU to the usual suspects: Ed Gaffney, Eric Ruben, Deede Bergeron, Pat White, and Lee Brockmann. Thanks also—and always—to Steve Axelrod, who is a different kind of agent than are Decker and Nash, but a super one just the same.

A giant, glittering, sequin-covered thanks, complete with fireworks and a thousand-voice "Hallelujah Chorus," to my editor Shauna Summers. Working with Shauna is a wonderful gift.

Thanks to Linda Marrow and everyone at Ballantine for getting this book into my readers' hands as quickly as possible.

Thanks to Michelle Gomez for providing a mountain of information about Kaiserslautern, Germany; to Karen Schlossberg, for letting me borrow Eric on her birthday and at other inconvenient times; and to fellow author Alesia Holliday for being brave enough not just to climb into the minivan with us, but to treat us to a trip to Graceland, too. (Thank you. Thank you very much.)

Thanks to Tina Trevaskis for being *way* overqualified and incredibly awesome and reliable.

Thanks to Reserve Navy SEAL Chris Berman for giving my readers a chance to meet a real hero, and for those terrific calendars available at www.navysealscalendar.com. But my biggest thanks to Chris is for having the patience, kindness, and sensitivity (oh, he's shaking his head now!) to take a large group of my readers—some who haven't ventured down this path ever before—on a journey to physical fitness. I'll be there in spirit when this group attends Chris's Navy SEAL Women's Fitness Camp (www.navysealswomensfitness. com) in California this June!

Thanks to the gang on the bb and to all my reader and writer friends, new and old.

When I write fiction, I can't read fiction. It's more than just a fear that I'll end up sounding like someone else. It's because I'm one of those readers who, when I start a good book, can't put the darn thing down until I reach the end. (And then it's 3:00 a.m. and I've written zero pages of my own book!)

But I can and do read nonfiction while I'm writing, and I'm particularly fond of WWII military history. During the course of writing *Flashpoint,* I went on a binge with the men of the 506th Regiment, 101st Airborne Division—both Able Company as well as Easy Company's famous "Band of Brothers."

Their exploits and sacrifices during WWII have nothing to do with *Flashpoint* and everything to do with my staying sane while writing this book.

With that said, a special thanks to Dick Winters and his men, to Tom Hanks and *his* men, to my son, Jason, for the great Christmas gift, and to Patricia McMahon for picking up that copy of Don Burgett's *Currahee!* several years ago because it looked like something I might like to read someday.

Last but not least, thanks to my daughter, Melanie, for the wonderful poem and for making me so proud!

As always, any mistakes I've made or liberties I've taken are completely my own.

FLASHPOINT

CHAPTER
ONE

LATE SPRING
MARYLAND

BEFORE TONIGHT, the closest Tess Bailey had come to a strip club was on TV, where beautiful women danced seductively in G-strings, taut young body parts bouncing and gleaming from a stage that sparkled and flashed.

In the Gentlemen's Den, thousands of miles from Hollywood in a rundown neighborhood north of Washington, D.C., the mirror ball was broken, and the aging stripper on the sagging makeshift stage looked tired and cold.

"Whoops." Nash turned his back to the noisy room, carefully keeping his face in the shadows. "That's Gus Mondelay sitting with Decker," he told Tess.

Diego Nash had the kind of face that stood out in a crowd. And Nash obviously didn't want Mondelay—whoever he was—to see him.

Tess followed him back toward the bar, away from the table where Lawrence Decker, Nash's longtime Agency partner, was working undercover.

She bumped into someone. "Excuse me—"

Oh my God! The waitresses weren't wearing any shirts. The Gentlemen's Den wasn't just a strip club, it was also a topless bar. She grabbed Nash's hand and dragged him down the passageway that led to the pay phone and the

1

restrooms. It was dark back there, with the added bonus of nary a half-naked woman in sight.

She had to say it. "This *was* just a rumor—"

He pinned her up against the wall and nuzzled her neck, his arms braced on either side of her. She was stunned for only about three seconds before she realized that two men had staggered out of the men's room. This was just another way for Nash to hide his face.

She pretended that she was only pretending to melt as he kissed her throat and jawline, as he waited until Drunk and Drunker pushed past them before he spoke, his breath warm against her ear. "There were at least four shooters set up and waiting out front in the parking lot. And those were just the ones I spotted as we were walking in."

The light in the parking lot had been dismal. Tess's concentration had alternated between her attempts not to catch her foot in a pothole and fall on her face, and the two biker types who appeared to be having, quite literally, a pissing contest. Not to mention the unbelievable fact that she was out in the real world with the legendary Diego Nash . . .

They were now alone in the hallway, but Nash hadn't moved out of whispering range. He was standing so close, Tess's nose was inches from the collar of his expensive shirt. He smelled outrageously good. "Who's Gus Mondelay?" she asked.

"An informant," he said tersely, the muscle in the side of his perfect jaw jumping. "He's on the Agency payroll, but lately I've been wondering . . ." He shook his head. "It fits that he's here, now. He'd enjoy watching Deck get gunned down." The smile he gave her was grim. "Thanks for having the presence of mind to call me."

Tess still couldn't believe the conversation she'd overheard just over an hour ago at Agency headquarters.

A rumor had come in that Lawrence Decker's cover had been blown and there was an ambush being set to kill him.

The Agency's night shift support staff had attempted to contact him, but had been able to do little more than leave a message on his voice mail.

No one in the office had bothered to get in touch with Diego Nash.

"Nash isn't working this case with Decker," Suellen Foster had informed Tess. "Besides, it's just a rumor."

Nash was more than Decker's partner. He was Decker's friend. Tess had called him even as she ran for the parking lot.

"So what do we do?" Tess asked now, looking up at Nash.

He had eyes the color of melted chocolate—warm eyes that held a perpetual glint of amusement whenever he came into the office in HQ and flirted with the mostly female support staff. He liked to perch on the edge of Tess's desk in particular, and the other Agency analysts and staffers teased her about his attention. They also warned her of the dangers of dating a field agent, particularly one like Diego Nash, who had a serious 007 complex.

As if she needed their warning.

Nash sat on her desk because he liked her little bowl of lemon mints, and because she called him "tall, dark and egotistical" right to his perfect cheekbones, and refused to take him seriously.

Right now, though, she was in his world, and she was taking him extremely seriously.

Right now his usually warm eyes were cold and almost flat-looking, as if part of him were a million miles away.

"*We* do nothing," Nash told Tess. "*You* go home."

"I can help."

He'd already dismissed her. "You'll help more by leaving."

"I've done the training," she informed him, blocking his route back to the bar. "I've got an application in for a field agent position. It's just a matter of time before—"

Nash shook his head. "They're not going to take you. They're never going to take you. Look, Bailey, thanks for the ride, but—"

"Tess," she said. He had a habit of calling the support staff by their last names, but tonight she was here, in the field. "And they are too going to take me. Brian Underwood told me—"

"Brian Underwood was stringing you along because he was afraid you would quit and he needs you on support. You'll excuse me if I table this discussion on your lack of promotability and start focusing on the fact that my partner is about to—"

"I can get a message to Decker," Tess pointed out. "No one in that bar has ever seen me before."

Nash laughed in her face. "Yeah, what? Are you going to walk over to him with your freckles and your Sunday church picnic clothes—"

"These aren't Sunday church picnic clothes!" They were running-into-work-on-a-Friday-night-at-10:30-to-pick-up-a-file clothes. Jeans. Sneakers. T-shirt.

T-shirt . . .

Tess looked back down the hall toward the bar, toward the ordering station where the waitresses came to pick up drinks and drop off empty glasses.

"You stand out in this shithole as much as I do wearing this suit," Nash told her. "More. If you walk up to Decker looking the way you're looking . . ."

There was a stack of small serving trays, right there, by the bartender's cash register.

"He's my friend, too," Tess said. "He needs to be warned, and I can do it."

"No." Finality rang in his voice. "Just walk out the front door, Bailey, get back into your car, and—"

Tess pulled off her T-shirt, took off her bra, and handed both to him.

"What message should I give him?" she asked.

Nash looked at her, looked at the shirt and wispy lace of bra dangling from his hand, looked at her again.

Looked at her. "Jeez, Bailey."

Tess felt the heat in her cheeks as clearly as she felt the coolness from the air-conditioning against her bare back and shoulders.

"What should I tell him?" she asked Nash again.

"Damn," he said, laughing a little bit. "Okay. O-*kay*." He stuffed her clothes into his jacket pocket. "Except you still look like a Sunday school teacher."

Tess gave him a disbelieving look and an outraged noise. "I do *not*." For God's sake, she was standing here half naked—

But he reached for her, unfastening the top button of her jeans and unzipping them.

"Hey!" She tried to pull back, but he caught her.

"Don't you watch MTV?" he asked, folding her pants down so that they were more like hip huggers, his fingers warm against her skin.

Her belly button was showing now, as well as the top of her panties, the zipper of her jeans precariously half pulled down. "Yeah, in all my limitless free time."

"You could use some lipstick." Nash stepped back and looked at her critically, then, with both hands, completely messed up her short hair. He stepped back and looked again. "That's a little better."

Gee, thanks. "Message?" she said.

"Tell Decker to stay put for now," Nash ordered. "They're not going to hit him inside. Don't tell him that—he knows. That's what I'm telling *you*, you understand?"

Tess nodded.

"I'm going to make a perimeter circuit of this place," he continued. "I'll meet you right back here—no, in the ladies' room—in ten minutes. Give the message to Deck, be brief, don't blow it by trying to tell him too much, then get your ass in the ladies' room and stay there until I'm back. Is that clear?"

Tess nodded again. She'd never seen this Nash before—this order-barking, cold-bloodedly decisive commander. She'd never seen the Nash he'd become in the car, on the way over here, before either. After she'd made that first phone call, she'd picked him up downtown. She'd told him again, in greater detail, all that she'd overheard as they'd headed to the Gentlemen's Den. He'd gotten very quiet, very grim, when his attempts to reach Decker on his cell phone had failed.

He'd been scared, she'd realized as she'd glanced at him. He had been genuinely frightened that they were too late, that the hit had already gone down, that his partner—his friend—was already dead.

When they got here and the parking lot was quiet, when they walked inside and spotted Decker still alive and breathing, there had been a fraction of a second in which Tess had been sure Nash was going to faint from relief.

It was eye-opening. It was possible that Diego Nash was human after all.

Tess gave him one last smile, then headed down the hall toward one of those little serving trays on the bar. God, she was about to walk into a room filled with drunken men, with her breasts bare and her pants halfway down her butt. Still, it couldn't possibly be worse than that supercritical once-over Nash had given her.

"Tess." He caught her arm, and she looked back at him. "Be careful," he said.

She nodded again. "You, too."

He smiled then—a flash of straight white teeth. "Deck's going to shit monkeys when he sees you."

With that, he was gone.

Tess grabbed the tray from the bar and pushed her way out into the crowd.

Something was wrong.

Decker read it in Gus Mondelay's eyes, in the way the heavyset man was sitting across from him at the table.

Although it was possible that the *wrong* he was reading was due to the four beef enchiladas Mondelay had wolfed down at Joey's Mexican Shack twenty minutes before meeting Decker here.

But Deck didn't trust Mondelay any farther than he could throw him. And something about the sound of the man's voice when he'd called to set up this meeting with Freedom Network leader Tim Ebersole had made Decker leave early enough to follow Mondelay as he left work, and to trail him over here. But aside from the Shack, Mondelay hadn't made any other stops before arriving at the Gentlemen's Den. He hadn't talked to anyone on his cell phone either.

Mondelay gestured for Decker to lean closer—it was the only way to be heard over the loud music. "Tim must be running late."

Jesus, Mondelay had a worse than usual case of dog breath tonight.

"I'm in no hurry," Decker said, leaning back again in his seat. Air. Please God, give him some air.

Gus Mondelay had come into contact with the Freedom Network while serving eighteen months in Wallens Ridge Prison for possession of an illegal firearm. The group's name made them sound brave and flag-wavingly patriotic, but they were really just more bubbas—the Agency nickname for homegrown terrorists with racist, neo-Nazi leanings and a fierce hatred for the federal government. And for all agents of the federal government.

Such as Decker.

Even though Deck's specialty was terrorist cells of the

foreign persuasion, he'd been introduced to informant Gus Mondelay when the man had coughed up what seemed to be evidence that these particular bubbas and al-Qaeda were working in tandem.

Those insane-sounding allegations could not be taken lightly even though Deck himself couldn't make sense of the scenario. If there was anyone the bubbas hated more than federal agents, it was foreigners. Although the two groups certainly could have found common ground in their hatred of Israel and the Jews.

So Dougie Brendon, the newly appointed Agency director, had assigned Decker to Gus Mondelay. Deck was to use Mondelay to try to work his way deeper into the Freedom Network, with the goal of being present at one of the meetings with members of the alleged al-Qaeda cell.

So far all Mondelay had given him were leads that had gone nowhere.

In return, Decker sat with him night after night, watching emotionally numb women gyrate unenthusiastically in one sleazy strip club after another where he was assaulted by crappy rock music played at brain-jarring decibels. He, of course, paid for the drinks.

Mondelay made the come-closer-to-talk gesture again. "I'm going to give Tim a call, see what's holding him up," he said as he pried his cell phone out of his pants pocket.

Decker watched as the other man keyed in a speed dial number, then held his phone to his face, plugging his other ear with one knockwurst-sized finger. Yeah, that would help him hear over the music.

It wouldn't have been quite so awful to sit here if only the DJ played some Aerosmith every now and then.

Or if the strippers or waitresses in this place bothered to smile—Jesus, or even scowl, for that matter. But their perpetually bored expressions were depressing as hell. They didn't even bother to be pissed at the fact that they were being exploited.

Mondelay sat back in his chair as whomever he was calling picked up. Decker couldn't hear the conversation, but he could read lips. He turned his head so that Mondelay was right at the edge of his field of vision.

What the fuck is taking so long? Pause, then, *No way, asshole, you were supposeda call me. I been sitting here for almost an hour now, waiting for the fucking goat head.*

Huh?

Fuck you, too, douche bag. Mondelay hung up his phone, leaned toward Decker. "I got the locale wrong," he said. "Tim and the others are over at the Bull Run. It was my mistake. Tim says we should come on over. Join them there."

No. There was no way in hell that Mondelay had been talking to Tim. Decker had heard him on the phone with Tim in the past, and it had been all "Yes, sir," and "Right away, sir." "Let me kiss your ass, sir," not "Fuck you, too, douche bag."

Something was rotten in the Gentlemen's Den—something besides Mondelay's toxic breath, that is.

Mondelay wasn't waiting on any goat head. He was waiting for the *go ahead.* The son of a bitch was setting Decker up.

Mondelay began the lengthy process of pushing his huge frame up and out of the seat.

"You boys aren't leaving, are you?"

Decker looked up and directly into the eyes of Tess Bailey, the computer specialist from the Agency support office.

But okay, no. Truth be told, the first place he looked wasn't into her eyes.

She'd moved to D.C. a few years ago, from somewhere in the Midwest. Kansas? A small town, she'd told them once when Nash had asked. Her father was a librarian.

Funny he should remember that about her right now.

Because, holy shit, Toto, Tess Bailey didn't look like she was in small-town Kansas anymore.

"There's a lady over at the bar who wants to buy your next round," Tess told him as she shouted to be heard over the music, as he struggled to drag his eyes up to her face.

Nash. The fact that she was here and half-naked—no, forget the half-naked part, although, Jesus, that was kind of hard to do when she was standing there half-fricking-naked—had to mean that Nash was here, too. And if Nash was here, that meant Decker was right about Mondelay setting him up, and he was about to be executed. Or at least kidnapped.

He glanced at Mondelay, at the nervous energy that seemed to surround the big man. No, he'd gotten it right the first time. Mondelay was setting him up to be hit.

Son of a bitch.

"She said you were cute," Tess was shouting at Decker, trying desperately for eye contact. He gave it to her. Mostly. "She's over there, in the back." She pointed toward the bar with one arm, using the other to hold her tray up against her chest, which made it a little bit easier to pay attention to what she was saying, despite the fact that it still didn't make any sense. Cute? *Who* was in the back of the bar?

Nash, obviously.

"So what can I get you?" Tess asked, all cheery smile and adorable freckled nose, and extremely bare breasts beneath that tray she was clutching to herself.

"We're on our way out," Mondelay informed her.

"Free drinks," Tess said enticingly. "You should sit back down and stay a while." She looked pointedly at Deck.

A message from Nash. "I'll have another beer," Decker shouted up at her with a nod of confirmation.

Mondelay laughed his disbelief. "I thought you wanted to meet Tim."

Decker made himself smile up at the man who'd set him

up to be killed. Two pals, out making the rounds of the strip clubs. "Yeah, I do."

"Well, they're waiting for us now."

"That's good," Decker said. "They can wait. We don't want to look too eager, right?" He looked at Tess again. "Make it imported."

Mondelay looked at her, too, narrowing his eyes slightly—a sign that he was probably thinking. "You're new here, aren't you?"

"He'll have another beer, too." Decker dismissed Tess, hoping she'd take the hint and disappear, fast.

Mondelay was in one hell of a hurry to leave, but he was never in too much of a hurry not to harass a waitress when he had the chance. "Whatcha hiding there, honey?"

"I'll get those beers."

Tess was just a little too late. Mondelay had already caught the bottom of her tray, keeping her from leaving. He tugged on it, pulling it away from her, and she let him, but not because she wanted to. She was still smiling, but she wasn't a good enough liar to hide her discomfort completely. Decker had to look away, hating the fact that she was subjecting herself to this, for him.

Yeah, who was he kidding here? She was doing this for James "Diego" Nash.

"How long've you worked here?" Mondelay asked her.

The volume of the music dropped as the routine ended and the stripper left the stage. There'd be about ten minutes for their ears to recover before the next woman started to dance.

"Not very long," Tess said. It was still noisy, but she didn't have to shout quite so loudly anymore.

"You need to work on your all-over tan."

"Yeah," she said, cool as could be. "I know."

"Let her get those beers," Decker said.

"I'd throw her a bang," Mondelay said as if Tess weren't even standing there. "Wouldn't you?"

Deck had been trying to pretend that a woman who was pole dancing on the other side of the bar had caught his full attention, but now he was forced to look up and appraise Tess, whom he knew had a photo of her two little nieces in a frame on her desk along with a plastic action figure of Buffy the Vampire Slayer. He knew it was Buffy because Nash had asked her about it once, and she'd told them it represented both female empowerment and the fact that most people had inner depths not apparent to the casual observer.

Decker felt a hot rush of anger at Nash, who, no doubt, had been taking his flirtation with Tess to the next level when the call came in that Decker needed assistance. He wasn't sure what pissed him off more—the fact that Nash had sent Tess in here without her shirt, or that Nash was sleeping with her.

"Yeah," he said now to Mondelay, since they'd been talking about the waitresses in these bars like this all week. He gave Tess a smile that he hoped she'd read as an apology for the entire male population. "I would also send her flowers afterward."

"Tell me, hon, do women really go for that sentimental bullshit?" Mondelay asked Tess.

"Nah," she said. "What we really love is being objectified, used, and cast aside. Why else would I have gotten a job here? I mean, aside from the incredible health plan and the awesome 401(k)."

Decker laughed as she finally managed to tug her tray free and headed toward the bar.

He watched her go, aware of the attention she was getting from the other lowlifes in the bar, noting the soft curve of her waist and the way that, although she wasn't very tall, she carried herself as if she stood head and shoulders above the crowd. He was also aware that it had been a very long time since he'd sent a woman flowers.

They were in some serious shit here. Whoever set up this ambush had paramilitary training.

There were too many shooters in position around the building. He couldn't take them all out.

Well, he could. The setup was professional, but the shooters were all amateurs. He *could* take them all out, one by one by one. And like the first two he'd encountered, most of them wouldn't even hear him coming.

But Jimmy Nash's hands were already shaking from clearing that roof. A cigarette would've helped, but last time he'd quit, he'd sworn it was for good.

He washed his hands in the sink in the men's, trying, through sheer force of will, to make them stop trembling.

It was that awful picture he had in his head of Decker gunned down in the parking lot that steadied him and made his heart stop hammering damn near out of his chest.

He'd do anything for Deck.

They'd been Agency partners longer than most marriages lasted these days. Seven years. Who'd have believed *that* was possible? Two fucked-up, angry men, one of them—him—accustomed to working alone, first cousin to the devil, and the other a freaking Boy Scout, a former Navy SEAL. . . .

When Tess had called him tonight and told him what she'd overheard, that HQ essentially knew Decker was being targeted and that they weren't busting their asses to keep it from happening . . .

The new Agency director, Doug-the-prick Brendon, hadn't tried to hide his intense dislike of Jimmy Nash, and therefore Decker by association. But this was going too fucking far.

Jimmy used his wet hands to push his hair back from his face, forcing himself to meet his eyes in the mirror.

Murderous eyes.

After he got Decker safely out of here, he was going to hunt down Dougie Brendon, and . . .

And spend the rest of your life in jail? Jimmy could practically hear Deck's even voice.

First they'd have to catch me, he pointed out. And they wouldn't. He'd made a vow, a long time ago, to do whatever he had to do, so that he'd never get locked up again.

There are other ways to blow off steam. How many times had Decker said those exact words to him?

Other ways . . .

Like Tess Bailey.

Who was waiting for him in the ladies' room. Who was unbelievably hot. Who liked him—really liked him. He'd seen it in her eyes. She pretended to have a cold-day-in-July attitude when he flirted with her in the office. But Jimmy saw beyond it, and he knew with just a little more charm and a little bit of well-placed pressure, she'd be giving him a very brightly lit green light. Tonight.

He'd let Decker handle Doug Brendon.

Jimmy would handle Tess.

He smiled at the pun as he opened the men's room door and went out into the hallway.

Tonight he would give Tess to himself as a present. Under normal circumstances, he would never get involved with someone from support. But these weren't normal circumstances.

His current state of happiness wasn't completely a result of the adrenaline charging through his system from clearing the roof. When Tess had called, he'd been looking forward to getting naked with a very lovely young tax attorney named Eleanor Gantz.

Who wasn't likely to welcome him back anytime in the

near future. He'd left her without a word of explanation when he'd heard Decker was in danger.

Although, truth be told, he couldn't quite remember what she looked like—his memory was dominated by Tess Bailey in those half-unzipped jeans and nothing more.

Ouch. Who knew?

Jimmy pushed open the ladies' room door, expecting to see her, live and in person. But she wasn't there. *Shit.* He checked the stalls—all empty.

It sobered him fast and he stopped thinking about the latter part of the evening, instead focusing on here and now, on finding Tess.

He spotted her right away as he went back into the hall. She was standing at the bar. What the Jesus God was she doing there? But then he knew. Decker and Mondelay had ordered drinks.

And he hadn't been specific enough in his instructions, assuming "Get your ass in the ladies' room" meant just that, not "Get your ass in the ladies' room after you fill their drink order."

The biggest problem with her standing at the bar was not the fact that she was bare breasted and surrounded by drunken and leering men.

No, the biggest problem was that she was surrounded by other bare-breasted women—i.e., the real waitstaff of the Gentlemen's Den. Who were going to wonder what Tess was doing cheating them out of their hard-earned tips.

And sure enough, as Jimmy watched, an older woman with long golden curls, who looked an awful lot like the figurehead of an old sailing ship—those things had to be implants—tapped Tess on the shoulder.

He couldn't possibly hear USS *Bitch-on-Wheels* from this distance. Her face was at the wrong angle for him to read her lips, but her body language was clear: "Who the hell are *you*?"

Time for a little secondary rescue.

He took off his jacket and tossed it into the corner. No one in this dive so much as owned a suit and his was ruined anyway. He snatched off his tie, too, loosened his collar, and rolled up his sleeves as he pushed his way through the crowd and over to the bar.

"Oh, here he is now," Tess was saying to Miss Figurehead as he moved into earshot. She smiled at him, which was distracting as hell, because, like most hetero men, he'd been trained to pick up a strong positive message from the glorious combination of naked breasts and a warm, welcoming smile. He forced himself to focus on what she was saying.

"I was just telling Crystal about the practical joke—you know," Tess said, crossing her arms in front of her, "that we're playing on your cousin?"

Well, how about that? She didn't need rescuing. The Figurehead—Crystal—didn't look like the type to swallow, but she'd done just that with Tess's story.

"Honey, give her a little something extra," Tess told him, "because she lost that tip she would have gotten."

Jimmy dug into his pocket for his billfold and pulled out two twenty-dollar bills.

Tess reached for a third, taking the money and handing it to her brand-new best friend. "Will you order those two beers for me?" she asked Crystal.

The waitress did better than that—she went back behind the bar to fetch 'em herself.

Tess turned to Jimmy, who took the opportunity to put his arm around her—she had, after all, called him honey. He was just being a good team player and following her lead, letting that smooth skin slide beneath his fingers.

"Thanks." She lowered her voice, turning in closer, using him as a way to hide herself—from the rest of the crowd at least. "May I have my shirt back?"

"Whoops," he said. Her shirt was in the pocket of his jacket, which was somewhere on the floor by the restrooms. That is, if someone hadn't already found it and taken it home.

" 'Whoops?' " she said, looking up at him, fire in her eyes.

As Jimmy stared down at her, she pressed even closer. Which might've kept him from looking, but sure as hell sent his other senses into a dance of joy. It was as if they shared the same shirt—she was so soft and warm and alive. He wanted her with a sudden sharpness that triggered an equally powerful realization. It was so strong it nearly made him stagger.

He didn't deserve her.

He had no right even to touch her. Not with these hands.

"Are you all right?" Tess whispered.

Caught in a weird time warp, Jimmy looked down into her eyes. They were light brown—a nothing-special color as far as eyes went—but he'd always been drawn to the intelligence and warmth he could see in them. He realized now, in this odd, lingering moment of clarity, that Tess's eyes were beautiful. *She* was beautiful.

An angel come to save him . . .

"No," he said, because for that instant he hated the idea of lying to her, and it had been a long time since he'd last felt anywhere close to all right.

Her eyes widened, and he knew that she'd spotted the blood on his shoe and the hole in his pants—number three on the roof had fought back—and assumed he'd been hurt. In truth, his physical health was the last thing he'd been thinking about.

But then Crystal put two bottles of beer on the bar, and Tess turned to thank her, and reality snapped back around. And she wasn't angelic or even beautiful anymore—she was merely Tess Bailey from support, kind of pretty in an interesting way. Her smile was crooked and her nose was rather oddly shaped and her face was too round—she'd probably have jowls before she turned fifty.

Of course, right now the combination of interesting plus half naked made her look sizzling hot. And since right now was all that ever mattered to Jimmy, he pushed away the last lingering residuals of brightness that had momentarily dazzled him.

He *was* going to go home with Tess tonight. She didn't know it yet, but it was a given. She wasn't going to save him, though. At least not more than temporarily.

He was too far gone for that.

As for what he did or didn't deserve . . . Real life was nothing like the movies, where villains were punished for their sins, and the righteous triumphed.

Which was damn lucky for him.

"Do you need me to get Decker?" When Crystal moved off, Tess's full attention was back on him—her concern something he could have reached out and held in his hands.

"No, I'm fine," Jimmy said, because she was looking at him as if he'd lost it. Crap, maybe he had for a minute there. "Really. Sorry." He kissed her, just a quick press of his lips against hers, because he didn't know how else to erase the worry from her eyes.

It worked to distract her—God knew it did a similar trick on him.

He wanted to kiss her again, longer, deeper—a real touch-the-tonsils, full fireworks-inducing event—but he didn't. He'd save that for later.

And Decker always said he had no willpower.

"I'm really fine," Jimmy said again, and forced a smile to prove it. "It's just a scrape."

He didn't know that for sure—he hadn't bothered to stop and look. Still, he'd managed to run back down the stairs. His injury couldn't be *that* bad.

He looked out at the crowd, trying to get a read on who was shit-faced drunk—who would best serve as a catalyst for part two of tonight's fun.

"Did you find a way to get Decker out of here?" Tess asked. He could see that he'd managed to confuse her. She was back to folding her arms across her chest.

"Yeah, I cleared the roof." He wondered if she had any idea what that meant. He glanced back at the room. There was a man in a green T-shirt who was so tanked his own buddies' laughter was starting to piss him off.

But Tess obviously didn't understand any of what he'd said. "The roof? How . . . ?"

"I called for some help with our extraction." Jimmy explained the easy part. "We'll be flying Deck out of here—a chopper's coming to pick us up—but first we need a little diversion. Have you ever been in a bar fight?"

Tess shook her head.

"Well, you're about to be. If we get separated, if I can't make it back over here, keep to the edge of the room. Keep your back to the wall, watch for flying objects, and be ready to duck. Work your way around to that exit sign—the one that's directly across from the front entrance." He pointed. "Behind that door are stairs. If you get there first, wait for me or Deck. Don't open that door without one of us—is that clear?"

She nodded.

"Oh, and there's one more important thing," he said. "Will you have dinner with me tomorrow night?" *You may feel a little pressure. . . .*

Tess laughed her amazement.

"Don't answer right away," Nash said. "Give yourself time to think it over."

He'd obviously caught her completely off guard. Good.

"Diego, I—"

"Heads up," he interrupted.

Because here came ol' Gus, right on cue, searching for Tess, wondering what the fuck was taking so long with their beers, impatient to send Decker to the parking lot where he'd be filled with holes, where he'd gasp out the last breath of his life in the gravel.

And here came Deck, right behind him, the only real gentleman in this den of bottom-feeders, ready to jump on Gus's back if he so much as looked cross-eyed at cute little Tess Bailey from support.

"When I knock over that guy sitting there with the black T-shirt that says 'Badass,' " Nash instructed her, meeting his partner's gaze from across the room just as Gus spotted him with Tess. Gus reacted, reaching inside of his baseball jacket for either his cell phone or a weapon—it didn't really matter which because he was so slo-oh-oh, and Deck was already on top of him, "lean over the bar and shout to your girlfriend Crystal that she should call 911, that someone in the crowd has a gun. On your mark, get set . . ."

Fifteen feet away, Decker brought Gus Mondelay to his knees and then to the floor, which was a damn good thing, because if it had been Nash taking him down, he would have snapped the motherfucker's neck. "Go!"

Decker knew the drill.

After he relieved Mondelay of both his weapon and his cell phone and brought him, with a minimum amount of fuss, to an unconscious state, he was more than ready to vacate the premises as quickly as possible.

"Green shirt, two o'clock," Nash shouted, giving Deck a target that was easy to spot, easy to hit.

After working together for seven years, he and Nash had the fine art of starting a bar fight down to a science. Find two angry drunks sitting fairly close together in the crowd. Knock into them both at the same time, taking them down to the floor, if possible. Come up loud, accusations flying, and start swinging.

Nash had an uncommon ability to determine a person's flashpoint in just one glance. Man or woman, he could see 'em, read 'em, and play 'em to his full advantage.

That was no small skill to have in their line of work.

True to form, it was only a matter of moments before the fight between Green Shirt and Badass escalated into something even the bouncers couldn't control. Tables were being knocked over, pitchers and mugs were flying, pool cues were being broken, chairs hefted and thrown.

It was a solid eight on a scale from one to ten—five being sufficient diversion for an escape.

Graceful as a dancer, Nash wove his way through the crowd, grabbing Tess Bailey as he headed for what Decker knew to be a fire exit.

Tess was still without a shirt, a fact that couldn't have escaped Nash's attention.

Instead of heading down and out, they took the stairs up, which was an interesting alternative.

Nash read his mind and answered the question as they continued to climb. "There's an army in the parking lot, so I called for a budget buster."

That was the Agency nickname for a helicopter extraction. Helos were expensive to keep in the air.

Nash had been pushing Tess in front of him, but now he stopped her from going out the door and onto the roof. "Get behind me," he ordered as he handed her his shirt. About time—Decker had been on the verge of offering her his own T-shirt.

Although Tess didn't seem to notice that Nash's chivalrous action had come about ten minutes too late. In fact, she was looking at Nash the way women always looked at Nash, particularly after he gave her a smile and leaned in closer to say, "You were great down there."

It was so typical. They weren't even out of danger and Nash was already setting up the getting laid part of his evening.

Decker would have laughed, but this was Tess Bailey that his partner was messing with. Not only that, but there was something off about Nash tonight, something squirrelly, something . . . brittle. It was almost as if he were going through the motions, or maybe even playacting what was expected of him.

Deck could hear the sirens of the local police as they approached, called in to break up the bar fight. They were an additional diversion and added protection. With five cop cars in the parking lot, only the craziest sons of bitches in the Freedom Network would attempt a shot at the Agency helo that was coming to scoop them off the roof.

"We need to keep our eyes open—it's been a few minutes since I cleared this area," Nash told them, and just like that, Deck knew.

Something ugly had gone down when Nash cleared the roof of any potential shooters.

Decker would never know what had happened. He and Nash didn't talk about things like that. Sure, Deck could try to bring it up, but the most he'd hear was "Yeah, I had a little trouble. It wasn't anything I couldn't handle."

Except Decker wasn't buying that anymore. Yes, without a doubt, his partner could handle any form of violence thrown at him and come out on top, or at least alive. But that was significantly different from the psychological *handling* that was required in this business. It was how Nash was handling the aftermath of violence that was worrying him.

"Here we go," Nash said, firing another smile at Tess. The helo was out there. Deck could hear its thrumming approach. "Stay close."

Nash met Deck's eyes, and Deck nodded, his weapon drawn, too. They kicked open the door.

There was no one up there, no resistance. They were inside the helo and heading quickly out of the area in a matter of seconds.

It was impossible to talk over the noise from the blades, but as Decker watched, Nash leaned in to Tess, speaking directly into her ear.

She laughed, then moved even closer to say something back to him.

His turn again, and to whatever he'd said, she had no immediate response. There was a significant amount of eye contact though, particularly when Nash reached out and finished buttoning up that shirt he'd given her.

Maybe Nash would talk to Tess tonight—tell her the things he couldn't put into words and say to Decker.

Or maybe he'd simply use her for sex until the scent of death wasn't so strong in his nostrils anymore, until he thought he'd "handled" whatever it was that he'd had to do tonight to save Decker's life.

Tess was watching Deck from across that helo cabin, and he made himself smile at her, hoping that she was using Nash as completely as Nash was using her, wishing she could read his mind and heed his unspoken warning.

But maybe she could, because she glanced at Nash, looked back at Decker, and made something of a face and a little shrug. Like, *Yeah, I know exactly what I've gotten myself into, but really, can you blame me . . . ?"*

No, he couldn't. He just wished . . .

Decker wished Nash would take Tess home and talk to her about what had happened out on the roof tonight, instead of nailing her.

Although he knew damn well that his motives for wishing that weren't entirely pure.

CHAPTER
TWO

Tess hung up the phone.

She couldn't believe it.

Brian Underwood didn't even have the balls to call her into his office and tell her the news to her face. He'd left a lousy *message* on her voice mail.

"Yeah, Bailey, it's Brian. Sorry to make this a phone call, but it's twenty-two hundred"—military speak for ten at night. Underwood had never been in the Armed Forces, but he liked people to think that he had—"and this memo just crossed my desk. I've got a busy day tomorrow and I didn't want it to get lost in the shuffle, especially since I know you've been waiting on this info for a coupla weeks. Long story short, they turned you down for that field position. But hey, that doesn't mean you can't apply again in six months. There's always next time, right? And in the meantime, your work with support is of vital importance. . . ."

If they hadn't accepted her this time, when there were still two additional positions that needed filling ASAP, Tess knew she was never going to leave the support office. She would still be here when she was sixty-five, like Mrs. O'Reilly, four cubicles down. And while she could, indeed, appreciate the vital importance of her work, this was not the job she wanted—and it wasn't the job she'd been promised when she'd signed on.

But Tess was never going to be promoted into the field.

Diego Nash had been right.

Somehow that made it sting even more. She didn't want Nash to be right—not about this, not about anything. But most of all, she didn't want to do so much as even *think* about him ever again.

Fool.

Not him—her. She was the fool. Not for letting him in that night. No, she knew exactly what she was getting—a one-night stand—when he'd asked to come up and she'd said yes.

She was a fool for thinking they'd actually connected. Somehow, something had happened to her brain after he'd kissed her in her kitchen. God, what a kiss. But sometime after that kiss and before the next morning, when she'd woken up, alone—and moronically surprised that he'd vanished with no word, no note—she'd fallen prey to Stupid Woman syndrome.

She'd slept with a man who was known as a player. She'd known that about him before she'd unlocked her apartment door. She'd accepted as fact that they were going to have nothing more than a fling.

And yet somehow she'd ended up thinking that this time it had been different. This time it had been meaningful. This time it had been special. This time he'd still be there in the morning—in fact, he'd be there for thirty-five years of mornings to come.

Yeah, right.

Fool.

And she was an even bigger fool for the way her heart still raced when the phone rang. What did she really think? That after two months of dead silence, Nash was suddenly going to call?

Flowers had arrived the very next morning. But they were from Deck. The card had a short message, in Decker's own neat handwriting: "Thank you for going above and beyond the call of duty." Tess knew his handwriting well. She'd processed many of his requisition sheets over the past few years. And in case she'd had any doubt, he'd signed it, "Lawrence Decker."

On Monday, there was an email in her inbox that Decker had sent to the assistant director—a glowing recommendation that Tess be promoted to a field position. He'd written a brief note at the top of the copy he'd forwarded to her. "I'm not sure how much this will help."

She'd sent a reply, just a short "Thank you," but the email had bounced back to her—a sign that the system was freaking out again. It bounced a few days later, too, when she'd tried to resend.

At that point, she'd actually become scared, thinking that Nash and Decker might be dead. They hadn't been into the office since that night. No paperwork had come through with their names on it either.

As the days continued to pass, she'd done some digging and found out to her shock that they'd left the Agency. Resigned. Just like that. They were gone and they weren't coming back. Like most of their work in the field, their departure had been quiet. Covert.

Tess had dug further, actually hacking into accounting, to find out that a rather substantial severance payment had been sent to Nash, care of a small hotel in Ensenada, Mexico, on the Pacific coast.

He was not just gone, he was *gone*. As in thousands of miles away.

And he hadn't bothered to send her so much as a postcard with an insincere "Wish you were here."

That had been a bad day, too. One of her all-time worst ever. Although today was coming pretty close to matching it.

It wasn't even nine a.m., but Tess had to get out of here. She grabbed her purse from the bottom drawer of her desk. Most of her colleagues were still arriving, but her workday was over.

No. Correction. Her Agency career was over.

She took the framed snapshot of her nieces and her piece of the Berlin Wall—too small to be effective as a paper-weight but heavy with importance and laden with history—her favorite pen, and her Jean-Luc Picard, Psyduck, and Buffy action figures from her desktop. That was all she wanted—the stupid lemon mints that Nash had liked so much could stay for the next naive recruit.

She took forty-five seconds to type up a letter, another ten to print it out.

Brian was already in his office, door closed, hiding from her. His administrative assistant, Carol, tried to intercept, but Tess wasn't about to be stopped. Unlike Brian, she needed to deliver this message face-to-face.

She knocked and opened the door without waiting for his go-ahead. He was on the phone, and he looked up at her, the surprise on his broad face morphing instantly into recognition and guilt.

Yeah, he should feel guilty—making promises that he had no intention of keeping.

"Hang on, Milt," he said into the phone, then put his hand over the receiver. "Bailey. You're upset. Of course. Why don't you take the day off?" He glanced toward the door, where his assistant was hovering. "Carol, will you check my schedule for this week and see when I have a spare twenty minutes to sit down and talk to Tess?"

Twenty minutes. This was her life, and he was going to give her twenty minutes of "Try again in six months" later in the week—when she knew for damn sure that right now he and Milton Heinrik were discussing nothing more important than a trade in their fantasy baseball league.

"I quit," she said. She handed it to him in writing, too, and walked out the door.

KAZABEK, KAZBEKISTAN

Kazbekistani warlord Padsha Bashir had a firm grasp of the English language. He'd honed his language skills while attending college in the States. It seemed almost ludicrous that one of the most feared warlords in this country was an alum of Boston University; a member of the class of '82.

Sophia stood impassively as the other women prepared her for this morning's encounter, dressing her in a gown of sheerest gauze, brushing out the tangled knot of her just-washed hair. She didn't bother to resist the dabs of perfume placed between her breasts and along her throat. She was saving her strength for the nightmare that was coming.

The gown was cool against her skin. It was not an unpleasant sensation.

Somehow that and the fact that the sun was up and streaming in through the palace windows made this seem even more surreal, and that much harder to bear.

But terrible things could happen in the sunlight. It had been a sunny morning, too, on that day when—

Sophia opened her eyes to escape the memory of Dimitri's head rolling across the ornately tiled palace floor—or at least to try to escape the grisly image for a while.

If she survived this coming day, she'd surely see the gruesome sight of Dimitri's mouth open in a silent scream the moment she fell asleep. It was a nightmare image she would remember forever, even if she lived to be a hundred and ten.

What had the floor, the room, looked like to Dimitri? Had he seen her in those last few seconds of his life as she gasped with horror?

Death by beheading came fast, but did it come fast enough?

Sophia couldn't stop thinking about it.

And little wonder, since every time she came face-to-face with Bashir, he had that very same deadly sharp sword close at hand.

He placed it on the table near his bed, and, when she was led into the room, he would never fail to demonstrate to her just how sharp it still was.

His message was clear. If she failed to please him—this bastard who'd killed her husband—her head would be next to roll across the floor.

Two of the women moved the mirror closer so Sophia could see herself—as if she cared.

They'd dressed her in white again. With her blond hair and fair skin, in that nearly transparent gown, she looked like some kind of MTV version of a virgin sacrifice.

Virgin, hah. The truth was that Bashir liked women dressed in white because it contrasted with the red of their blood.

Sophia didn't know if she would still be alive an hour from now. All she knew for sure was that she was going to bleed.

CASA CARMELITA, ENSENADA, MEXICO

Tess Bailey was back in his bed.

Although *back* wasn't quite correct, since that one night Jimmy had spent with her had been in *her* bed, in her cozy little apartment with that kitchen with the cow wallpaper, out in Silver Springs, Maryland.

"Nash."

But the difference between Tess's bed and his didn't matter now, because she was here and she was naked and she was warm and she was willing and God, God, God, he wanted her.

"I'm here," she said as she kissed him, as she opened herself to him. "It's okay, Jimmy, I'm here. . . ."

He pushed inside of her, nearly blind with need, and oh, holy sainted mother of—

"Nash."

Jimmy opened his eyes to see Lawrence Decker standing over him. He sat up and his head nearly exploded, but he still managed to take in the fact that he was quite definitely alone in his hotel room bed, that the sun was streaming in through the window blinds, that the ceiling fan overhead was on high, that his mouth was impossibly dry . . .

And that if Deck had been an assassin, Jimmy would, without a doubt, be exceedingly dead right now.

It was not his finest hour.

"Hey," Jimmy greeted him, his voice sounding rusty to his own ears. "You changed your mind about that vacation, huh?"

"Not exactly." Deck glanced at the two empty bottles of tequila sitting on the bedside table. "You stopped answering your cell phone."

"Ah," Jimmy said. "My batteries ran out."

"A week ago?"

"Yeah, well." He shrugged. "You know how it is on vacation. You stop wearing a watch, stop charging the phone."

He looked at Decker standing there in his T-shirt and those army green fatigues with all those pockets, looking almost exactly the same as he'd looked that day they'd first been introduced. *And this is Chief Lawrence Decker, formerly of SEAL Team One.* What was it about former SEALs, former Rangers? They had a look to them, an edge, that they never lost. It had been, what, seven and a half years since

Deck left the teams, yet he still walked, talked, moved, stood, even breathed like a Navy SEAL.

"Or maybe you don't know how it is," Jimmy added.

When they'd worked together at the Agency, Decker never took vacations.

"Are you all right?" Decker asked. It was the closest he'd get to mentioning those bottles.

With his hair-colored hair and his eye-colored eyes, his pleasantly featured face, his relatively vertically challenged stature and bantam-weight build, Decker was the poster child for average.

"I'm great." Jimmy swung his legs out of bed, pushed himself up—Christ, his head—and staggered into the bathroom.

"You don't look great." Decker raised his voice slightly to be heard from the other room.

Jimmy flushed the toilet and moved to the sink, splashing his face, drinking from a water bottle he kept nearby, swallowing some painkiller at the same time.

He winced at his reflection in the mirror as he supported himself with both hands on the edge of the sink. He looked—and felt—like walking roadkill.

Decker, always thoughtful, waited until he turned off the water to say, "I got a call from Tom Paoletti."

And there it was.

The reason Jimmy had stayed here in Mexico for all these weeks.

Lawrence Decker was a man with a future—and he needed to move into that future unencumbered by ghosts from the past.

Jimmy turned away from the mirror, taking his towel with him into the bedroom, drying his dripping face. "I told you he'd call. Congratulations. When do you start?"

And what the hell took Tom Paoletti so long to call? But he didn't bother to ask that because he already knew. *He* was what took Tom Paoletti so long. Pizza and beer. Thunder and lightning. Decker and Nash.

You couldn't have one without the other.

Or so people thought.

But pizza went down just fine with tequila, too.

Decker, as always, didn't miss a note. He caught Jimmy's intentional *you*.

And gently volleyed back a plural. "He wants us to come to San Diego," he said. "As soon as possible."

Us. Jimmy sat on the bed, exhausted and still half drunk. "I don't know, Deck. I'm a little tied up right now."

Decker nodded, as if that weren't the biggest load of bullshit he'd ever encountered. "I could really use you," he said. "Tom's looking to send a team of civilians into Kazbekistan."

Kazbekistan. Yeah, right.

There was no way anyone from the West was crossing over the K-stan border without some seriously expensive equipment. Such as HALO gear—including an extremely high-altitude aircraft to jump out of.

Decker was, no doubt, attempting the age-old practice of bait and switch. He knew Jimmy wouldn't rest easy with the idea of Deck heading into the hotbed of terrorist activity known in the Spec Ops world as "the Pit" without someone to watch his back. But as soon as they got to Tom Paoletti's office, Jimmy would find out that the job was really in Sandusky. Some dot com geeks with more money than God wanted to feel important and install a high-tech security grid in their corporate headquarters.

"Kazbekistan," Jimmy repeated.

Deck nodded.

Jimmy laughed—softly, so his head wouldn't split in two. "You are such a fucking liar. But yeah. Okay. I'll go to Kazbekistan. You go get the plane tickets from Tom Paoletti. I'll wait here."

Decker's response was to cross to the ancient television that was on and flickering, volume muted. He flipped stations until he found a cable news channel and turned up the sound.

English subtitles scrolled across the bottom of the screen as the anchor delivered the story in Spanish spoken too quickly for Jimmy to follow. The graphic behind the woman said *Terremoto* in crumbling letters. ". . . six point eight on the Richter scale, with the epicenter of the devastating earthquake just north of downtown Kazabek."

Holy Mary, Mother of God. The death toll was going to be in the tens of thousands. Jimmy leaned closer.

"For the first time in five years," the anchor—a hot bleached blonde with big lips—announced, "Kazbekistan's borders are open to Western relief workers."

"It would save time," Deck told Jimmy, "if you just came with me to San Diego."

KAZABEK, KAZBEKISTAN

Sophia had her eyes closed—it was always easier with her eyes closed—when the earthquake hit.

At first she, like Bashir and his men, thought they were under artillery attack.

It certainly felt like some kind of bombardment, the way the building shook and windows rattled.

Everything happened so quickly.

A half-dozen guards burst into the room.

Bashir shoved her roughly aside and she fell onto the tile floor, her head hitting with a jarring crack.

It felt as she'd imagined it would, only unlike Dimitri, she still had her head attached to her neck.

Bashir shouted to the guards as he scrambled for his

clothes, ordering them to sound the alarms, and they rushed back out of the room. . . .

Leaving her alone with the warlord, whose back was to the table beside his bed. It was the same table upon which he'd put his sword after demonstrating to her just how razor-sharp it still was.

She'd lived through a massive earthquake before in Turkey, and unlike Bashir, who was convinced he had an enemy to repel, she began to suspect that was what this was. But bombardment or quake, it was the break for which she'd been waiting two long months.

Sophia grabbed the sword.

She didn't have the upper body strength to behead Bashir with one mighty stroke, as much as she would have liked to do just that unto him. As he had done unto others.

Instead she lunged, throwing all of her weight into it.

Even so, she didn't manage to run him clean through. Still, it stopped him, his scream of pain lost among all the other cries echoing through his palace.

He fell to his knees, and Sophia grabbed the bedcover and ran to the door. The entrance to Bashir's chamber was usually guarded, but everyone—guards and servants alike—had fled. She wrapped the folds of fabric around her, turning it into a makeshift burka and hiding the blood on her gown.

She made it to the front door, where a crowd of people was pushing to get outside, where uncovered women were being turned back, despite the fact that a portion of the palace roof had already caved in.

Sophia covered her head and face and slipped out onto the street, into the dust rising up into the blue morning sky, and ran.

CHAPTER
THREE

SAN DIEGO, CALIFORNIA

TOM PAOLETTI slid a photograph across the table in the conference room of his offices at Troubleshooters Incorporated. "Ma'awiya Talal Sayid."

Decker picked up the photo as Jimmy sat forward to get a look. "When and where was this taken, sir?" Deck asked.

"Kazabek," Paoletti told them in a voice that revealed his New England roots. "Today. About thirteen hundred local time."

Deck passed the photo over, and Jimmy took a closer look at the man who was known to be a top al-Qaeda operative. "Is he . . . ?"

"Dead," Paoletti finished for him. "Yeah. Courtesy of the quake." He pushed more photos toward them.

Jimmy leaned forward again. None of the news stations had footage or even photos of the devastation in Kazbekistan—reporters from the West hadn't been allowed into the country for years.

In these photos, the skyline of the city—an architectural blend of ancient and new—had been radically changed. The Kazabek Grande Hotel still stood, a testament to the Westernization of the tiny country in the late 1970s. But the office building next to it had partially crumbled. In the foreground of the photo, many of the older structures—

35

homes similar to that of Jimmy's longtime contact Rivka and his wife, Guldana—had been reduced to rubble. It looked like parts of Baghdad and Basra after the war in Iraq.

"I'm sorry—I know both of you have friends in Kazabek."

Jimmy looked up into Paoletti's eyes. The compassion and understanding he saw there was not feigned.

"The situation's bad. Sewer pipes broke—water's contaminated in most of the southern sectors. WHO's trying to get involved—southern Kazabek's an epidemic waiting to happen. Power's out, cell towers—the few that were left—are down. And the local warlords are still killing each other and anyone who looks at them cross-eyed." Paoletti smiled. "I'd make one hell of a travel agent, huh? Bottom line, this job is going to suck."

"We've both been to K-stan before, sir," Decker told him. "Conditions there have never been good."

"Yeah. I served a short sentence there myself," Paoletti said. "And you don't have to sir me. We're not in the Navy anymore, Deck."

When Jimmy had walked into this office, nothing about this place had impressed him. The building itself was low-rent, the furniture ugly, and the receptionist's desk empty. Tom Paoletti's new company specialized in personal security, but at first glance it looked as if Troubleshooters Incorporated needed a little rescuing itself.

But then Paoletti—the former commanding officer of SEAL Team Sixteen—had come out of the back office and shook his and Deck's hands, and Jimmy knew instantly why the man was a Spec Ops legend.

He had that same je ne sais quoi that Decker did—the same golden aura. It danced and glowed about him and proclaimed him a true leader of men. Of women, too, although Jimmy would bet big money that most women followed Tom Paoletti around for a different reason entirely.

And this was despite the fact that, in another couple of years, he was going to be billiard-ball bald.

Deck's still-thick head of hair wasn't the only difference between the two men. In fact, besides that rare leadership quality they shared, they really weren't that much alike.

Paoletti's quietness was easygoing. There was a contentment to him, a sense of peace, a comfortable-inside-his-skin quality that could be found only in someone who—at least most of the time—liked the man he saw in his bathroom mirror each morning.

Decker's watchful quiet, on the other hand, seemed to hold an undercurrent of danger. He was like a gunslinger from one of those old Westerns Jimmy had watched as a kid. Quiet and even polite, but with something in the way he sat or stood that let the world know this was not a man to mess with.

And if he *was* messed with, look out.

And yet, at the same time, Deck could, with very little effort, make himself completely invisible.

That was something Jimmy particularly admired, since invisibility in a crowd wasn't high on his personal list of easy tricks.

He suspected it wasn't on Paoletti's either. But right now the man was silent, just letting Decker take a longer look at the photographs he'd given them.

Deck knew Paoletti from his years with the SEAL teams. In the rental car on the way to this meeting, when Jimmy had been speculating on the nature of this assignment, Deck had turned to him and said, "I'd sign on just to shine Commander Paoletti's shoes."

It was one hell of an endorsement.

"Where did these pictures come from?" Decker asked Paoletti now. "Who's the photographer?"

"The client sent them to me," he replied. "I can't be more specific than that."

"Understood." Deck finally put the photos down on the table. "They're looking for Sayid's laptop."

It wasn't a question, but Paoletti nodded. He glanced at Jimmy, checking to see if he was up to speed.

He was, indeed. Al-Qaeda leader Ma'awiya Talal Sayid carried a laptop that was believed to contain a gushing fountain of information—maybe enough to clue in the West to the next terrorist target. Of course the key word there was *believed*.

"Does your client—let's call them the Agency for short—have any proof that this mystical laptop isn't just a rumor?" Jimmy asked. "Or that it contains more than the latest versions of Pac-Man and Solitaire?"

"Nope," Paoletti told him, with a coolness in his eyes that let Jimmy know his easygoing friendliness was for Decker and Decker alone. Paoletti still hadn't decided whether he and Nash would be buddies. Which was different from most people's prejudgment. Most people filed Jimmy in their troublemakers folder before even meeting him.

"And let's not call the client anything but the client," Paoletti added. "They like it better that way."

"Especially since you haven't got your Cone of Silence up and working," Jimmy said with a deliberate glance around the room, letting Paoletti know that he, too, hadn't yet decided if he was going to climb in bed with the former SEAL. So to speak.

Paoletti laughed, getting both the *Get Smart* reference and Jimmy's unspoken message, which was another point in his favor. "Yeah, well, we moved into this office two months ago and I haven't had time to hire a receptionist, let alone set up some kind of shielded room." He included Deck in the conversation. "I'm turning work away, Chief— I can't keep up with the demand. Lot of people traveling overseas want an armed escort these days. Even domestically, there's a huge call for additional security, evacuation plans, that type of assignment. And those are just the corporate clients. But this job . . . this one's important. The client can't send in their own, um, employees—the U.S.–K-stani relationship has deteriorated beyond repair and if those *employees* were discovered, there could be real trouble. I don't think that's news to either of you."

It wasn't. It had been more than three years since Jimmy had gone into K-stan with Decker on an Agency assignment. "And yet someone eliminated Sayid," he commented.

"No. Mother Nature eliminated Sayid. His death was from internal damage, believed to be caused by a collapsing building," Paoletti informed them. "He apparently crawled free and found his way to a hospital before he died. We have no idea where he was at the time of the quake, or if his laptop is still there in the rubble. Even if it is, it could be destroyed or damaged."

"Which hospital?" Deck asked.

Paoletti shook his head. "We don't even know that."

Deck glanced at Jimmy, who sat forward to look more closely at the two pictures of Sayid. They were both the same photograph, but one had been cropped and enlarged so that the terrorist leader was in close-up. The original shot showed a long line of injured people in makeshift beds, really no more than pallets on the floor, in an ornately tiled room being used as a temporary hospital ward.

"This is the lobby of the Hôpital Cantara," Jimmy told Decker. "Near Kazabek's City Center." He glanced at Paoletti, resisting the urge to bat his eyelashes. *So do you love me yet?*

"You're that certain?" the former SEAL CO asked.

"I went there a few years back to get some stitches," Jimmy told him.

Paoletti lifted an eyebrow. "I thought you Agency types were like the SEALs and stitched yourselves up."

"In my large intestine," Jimmy added. He often got dinged

up out in the field, a result of playing hard and rough, but that time he'd been stabbed.

I can't believe you call getting stabbed "dinged up." Tess Bailey's voice echoed in his head from that night, two months ago. He'd answered, *There's a big difference between getting dinged and stabbed.* She hadn't believed him, but it was true.

The barely noticeable ding Jimmy had gotten on the night Tess had helped him keep Decker from being gunned down in the parking lot of the Gentlemen's Den was very different from the injury that had brought him to the Cantara hospital.

He'd been jumped. Three to one—odds he normally wouldn't have blinked at, but one of 'em had a knife that Jimmy hadn't seen until it was almost too late. He'd stopped the blade from going into his chest, instead catching it lower, in his gut.

That had hurt. But it hadn't killed him. It *had* warranted that trip to the hospital, though. Which was serendipitous, since he could now give a positive ID to the location of Sayid's body.

"I sat in that lobby for ten hours," Jimmy told Paoletti. There had been that many people there who were more seriously wounded than he was. It was just another night in Kazbekistan. He tapped the picture. "This is L'Hôpital Cantara. No question in my mind."

Paoletti nodded. "I'm putting together a team," he said, "to enter Kazbekistan as earthquake relief workers, and to find and extract Sayid's laptop."

Decker nodded, too. "Who's your team leader, sir? Starrett?"

A Texan by the name of Sam Starrett, also formerly of Navy SEAL Team Sixteen, was a major player in Paoletti's new company, as was Starrett's wife, former FBI agent Alyssa

Locke, whose beauty was as legendary as her sharpshooting skills. Jimmy had hoped to meet the two of them today.

"Sam and Alyssa are both out of town," Paoletti told them. Of course, "out of town" meant something a little different for his employees than it did for most people. "I was hoping you'd lead this team, Deck."

Whoa. This wasn't just a job offer—this was an open door. Paoletti was offering Decker a new career.

But Deck, being Deck, didn't leap up and start doing cartwheels. He just nodded as if he were thinking about it, as if he might actually say no. He finally glanced at Jimmy before asking Paoletti, "What size team are you hoping to send over?"

"I'd like to send a battalion, but I just don't have the manpower," Paoletti said. Rumor had it he was recruiting as fast as he could. But recruiting took time. Background checks could be a real bitch.

Jimmy knew what his own background check had revealed. Nothing of substance. A name, a social security number, a date and city of birth. A two-word message: *Access denied.*

And just enough rumors to warrant that coolness in Tom Paoletti's eyes.

He was actually surprised that Paoletti hadn't asked to speak to Decker privately. Of course, there was still time for that.

"I've got two men who've worked with me for the past few months who are already en route to Kazabek—Dave Malkoff and Vinh Murphy," the former SEAL CO continued. "Normally I would've asked for your approval as team leader before sending them out, but I couldn't wait. Murph spent ten years in the Marines; Dave was with the CIA."

"I know them both," Deck said.

So did Jimmy. Murphy was cool, part African-American,

part Vietnamese, with just enough Irish thrown in to make things completely confusing to anyone walking into a room and looking for a guy named Murphy. But CIA agent— former CIA agent, apparently, since he was now working for Paoletti—Dave Malkoff was a complete head case. He was a bundle of raw nerves in need of some serious decaffeination. And a new wardrobe. He made the MIB squad look colorful.

"Nash isn't a big fan of Malkoff's," Decker told Paoletti, "but I'm okay with him. And Murph's solid."

"I'd also like to send along a computer specialist," Paoletti told them, "but there's a real shortage of skilled people. I got a call just this morning from a comspesh who's had field training, but no experience. I know that's not ideal. And I've never worked with her myself so I can't vouch for—"

"Her?" Jimmy interrupted. Whoops. Deck was giving him a look. "Excuse me." He threw in a little extra respect. "Sir. You're actually considering sending a woman into Kazbekistan?"

Sending female agents into K-stan hadn't been done without a great deal of angst five years ago, before the armpit of a country had had a regime change. And over the past few months things had gotten even worse there. Even the most basic of women's rights had been flushed down the toilet.

"She wouldn't be my first choice," Paoletti said. "If I *had* a choice. Like I said, I haven't worked with this comspesh, I haven't even met her. But I'm pretty sure you both know her. She just left the Agency."

A comspesh that he and Deck knew from the Agency who'd had field training? Oh, no. No, no.

"She worked in the support office." Paoletti shuffled through the papers in front of him. "Her name's . . ."

Not . . .

"Tess Bailey."

Oh, shit.

Paoletti looked sharply up at Jimmy. "Problem, Nash?"

Had he said that aloud?

Apparently he had, since Deck was looking at him, too.

"No," Jimmy lied automatically before his brain fully kicked in. There were a lot of problems with Tess Bailey joining the team, and only one of them related to the fact that he'd spent the night with her two months ago and then left town without calling, without emailing, without a single word.

"Well, actually yes," he quickly countered. "She's great. Don't get me wrong, Tess Bailey is really, *really* great. Good person. Smart, resourceful . . . But like you said, she's got no experience out in the field." He looked from Decker to Paoletti. "None. Whatsoever."

"Everyone's got to start somewhere," Decker pointed out.

"Yes. Yes, they do." Jimmy turned to face his partner, giving him an SOS message with his eyes. Whose side was he on here? "In Kansas City. Or Lincoln, Nebraska. Lincoln's a great place to start fieldwork. Not Kazbekistan."

Christ, he was going to pop a vein. He forced himself to take a deep breath. There was no way anyone in their right mind was going to send Tess Bailey and her cute little freckles to K-stan, the country that bore the nickname "the Pit." As in Shit Pit. As in the putrid stink of the worst side of humanity.

"Tom. May I call you Tom?" Jimmy didn't wait for Paoletti to give him permission before continuing. "Seriously, Tom, this is a woman who grew up on a farm in Iowa. We're talking Middle America. Cornfields and blue skies. And she looks it, too. She has no chance of blending in in Kazabek. I mean, she might as well walk off the plane waving an American flag and singing 'Yankee Doodle.' I'm telling you, she looks like she stepped out of a Disney movie."

"I don't know what Disney movies you've been watching," Decker said, giving Jimmy a smile that was grimly amused. "But I disagree." He turned to Paoletti. "I think Tess Bailey would do just fine. Like Nash said, she's smart and resourceful. In my opinion, she's ready for the real world. When did she leave the Agency?"

Jimmy clenched his teeth, squelching a sound of pain. Decker was screwing him. And on purpose, too, if he correctly read the meaning of that smile.

"Just today," Paoletti reported. "Apparently she got passed over for a field position again. She's been trying to break out of support for a while."

"Maybe there's a good reason she was passed over," Jimmy pointed out.

Paoletti turned to look at him. "Is there anything specific you know about her that would—"

"Yes," Decker answered the man before Jimmy could even open his mouth. "The reason she was passed over is that she's damn good at what she does while sitting at a desk. She's a hacker, sir. She's practically hardwired into her computer. It's poetic, what she can do. She was working as part of a tiger team while she was in college—that's how she got recruited by the Agency. They were bluffing when they turned her down—I know this for a fact. It's been the Agency's experience that most women will settle for support, or even just keep following the rules and applying for fieldwork indefinitely, but apparently she called their bluff and walked. Good for her."

Paoletti laughed his surprise. "I guess you like her for this slot."

But Decker wasn't ready to laugh about this. "Not so much for this particular job, sir. I'm with Nash—I'd rather not bring a woman into K-stan unless there's no other choice. But you definitely want her as a permanent member of your team."

Whoa, what was Decker saying? Permanent? Jimmy couldn't imagine going to K-stan with Tess, let alone working with her on a permanent basis.

Although, wait. Breathe. He himself was only in for this one assignment. He was going to Kazbekistan because he'd told Deck he would. But afterward, he was going to disappear again—this time someplace where Decker wouldn't find him.

"The Agency's going to come back to Tess with an offer," Decker told Paoletti. "And they're going to do it soon. If you want her—and you do, believe me, sir—you better grab her while you can. Bring her in for an interview—fast."

A buzzer sounded from the outer office, but Paoletti didn't move. He just gave Deck a long, measured look. The buzzer sounded again. It was the doorbell. Without a receptionist out front, the door to the street was kept locked. It sounded a third time before he finally spoke. "Are you involved with this woman, Chief?"

Deck looked surprised and then . . . embarrassed? He glanced at Jimmy before answering. "Did I say something that implied I was—"

"No, you didn't." Paoletti cut him off, looking at Jimmy, too, speculation on his face.

Jimmy tried to look only mildly interested—as if this conversation about Tess Bailey wasn't making him want to squirm in his seat.

"And frankly," Paoletti added, "I shouldn't have asked. It's not my business. You just seem to know her rather well, and it reminded me of . . ." He shook his head. "It doesn't matter."

But it obviously did matter to Deck. "I worked with Tess, sir," he said, "and I don't fraternize."

"This isn't the Navy," Paoletti pointed out. "I don't have any rules about what my people do on their time off. And as far as I'm aware, the Agency didn't have those kinds of restrictions either."

"As a rule, sir, I keep intimate relationships separate from work."

Unlike some asshole whose name just might be Nash. Or mud. The two were apparently synonymous. Decker's message to Jimmy was loud and clear, even without the pointed look.

The office telephone rang. "Excuse me," Paoletti said, and picked it up. "Paoletti."

Jimmy took the opportunity to lean toward Deck. "I'd like to point out that, also as a rule, you never get laid."

Deck didn't bother to respond.

"Great," Paoletti said into the phone. "I'll be right there to let you in." He pushed himself to his feet and dropped another bomb, this one of devastating proportions. "Tess Bailey's out front. Her flight got in early."

Jimmy didn't so much as blink. Mentally, he'd jumped out of his seat and run right through the wall into the back parking lot—like Wile E. Coyote used to do on the Road Runner—leaving behind a hole in the shape of a desperately fleeing man. Physically though, he didn't move an eyelash.

"That fast enough for you, Chief?" Paoletti smiled at Decker.

As the former SEAL CO vanished into the outer office, Decker turned and looked at Jimmy. His eyes were decidedly chilly.

"You didn't call her after we left the Agency, did you?" Deck guessed correctly, although it was a mystery how he suddenly knew that. Because Jimmy was still not reacting to Tess's unexpected appearance. Not at all. Nothing, nada, zip. No expression whatsoever. "You didn't tell her where you were going, you just left town, no word."

It was pointless to lie. "Yeah." Crap, how was he going to handle this?

"You are such an asshole." Deck was going to be no help. He was genuinely pissed at Jimmy.

It didn't happen often, but when it did—look out.

"Yeah, I know." He *was* an asshole. Had he really thought he'd simply never run into Tess again? Had he honestly believed it would be that easy?

"You know what I never do?" Deck said flatly. "I never find myself in the awkward situation of having to work with someone I've screwed, both literally and figuratively. Jesus, Nash."

Jimmy could hear Tess's voice in the outer office—her laughter as she responded to the lower rumble of Paoletti's voice. Shit. *Shit.* Any second she was going to walk in here and . . .

"You don't have to worry," Decker told him. "Not right now, anyway. She's a professional—she's going to behave like a professional. It's later, when she gets you alone—"

Oh, Holy Christ. "Don't let her get me alone." Jimmy broke down and begged.

"Fuck you," Decker said, and actually meant it. He stood up, headed toward the door that led to the outer office. "I'm not just going to *let* it happen, asshole. I'm going to help set it up."

"No, Deck, listen," Jimmy said. "You don't get it. . . ."

But what could he possibly say to make Decker understand when he himself didn't even fully comprehend the reason he'd run so hard and fast from Tess?

But Decker wasn't waiting for him to try to explain the inexplicable.

He was already gone.

CHAPTER
FOUR

DECKER INTERCEPTED Tess and Paoletti before they came into the conference room.

"Hey, Tess," he said, holding out his hand for her to shake. "How've you been?"

She was surprised to see him. Genuinely pleased, too, with a wide smile that was sincere. "Lawrence Decker! I didn't expect to see you in San Diego."

She took his breath away, she looked so good. Healthy, with high energy. Happy. As if she hadn't spent the past two months pining away after Nash. Of course, maybe she hadn't. Maybe she hadn't even noticed when he'd left.

Her brown hair was cut short—even shorter than it had been that night she and Nash had saved his ass at that strip club outside of D.C. She was dressed more formally now in a feminine version of a business suit, a crisp white shirt buttoned nearly to her throat. It was a far cry from those half-undone jeans and nothing else, but okay, thinking about that was seriously inappropriate right now. Decker was certain that a perceptive woman could always tell when a man was remembering what she looked like naked.

And Tess was extremely perceptive.

"Yeah," he said, thinking instead about Nash sitting in that conference room. "We just flew in this morning."

She picked up on that *we*, and her expression changed. It was subtle—she was good at masking it—but her entire body seemed to tense. So much for hoping that she hadn't noticed when Nash left.

God damn Nash. Deck promised himself to take the son of a bitch into the sparring ring as soon as possible—and beat the shit out of him, under pretense of physical training.

Of course, Decker would get equally thrashed, but maybe he deserved it, too. He should have said something to Nash three years ago, when Tess first came to work at support. Something like, "Hey, I really like this one."

And then Nash would've kept his hands off of her.

Of course, so would've Decker.

Because Nash was right about one thing. Refusing to mix work and sex, and then working 24/7, pretty much meant a total lack of sex.

Decker was going to have to do something about that in the very near future.

Right now he turned to Tom Paoletti. "If you want, Nash and I could step outside for a while, let you talk to Tess privately."

This was the equivalent of a job interview for her. He tried to imagine doing an interview with Emily in the room. Well, okay, bad example, because on some levels he'd been relieved when she'd moved out of their apartment. But still . . .

"No, let's keep you part of this," Commander Paoletti said, leading the way back into the conference room.

Deck watched as Tess braced herself. She took a deep breath, stuck a pleasant smile on her face, and . . .

Nash was on his feet, looking equally casual, hands in his pockets. He greeted Tess with a completely impersonal smile. "Tess Bailey. What a surprise."

"I bet," she said. "How are you? How was Mexico?"

As Decker watched, something flickered in her eyes, and

he knew she'd just realized that she'd given something vital away.

Nash hadn't told her he was going to Mexico. Which meant that she'd cared enough to look for him after he'd left.

Deck could see from the way Nash was standing, from his "Oh, uh . . . It was . . . uh, great," that he'd picked up on that info, too.

He wondered if Nash had taken Tess's seemingly innocent question one step further and realized that not only had she looked for him, but she was good enough to find him.

And intelligent enough not to pursue him.

"That's . . . great," Tess said. "You look like you got some rest. I'm glad."

She really meant it. She really *was* glad.

Decker couldn't have loved his partner more if he were his own brother, but never before had he wanted quite so badly to break Nash's nose.

But then he looked over and realized that Nash knew she meant it, too. And the son of a bitch was actually shaken. Tess and Commander Paoletti probably didn't notice it, but Decker sure as hell did.

And wasn't *that* interesting? Nash. Shaken.

They all sat down, and Decker sat back and watched everyone's body language as Paoletti—as easygoing and relaxed as ever—explained about the earthquake and the missing laptop. Tess—feigning casual comfort and sitting in a position that signaled she was interested in this job and open to all possibilities—asked questions and made comments that let them all know she was completely up to speed on both al-Qaeda and Kazbekistan, and entirely capable of holding her own as a member of the team.

Nash was very, very quiet. Normally never going for long without some comment or joke, he simply sat and listened while Tess answered Paoletti's inquiries about why she'd left the Agency, about her training, about her background.

He was completely motionless and closed. Legs and arms crossed, shoulders tight. He looked as if he might explode, if someone held a burning match to him.

Tess had plenty of questions for Tom Paoletti, too, about Troubleshooters Incorporated.

"This team you're building for this assignment in K-stan, is it a permanent grouping of personnel?" she asked. In other words, if she signed on now to work with Decker and Nash, would she be working with Decker and Nash forever and ever, amen?

"No," Paoletti told her. "Each team will be created from the larger pool of personnel, depending on the needs of the assignment and the preferences of the individual team leader."

Tess looked at Decker, one eyebrow raised. "And you honestly want me on your team for this assignment?"

Decker shifted in his seat. "Honestly?" he said. "No."

She blinked at him, then laughed, turning to look questioningly at Tom Paoletti.

But Deck wasn't done. "No one in this room wants to send a woman to Kazbekistan. But we need a comspesh, and our choice seems to be either you or no comspesh at all."

Tess nodded, meeting his gaze again. "I appreciate your honesty. As a woman, I'm not particularly happy at the thought of going there. On the other hand, I *am* completely thrilled at the idea of participating in such an important assignment. If we can locate that laptop and gain access to al-Qaeda's plans . . ." She looked at Paoletti again. "If you're offering me this job, I accept."

Nash suddenly spoke up. "What about Mike Giacomo?"

"Gigamike?" Decker laughed. Nash despised Gigamike Giacomo.

"Yeah," Nash said. "Sure, he's an idiot, but no more so than freaking David Malkoff. Gig's a comspesh and he's male."

"I don't want him on my team." Deck put finality in his voice.

There was silence then. Paoletti had definitely picked up on the tension in the room. But he just sat back, watching.

"There are steps we can take to ensure Tess is as safe as possible," Decker continued.

"Yeah, except at night, because as an unmarried woman, she can't sleep in the same room with us." Nash was done being silent. "Depending on where we're staying, there's a chance she might even be housed in a different building than we are—"

Tess cut Nash off. "So I'll go in as a married woman. Who'll know that I'm not?"

"That'll work only if you pretend to be married to one of us," Decker pointed out. He looked at Paoletti. "But that's a good idea. If we can get Tess a new passport and papers on short notice . . ."

Paoletti nodded. "I'll get whatever documents we need."

"Then one of us can pretend to be her husband and be with her at all times," Deck said.

"It can't be Decker," Nash said to Paoletti, to Tess. "Too many of our contacts in Kazabek think he's got a K-stani wife back here in the States."

That was true. In the past, Deck had worked hard to establish an identity, a cover, on his frequent trips to K-stan. He'd created Melisande, his fictional wife, and it had helped him gain acceptance and trust. To show up now with a different "wife" would be the equivalent of tattooing the words "I am an agent of the U.S. government" on his forehead. Even now, three years after his last visit.

"And it can't be Dave Malkoff," Nash continued. "No one in their right mind would believe Tess would marry him. Our cover would be blown before we even got out of the airport."

Tess cleared her throat and crossed her legs. "I don't know Dave, so I'm not sure whether you're insulting me or—"

"Him," Nash said quickly. "I'm insulting him."

"Dave *is* lacking in certain social skills," Decker told her.

"He's a freak," Nash said bluntly, going for truth over tact. "And he looks and acts like a total geek."

"So what?" she argued. "People fall in love and get married for all different reasons. Maybe he's great in bed. In my experience, just because a guy isn't *GQ* handsome doesn't automatically mean he's not great in bed. And vice versa."

O-kay. Decker didn't dare look at Nash. *And vice versa.* He didn't want to begin to speculate about the subtext of *that* message.

Tess broke the silence. "Well, I sure know how to stop a conversation cold, don't I? My comment was inappropriate, and I'm sorry, but it really annoys me when people are judged on their appearance."

"Dave Malkoff is a freak because he's a freak," Nash told her in that completely calm voice he used when he was hiding an emotional reaction. "He's book smart, but if someone didn't remind him to go home, he'd starve to death in his office. The fact that he looks like a geek is secondary to—"

"It can't be Dave," Paoletti interrupted the discussion. "*Or* Murphy. So we might as well get that idea off the table. They're already en route to Kazabek. They're out of the loop. They both spent significant time in K-stan before the borders were closed—I have no way of knowing what kind of cover they already have in place. I apologize for not having that information." He looked at Nash, and he didn't look entirely happy. "It'll have to be you."

Decker was watching Tess. She kept her face carefully blank.

Nash was noticeably silent again, too.

"Is that going to work?" Decker asked them both.

"If Tess is going, in order for her to be safe, it'll have to work," Nash said. He even managed to smile. "Won't it?"

"I can make anything work," Tess agreed. "Particularly for the short term."

"Good," Paoletti, standing up. "Figure out a cover story. Chief, with me in my office. Now."

Tess sat at the receptionist's desk in the outer office of Troubleshooters Incorporated, flipping through the packet of information on Kazbekistan that Tom Paoletti had emailed to her, waiting for Jimmy Nash to come out of the bathroom.

She'd already read it twice. And she'd done extra extensive research on the country, downloading info from the State Department and other Web sites for savvy travelers onto her laptop. She'd studied it all on the flight to San Diego.

She couldn't believe how quickly this had happened. She'd called Tom Paoletti on the rumor that he was looking for people. He'd actually answered his own phone, they'd had a conversation, and she'd faxed over her résumé. He'd called her ten minutes later to tell her he had a job he wanted her to consider and that there was a plane ticket waiting for her at Dulles so they could meet face-to-face.

At the time, he hadn't mentioned Lawrence Decker or Diego "My name's Jimmy" Nash.

And here came Nash now, his carefully polite smile—more suitable for strangers than people who had been naked together—perfectly in place.

This entire assignment had the potential to be one giant, embarrassing ball of pain. For both of them.

But particularly for her.

"I didn't know you were going to be here," she said point-blank. It seemed a far better route to take than avoidance. Ignoring the anvil that was hurtling down from the sky could only work for a limited time. And she didn't want him to think she'd followed him here.

Especially since she'd already given away the fact that she'd gone looking for him, at least electronically, by asking about Mexico. Boy, for a Mensa member, she could be a total imbecile. She felt the need to explain that further. "I had no idea you and Decker were leaving the Agency. I was worried when you dropped off the map, so I checked around and found out . . . It wasn't because I wanted anything else from you."

"I know," Nash said. She couldn't tell if he was lying. "I also know you've wanted to go into the field for a long time, so . . ."

"Here I am," she said.

"Yeah. Here you are." He sat down across the wide expanse of the desk from her. "I'm sorry I didn't call you."

Tess rolled her eyes. "No, you're not. You're sorry that you're forced to work with me now. You're sorry you didn't foresee that possibility. I'm into honesty, Nash, remember?"

"Yeah." He met her gaze only fleetingly. "I, uh, do remember." He laughed softly. "God, this is awkward."

"Why?" she asked, and this time he really looked at her, with wariness and disbelief in his eyes, neither of which he tried to hide from her. "I'm serious," she added. "Why should this have to be awkward?"

Apparently she'd rendered him speechless.

"I don't know about you, but I had some really great sex that night," she told him. "It was incredible. You're very good in bed. I'm sorry if I implied otherwise when we were talking about Dave Malkoff—you just really pissed me off. And yeah, okay, it's true, the first time *was* a little quick, but you more than made up for it later—"

"Tess, stop. Look, you have every right to be angry—"

"But I'm not," she said. "I'm really not. I'm just . . . Yes, okay, I *am*, but not about what you think. I didn't even realize it until Decker said you were here, until I saw you again." She closed her eyes, wishing there was an easy way to explain. "I didn't expect you to call me because we had sex that night, Jimmy. I expected you to call me because, well, I thought we were friends."

Tess opened her eyes and he was staring at the floor, jaw muscles jumping. When he glanced at her, his eyes were filled with chagrin. If it was an act, it was brilliant.

"Are we really going to be able to do this?" he asked.

"I am," Tess said. "I've wanted this for too long to walk away from it now. And unless you're going to let Decker go by himself into a city that's been labeled 'the terrorist capital of the world'—"

"I'm not," he said.

"Well, there you have it," she said. "It looks like we're going to do this."

They were both silent then. Nash was looking at her now, really looking at her. He'd looked at her that same way, that night—as if he liked what he saw. And as if that surprised him.

They both spoke at the same time, both cut themselves off.

"I'm sorry," Nash said. "Go ahead."

"No, you go," she said.

"I was just going to ask if there was any way we could be friends again."

Yeah, *right*. "Well, that depends on your definition of friends," Tess countered evenly instead of bursting into disbelieving and near hysterical laughter. "Because I was just going to say that there's absolutely no way I'm ever going to sleep with you ever again. Not in this lifetime."

He nodded. "Of course. I . . . I understand."

Did he really? Tess doubted it. But there was no way she was going to explain that she couldn't keep sex separate from her emotions—the way he did—without revealing that she'd fallen a little bit in love with him that night. She might've been able to keep her heart out of it if it really had been a casual encounter—just relatively superficial small talk, some laughter, and an orgasm or two—the way she'd expected. But Nash had *talked* to her. He'd said things she'd never expected to hear him say.

They'd connected.

Correction—she'd thought they'd connected. He'd merely played her. Although why he'd done that, she wasn't sure. She'd made the first move—he had to know she was more than willing.

But maybe Jimmy Nash had gotten to the point where sexual conquests weren't enough. Maybe he didn't get off unless he knew he was going to break someone's heart.

Although hers had only been cracked.

"So," she said now. "Tell me what I need to know about you to pass myself off as your wife. Have we been married for long? What's my name?"

"My cover was that I was unattached, so you can keep Tess," he said. "It's easier that way. Although you'll be Tess Nash, of course, to drive home the fact that we're together."

"But Nash isn't your real name," she started to say, and as he glanced at her, she saw surprise and even wariness in his eyes. No doubt he was wondering if, as a comspesh, she'd had access to his Agency file. His *real* Agency file, not the one that proclaimed *Access denied*. She had, after all, tracked him to Mexico. That hadn't been easy to do. "Never mind. Off topic. It's inconsequential. I'm sorry, go on."

She realized that he was more put off by her being here than he was letting on. And he was less rested and relaxed than she'd thought at first, too. He kept rubbing his forehead and the bridge of his nose.

"It's been three years since I've been in Kazabek," he said. "But I think it's better to say we met just a few weeks ago."

"Weeks?" And after knowing each other such a short time, they were already married?

"Yeah." Nash didn't seem to think that was far-fetched. "They know me in Kazabek as James Nash. I'm the director of a not-for-profit organization called People First," he told her.

"James," Tess said, "not Jimmy?"

My name's Jimmy.

He met her eyes only briefly, and she knew he remembered telling her that, too. They had both been naked at the time.

"No." He cleared his throat, went on. "The story is that I was hired by PF right out of college. Which, by the way, was right down Mem Drive from you. I went to Harvard."

During the interview, she'd told Tom Paoletti that she'd attended MIT. "Really?"

"Yes, really. Is that so hard to believe?"

"No," she said swiftly. "I just . . . I had no idea." His file hadn't mentioned Harvard, but of course, it wasn't that sort of file. "When were you there? Maybe we could say we met in Cambridge, you know, and were friends for years before—"

"I was there right after I participated in that manned spaceflight to Mars," Nash told her.

Tess stared at him. He was just such a good liar, it was hard to know what was truth and what was cover story. What was real and what was make-believe.

"Where did you really go to school?" she asked.

"Harvard," he said. But then he added, almost gently, "*Really* is relative. The only *really* you need to be concerned with is the one that drives our cover story. Which is I went to Harvard, graduated fifteen years ago, worked for People First ever since."

"You worked for the Agency for fifteen years," Tess said aloud, and he paused. He was clearly wondering how she knew that, and she then realized that this wasn't public knowledge.

"You told me," she reassured him. He wasn't the only one who knew how to lie.

But like most liars, he was extra suspicious. "When?"

"How should I know?" she said with an eye roll that expressed just the right amount of exasperation. "You came into support and sat on my desk only 854 times in the past three years. It was one of those times."

If she'd been specific—May 14, 2002, at 3:30 in the afternoon—he would've known she was making it all up.

Instead he nodded. "Here's the deal, okay? We met three weeks ago, in D.C."

"Not while we were at school?" Tess asked. "It seems perfect—"

"It's not. There'd be too many years of ancient history to keep straight. We met three weeks ago, while I was in town for a conference," Nash told her. "People First is based out of Boston, but I travel a lot. Particularly to D.C. Where you live . . . doing what?"

"Working for a dot com?" It was what she probably would have done if she hadn't been recruited by the Agency. "How about . . . After MIT, I worked for a dot com that peaked big, but then died," Tess suggested. This was kind of fun. Or at least it would have been if she'd been playing this game with anyone but Nash. "It gasped its last breath a year ago. I'm so, *so* sick of computers, I decided to go back to school, right there in D.C. To law school."

"Are you really sick of computers?" he asked.

Tess gave him a look. "Harvard?"

Nash nodded, smiled. "You're good at lying."

"Thank you," she said. "I think." Of course, coming from the Liar King, that was probably the highest praise.

They were both silent then. So exactly how did they meet, Tess the law student and James the head of a not-for-profit organization, three very short weeks ago?

That particular detail—three weeks and then, bang, a wedding—still seemed weak to Tess.

Across the table, Nash rubbed his forehead.

"Headache?" she asked.

"Yeah." He smiled ruefully. "Hangover."

Ah. "It might help if you drink some water." She fished in her bag for the extra bottle she'd bought at the airport, slid it across the desk to him. "Here."

She'd surprised him. "Wow," he said. "I'm—" He shook his head. "Thanks."

"How about if I was doing work-study as a legal assistant for a firm—you know, pro bono law for not-for-profit groups," Tess said as he opened the bottle and drank. "Maybe one of our clients was People First. And that's how we met."

"No," he said, wiping his mouth with his hand. "I mean, yes, that's excellent, but let's not have your firm connected with People First. It would be too easy for someone to check and see that there's no record of . . . We could do it if we had more time to set it up, but we're on a plane to Kazabek in just a few hours. Let's say instead that you hadn't heard of PF until you met me. What if . . . you had a meeting with a pro bono client who was attending that same conference. Your meeting was in the hotel bar."

"But he didn't show," Tess said.

"Yeah. I walked in, saw you sitting there alone, and it was love at first sight. And here we are, three weeks later. Married."

Tess looked at Jimmy Nash, with his perfect hair, his bedroom eyes, his broad shoulders, and his washboard abs—oh, she couldn't see them now, but she knew they were there beneath his shirt. "Is anyone really going to believe that? We meet and we're married in just a few weeks?"

"Yeah, and it'll help explain why we don't know each other all that well. That's important, unless you want to spend hours on the flight memorizing brands of toothpaste and deodorant, favorite foods, favorite movies, whether you like anchovies on your pizza—"

"Definitely not—to both of those things. The memorizing and the anchovies."

"I figured as much," he said. "The anchovies, I mean."

"I suppose you like them."

"Absolutely. Live large, I always say."

"Anchovies are small. And awful," Tess pointed out. "And people don't really get married after knowing each other for only a few weeks."

"Sometimes they do. We're going to Kazabek, Tess, not L.A. There's not a lot of premarital sex happening there. People get married before they get busy—and likewise, people who want to get busy get married first. You know, women have been sentenced to death for adultery there—even women who were raped."

Tess nodded. "I do know. I've read the packet of information on Kazbekistan that Tom Paoletti gave me."

"Then you also know that their women's rights movement has recently regressed about two hundred years," he said.

"Yes, I do."

"Whenever you're outside, you need to be covered." Nash had on that same concerned face she'd first seen in the car, two months ago, on the way to rescue Decker at the Gentlemen's Den. He was using the same commanding officer voice. These were orders he was giving, not suggestions. "Down to your ankles and wrists and up to your neck."

"So much for my budding career as a topless waitress."

Nash was not amused. "I'm serious."

"That's very apparent."

"Even if it's a hundred degrees in the shade."

"I'm clear on that," Tess told him. She resisted the urge to salute.

"You'll have to carry a scarf whenever you go out, too," he said. "In case you're stopped and asked to cover your head."

"Yes, I read that. In the packet."

"Some people don't read the packet."

"I did."

"There are parts of the country where women have to wear a burka and veil," Nash told her.

"Some parts of the capital city, too. And some women in Kazabek actually choose to wear burkas all the time. Or at least so I understand, after having read the packet," Tess said.

"Think of this as a test," he told her.

"You mean, a pop quiz on the reading material, or more of a 'How long will it take before Nash drives me nuts' kind of test?"

"This is your first time out there." As if he had to remind her. "I'm going to be on top of you every minute. You don't like it when information is repeated? Too bad. I'm going to make damn sure that you know everything you need to know to keep from getting hurt or, yeah, even killed. People can die in the field, Tess."

She did know that.

"And if you want to have a contest to see who drives who crazy first," Nash continued, "well, congratulations, you're already winning." He stood up. "Do you have other clothes with you? Because you can't wear that to K-stan."

"Yes, I know. These are interview clothes. I have a suitcase in the rental car."

"You can't take a suitcase to Kazbekistan."

"Yes, I know that, too. I just wasn't sure how many changes of clothing to bring, so—"

"Get ready to smell bad," he told her. "Figure that your entire wardrobe's got to fit in that shoulder bag you're carrying. And don't overload it, because you'll be carrying my bag, too."

Tess laughed. Of all the . . . "Look, Nash—"

"You should get used to calling me James."

"James," she repeated. "I know that you're trying to frighten me off, but it's not working. You may not know my brand of toothpaste or my favorite movie, but haven't you caught on, maybe even just a *little* bit, that I don't scare easily?"

"Colgate regular and it's probably a toss-up between *Moulin Rouge, The Philadelphia Story,* and *Casablanca,*" he reported, smiling briefly at the expression of surprise that she couldn't keep from her face. "I was in your apartment, remember?"

Yeah, like she'd ever forget. "Snooping among my DVDs?"

"No, just keeping my eyes open."

"While you snooped among my DVDs." After she'd finally fallen asleep, he must've stopped to look while he was on his way out the door, because she'd been with him every other moment and they'd been nowhere near her entertainment center. Funny, she would have thought he would have been in an enormous hurry to escape before she awoke. Instead he'd stopped to look at her things.

"I meant what I said about packing light," Nash told her now. "You really are going to be carrying my bag."

"Isn't that overdoing it a little in terms of following Kaz-bekistani customs?"

He lifted the bottle she'd tossed to him, toasting her before he finished off the last of it. "I'll be carrying our water."

Ah. Bottles of water would definitely be much heavier than clothing.

"Go and get your suitcase, Mrs. Nash," he said. "I'll help you figure out what to bring."

Mrs. Nash.

Hearing that from his lips was just too weird.

CHAPTER
FIVE

DECKER WATCHED Nash watch Tess Bailey browsing in the airport bookstore.

Nash looked up, feeling Deck's gaze.

Decker shook his head in disgust, and Nash played dumb. "What?"

It was only because he asked that Decker answered. "You're an asshole. Two months—and you didn't call her once. And now you get to pretend to be her adoring husband?"

Nash was going to share a room with Tess, which by nature would generate intimacy. Add in the adrenaline inherent in a dangerous mission, plus the romance of being in an ancient, foreign city . . .

"It's a tough job," Nash said, trying to turn it into a joke, "but someone's got to do it."

"Yeah, well, do more than pretend, and I'll beat you until you bleed."

Nash looked at him.

"Yes," Decker said. "I *am* serious."

"Well, I'm not," Nash said. "I was just kidding. I'm not going to take advantage of her. I mean, not that she'd let me." He looked over at Tess. "Although, holy Mother of God, I forgot just how hot she was."

Decker shook his head. Hot. Tess Bailey was beautiful

and brilliant. She was funny, and enthusiastic, and brave. She was so much more than merely hot.

And Nash had walked—no, run—away from her.

"What the fuck is wrong with you?" Decker asked.

Nash met his gaze only briefly. It was hard to tell if that was because he was uncomfortable with the direction their conversation was going—they didn't talk like this, not about things that mattered—or if it was because he couldn't keep his eyes off Tess. "That was a rhetorical question, right? I mean, you don't want me to make a list or anything. . . ."

"I thought you didn't mess with women who worked support." Decker knew this was senseless. Talking about it wouldn't change what had happened.

"I didn't," Nash said. "I mean, I never did before. It was just . . . It was that one crazy night."

Wait a minute. "One night?"

"Yeah."

Decker could feel his blood pressure rising. "You had a one-night stand. With Tess Bailey." *Fuck.* He'd thought Nash's fling with Tess had been going on for a while. "That night at the Den."

"Yeah," Nash said. "I mean, well . . . You saw her."

"Yes," Decker said. "Yes, I did."

"How could I say no?"

Jesus, Nash was practically drooling as he watched Tess.

Decker got right up in his face, but he kept his voice low. "I meant what I said before, douche bag. You so much as *touch* her again, and I *will* beat the living shit out of you."

Nash was amused. "Shit, Deck, you sound like I slept with your girlfriend." He stopped laughing and actually looked shocked. He did a double take, looking from Deck to Tess and back in disbelief. "Did I sleep with your girl-friend?"

Okay, now they'd managed to dive headfirst into territory Decker didn't want explored. "No. Forget it, all right?"

He turned away, and Nash let him go. But then he followed. "I swear to God, I didn't know."

Decker gave up. "Look, she wasn't my girlfriend. She's not my girlfriend. She's never going to be my girlfriend."

"She could be."

"No," Deck said. "Even if . . ." He laughed his disgust. "I'm her team leader now."

"To hell with that."

Decker just shook his head.

"I'm sorry."

"Life goes on," Decker said.

Nash was back to watching Tess. He sighed. "Shit."

"Tom Paoletti gave me an additional job to do while we're in Kazabek," Decker told him. "He asked me not to mention the details to anyone else—including you." That got Nash's full attention.

"That figures," he said. "I could tell he didn't really like me."

"Give him time," Decker said. "He's naturally got some questions about you."

"So that's what the closed door was about. This secondary assignment, and him asking you questions—like are you sure you can trust me?" Nash's laughter sounded remarkably real. If Decker didn't know him so well, he would have been certain that Nash didn't give a damn.

But Deck knew that it bothered him. Nash pretended that he found it all amusing, but he was particularly sensitive to some of the nastier rumors that circulated about him.

"Yeah," Decker said. "I told him that as long as we paid you enough, you wouldn't flip to the other side."

"Screw you!" This time Nash's laughter was real.

Decker smiled. In truth, Tom hadn't asked the trust question that everyone usually always asked about Nash. He hadn't had to—he was a smart man who knew he'd gotten enough of an answer when Deck had told him he didn't keep secrets from Nash, that anything Tom told Decker would find its way to Nash's ears, no exception.

Well, okay. Maybe Deck would keep it secret if Tom wanted to throw Nash a surprise birthday party. But probably not, because Nash hated being surprised.

So if Tom didn't like that, well, Deck wished him luck with the new company and this mission, but . . .

Tom had told him to chill out and sit back down.

"He asked me to look up a guy named Dimitri Ghaffari," Decker told Nash now. "See if he and his American partner are good candidates for recruitment to Tom's team. We don't have a name for the partner—in fact that could be something Ghaffari made up to build his reputation. It rings of urban legend: Ghaffari and his rich American backer.

"Tom doesn't know much about him, but Ghaffari's name has come up often enough over the past few years. Apparently he did import/export out of a home base in Kazabek. Business has tanked since the K-stani government deteriorated."

The warlords who were running most of the country these days wanted to keep the West out, and people like Ghaffari had made a living bringing it in.

Ghaffari could well be looking for work, and his loyalties no doubt would be on the side of those who supported capitalism.

"He might've been killed in the quake," Nash pointed out.

"Yeah."

"Everyone we know in Kazabek might've been killed in the quake."

"Yeah." That was a sobering thought.

"This assignment already blows," Nash said.

"Yeah," Decker agreed. But if that laptop was real, and

there was even the slimmest chance that it was somewhere in the rubble, with even just the smallest portion of its hard drive intact . . .

"You have any nickels on you?" Nash asked. "We're flying in to Ikrimah, and, well, I usually have enough time to pick up a few rolls of nickels from the bank."

Decker dug through his pockets. He had only a few mixed in with the pennies and dimes. He gave them to Nash. "Maybe the bookstore has an extra roll."

"Ah." Nash managed to smile. "Good idea." He looked over at Tess again, but then caught Decker watching him. "I honest to God didn't know about . . ." He shook his head.

"There was nothing to know," Decker said, and went to help Tess find a book to read on the flight.

KAZABEK, KAZBEKISTAN

The first aftershock had caught her unprepared. Sophia had forgotten how intense it could be, much like another earthquake itself.

After escaping Padsha Bashir's palace, she'd found her way to the old Hotel Français, near City Center, where she had lived with her parents when she was barely ten years old, an entire lifetime ago. The hotel had been crumbling and in ill repair even then, and she'd heard two months back—before she'd foolishly accepted Bashir's invitation to that ill-fated luncheon where Dimitri had been served his final meal—that the Français had shut its doors. The old wreck had been sold and was scheduled to be either restored or demolished in the very near future.

But Sophia had lived in Kazabek for long enough to know that the very near future could be any time between the end of the year and the end of the decade. It wasn't likely to be sooner, because, in K-stan, changes of that magnitude took time.

And sure enough, the building was still standing. Part of the roof had decayed, but as she made a slow circuit of the rambling place, she could see that the walls weren't cracked—at least no more than they had been before.

The basement door was locked, but locks had never been a challenge for her. She opened it without doing any damage. No one would know she'd gone inside.

The entire hotel was empty, all of the furnishings and wall hangings missing, and all the towels and the maids' uniforms that had lined the little corridor by the laundry room gone.

On the first floor, outside what had once been a restaurant, she found the ladies' washroom. Comprised of two small rooms, one a former sitting area, now empty, the other filled with sinks and stalls, it had a door that locked, a cool tile floor, and most important, windows way up high on the interior wall, looking out over the center courtyard. If she burned a candle in there at night, the light wouldn't be seen from the street.

If she had a candle.

The water, amazingly, still worked. It came, with a gush of rust and slime, from the faucet of one of a row of sinks that lined one mirrored wall.

Sophia let it go until it ran clear and then she drank. She washed using the soap still in the glass globes—apparently not everything had been taken from the hotel. The soap was thick and congealing from age and evaporation, but she used it to wash not just her torn and bleeding feet and the most recent cuts on her arm where Bashir had reminded her of the sharpness of his sword, but all of her. Everywhere he or one of his horrible friends ever touched.

She even washed her hair, wanting to be rid of the perfumed scent of the palace.

She had virtually nothing but the nearly transparent white gown and the sheet—she washed those, too—that she'd wrapped herself in after killing Bashir. No real clothes, no passport, no papers, no money, no food. No friends who would be willing to help her.

Because Bashir's nephews would seek revenge. The entire city would be searching for her, eager for the reward. It would be a big reward—the kind that could turn her friends into her worst enemies. With her blond hair, she had to be careful. She'd be easy for anyone to spot.

After checking that the door was locked, she wrapped herself in that wet sheet and lay down on the tile floor, exhausted and needing to sleep.

And, for the first time in months, able to sleep.

She may have had nothing, but she had water and she had her freedom.

Mere hours ago she'd been little more than a prisoner, a slave to a man she despised. Compared to that, she was now far richer than her wildest dreams.

WORLD AIRLINES FLIGHT 576, SAN DIEGO TO HONG KONG

Tess looked up from her book to see the flight attendant standing in the aisle of the plane with a tray of champagne flutes.

The only seats available at such short notice on this intercontinental flight had been in first class. What a shame.

Tess smiled and shook her head—no thanks—and, ignoring the murmur of voices around her, returned her attention to her book.

It was a somewhat anemic spy thriller that had been written during the Cold War. The hero was a James Bond type who reminded her a little of Jimmy Nash. He was tall, handsome, and extremely skilled, clever with a dry wit. But like most fictional secret agents, this character never, ever whined and complained to his support staff.

It was remarkable how often authors left out those particular moments—the scenes where the superagent comes striding into the office, scowling at everyone and demanding to be told why no one had let him know *before* he went to Turkey that his credit card had expired last week.

Yeah, Tess would've liked to read the scene where Miss Moneypenny pulls the e-memo titled "See Me NOW About Your Credit Card's Impending Expiration" from James's email box, prints it out, and hands it to him, then tartly asks him what more he would like her to do to keep him informed, especially when he's too busy wining and dining some babe in a black leather catsuit to read his blasted email.

She looked up as Nash returned from the bathroom and, with a smile, slipped past her into the window seat. The difference between no Nash and Nash was like night and day, and she had to force her gaze back to the open pages of her book. Reading with him sitting beside her was a challenge. The man had an enormous presence.

He could fill an entire room—let alone the small first-class cabin of a commercial airliner—with just a smile.

It was similar to the way he'd filled the car that night, as he'd driven her home.

She'd left her own car in the parking lot at the Gentlemen's Den, and wouldn't be able to pick it up until morning. That bar fight Decker and Nash had started had escalated, and the entire street was blocked with police and emergency vehicles.

The helicopter that scooped them from the roof of the strip club had brought them to Agency headquarters, where Nash had quickly claimed the keys to the last of the loaner cars in the lot.

"Come on, I'll give you a lift," he'd told her.

But Tess had hesitated before climbing in. "Don't you have, like, other things to do?" she'd asked. "Debriefings . . . ?" Didn't Decker need him?

But Nash had smiled his best smile. And the combination of that smile plus the white tank-style undershirt—she still had on his dress shirt—that hugged his chest and showed off his muscular shoulders and arms actually made her heart skip a beat. Her response to him had been both tacky and clichéd, but true.

So she'd gotten into the car. Accepted the ride. With her eyes wide open.

Tess couldn't remember what they'd talked about on the way to her apartment. Nash was good at keeping a conversation going, though, at keeping it light and easy.

There had actually been a parking space open in front of her building. Was it possible he'd arranged that, too? Or maybe he was just born lucky. He'd parallel parked the way he did everything—with confidence and skill.

"I'll walk you up." He didn't ask, he told her. Tess looked at him, and he smiled very slightly. "That way you can give me back my shirt."

She didn't want or need any excuse to let him come up.

But she just smiled back at him as they got out of the car and went up the steps, as she unlocked her apartment door and led him inside.

"Can I get you something besides your shirt?" she asked, unfastening the buttons as she went into the kitchen, starting at the bottom and working her way up. "Beer, soda . . . ?" Condom?

Was she really going to do this?

"A beer would be great." Nash, tall, dark, and almost unbelievably gorgeous, followed her.

Yes, she *was*.

The apartment's last tenants had redone the kitchen with

a cow motif gone mad, and he clashed with the kitschy wallpaper and stenciled cabinets. It was like seeing James Bond in bed with the cast from *Oklahoma!*

"Cute," he said as he looked around him.

"Yeah, right," she said, reaching into the refrigerator for two bottles of beer. "Try living with it." She twisted off the tops. "I eat out a lot."

Not quite the truth, unless *out* could be defined as the takeout she ate at her desk at work, eyes on her computer screen.

Still, as far as comparisons went, she *was* closer to Bond than Aunt Eller. And after she handed him one of the beers, she proved it.

Because she also handed him his shirt, taking him completely by surprise for the second time that night.

Her audacity made her own pulse race, but really, they both knew damn well why he'd come upstairs. And if she'd had any doubts at all, they were erased by the look that was now in his eyes, and by his smile.

It was a real smile, not one of those loaded-with-meaning player smiles that he'd been giving her most of the night.

"I don't like playing games," she told him. "Let's be honest about what this is, okay?"

Nash laughed. "Thirty seconds ago I knew what this was," he admitted. "I have to confess that I don't anymore. I . . . I really like you, Tess." He looked away from her as he laughed again, as if his words had surprised him as much as they'd surprised her. Surprised and maybe even embarrassed him.

Of all the things she'd expected him to say . . .

Tess put her beer back down on the counter and reached for him, and then, God, his arms were around her and she was kissing Diego Nash.

Who really liked her.

"Tess," he gasped as he kissed her harder, deeper, again

and again, as he pressed her closer to him, so that she couldn't miss the fact that he was fully aroused. "You don't know how badly I've wanted to do this. How much I need . . ."

There was a desperation to both his mouth and hands that she hadn't expected, a clumsiness broadcasting a lack of control that thrilled her. She'd imagined that making love to Nash would be exquisite, but that it would be something he would do to her. She imagined he'd remain cool and almost aloof, as much a pro at this as at everything else he did, while she was the one who would come undone.

Instead he nearly broke the zipper of her jeans, swearing and apologizing until she shut him up by kissing him again. He even tripped over his own pants in his haste to remove them while she led him down the short hall to her bedroom.

She didn't have to remind him of their need for a condom, but she did have to help when he fumbled with it, and then . . .

The sound he made as he filled her made her laugh aloud, but then he kissed her hard, harder, as he drove himself into her again and again and again. It was only because she was so turned on by the raw, nearly mindless intensity of his passion that she came, too, in a hot rush, when he climaxed.

"Earth to Tess," Nash said, and she realized he'd reached past her and taken two glasses of champagne from the flight attendant's tray, and was now holding one in each hand. God only knows how long he'd been attempting to get her attention, while she'd been thinking about . . .

"Sorry," she said, nearly dropping her book as she reached to take one, trying not to let their fingers touch, but unable to prevent it. Oh, God.

He toasted her before taking a sip. "Here's to us."

"To . . . ?"

"It's our one-week anniversary."

Ah, yes. That. "To us," she echoed.

"That must be a really good book," he said.

"Yeah." She took another sip of the wine. It steadied her enough to be able to smile at him somewhat vaguely—the kind of smile someone would give someone else when they were completely engrossed in a book.

Nash had gotten a pillow and blanket from somewhere, and after polishing off his champagne—tossing it back like a glass of whiskey—he settled back in his seat. "Wake me when we start our approach into Hong Kong."

He was going to sleep now, thank God.

Tess lifted her book—and realized she'd been holding it upside down. Perfect.

Nash didn't have his eyes closed yet—damn it. But he wasn't laughing at her. "I know what you're thinking about," he said.

Okay. Don't panic. Unless he was a mind reader, he couldn't possibly know. "Really?" she said, praying he truly wasn't a mind reader.

"Your first time out there," he said. "Heading to Kazabek. It's okay to be scared. It's normal."

"Ah." He'd thought she was thinking about their assignment. "I'm ready for this, you know."

He nodded, just looking at her.

So she asked him, "Were you scared? Your first time out?"

"I was too young and stupid to be scared," he told her—a real surprise. She hadn't expected him to say anything at all. Let alone that.

But then he closed his eyes, which was exactly as she'd expected, exactly as she'd intended.

Didn't it figure that, as desperate as she'd been just moments ago for him to stop looking at her like that, she now wished for the exact opposite?

"How old were you?" she asked.

His eyes opened and he gazed at her for several long moments before he spoke. "First time People First sent me to Kazabek was in . . . it must've been 1997. I was twenty-eight."

"That's not what I meant," she said.

"I know," he said, and closed his eyes.

CHAPTER
SIX

IKRIMAH, KAZBEKISTAN

WILL SCHROEDER climbed onto the bus.

Jimmy could not believe it.

He was definitely on some kind of weird bad luck streak.

He'd slept through most of the flight to Hong Kong. The flight here to Ikrimah had also been relatively uneventful—considering he was sitting inches away from Tess Bailey the entire time.

During the last few hours of the trip, he and Tess had drilled procedures and done a whole lot of worst-case-scenario type war-gaming. He was now as convinced as he'd ever be that she knew what to do and where to go if Godzilla attacked Kazabek and they were temporarily separated from each other in the panicking crowd. She also knew what to do in the event of a permanent separation—such as if Godzilla went and stepped on him.

And he'd repeated, ad nauseam, the importance of checking for the all-clear signal anytime she returned to their K-stani home base. Deck usually used a short length of rope hanging innocently from the knob of the main door. Tess should never walk in, even to an area that otherwise seemed secure, without checking to make sure that that rope was there. Checking for it needed to be an instant habit, and she assured him she would not forget.

But never once, during all the hours that they'd spent talking, had Jimmy leaned in close and told her, "Hey, you know what? Decker has a thing for you."

There had been a moment, on the flight to Hong Kong, before he'd slept off the last of his hangover, that would have been perfect. But had he used the opportunity to bring up Deck?

No, he had not.

And once they'd gotten off the plane here in Ikrimah, a hundred miles from Kazabek, there had been no time to say much of anything at all.

Ikrimah was a nightmare. The situation had gotten dire since the last time he'd been here. This was the second-largest metropolis in K-stan, and it was filled with people who wore their hopelessness and fear deeply etched into their faces.

Their very lean faces.

These people were starving. But they hadn't been rocked by an earthquake, so all of the aid was going straight to Kazabek.

Or maybe it wasn't.

Only half of the supply crates that Tom Paoletti had procured seemingly out of thin air—the man definitely had some powerful connections—had made it through. According to the airline, the others were "still in transit." Talk about a royal pain in the balls. Unless they got really lucky and the gaping cracks in the Kazabek Airport runways got patched in the next few days, they were going to have to return to this airfield, way out here in terrorist country, later in the week to pick them up.

Of course, "still in transit," was corporate code for "Oops, we screwed the pooch and have absolutely no idea where on this vast planet your missing luggage might be." A trip back to Ikrimah was probably not going to be necessary.

Because, ten to one, the crates had already been appropriated by the K-stani warlords who ran the local black market.

Vinh Murphy, who with Dave Malkoff had met them at this airport, had been in charge of getting the surviving supplies to the bus. But as they passed through the open-air terminal, Jimmy managed to lose yet one more crate. It was marked "Rice," and he misplaced it in Nida's vicinity.

The burka-clad K-stani woman had set up her jewelry stand right there on the sidewalk, where she'd done business every day for the past five years since her husband had died. She had four impossibly small and solemnly obedient children assisting her today, instead of her usual three.

Jimmy quickly picked out a beautifully crafted bracelet and then a necklace, paying for them both in American money and in rice. He knew things were bad in K-stan when Nida didn't argue as much as she usually did, insisting that he was paying too much. Instead her eyes filled with tears, and she slipped a matching pair of earrings into his bag.

He had had to run to catch up to the others. They were in the process of lashing down their supplies on the roof of the ancient rattletrap of a bus that would ferry this latest contingent of relief workers south to the capital city of Kazabek.

Finally they were on board and ready to go—only three hours behind schedule, which was pretty damned miraculous.

That was when Will Schroeder, known in some circles as the Antichrist, made the scene.

Jimmy saw Schroeder's familiar red hair from where he was sitting with Tess, way in the back, as the prick lugged his duffel bag up the steps and past the driver.

"Oh, shit," Jimmy said, and three or four of the God Squad—devoutly religious men and women who bounced from one disaster site to another—turned to give him the profanity stare.

Yeah, yeah, he was going to hell. Tell him something he didn't know.

Deck was across the aisle and up four rows, sitting next to Murphy. He spotted Will Schroeder, too, and turned invisible.

That was always amazing to watch. Jimmy wasn't exactly sure how Decker did it, but he definitely became less . . . there. There was no other way to describe it. He took up less space—he actually got smaller. He slumped, hunched, contracted—whatever he did, it was freaking effective. It was possible that he somehow slackened the muscles in his face, too, and that, combined with pulling his hat down over his eyes, was the final touch. His own mother would have looked right past him.

Jimmy did the only thing he could do—he ducked down and hid behind the nearest woman. Who happened to be Tess.

Who also appeared to understand the situation without any kind of spoken explanation. She leaned back, effectively hiding him from Will's view, and pretended to be asleep, draped against him. All he had to do was turn his head a little, and his face was buried in her hair.

Hair that, despite the endless hours of relentless travel, still managed to smell unbelievably good.

The bus moved forward with a hiss of releasing brakes, and they were on the road.

An extremely potholed road, over which they lurched and bumped. Tess braced herself with one hand high on his thigh.

"Sorry," she said, pulling back as if she'd been burned.

It was not the first time she'd put her hand in that particular spot.

Don't think about that night. She was sitting much too

close for him to start entertaining memories of the way she'd given him back his shirt while they were standing in her overly dairy-cowed kitchen. Now was definitely not the time to recall just how desperate he'd been to lose himself in her, how mind-blowing it had been to do just that.

Because although Tess was willingly letting him hide behind her, she was trying to do it by touching as little of him as possible.

Jimmy risked a look toward the front of the bus.

Sitting beside some unrecognizable, bland little relief worker who was wearing Decker's shirt, Murphy was a human monolith at rest. He was about as nonplussed as Stonehenge.

Jimmy would bet his entire stock portfolio that Murph and Will Schroeder had never been introduced. Because Murphy—who could have been the love child of Tiger Woods and Andre the Giant—wasn't the kind of guy you could meet and then forget.

Dave was up toward the front of the bus, a few seats behind the driver, no doubt because he'd gotten food poisoning during his stopover in Turkey—what a typical Dave Malkoff thing to do. He probably thought the bus wouldn't lurch so much if he sat near the front.

Dream on, Dave. This was K-stan, where fixing the shock absorbers was the dead last thing on the local bus company's maintenance priority list, just beneath fixing the bullet holes in the windows.

Will Schroeder was sitting several seats behind Dave—whom he apparently didn't know, or didn't recognize.

Which wasn't really that absurd a possibility. Jimmy himself hadn't recognized Dave when they'd come face-to-face at the baggage claim area just a few hours ago.

Dave had, apparently, taken his departure from the CIA as an opportunity to embrace his inner grunge rocker.

His hair was shaggy and long enough in the back to be

pulled into a ponytail. He hadn't shaved in at least a week. He wore jeans and a T-shirt that said "Bite Me," neither of which fit his wiry frame particularly well, but both of which were a radical change from the Joe Friday designer line of cheap-as-shit black suits that he'd worn as his uniform in the past.

If Jimmy hadn't known about the food poisoning, he would have guessed that Dave was completely stoned. He was sitting with his head lolled back and his body boneless—totally relaxed. In fact, he'd even smelled a little like the local weed. It was freaky.

Who are you and what have you done to Dave "Puckerfactor Five Thousand" Malkoff?

It was either *Twilight Zone* time, or weird Dave had created one damn good cover.

"Who is he?" Tess asked, her breath warm against his neck. She was talking about Will, of course. "Red hair, right?"

From his hiding place behind Tess, Jimmy could see only the back of the evil one's head, but it sure seemed as if he were planted in his seat. He'd taken out a book and was reading.

He maneuvered his mouth closer to her ear. "He's a *Boston Globe* reporter. His name's Schroeder."

She nodded. "Does he know you?"

"Yeah. He knows I'm no relief worker—Deck, too," Jimmy told her. "But then again, neither is Schroeder."

It was entirely possible that half of the people on this bus were reporters. K-stan had a no-media, no-cameras rule that was strictly enforced, and everybody and their CNN reporter brother were using this admittance of Western relief workers as a way into the country.

Of course, the fact that they were letting in relief workers from the West at all was a sign of just how terrible the situation was in Kazabek.

Tess shifted so that she could speak to Jimmy even more quietly. In fact, her lips brushed his ear as she spoke.

"Even if he sees you, he won't blow your cover, because if he does, you'll blow his," she concluded, quite correctly.

His turn to put his mouth near her ear. He resisted the overwhelming urge to lick her. "Yeah, but once he sees we're here, he'll be on us like a dog in heat. He's probably come for the disaster story, but it won't take much for him to realize there's something bigger going down."

"So he not only knows you're not a relief worker . . ." Tess said.

"Deck and I were sent to Bali shortly after the night-club bombing," Nash told her. "We, uh, interacted with Schroeder there. He'd have to be an idiot not to know that we were working for the government. And he's no idiot."

Tess was silent for a moment. He could feel her breathing, feel her thinking. Finally she turned her head, her mouth again touching his ear. Christ, was she doing that on purpose?

Maybe she was. And maybe tonight . . .

But, "Sorry. The bus keeps . . ." She pulled back a little. "Do you really think we'll be able to get off this bus without him seeing you?" she asked. "Once we disembark, I won't be able to hang all over you like this. Public displays of affection are a big no in the streets—or so I read in my information packet on Kazabek. You know, the one you didn't really expect me to read?"

"You're so funny," he murmured.

She laughed softly, and he was rocketed back in time to her bedroom. She was beneath him, out of breath, her legs still wrapped around him, her eyes dancing. . . .

"So what's the plan?" she asked now.

They would get to Kazabek, hire a truck to take them to Rivka's house, unload their equipment, have a little dinner, and then go into their bedroom and . . .

And not jump each other.

How could he be thinking about sex after that conversation he'd had with Decker outside the airport bookstore? Forget the threat of a beating—that was inconsequential. What mattered was that Decker had a thing for Tess. And despite his claims that it was too late for any kind of relationship between them, Jimmy was determined to make things right.

He wouldn't be jumping Tess tonight or any other night. Even if she begged him to. Which was about as likely as Elvis parachuting out of an alien spacecraft, onto the fifty-yard line of the Super Bowl and breaking into "Burning Love." No, if Elvis came back, he'd definitely start the gig with "Heartbreak Hotel."

"We'll wait for him to get off the bus first," Jimmy told Tess. "Most people are always in a hurry."

"And we're not?"

He knew she was thinking about that laptop computer, potentially filled with all that information about impending terrorist attacks, sitting somewhere in the rubble.

"Sometimes you get farther by watching and waiting." Jimmy laughed. It was funny—that was usually what Decker said to him. But really, the last thing they wanted was a reporter—*this* reporter—figuring out why they were here. And it wasn't as if they could just make Will Schroeder disappear.

Well, actually, they could. *He* could. Quite easily, in fact. *Too* easily.

Tess once again was quiet, as if she'd picked up on his sudden change in mood, and the bus bounced its way toward Kazabek. It seemed impossible that anyone could sleep on this thing, but her silence stretched on and on for five minutes, ten minutes, fifteen.

But then Jimmy realized she wasn't asleep. She was looking out the window. The sun hung in the brilliant blue sky, making the desolate, rocky hillside strikingly beautiful. Of course, not everyone saw it that way.

"You love it here, don't you?" Tess said softly, and he looked down to see that she was watching him now instead of the scenery.

"Yeah," he admitted. He was only answering a simple question. He wasn't sure why it felt as if he were giving her a piece of his soul.

The bus swayed hard to the right as the driver swerved to avoid a deep hole in the dirt road.

"Hold on," Jimmy said as his arms tightened around Tess, as he held her even closer to keep her from hitting her head on the hard back of the seat.

She braced herself, too, her hand briefly on his thigh again, before she grabbed the seat in front of them.

"Careful," he said, the warning as much for himself as it was for her.

KAZABEK, KAZBEKISTAN

Jesus.

Jesus. As Decker stared out the bus window, he could feel Murphy leaning closer to look over his shoulder.

Up toward the front of the bus, Will Schroeder from the *Boston Globe* had put his book down.

After interminable hours on the road, even the five relief workers from Hamburg had stopped their relentless singing of German folk songs as they, too, gazed out at the devastation.

Kazabek—at least this northernmost part of the city—had become piles of rocks and crumbling mortar.

The streets were barely passable, and the bus had to slow almost to a crawl.

Grimy children stared at them from perches atop the ruined buildings, while their parents dug through the rubble that had once been their homes.

In a former marketplace, bodies were laid out, lined up row after row after row.

Another open square had been turned into a temporary hospital, with tents set up to protect the wounded from the hot sun. But there were nowhere near enough tents or medical personnel, and people sat or even lay right on the hard ground, dazed and disoriented, some still covered with blood.

And then there was nothing but block after endless block of devastation.

Murphy saw it at the exact second Deck did—four men running from a side street, shouting and gesturing toward the bus.

Murph got to his feet, already opening the bag that held the arsenal of weapons he'd somehow acquired in Ikrimah, readying to repel an attack.

Dave Malkoff, too, was up and over by the bus driver, prepared to launch out the door, if necessary. Decker hadn't even seen the man move.

"Don't slow down," he heard Dave instruct the driver, who kicked it into a higher gear.

But then Nash stood up from his seat in the back. "Stop the bus!" he called out both in English and the local K-stani dialect. "They're saying they've uncovered a school!" He was by an open window and had no doubt been able to make out the words that the men had been shouting as they drove past. "It was buried under debris. Another building fell and . . . They've finally dug through and part of the school's intact. There are children inside—still alive! They need this bus!"

Decker stood then, too. "Dave!" he shouted.

Everyone was talking at once, so he didn't hear what the former CIA agent said to the driver. All he knew was that the bus skidded to a stop and was put into reverse. With a whining of gears, they began backing up.

When he glanced again toward the front of the bus, he saw that Dave Malkoff had commandeered the driver's seat.

"Gather up all your gear and take it with you," Nash was shouting over the babbling. "God willing, they're going to need every seat."

Murphy was already pulling duffels and backpacks down from the overhead racks.

The bus jerked to a stop, and Decker saw exactly what three of the men chasing them were carrying in their arms.

Injured children.

Will Schroeder was standing in the aisle, looking from Nash to Decker, a lopsided grin on his face. "Well, isn't this a happy surprise," he said.

"Get your ass off the bus and help these people," Deck ordered the reporter as he pushed past him.

"Right," Will said, following him out onto the dusty street. "Because that's what we're all here to do. To help these people. Except Nash. We all know why he's here." He turned to Nash, who was right behind him. "Hey, Jim. Fuck anyone's wife lately?"

Nash ignored him, catching Decker's eye. "I'll set up triage."

"Good."

Nash pushed past Schroeder to help organize the milling relief workers into teams. "Anyone with a medical background," he shouted above the chaos. "First aid training included. Follow me."

"Murph!" Decker called for the big former Marine. "Find our supplies!" If those kids had been buried since the quake, they had to be in desperate need of water.

Tess was thinking along the same lines, and as Murphy broke open a crate filled with bottled water, she was right there. She hefted four whole cases and started toward the cleared entrance to the school, staggering slightly under the weight.

"Yo, Red," she said to Will Schroeder, who was still standing by the door of the bus, just watching the activity. "Yeah, you! Make yourself useful." She dumped two of the cases of water into the reporter's arms.

Decker wasn't too far behind them with more water, but as he approached the entrance, Tess was already coming back out.

The look on her face was one he knew he would remember all his life.

"They can hear a tapping sound," she told him. "There are more kids alive, I think probably in the basement. But in order to get to them . . . God, Deck, I think we're going to need a hundred body bags."

CHAPTER
SEVEN

"IT'S ANOTHER girl," Tess said.

Khalid murmured his thanks as he took the body from her and laid it tenderly on the worn boards of the wagon bed, making sure the child's face was covered.

"Amman probably made it down into the basement," Tess said, as she'd said each time she'd made another terrible delivery out here from the ruined school building. God, it was hot in the sun—even hotter than it was inside the school.

"But he may not have," the Kazbekistani boy said, just as he, too, said each time.

She looked into his eyes. She was more tired than she'd ever been in her life, but he was beyond exhausted. He'd been here since the quake hit, helping first by clearing the rubble and now by transporting the dead through this relentless heat to a mortuary that had been set up in a park down the street. It had been far more than forty-eight hours since he'd last slept.

Although he was at most sixteen years old and slight of stature and build, to call Khalid a boy wasn't quite accurate. He'd told her he'd been working to help support his family since his father had died three years earlier.

Khalid's English was remarkably good. He'd learned it at school, when he was younger, he'd told her one of the times she'd brought the body of yet another little K-stani girl out to his waiting wagon. He'd attended this very same school, where she'd been assigned the difficult task of removing bodies from the rubble, where he'd come searching for his little brother, Amman.

The relief workers were no longer allowing family members near the ruins of the building—the parents' understandable grief at finding their children's bodies was hampering the rescue effort that was still under way.

Khalid had gotten around that by pretending to be just another volunteer—and one with a horse and wagon at that.

"Enough of the floor is clear now," Tess reported, knowing that he wanted desperately to be inside that school, to see with his own eyes the progress that was being made. "They're about to cut a hole through to the basement."

It was hoped that most of the nine hundred children who attended this school had been led down to safety in an old bomb shelter when the earthquake first hit.

"And they're sure that doing this won't bring the rest of the building down on top of them?" Khalid asked.

"Yes." Tess was able to answer with complete certainty. "I know the men who've taken charge of the rescue operation. If anyone can get those kids out safely, they can."

Another relief worker appeared, his arms filled with another awful burden.

Khalid moved to meet him, taking the body from the man's arms. He flipped back the shroud to check the child's face, covered it again, glanced at Tess, shook his head slightly. It was another girl. "Thank you," he told the man.

"Well, you're not at all welcome." It was Will Schroeder, the reporter, his red hair dulled from the relentless dust. He looked as shell-shocked and exhausted as Tess felt, sweat making paths down the sides of his grimy face. But unlike the female relief workers, he was wearing shorts and a T-shirt.

Khalid took a step back, as if Will had struck him. "I beg your pardon, sir."

"No, kid . . ." Will wearily rubbed his forehead with the back of his forearm. The surgical gloves he was wearing were far from clean. "I meant . . . This is not the time or place to be so goddamn polite. Don't thank me for handing you a dead seven-year-old."

"Forgive me, sir," Khalid murmured, placing the child next to the others. "It is our way."

Dear Lord, there were so many of them. None were Amman, but every one of them was someone's little brother or sister, someone's precious child.

Will was gazing at the back of the wagon, too. "Look at that. You know, your way is totally fucked."

There was an answering flash of anger in Khalid's dark eyes. "Perhaps you would prefer if I acted more American. 'Who did this awful thing?' 'An earthquake, sir.' 'Who caused this earthquake?' 'God, sir.' 'Find where God lives—we must invade! A preemptive strike before He does this to us, too!' "

Will laughed his disgust. "Oh, *that's* sweet. Go on and throw stones—"

Tess stepped between them. "This isn't helping. We're all being pushed beyond our limits—"

He spoke right over her, glaring at Khalid. "—because we all know you and your country have *so* much to be proud of!"

"Not so much as *you*!"

"For God's sake, both of you! This isn't about politics— it's about *dead children*!"

Khalid turned away, but Will was still practically quivering with anger.

"You think this isn't about politics?" he asked. "Look at that wagon," he ordered Khalid, raising his voice. "Just look at it! What do you see? Don't you notice anything special about your cargo? Or is it just another load to carry, another chance to earn a fast buck?"

"Stop that!" Tess took off her gloves, took his arm, trying to tug him back toward the school and away from Khalid. "He's a volunteer, and you know it! It's costing him to help—he still needs to feed that horse, and on what, God only knows!" She stepped closer to Will, lowered her voice. "Show a little compassion. His brother's somewhere in that school."

Will pulled free. "Well, he doesn't have to worry. His brother's probably safe in the basement." He turned to speak directly to Khalid. "We just uncovered the basement door. And the bodies of about twenty more girls who were *locked out*." He spat the words. "Because God forbid they occupy the same fallout shelter as the boys, use up all the air, eat all the supplies . . ."

Dear God.

"Look at that wagon," Will told her again. "Those are mostly girls."

He was right. Tess had carried out body after body, and they *were* nearly all . . . Dear God.

"Someone told me that out of nine hundred kids in this school, only about sixty were girls. They were taught in their own special classroom, carefully segregated from the boys. Their parents paid nearly three times as much for them to attend, and considered themselves lucky that their daughters were getting any kind of education at all. Lucky, yeah." Will laughed, but it was a terrible sound. "The teachers brought the boys into the basement and goddamn *locked* the *door* on the girls."

With one final accusing look at Khalid, he headed back toward the school.

Tess felt sick. "They couldn't have done that."

Khalid didn't say anything, but the look on his face told her that they, indeed, could have.

"Dear God." She followed Will more slowly into the school where the stench of death just kept growing stronger in the late afternoon heat. Twenty more bodies, he'd said. All girls.

Tess was dripping with sweat. It was running in a stream down the backs of her legs, soaking through her clothes. Local rules, the same ones that kept boys and girls from sharing a classroom—or a shelter during an earthquake— dictated that women be covered at all times. She couldn't so much as roll up her long sleeves.

The heat and the news that Will had just shared made her light-headed, but her discomfort, she knew, was nothing compared to that of the women waiting just down the street for that next wagon, about to find out that their children—their daughters—were dead.

"Hey."

Tess looked up to see Nash coming toward her. He was moving fast, as if he thought he might have to catch her. Truth was, she *was* feeling faint.

"You okay?" he asked, concern in his eyes.

She started to nod yes, but couldn't do it. "I think I might throw up."

"Yeah," he said, taking her arm and pulling her out of the path of traffic. "I know the feeling. You just heard about that locked door, huh?"

She nodded, searching his eyes. "Is it true?"

"Come on, sit down. Here . . ." Nash led her all the way back outside, to an area beneath a sheet someone had set up to provide shade. "Sit," he ordered, pulling her down onto a pile of concrete blocks. "Where's your water bottle?" He didn't wait for her to answer. He just turned, shouting, "Dave!"

"I just had some," she told him.

"You need more than some." He knelt in front of her, pulling her shirt up and out of her pants and fanning the fabric so that air moved against her body. "Look at you. You're boiling over. You need to be pouring water down your throat pretty much continuously in this heat. Desert rations are—"

"Minimum one and a half gallons a day," she finished for him. "I know. I read the packet."

Nash didn't laugh. He didn't even smile. "Did you do the math, too? Because that works out to about a bottle every hour. Come on, Tess, use that big brain that's in your head. You should be carrying around a bottle of water—and you know it."

"Yeah, well, guess what? I've been carrying around other things," she retorted hotly, glad for the anger that surged through her, knowing that without it, she might've started to cry.

And Nash knew it, too.

It was pretty remarkable. On him, the dust and the sweat actually looked sexy. It made his dark hair appear as if he were going gray, which, when it finally happened for real, was only going to succeed in making him even better looking than he already was.

Which was saying something.

If he was tired, if he felt like crying, too, he didn't let it show. He had a haphazardly bandaged gash on his right forearm that must've hurt something fierce, and a scrape on his cheek.

It must've hurt . . .

I get dinged up a lot. She heard an echo of his voice from that night he'd come up to her apartment. They'd talked about things she hadn't expected him to talk about. He'd told her how he'd gotten injured on the roof of the Gentlemen's Den. He'd been stabbed in the leg, although he brushed it off as inconsequential, calling it "getting dinged up." He'd told her—although not in so many words—that he often got dinged up. On purpose.

Tess was no expert, but she suspected that Jimmy Nash used physical injuries to drown out emotional pain.

She touched his hair, his cheek, knowing that even though he didn't show it, this day had to be as hard for him as it was for the rest of them. "What happened to you?"

"Nothing," he said. "I tripped and . . . It was nothing."

He was on the verge of a full-scale retreat, but Tess stopped him by putting her arms around him. She knew she wasn't supposed to, and she certainly didn't want to give him the wrong idea, but she couldn't help herself. She needed the contact. The comfort. And she knew that, as much as he pretended otherwise, he needed it, too.

Jimmy Nash tensed for only a fraction of a second before he put his arms around her and held her just as tightly.

He smelled good. How on earth did he manage to smell good? And, oh, God, it felt so nice to be in his arms again. He'd put his arms around her on the bus, but it hadn't been like this.

She wasn't in love with him—she was smarter than that—but in that moment, she knew the truth. She could have loved him. Big-time. He was a fool for having thrown that away.

"I'm sorry," he whispered, as if he could read her mind. But she knew he was probably apologizing for countless other things. The heat. The horror. The injustice.

"She okay?"

It was Dave. Jimmy let go of her to take two bottles of water from him. "Thanks."

"She's fine," Tess said, forcing a smile as—shit! Some of her tears had escaped—she quickly wiped her eyes.

"She heard about the door," Jimmy told Dave as he opened one of the bottles and handed it to her.

Dave looked at her as she sipped the water, sympathy in his eyes. He had a face that didn't quite match his long hair, kind of like Tom Hanks in *Castaway*. "Don't go back there," he told her. "It's grim. It's . . ." He shook his head. "We can move them in stages. I'll bring them out here, you can take them the rest of the way to the wagon."

"That's not necessary," Tess said.

"Yes, it is," Dave said.

He was gone then, as quickly as he came, leaving Jimmy sitting in the dust in front of Tess, watching her drink her water.

"So it *is* true," she said. "That the door was locked."

He nodded. "Do yourself a favor and don't go back there."

"I'm not a child," she told him. "You don't need to protect me."

"I know. I also told Deck not to go back there. He doesn't need to see this either," Jimmy said. "And believe me, I don't think of him as a child." He looked away from her, over toward Khalid and the wagon, as if he were deciding whether or not to tell her something. But when he spoke, all he said was, "You know, you and Decker have a lot in common."

The high-pitched whine of the floor being cut made it impossible for her to respond to that. Jimmy pushed the water bottle up toward her mouth, tucked a stray piece of hair behind her ear.

But then he moved back. He was looking at something over her shoulder, and she turned to see Will Schroeder watching them as he went past.

"He knows who we are," Tess said.

Jimmy didn't try to speak over the noise. He just nodded.

The saw finally shrieked to a stop. "Why is Decker doing that? Why can't we just open the basement door?" she asked.

"There's a fallen beam leaning up against it," Jimmy told her. "It could jeopardize the structural integrity of the building if we move it. At least that's what Murphy said. I had no idea, but he's some kind of engineer." He laughed. "Who would've guessed? You learn something new every day, huh?"

You do, indeed.

Tess had learned quite a bit that very afternoon. She'd learned that although there was a great deal of bad in the world, there was also good. And it sometimes came from the most unexpected places.

She'd followed Jimmy at the Ikrimah airport terminal and watched him approach a Muslim woman who had a blanket on the ground covered with some of the most beautifully crafted jewelry she'd ever seen.

Jimmy had selected a bracelet. Tess didn't speak the language, but she understood the conversation just from watching. The woman told him that the rice was too much payment for what he was buying.

He picked out a necklace then, too, giving the woman that roll of nickels he'd gotten from the bookstore in the San Diego airport. Tess had puzzled over that for a long time on the flight. What on earth did Jimmy Nash want with forty nickels?

Now she understood.

Those coins were what this woman used to make her jewelry. She must melt them down and . . .

Jimmy had asked the woman something, gesturing toward one of the children. The woman pulled the child closer—a dark-haired little boy who couldn't have been more than four years old.

As Tess watched, Jimmy greeted the boy, even shook his hand. He then passed out candy bars to all of the children. He had only three, but none of them complained about having to share the treat.

"He is my sister's child," Tess heard the woman say to Jimmy in heavily accented English, glancing back at the littlest boy. "He doesn't speak American. His mother is very sick. He doesn't know it, but he will soon be my child."

"Doesn't he have a father?"

"His father died in the same factory explosion that killed my husband."

"I'm sorry," Jimmy told her. "Just what you need—another mouth to feed."

"He is a gift from God," she said quietly. "With a very small mouth." The smile she gave him was tremulous. "And I now have rice enough to fill it. Bless you for your kindness and charity."

"There's no kindness or charity here," Jimmy told her, almost as if she'd insulted him. "Just fair payment."

But Tess and the K-stani woman both knew otherwise.

Jimmy was looking at Tess now, eyes filled with concern in that face that he'd gotten dinged up, probably on purpose. "You okay?" he asked. "You kind of zoned off for a second there."

"Yeah. Yes. I'm fine. I was just thinking about . . ." She didn't want him to know that she'd seen him giving away that rice. He would be embarrassed. And he would also think she'd been following him, which she had been. Sort of. Not the way he'd think, but she would end up embarrassed, too. She stood up. "I should get back to work. You should, too."

"Yeah." He just stood there, looking at her, as if he were going to say something more. But he didn't.

"This sucks," she finally said. "I never imagined anything could be this bad."

"Yeah, well, welcome to Kazbekistan," Jimmy said. "I don't suppose I could talk you into catching the next flight home?"

"Not a chance," Tess said.

His smile touched his eyes. "Yeah, I didn't think so."

* * *

Sophia was getting robbed.

The pawnshop owner put the ring down on the counter. "Two hundred. That's my final offer."

"Kind sir." Sophia kept her voice even, low, respectful. Disguised. She'd done business with him before—months ago. She was grateful now for the burka and veil that covered all but her eyes. He was a bastard and a thief, and if she could have, she would have gone somewhere else. Anywhere else. But his was the only shop open. Probably for this very reason—so he could have his turn thieving from the thieves who had used the quake's aftershocks exactly as she had.

Sophia had used the second aftershock to steal a robe and burka, some pillows and blankets, jewelry, food, candles, and even a nifty little pair of his and hers handguns from an undamaged house in a well-to-do neighborhood.

The Kazbekistani family who lived there all ran outside when the walls again began to shake, so she'd slipped in through the open back door. As they'd stood in the street with their neighbors, talking, shouting, a baby crying, dogs barking, she'd helped herself to things they probably wouldn't even notice were gone.

Well, except for this ring. "The value of this ring is a thousand times that."

"Two hundred," he said again. "Take it or leave it."

Sophia needed cash, lots of it, if she was going to buy the false papers and ID cards she'd need to get out of Kazbekistan.

But she needed, even more, for her head to remain attached to her neck.

If she caved in to this pawnbroker's insulting offer, he would know how truly desperate she was. She might stand out in his mind. Yes, she was wearing a heavy veil, but her eyes were blue. And while blue-eyed Kazbekistanis were not unheard of, they were certainly noteworthy.

And if word of a blue-eyed thief got back to Padsha Bashir's nephews, they'd know she was still in Kazabek. The only reason she hadn't fled into the mountains was this ridiculous sense of hope—that the Western relief workers flooding the city meant that the American embassy would soon open its long-closed doors. That old friends might finally return and provide the help she desperately needed.

But each time she checked, the doors to the old embassy building in Saboor Square were still boarded shut.

Without another word, Sophia took the ring from the counter, pulled the burka's heaviest screen over her eyes, and went out into the street.

Tess was already sleeping in the back as Jimmy climbed up and into the driver's seat of Khalid's wagon.

She was asleep sitting up, leaning back against the hard wooden sideboards, Dave Malkoff's head in the softness of her lap, her hand in Dave's hair.

Dave had his eyes closed, too. His food poisoning was significantly more severe than he'd let anyone believe, and Jimmy couldn't help feeling respect for the man. Dave had worked tirelessly all day, without a single complaint, as they'd dug more than six hundred surviving boys out of that basement bomb shelter. He'd just stepped aside, dropped to his hands and knees, and quietly communed with the dust and dirt when necessary.

In the past, when Jimmy had done the food poisoning tango himself, he'd been able to do little more than lie in bed and moan. So, okay, yeah. He was impressed. And a little jealous of that hand in the hair thing. Jealous and impressed. By Dave Malkoff. It was surely a sign of the coming apocalypse.

Vinh Murphy climbed up beside him, and the ancient cart creaked and groaned under the big man's weight. "Yo, Nash, you really know how to drive this thing?"

"Yes, I do."

Murphy looked at him and laughed. His eyes actually twinkled—a giant Asian-African-American leprechaun. "Yeah, right."

Murphy had two basic modes. Silent and watchful, which played to most of the world as just this side of comatose, and amused. It was hard not to laugh, too, when Murphy was laughing, probably because he wasn't ever mean-spirited. Murphy didn't laugh *at* anyone—he laughed at the world around them.

"You know, Khalid had no trouble believing me," Jimmy told him.

"Khalid is, like, twelve years old. Besides, he wanted to go to the hospital with his brother," Murphy pointed out. "You could've told him you were the Queen of England, man, and he would've kissed your ring and asked you for a knighthood."

Khalid had wept with joy when Amman had been carried from the basement with nothing more serious than a sprained wrist and a bad case of dehydration. He'd needed to go to the hospital to get checked out, but the little boy wouldn't stop clinging to his brother's neck.

Jimmy had suggested Khalid trust him to drive his horse cart to Rivka's house, where they were planning to stay. Khalid could go to the hospital with his brother and pick up both horse and cart the next morning.

The boy had extracted a number of promises from Jimmy. He promised to feed and care for the horse and to lock up the cart in Rivka's yard. He also promised that he'd handled a horse and cart before.

"Okay, James," Decker called softly to him now from the back of the wagon. "We're good to go."

"Yeah, James," Murphy said. "Pedal to the metal, man. I told Angelina I'd try to call her tonight, and cell towers

are still down in this part of Kazabek. I'm hoping something's been restored in the wealthier part of the city."

"Don't count on it." Jimmy smacked the reins loosely
against the back of Khalid's horse, Marge. As in Marge
Simpson. Hooray for satellite TV.

Marge glanced back at him in mild annoyance, but otherwise stood there.

Come on. He'd seen it done this way in the movies.
Jimmy tried again. "Giddyap."

The horse's ears flickered. He—Marge was a gelding, go
figure—didn't even bother with the WTF look this time.

Murphy knew when it was not a good idea to laugh.

"So, okay," Jimmy said. "Maybe I was exaggerating a
little."

Murphy turned toward the back. "Maybe we should
wake up Tess. She's from Iowa—"

"She hasn't lived in Iowa since she was ten," Jimmy said.
"And believe it or not, there are a lot of people in Iowa
who've never even touched a horse."

"She told me she was from Greendale. That's farm country."

"Yeah, but she lived in town," Jimmy told the big ex-
Marine. "Her father worked at the public library. Right on
Main Street. Not a horse in sight."

Although she did have both a swing and a porch to swing
from at that house in Greendale. God. Green-freaking-dale,
Iowa.

"Maybe she had friends who had—"

"Let's let her sleep." Jimmy handed the reins to Murphy
and climbed down from the cart. He could do this. How
hard could it be?

He hadn't been lying completely when he'd told Khalid
he knew a thing or two about horses. He and Deck both
had gone in for special training after horses had proven a
handy mode of transportation for the Spec Ops teams dur-

ing Operation Enduring Freedom in Afghanistan. They'd both learned how to ride, as well as how to care for horses.

The cowboy who'd taught the class had told them that A) horses were smart, and B) they would immediately know it if you were inexperienced. They'd then proceed to dis you totally.

Jimmy approached dead on and looked the horse in the eye. "Stop fucking with me," he said. Then he said it again in the local dialect.

The horse was not impressed.

Jimmy resisted the urge to lift his shirt and flash Marge a glimpse of the sidearm he had tucked into the top of his pants. Murphy had scored a whole bagful of weapons in Ikrimah and had distributed them to the entire team. A quick look at the old 9mm was often enough to get stubborn humans to shake a leg.

The horse shook his head to dislodge a fly.

Maybe this thing needed a running start. Jimmy had seen Khalid leading the horse. He grabbed the horse's bridle in a likely looking spot and pulled.

Okay. Now they were moving. Of course, Jimmy was walking, too, which sucked. It was probably twelve miles to Rivka's. It would be bad enough to have to sit on that hard bench up front, holding the reins. Especially when he wanted to be in the back, with his head in Tess's lap.

He got them up to speed and attempted to climb back into the moving cart.

Which wasn't the easiest thing in the world to do, especially after all those hours spent clearing rubble.

Of course, the horse made it easier by courteously coming to a full stop.

"Shit."

Murphy gave the reins a try.

Nada.

Again.

No movement.

Jimmy heard Deck sigh from his seat in the back of the cart. Or maybe he didn't hear it. Maybe he just imagined it. Whatever the case, it was motivating.

He climbed out of the cart.

"I think he's tired," Murphy said.

"No kidding." Jimmy returned to the eating end of the horse and got the wagon rolling again.

They lurched and squeaked and clopped past Will Schroeder, who was sitting by the side of the road with his duffel bag, his head in his hands.

He wasn't alone. Jimmy realized there were quite a few people who had been on that bus from Ikrimah sitting there, looking shell-shocked after having helped recover the bodies of those children from that school.

They were probably all reporters, most of whom had never seen the aftermath of an earthquake in a third-world country up close and personal like this. At best, they'd stood on the fringes of the destruction with their news cameras and reported death tolls in hushed tones, without really comprehending what those numbers meant.

Today it had been spelled out for them quite clearly.

Picking a path through the rubble and ruins, Jimmy led the horse and wagon down a street he barely recognized but knew had to be Rue de Palms.

"Okay, Marge," he murmured to the horse. "I guess I'm going to walk it with you."

Twelve miles wasn't all that far.

CHAPTER
EIGHT

TESS WOKE to the extremely odd sensation of being carried. She opened her eyes to find herself moving through a doorway into a house with a low ceiling.

Jimmy Nash was holding her, her head tucked against his chest. He had one arm around her back, the other beneath her knees.

"Whoa," she said. "What are you doing?"

"Sorry," he told her as he took her farther into a rustic-looking kitchen and set her down. "I tried to wake you, but you were completely out. I had to get you inside because a curfew's being enforced, and we're already nearly an hour beyond it. We've been traveling with a police escort for the past twenty-five minutes."

Tess looked around. There was only one oil lamp burning. Set on a big table in the center of the room, it threw shadows against walls that were quite possibly made of mud.

Murphy and even Dave were carrying the supplies in from the wagon, stacking crates neatly on one side of the room.

"Rivka's not here. He left a note," Decker reported, after poking his head into a curtain-covered doorway back by what looked to be an earthen oven and an ancient cast-iron stove. "His son-in-law is in the hospital. He and Guldana went to keep their daughter company—he wasn't sure if they'd be back before curfew."

"Apparently not," Jimmy said. He smiled at Tess. "If Rivka were here, we'd know it."

Decker handed him the note, then went out to help Murphy and Dave unload the wagon.

Tess tried to follow, but Jimmy caught her arm. "Head scarf," he said. "The police are still out there."

"It's in my bag," she said. Which was in the wagon.

"I'll get it," he said, quickly skimming the note.

Tess moved closer to the window so that she could see outside. The night was dark, but someone had set a lantern on the front bench of the wagon. It lit Dave's face eerily as he helped Murphy and Decker negotiate a particularly large crate from the wooden bed.

The yard was small and fenced in—just a dusty patch of land between this house and what looked like a barn.

"Rivka's cleared a space for you in the pantry."

Tess turned to see Jimmy pointing toward the curtained room that Deck had peeked into.

"He got the message that we had a woman with us, but he doesn't seem to understand that you're my wife. Maybe I wasn't clear about that," he added.

Along with leading the rescue efforts at the school, Jimmy and Deck had also managed to send a message to a Kazbekistani friend, asking him to help them find accommodations. But housing in this city was at a premium, and the best that that friend, Rivka, could do was offer them his own kitchen floor.

Which wasn't great in terms of setting up her computer and other communications equipment. Tess looked behind the curtain—the pantry was barely big enough for her to sleep in. But this entire situation was a significantly better alternative than, say, the barracks-style housing over at the old U.S. Army base. There'd be even less privacy there. They needed to be able to come and go at will.

Jimmy laughed. "Hey, I just carried you over the threshold, didn't I?"

"Isn't that supposed to mean that now we'll have good luck?" Tess asked. They could use some. They were going to need it to find that laptop in what was left of this battered city.

There was a long crack in one of the kitchen walls, but other than that, this house and the nearby barn had survived the quake. Apparently, others in this neighborhood had not fared quite so well.

"I'm not sure, but I think it's probably more of a tradition having to do with the fact that as my wife you're considered my possession," Jimmy said.

"Nice," Tess said. "I'll keep that in mind—ix-nay on the eshhold-thray. You know, in case I ever do get married for real."

Jimmy had started for the door, but now he turned around. He came all the way back to her and even put his arms around her, pulling her in for what probably looked like an embrace. To anyone who couldn't hear the chill in his voice, that is.

"That's the dead last time you say anything like that in an unsecured area," he said almost inaudibly, directly into her ear. "Do I make myself clear?"

He was serious. She tried to remember what she'd just said. *Married for real.* Oh, God.

"We're married. I'm your husband. You're my wife," he continued still in that near-silent voice. "Even when we're alone. Especially when we're alone, because until we sweep for bugs, we may not really be alone." He pulled back to look at her.

Tess nodded. "I'm sorry," she told him silently. She knew this. She'd even prepared for it.

"I know you're tired," Jimmy said into her ear. "I am,

too. It was a bitch of a day. But think, Tess. Always think first. Before you say or do anything."

She nodded again.

"I'll get your scarf."

He finally released her and went out the door, and Tess sat down heavily on one of the benches that lined the thick wooden table. He was right. She hadn't been thinking. At all. She'd really blown it.

Decker was across the room, helping Murphy stack another crate along the wall. He was watching her, so she squared her shoulders, plastered a smile on her face, and stood up and went over to see what she could do to help while stuck here inside.

Deck met her halfway. His clothing and face were still streaked with that pervasive yellow-brown dust. He'd been the first one down into that basement, the first person those trapped children and teachers had seen, an angel come to lead them out of the darkness and into the light.

Then, as he did now, he'd looked American. Quietly strong and confident, with a nearly visible aura shimmering around him that spoke of a life lived with freedom from fear. Freedom and orthodontists for all—her team leader had a truly American smile with straight white teeth.

"You don't need to be a cheerleader, Tess," he told her now. "No one's going to be surprised if you let it slip that you feel bad after seeing what we've seen today."

"Oh," she said. "Yeah, I know."

Decker didn't believe her. "You did a good job out there," he said quietly. "Did Nash remember to mention that when he was dressing you down for whatever it was that you did or said that pissed him off?"

She sighed. "You saw that, huh?"

"Yeah." His eyes were unbelievably kind. "He can be an asshole when he's exhausted, and believe me, he's exhausted. Don't take it to heart."

"I did mess up," she admitted.

"So you learn from the mistake and move on," Decker said. "Don't dwell on it. Just don't do it again."

"I thought I was allowed to feel bad," she countered.

He laughed as he headed for the door. "Yeah, but only about the things that matter." He turned back, his smile gone just as quickly as it had appeared. "You know, no one's going to think less of you if you cry. It's good to let it out, especially after a day like today."

Tess nodded and crossed her arms. "I know you don't mean to be rude, but don't you think it's just a *little* offensive to say something like that to me? I mean, would you really tell Murphy or Dave that they should cry?" Or Nash, who probably needed to hear that more than any of them?

"Yeah," he said. "I not only would, but I did. Dave Malkoff's out in the wagon right now, weeping like a baby."

"Really?" Tess laughed at herself for believing him enough to ask. He was an awesome liar.

"Yes about saying it, no about Dave," Decker admitted, smiling again, too. He was an awesome liar with a killer smile. But what was real and what was an act? Was he playing the strong American for her, too? "But more's the pity he's not, huh?" His smile faded again. "This is going to be a long, tough assignment. Make sure you do what you need to do to take care of yourself." He stepped closer, lowered his voice. "I know this can't be easy for you, and I am sorry about that."

He was talking about her having to work with Jimmy Nash.

"I'm okay with it," she told him, but again, she could tell that he didn't believe her. And at this point, after all that she'd seen and done today, she wasn't sure she believed herself.

It was one thing to handle being so close to Nash in the

sterile environment of Tom's office or on an airplane. It was another entirely to be pushed beyond her emotional limits. God, they'd found the body of one little girl—she was probably twelve years old. . . . But she'd been one of dozens.

Decker looked over at Nash and Murphy, who were wrestling another crate through the door.

He cleared his throat and forced a smile that now only served to make him look as tired as he probably felt. "Well, let me know if there's anything I can do," he continued. "You know, to make this any easier."

"Hey, Tess," Nash called, and she looked over at him. He was just as dusty as Decker—and just as capable of playing a role and hiding his true feelings. What awful things had *he* seen today that had made him want to cry? Not that he ever would, not in a million years. "Catch."

He'd had her bag over his shoulder, and he tossed it to her now. She caught it. "Thanks."

"Get the rest of our personal gear inside, will you?" he said.

"Yeah." Her scarf was right there on top, and she pulled it out and put it on.

Tess turned back to Decker to thank him, but he'd already gone back to work.

The doors of the American embassy remained locked up tight.

Still, Sophia checked Saboor Square regularly for messages, all the while knowing that help wasn't going to come from that quarter.

If she wanted to get out of this country—and she did— she was going to have to rely on former business associates, such as Michel Lartet. A French ex-pat, Lartet ran an illegal bar and gambling casino from the basements of his various properties. The location of his establishment was rolling—always different from night to night—and it sometimes changed even within the course of a single night. It hadn't always been that way. But over the past few years, Lartet was kept on his toes by the ruling warlords like Padsha Bashir.

Although the former K-stani government had outlawed both alcohol and gambling, the officials assigned to enforce the law took bribes and payoffs. Not so Bashir and his compatriots.

Dimitri had always said that there was no payoff large enough for the warlords to allow Western contamination to remain within the borders of their country.

Out of all of her former friends and business acquaintances, Lartet was most likely to offer her aid. Or perhaps he would trade assistance for the promise of substantial payback. At least Sophia thought he would. She was not, however, willing to gamble her life on that.

And so she had devised a plan.

She found Lartet's bar easily. In fact, the people she'd asked implied that he'd been at this same location for quite a few weeks, which was a surprising turn of events.

These days, apparently, he was operating in the basement of a squat little building that housed a butcher shop above. Generators kept the freezers and refrigerators humming, even though the meat was probably stringy and exorbitantly priced.

The place wasn't full by Lartet's usual standards, but that was to be expected, considering it was after curfew.

As a woman in a burka, all but her eyes veiled, Sophia was noticed coming in, but quickly forgotten as she took a table in the shadows on the side of the room. She sat near a handful of other women, all prostitutes.

Prostitution was an extremely dangerous business in this country. Being caught was a guaranteed death sentence, one that was usually carried out by the woman's own family—brothers and father and male cousins.

Never mind the fact that many women turned to prostitution as the only means for feeding that very same family.

Sophia had come into Michel Lartet's bar, into this very room, dozens of times in the past eight years. But she'd come in as an American woman and had been welcomed as an equal. She'd take off her burka and robe once inside to reveal clothes she would have been arrested for wearing on the street. She sometimes wore shorts and a T-shirt, sometimes a slinky dress Dimitri had ordered for her—for him, really—from some catalogue.

She'd sat at the bar with the men, drinking and laughing. She'd noticed the women who kept on their burkas as they sat in the corner, and she'd understood why they might want to keep their faces hidden.

She'd also seen them leaving, one by one, with Lartet's patrons as the night drew to an end.

She'd never had much compassion for them before—women who'd let their lives get so out of control that they had to sell their bodies just to eat.

Just to survive for one more day.

Even as recently as mere months ago, she'd foolishly believed that she'd rather die than be reduced to such degradation. Sex without love. Sex with strangers. What woman with any self-esteem would resort to that?

Sophia had discovered as she'd lain with Dimitri's killer, with her husband's blood still splattered on her face, on her dress, in her hair, that there was little she wouldn't do to keep from dying.

And as the days turned to weeks turned to months, as her survival depended on her ability to "entertain" her sworn enemy and his loathsome friends, she realized she'd never understood just how insignificant sex really was, how little true meaning it held.

The poetry, the magic, the beauty—the fanciful concept of true love—was all a pathetic attempt to romanticize something that was nothing more than a basic biological function. Sex was no more profound than eating or sleeping or taking a dump.

Sophia sat now among the prostitutes in Lartet's bar, aware of the scornful glances she was getting from the other women. Before this, she'd never quite understood how the men who bought them for a night or an hour could differentiate one from another. They were all covered, enshrouded—the men could only guess what was underneath.

But now, as she sat among them, she realized that the Kazabek streetwalkers had their own variation of a New York City street hooker's garb. Instead of miniskirts and tube tops, they wore the sleeves of their robes pulled up just enough to reveal intricate artwork done in henna on their arms. They kept their hands on the tables in front of them, artfully arranged. Young, soft hands, wrists adorned with bracelets. They wore toe rings and toenail polish and, like their sisters on Forty-second Street, they wore remarkably high-heeled sandals.

Apparently the language of women's shoes was universal.

Sophia was wearing a stolen pair of flat leather sandals. They were a size too large on feet that were still swollen and red, sore from her barefoot run from Bashir's palace. She hoped that the message received from *her* shoes was a warning about possible infectious diseases.

Her own wrists were unadorned. She *was* wearing the ring she still hadn't managed to pawn—having chosen to arm herself with the ability to offer a bribe as well as one of those deadly looking little handguns she'd stolen. But she wore that ring turned around, the jewels hidden in her palm.

She caught another pointedly amused glance from one of

the other women and knew, with some relief, that if a client approached, she wouldn't be chosen first.

Not that she wouldn't appreciate the chance to separate some man from his money. Of course, the services rendered would be a knock over the head instead of a roll in the dust.

But as appealing as the idea seemed, she wasn't here for that.

She was here to watch Michel Lartet's response to the message she'd sent him—a written message he should be receiving any moment. She wanted to see his reaction to her note, see if he'd gotten wind of the reward that was surely on her head. She was eager to see if the promise of a huge amount of money was enough to bring him into his hated enemy's camp, or if he would be her salvation.

She was sitting close enough to the main bar to hear Lartet's booming voice.

He was telling a joke—badly. *A camel, a horse, and a zebra walk into a bar* . . . Lartet loved to tell jokes.

And Dimitri used to tease him mercilessly—the two men had been close friends—for always blowing the punch lines.

Sophia sat, with her hands in front of her on the table, ring carefully hidden, and waited.

After Jimmy finished tucking Khalid's horse into bed in Rivka's barn, he came into a kitchen that was decidedly empty.

Dave Malkoff was out in the stable. Clutching a bucket, he'd crawled into an empty stall to sleep, still terribly sick.

Tess had worried he'd be uncomfortable sleeping in the barn, but ol' Dave had been adamant about it. Jimmy had pulled Tess off the man when she'd looked as if she was settling in for a fight. He recognized where Dave's head was at. He knew that the only thing worse than being wicked-ass, groaning sick was to be wicked-ass, groaning sick within earshot of teammates. Teammates whose eyes Dave wanted to be able to look into over the next few weeks without wondering if they'd heard those nasty noises he was going to be making all night long.

Although, to be honest, each time Dave gave the old heave-ho, within earshot or not, Jimmy's respect for the man only climbed higher.

Jimmy had checked on him one last time after kissing Marge-the-gelding good night, and had found him sticking a needle into his arm. Dave was so freaking sick, he was actually giving himself an IV. It was just a saline drip to keep him from getting dehydrated, but still.

"I'll be okay by morning," Dave had said, looking up at Jimmy from the floor. The man was wrapped in blankets and shivering despite the eighty-five-degree Fahrenheit sweat-fest they were enduring. "Don't tell Decker."

Jimmy sighed as he shook his head. "I *am* Decker," he told Dave.

Who didn't understand. Of course, his teeth *were* about to rattle out of his head.

Jimmy spelled it out for him. "If I see or hear something, it's going to get back to Decker. There are no exceptions to that rule. If you're looking to hide something from Deck, you better hide it from me, too. I should also point out that hiding something—or trying to hide something—from Deck is the quickest way to find your ass. Because it'll be on the next flight home. You follow?"

Dave nodded. And took a deep breath, obviously ready to list the top ten reasons why it would be a mistake to ship him off to the nearest hospital.

Jimmy didn't let him make a single sound. "On the other hand, arguing with me is not the same as arguing with Deck, so save it for when you see him. Which, incidentally, probably won't be until tomorrow morning."

There was so much relief in Dave's eyes at that news, it

was as if Jimmy had told him that power was out, making the electric chair nonoperational.

"If you look like this in the morning—," Jimmy continued.

"I won't," Dave said.

Jimmy rephrased. This guy had bowling balls. "If you *feel* like this in the morning—"

"I'm feeling better already." Dave forced a smile. It was a worthy effort that was completely blown by his having to lunge for his bucket.

"I'll check on you later." Jimmy left Dave to his private conversation with the bottom of that plastic pail.

He passed Murphy going out as he went into Rivka's tidy house. Curfew, shmurfew. In fact, the curfew was a good thing. It would keep the streets clear of innocent civilians. Anyone out and sneaking about in the night was either dangerous or very dangerous.

Deck himself had ninja-ed out after helping Jimmy lock Khalid's wagon in the yard. Like Murphy, he was going into the heart of Kazabek to try to touch base with his various contacts, get a read on what the street people were talking about—not just the news but the rumors. You could learn a lot from rumors, if you knew how to read them.

Although Decker also had an additional agenda—to locate and talk to this Dimitri Ghaffari guy. Jimmy had no doubt that Deck was going to get right on top of that special assignment from Tom Paoletti.

Jimmy was a little jealous as he washed the day's grime from his face in Rivka's kitchen sink. He'd be getting ready to break curfew and go out himself if Rivka had been home or if Dave hadn't been so sick. But he wasn't about to leave Tess alone in an empty house.

Of course this meant that he and Tess were alone together in an empty house.

She'd already gone behind the curtain, into the tiny pantry

where Rivka had cleared just enough space for her to put her sleeping bag. If Jimmy was lucky, she was already asleep.

But the curtain moved—these days his luck was for shit—and she came out into the kitchen.

"Okay," she announced. "I'm ready."

Jimmy stared at her. She was dressed in basic evening black—minus the heels and pearls.

Black pants, black shirt, black nylon shoulder holster, black cammy paint covering up all those freckles . . .

Pippi Goes Commando.

He laughed. "No, you're not. Go wash your face and get ready for bed." Hindsight, which came immediately after he spoke, made him realize that just a little more finesse might've allowed him to avoid the shit storm that was now bearing down on him at high speed.

"Excuse me?" Tess said.

If real life had a sound track, that song that went, "You're Not the Boss of Me, Now," would have been playing. At a very high volume.

"Tess. Come on. You're exhausted," he said, even though it rarely worked to play the "Let's be rational" card after laughing in someone's face.

She stepped closer, close enough to kiss him—or to speak without being overheard. "So's Deck and Murphy," she pointed out practically inaudibly. "They've both gone to do their jobs. I'm going to do mine."

She would have moved away, but he caught her arm. "Your job is to not get yourself thrown into prison on the first night we're in Kazabek," he told her in less than a whisper, his mouth near her ear. "Your job is to still be in one working piece if and when we find . . . what we're looking for." The laptop. He was not going to use the L-word. Not ever. Not aloud.

Tess pulled free, held up one finger, then disappeared back behind the curtain. She came out seconds later carrying what looked like a dictating machine—one of those little hand-held jobs that used miniature cassette tapes. She pressed the button and a conversation between two people—a man and a woman—began playing.

Hey, that was his voice. And hers, too. What the hell?

He heard the Tess on tape mention the latest Tom Hanks movie, and he realized she must've taped the conversation they'd had at the airport. They'd had an extremely innocuous discussion about their favorite movies while they'd waited to board the plane—while Jimmy had tried not to think about that night he'd spent with Tess. Usually he enjoyed his memories of intimacies shared, but this time those thoughts made him feel restless.

She now set the tape player down on the table and stepped closer to him, but not as close as they'd been before.

Which was something of a shame.

"My job includes getting our computer system up and running," she said in a low voice as, on the tape, she chattered on about *Forrest Gump*. Anyone listening in would hear only that taped conversation. "With Internet access. We need communications, too. In case you didn't notice, both of our sat-com radios didn't make it over here. If I can get a satellite dish placed somewhere high enough, I can rig a comm system with our phones. We'll be able to keep in touch with one another as well as Tom—provided we're in range of the dish. This is important, Jimmy. And it's not something I can do when the sun's up."

"Well, I'm sorry." Jimmy tried to look it. It was hard. He was distracted by his own voice making some totally lame joke about Wilson the Volleyball in *Castaway* deserving the best supporting Oscar. On the tape, Tess's answering laughter sounded much too polite. "But Decker thought it would be best if you used tonight to depressurize. Get your feet underneath you, get some rest."

Her eyebrows had lifted, and she looked amused. "Decker said that?"

"Yes," he lied. "While we were locking down the cart. Out in the back."

"You know, that's odd, because I spoke to Decker, too, right before he left. And he gave me an absolute thumbs-up to go out and get that portable sat-dish in place." Tess swung a black backpack off her shoulder. "He even gave me this to carry it in."

Oh, crap. That was indeed Deck's bag. But . . . "You've actually got a sat-dish in there?"

"It folds. It's made from a special fabric, kind of like a kite," she told him. "There's a frame that opens up and snaps into place."

It was funny. This techno stuff—even just talking about it briefly like this—really turned her on. Tess Bailey was a true technogeek.

"The heaviest part of it is the power pack," she was telling him. "The whole thing's ultralightweight."

She'd been all lit up, just like that, two months ago when he'd raced her down the hallway to her bedroom.

"How do you anchor it?" Jimmy asked now. "What happens in a windstorm?"

"It's been known to fly away," she admitted. "But really, it more than makes up for that by being so easy to replace."

"You're kidding, right?" Jimmy scoffed, purposely dissing her glorious new technology. It worked to make her take a step back, away from him.

Which was a good thing, because whenever she stood so close, he had the urge to drop to his knees and beg her for a replay. And maybe even tell her the truth about why he'd never called her back: Because he'd wanted to call her. And hadn't *that* scared him to death. . . .

"We're coming up on dust storm season," he told her instead. "Usually there's only one per week, but this time of year there could be three or four. Or one long one that lasts six days."

"Like any piece of equipment, this system has got its disadvantages as well as advantages," she said. "I'll have to check it regularly and replace it when necessary. Personally, if I'm going to climb up the side of a building, I'd rather not be carrying a traditional sat-dish."

Climb up the side of . . .

Tess shouldered the bag, ready to head for the door.

Okay. Moment of truth. Should he stick to his claim that he spoke to Deck in the yard, call her bluff, and accuse her of being the one who was lying? It was so obvious that her story wasn't any more real than his, despite the fact that she had Deck's bag. It was just her style to ask to borrow it without telling Deck exactly what she wanted to use it for.

But before he could decide, she injected just the right amount of doubt in his mind by looking him directly in the eye and saying, "Deck said he wanted you to go with me. I told him I didn't need a babysitter, I know exactly where I'm going to place this—I took a look down the street when I was helping unload the wagon. There's an abandoned Catholic church not far from here that seems to have the right height to it. But he insisted. He doesn't want me doing this alone. Not the first time, he said. Which, okay, I can respect that. I don't necessarily agree, but . . . I know you're tired, Jimmy. I am, too. But Deck really does want our computers up and running as soon as possible."

Damn, she was good. *Not the first time.* That really sounded like something Decker would say. And then to end it with that little challenge. *I know you're tired, Jimmy.*

Yeah, he was tired and his feet freaking ached—that twelve-mile late-night stroll had really put the frosting on his pain cake—but he wasn't going to be able to fall asleep anyway. Damn it, after this afternoon, it was possible he was never going to sleep again.

Jimmy knew that he didn't move an inch, but something he did—or maybe it was something he didn't do—made Tess's eyes soften. She actually touched him, her fingers surprisingly cool against his face.

Cool, but far too fleeting. Jimmy didn't catch her hand, though. He didn't touch her at all.

"Thank you for being so great out there today," she said. "That was . . . challenging in so many ways."

No fucking kidding.

"You were wonderful with Khalid and Amman," she continued. "I just . . . I was impressed."

Wonderful. Great. Yeah, he was terrific—he had a real way with kids who were still alive. But today, too many hadn't survived.

"Decker told me it was okay to cry," she said, almost too quietly.

Did she honestly think . . . ? Yes, she did. He'd let her get too close once before, and now she thought . . .

Jimmy knew, without a doubt, that now was the perfect time to tell her. "Decker told *me* that if you weren't on his team, if you didn't work for Troubleshooters Incorporated, he'd be chasing you down the street."

He could see that he'd surprised the hell out of her with that—and possibly even offended her, too. So he pushed it even further. "When you get back to D.C., you're going to find a message on your answering machine from the Agency, offering you a field position. You could have it all, you know. The job you've always wanted. And Deck."

She gave him a look that clearly said *You are such a jerk.* "Are you coming? Because I'm going in two minutes, whether you're with me or not."

"I thought you just told me that Decker said—"

"Screw Decker. Screw *you*, Jimmy. I'm not going to play your mind games."

"Yeah, like you weren't trying to con me?" He touched her then, the same way she'd touched him. "Thank you for being so great out there today—"

She slapped his hand away. "I wasn't conning you. I was trying to—" She broke off. "*God.*"

"What?"

"Forget it."

"You were trying to what?"

"I don't know," she said. "Let you know that it was okay to talk about it. You're wired so tightly shut—"

"Yeah, well, where I come from, that's how you stay alive."

"Where *do* you come from?" she asked, looking hard into his eyes as if she'd find the answer there.

Her question stopped him dead.

"I know you're not really from Connecticut," she continued.

"What the fuck does it matter where I'm from?" Okay. Stop. Apologize. But he didn't get a chance.

"You're right. It doesn't matter. What matters is that I'm worried about you," Tess said. "And okay, maybe you can pretend that's just some female hormonal reaction to having slept with you, but Decker's worried about you, too."

He tried to shrug it off—all of it. Including the way that her visible flinch at his harsh words had made his stomach hurt. Including the way that she hadn't then turned from him, but instead took a step *toward* him. She was *worried* about him. And as for Deck . . . "Deck worries about everyone."

"He worries most about you," she said. "I see him watching you, and lately . . ."

"Okay, you win." Jimmy couldn't talk about this anymore. He couldn't even think about it. "Let's go get that sat-dish in place."

Once they went out Rivka's door, they'd have to be completely silent. Thank you, Jesus.

Tess turned away—probably to hide her triumphant smile. "You better get changed, then."

"Not a chance." That made her turn back to him, but he read only surprise on her face. She was either really good, or truly sweet and completely triumph free. "You're the one who needs to change," he told her.

She didn't comprehend.

"Play this little scenario out in your head," he said. "You're out on the street, creeping around after curfew, dressed like one of Delta Force—you've got everything but the combat vest and the AK-47. What do you think's going to happen if you get caught, looking like that?"

"I have no intention of getting caught."

She was serious. "If you have no intention of getting caught," Jimmy pointed out, "then you should have no need for a sidearm."

Tess lifted her chin as she informed him, "I know how to use it." With her eyes slightly narrowed as she gazed at him, she looked like Minnie Mouse doing an impersonation of Clint Eastwood.

Laughing at her right now would be bad.

But all he had to do was picture her stopped by one of Padsha Bashir's patrols and the urge to laugh vanished.

"I don't doubt that you do," he said. "But if we *do* get caught—and I'd like to point out that no one ever *intends* to get caught—you're not going to be carrying a gun. Or dressed like GI Jane. It won't fit with the story we'll use in case we do get caught, so go back there and put on the clothes you were wearing earlier today."

She didn't move.

"That wasn't a request," Jimmy said.

"What story?" she asked.

Jesus Christ. Okay. "We're newlyweds, it's been a rough day, we had our first fight. You ran out of the house, I followed." Jimmy made it up on the fly. " 'I'm so sorry, Officer, Tess completely forgot about the curfew. She was just so upset. You know how women can get, ha, ha, ha. I promise it will never happen again, sir.' "

"You know, with that kind of attitude toward women, it's a wonder that men in this country ever get laid."

"Women are property," Jimmy said. "You don't ask your horse if it wants to pull your cart today."

"God." Tess looked at him as if the oppression of women in third-world countries was his idea. She turned away, turned back. "What if they look in my bag and discover the satellite dish and power pack?"

"You must've taken the wrong bag at the airport. You've never seen this equipment before in your life. You thought you were grabbing your clothes."

She nodded. Turned away. But again she turned back. "What did we fight about?"

"I don't know," he said. "What do people who were just married fight about?"

Tess thought for a moment, then smiled. "You're an idiot," she said. "We had a fight because you're a total idiot."

She crossed to the table, waiting until her voice on the tape finished a sentence. ". . . like to see an action movie that ends, you know, after the nuclear bomb has been defused, with the heroine walking away from the hero's romantic overtures, saying, 'Yeah, right, like I want to spend the rest of *my* life in couples counseling. No thanks.' "

As Jimmy watched, Tess clicked off the machine and went behind the curtain to change her clothes.

CHAPTER
NINE

WHEN DECKER said, "Dimitri Ghaffari," the overwhelming response from the people of the street was "Michel Lartet."

Lartet ran a private "club" for Westerners who couldn't go a week—or a day—without a drink in the otherwise dry city of Kazabek. Decker didn't know the Frenchman personally, but he'd been to his establishment a time or two, back about five years earlier. It was right after a car bomb sprayed shattered window glass onto the patrons of the restaurant in the street level of the Kazabek Grande Hotel. Forty-seven people had been hospitalized, four had died.

And it could have been worse. The car's driver could have gotten even closer to the twenty-eight-story hotel and taken out that entire half of the building.

Needless to say, the Grande had shut down operations for the weeks it took to move the restaurant into the huge ballroom in the hotel's windowless basement.

During those weeks, business at Lartet's club had boomed.

Nowadays, the club was a whole lot less crowded. Not counting the recent influx of relief workers, there just weren't that many Westerners left in the country.

Which meant it was entirely possible Dimitri Ghaffari was gone, too. Out of all the people Decker had spoken to, none had seen Ghaffari in months. But they all agreed that if he was still in Kazabek, Lartet would most likely know how to find him.

Inside the "club," in the basement of a butcher shop, Decker took a table along the wall opposite the bar. Sitting there, with his back against the concrete blocks of the building's foundation, he could watch both the front and rear entrances with little effort.

He recognized Lartet behind the bar—he was a big man, with some excess bulk and not a whole lot of hair. Lartet had glanced up, taking note of Decker as he came in the door, but other than that, he didn't appear to pay him much mind.

Besides Lartet, there were nine other men in the place, most of them Europeans. One was American, and two were young K-stani men. They were dressed in decidedly Western garb, and appeared to be either good friends or employees of Lartet.

Out of the lot of them, only the American posed a potential immediate threat. He was staring at Decker, sizing him up. There were two bottles of vodka on the bar in front of him, one empty and one half-full.

Decker was picking up a heavy drunk-and-looking-for-a-fight vibe, so he met the man's glare for maybe three seconds—just long enough to let him know that he wasn't afraid. If the American was looking for an easy target to intimidate, he needed to look elsewhere.

And then he dismissed the guy. Deck purposely turned his attention to the five burka-clad prostitutes sitting quietly off to the side, while still keeping the American on the edge of his radar.

At first glance, based on the size of their feet, he would've bet that all the prostitutes were really women underneath those heavy robes. But only four of them were looking submissively at the tables in front of them. The fifth was surreptitiously checking him out.

Which probably meant she was either a man with small feet, or not Kazbekistani.

Lartet gave a nudge to one of the young men, gesturing toward Decker with his chin. The man slid off his barstool and approached.

"May I get you a beverage from the bar, sir?" he asked in flawless English.

The American and the fifth prostitute were no longer the only ones looking at Decker now.

"A beer." He answered in the local dialect, loudly enough for his entire audience to hear. "In a bottle or can. I'll open it myself."

Ahh. He could almost hear the murmur of approval as the entire bar seemed to take a breath and nod its collective head. Whoever he was, he drank like all the other ex-pats in this part of Kazabek. With extreme caution.

Although they didn't know him by name, he was one of them.

The American sitting at the bar stopped watching him so closely. The man didn't turn his back, he just turned down the volume of his glare.

The fifth prostitute was now pretending to gaze at the table in front of her like the others, but Decker knew she—or he—was really still scoping him out.

There was another possibility, of course. She could well be a K-stani woman, but one who had been raised in the West. Or maybe she was a newcomer to the trade, just recently gone into business, so to speak.

The waiter brought him his beer—foreign, exotic, and imported, a Bud Lite in a can—and ceremoniously washed off the top.

"Thanks," Deck said, this time in English.

He wiped the top dry with the edge of his T-shirt, popped it open, and took a swig.

He'd sit here, drink the beer, watch the room. When he

finished this one, he'd order another, and this time Lartet would bring it over himself.

Decker would invite him to sit. They'd start with small talk. The weather. The quake.

Dimitri Ghaffari. *Have you seen him lately?*

And maybe—if Decker picked up the right vibes and signals from Lartet—they'd then talk about al-Qaeda leader Ma'awiya Talal Sayid.

Decker took another sip of beer, glancing again at the fifth prostitute's feet. They were dirty and battered, as if she'd run barefoot over gravel, but they were definitely female feet.

Weren't they?

She was still watching him. Of course maybe she had some kind of super-pross sixth sense that told her he was a good target tonight—that he was disgusted with himself for continuing to think so relentlessly about Tess Bailey. Bailey was on his team, which made her untouchable. Period, the end. Deck was disgusted with Nash, too, for actually making him consider the possibility that Tess might be an exception to his unbreakable rule.

The truth was, it wasn't Decker's rule that was going to keep him from finding whatever it was he thought he might find in Tess Bailey's arms.

It was Tess herself who was going to keep that from happening.

She was still completely hung up on Nash. She was good at hiding it, but it was there.

No, Deck had missed any chance he'd ever had a long time ago.

And somehow that prostitute knew that. The same magical way she knew that tonight Decker was particularly desperate for sex.

Mindless, no-strings sex with some beautiful stranger.

It would help dull those images of dead children that

were cluttering up his head. It would replace those errant thoughts of Tess, of what could never be.

The fifth prostitute with the dirty feet and what had to be stolen sandals, because they were much too big, looked up at him from across the room.

Decker held her gaze as he finished his beer, as he felt his body respond to the glitter of her eyes. He'd never paid for sex before. Not ever.

Desperate or not, he wasn't about to start now.

He lifted the empty can, signaling the barkeep to bring him another beer, and the world started to shake.

"What the . . . ?"

"Aftershock," Nash said into Tess's ear.

They had slipped into an alley to avoid a passing peace-keeping patrol. Nash had pulled her behind a pile of bricks and building supplies. Together, they'd squeezed into an area that she would have had trouble fitting in by herself.

Nash's arm was around her waist—it helped if she thought of him as Nash, not Jimmy—and he held on to her as the earth shook.

She still couldn't believe what he'd said to her tonight.

Decker told me that if you weren't on his team . . . he'd be chasing you down the street.

Was that why Deck had hired her? Not because he thought she'd make a good field operative, but because he wanted to shag her? Had he and Nash talked about her, after she and Nash had . . . Oh, God. She could just imagine their conversation. *She's not all that pretty, and her thighs could use some toning, but she's low maintenance and she doesn't need a lot of foreplay.*

And wasn't *that* a very icky thought?

A shingle from one of the buildings that was sheltering them crashed onto the ground and shattered.

"Ow!" Nash said.

She hadn't thought it was possible, but he pulled her closer, tucking her head down and shielding her with his body.

"Ow! Shit!" he said. "We better run for the street. Keep your head covered! Stay close—"

She started to move, but just like that, it was over, and he caught her, holding her even more tightly. The sudden stillness was almost as freaky as the shaking had been when it first started.

"Are you all right?" Nash asked her. His voice sounded odd.

"Yeah. Are you?" She half expected him to make some kind of joking comment about the way the earth always seemed to move when they were in such close contact.

But "I'm fine" was all he said, pulling her out into the alley. Despite the curfew, people were spilling out of their houses and into the street.

There was more than just milling about in the open happening here—people were hurrying down the road, probably going to check on their grandmothers while they had the chance.

"This is great," Tess told Nash as they joined the crowd. "If we move fast, we can probably make it all the way downtown, to the Kazabek Grande Hotel."

Nash stopped short. "You said there was a church just down the street that was probably tall enough—"

"To get us phone coverage right in this area, yes," she said. "Its steeple is high enough do the trick. Probably. But if we want to be able to communicate from anywhere else in the city, the best place to put a dish is the roof of the Grande Hotel."

"It won't be after it falls down," Nash said. "Which it's going to do, any minute."

"Well, until it does, we'll have operational phones." Tess

started down the street but he didn't follow. She glanced back at him but didn't stop, and he finally ran to catch up.

"There's no way you're getting into the Grande," he said curtly. "That entire part of the downtown area was evacuated after the quake. All of the buildings have severe structural damage—one of them in that neighborhood already came down. The area's completely cordoned off."

"Yeah, Decker showed me that photo," Tess told him. "There's yellow police tape blocking off those streets. It's not going to be hard to get past that."

"Except if we cross that line, the police will think we're looters and we'll be shot on sight."

"Then we better not be seen." Tess sidestepped a toddler who had run, laughing, into her path. She was glad *some*-one was having fun tonight. She glanced back at Nash. "That *is* your specialty, isn't it?"

"Stop." He caught her arm. "This is bullshit. There's no way you cleared *this* with Decker. No way. I'm not letting you near the Grande. You want to prove how good you are, you're going to have to do it another way."

He was dead serious.

He was also bleeding.

"You're hurt," she realized.

Nash followed her gaze and reached up to touch his neck and then the back of his head. He winced and his hand came away red with blood, but he shrugged. "It's not that bad. Heads bleed more than—"

"You got hit by a tile," she guessed, and guessed correctly based on his reaction—or rather lack thereof, "hard enough to make you bleed. And it doesn't occur to you that might be something I'd need to know, so when you keeled over I'd at least have half a freaking *clue*?"

"It's not that bad," he said again, looking around to see who else might've noticed her rising voice. "It's just—"

"A ding," she finished for him. "Yes. Right. I know." She

was furious and terribly, terribly upset. If Decker had appeared out of nowhere, she would have hauled back and socked him. She wanted him to have hired her for this job because she was skilled, because she was a good field operative, not because he liked the way she looked without a shirt. That was something she'd have expected from Nash, but not Decker. Never Decker.

Damn it. Damn Decker.

And damn Jimmy Nash for being right about her wanting to prove how good she was. She was guilty of wanting to do some serious hotdogging.

And not just to impress him and Decker either.

"You were right," Jimmy said. "I should have told you. I really didn't realize how hard I got hit. I'm sorry."

And just like that, her anger was gone.

"I'm sorry because you were right, too," she whispered. Her eyes were filled with tears—where did they come from? Oh, God, she wanted that anger back, because this feeling of sadness, of sorrow, of hurt, of regret and wistful longing it had left in its place was not helping her at all.

All of the emotions of these last few minutes were teetering on top of those from this terrible day, from this week, from these months since she'd invited Jimmy Nash into her life. . . .

Please don't let her start to cry.

If he reached for her, she was going to break down completely.

But Jimmy kept his distance. "If we hurry, we can get the sat-dish on the church and get back to Rivka's in time to catch a few hours of sleep before dawn."

"Maybe you shouldn't sleep," Tess said, steeling herself. She could do this. She did *not* have to fall to the ground, weeping. And she could be concerned about this man because he was a teammate, no more, no less. "Not until Murphy checks you out. If you have a concussion—"

"I don't have a concussion." Nash actually laughed. "It's barely a scratch."

Ah. Scornful indignation came roaring back, thank God. "And you know this because you're some kind of genetic mutant who can see the back of your head?"

"I know this because if it were more than a scratch, it would be bleeding like hell."

"Funny," she said. "It looks to me as if you're bleeding like hell."

"Trust me," he said. "If I were—"

"Zip it," she ordered. "And sit down so I can see if your *ding* needs stitches."

The overhead lights continued to sway, long after the building stopped shaking.

It was the only sign in the bar that the aftershock had ever happened. No one reacted. No one got upset. No one so much as blinked.

Sophia watched as Michel Lartet brought two more cans of beer to the little American's table. There were two Americans in the club tonight—the big one at the bar who'd been there when she'd arrived, and this littler one who'd come in after.

The little one was definitely one of the relief workers. A do-gooder with no money. Although he probably had something in his wallet. He'd been looking at her as if he were considering taking her along when he left here tonight. That sort of purchase had to cost, didn't it?

She watched as the American invited Lartet to join him. The barkeep had just barely sat down when her messenger, a street kid named Asif, finally came in the door.

She'd started to think he wasn't going to show. She'd given him the note for Lartet and told him that Lartet would pay him to take an answering note back to her.

She'd made a plan to meet Asif in the chaos of the Saboor Square market in the morning.

It seemed the logical place to connect, considering she found herself going back there, morning, noon, and night. Foolishly hoping that she'd be rescued.

But knowing that she was going to have to rescue herself.

She'd given young Asif a burka and robe to wear. He'd protested, of course, as any teenage boy would when told to dress as a woman. She'd informed him he wouldn't be paid if he didn't wear it, if he didn't speak in a disguised, high-pitched whisper.

The promise of money made him consent.

Asif now handed Lartet the note. "Forgive me, sir," he hissed from beneath his veil. "It's urgent."

"Excuse me," Lartet said to the little American, and Sophia watched as he sat back in his chair and unfolded the piece of brown paper bag she'd written on. He held it up so it caught the light.

Lartet looked up from her note and over at Asif, his eyes narrowed. "Where did you get this?"

"From a stranger," Asif said, sotto voce and falsetto, as Sophia had instructed. "She told me to wait to deliver your reply—that you would give me a fifty."

Actually, she'd said Lartet would pay him twenty. Trust Asif to be greedy. That was money she would end up owing the Frenchman. With interest.

Lartet laughed. "A stranger? Surely you can make up a better story than that, Sophia." And then, moving faster than she'd dreamed a man of his size could move, he pulled off Asif's veil, revealing the boy's face.

Asif made all kinds of noises of outrage.

Sophia.

Lartet stared in genuine surprise at the boy's dark curls, at his straggly, teenaged beginnings of a beard. He'd expected her to be under that burka. He was not going to help her. On the contrary, if she had delivered her own message, which she'd actually considered doing, she would be held at gunpoint right now, about to be shipped across town to Bashir's nephews.

And suddenly it made perfect sense. The reason Lartet's club had been so easy to find, the reason he was no longer forced to hide his location.

Lartet was already working for Padsha Bashir.

He carefully folded the brown paper and put it into the front pocket of his shirt. He took out a pen and wrote her an answer on a cocktail napkin. What a fool. Even if she hadn't been here to see his attempted betrayal for herself, she would have known not to trust him just from that.

If he'd truly wanted to help her, he would have written right on her note, sending it back to her, making sure she knew he was being careful not to let proof that she was still in Kazabek fall into the wrong hands.

As Sophia now watched, he folded the napkin and handed it to Asif. Then he took out his wallet and gave the boy not a fifty note, but a full hundred.

"Tell her I've been worried about her," he instructed Asif. "Tell her I'm glad she's safe. Don't tell her I took off your veil, and there'll be more where that came from."

Asif pocketed both the napkin and the money and went back out into the night as Sophia tried not to clench her fists.

Sit still. Stay calm. Don't lose it—if she did, she could lose her head.

"Excuse me for just another moment," Lartet said to the little American, who'd watched the entire exchange without a single change in his emotionless expression.

Lartet then crossed the room, toward one of the two K-stani men at the bar. He leaned close, giving the young man in the blue shirt some kind of instruction.

And Sophia's note.

The man nodded, pocketed it. And went out the back door with a sense of purpose.

Sophia sat in silence.

But she wanted to scream. She wanted to stand up and run out of the club. She wanted to turn to the other women who were sitting at the tables near her and ask just how long Michel Lartet's club had been here, at this very same location.

Had it been two months?

Had he started working for Bashir two months ago?

Had Lartet been the one who had betrayed her? Had he been the one who had told Bashir that she and Dimitri had been working to reinstate a democracy in this country, working to put the warlords like Bashir out of business for good?

Had Lartet traded Dimitri's life and her freedom, her body, her heart, her very *soul*, for Bashir's protection?

Sophia closed her eyes to banish the image of Dimitri's head rolling across Bashir's palace floor. She opened her eyes against the memory of Bashir's stinking breath in her face as he grunted and pushed himself inside of her, against the too vivid picture of him using his razor-sharp sword to violate her mind just as thoroughly as he and his horrible friends had violated her body.

She wasn't sure how long she sat there, staring at her hands clenched in front of her on that table.

Lartet had gone back to sit with the little American. They were talking about the relentless heat, about the quake, about a betting pool that someone had started sometime in the past few days.

"For a hundred dollars American you can pick a date and a time," Lartet said. "And if the Kazabek Grande Hotel falls on your date and time, you win the pot."

Sophia's legs finally worked well enough for her to think about standing up.

"And if it never falls?" the American asked.

Lartet laughed his big booming laugh—the way he used to laugh with Dimitri. "I suppose you could bet that, if you want. Although then you'd have to wait for never to collect the pot, wouldn't you?"

Sophia pushed back her chair, knowing without a doubt that Lartet had killed Dimitri as surely as if he'd taken Padsha Bashir's sword and beheaded him himself.

"What's that pot up to?" the American asked, his voice like his face. Bland and unremarkable. Nothing special, nothing too noticeable. He glanced in her direction, though, noting her movement.

"Five thousand dollars," Lartet said. "And growing."

Sophia rose to her feet. Again, another flicker of the American's eyes in her direction.

But the American's attention was quickly back on Lartet. He smiled. "I'll think about it."

Lartet shrugged. "Okay. But don't wait too long."

"You know, I'm wondering if maybe you could help me out," the American said as Sophia headed toward the door. "I'm looking for a man name of Dimitri Ghaffari."

Sophia tried not to react. She didn't trip over her burka, she didn't falter. She hardly hesitated, yet the American's eyes were on her again.

She slowed down. Changed her route. Headed toward the back, toward the ladies' water closet.

Lartet was shaking his head, frowning and making a "don't know" face as she went past them. "I haven't seen Ghaffari in . . . gee, it must be months since he was in here last." He leaned in closer to the American and asked the question she was dying to have answered. "How do you know him?"

Sophia knew everyone Dimitri knew because he had been

her front. Their business, although it bore his name, had been all hers. He'd merely followed her script at business meetings with the men who wouldn't deign to make deals with a mere female. She would sit off to the side, in a burka much like this one she was wearing now, and laugh at them—all the way to the bank.

"He's a friend of a friend," the American said vaguely, "who owed Ghaffari some money. When he heard I was coming to Kazabek, he asked me to get in touch with him. He feels badly about not paying the loan back sooner, but he hasn't been able to make it past the K-stani border for close to three years now."

Lartet stood up. "I'm afraid I can't help you."

The American looked up at him. "If you see Ghaffari, let him know I'm looking for him. I'll try to stop back in, in a couple of nights."

Sophia pushed open the water closet door, then closed and locked it behind her. How long did it usually take a woman in a long robe to pee? She counted, as slowly as she could, to a hundred, then unlocked the door.

Just in time to see the little American climbing the stairs that led out of the club.

And to see Lartet pulling his second helper aside and speaking to him, much in the same way he'd spoken to the other young man.

This one nodded and headed out the door after the American.

Sophia tried not to hurry as she crossed the room, as she went up those stairs, too.

She pushed open the door that led out into the night. In the moonlight she could see the American heading south on the boulevard, Lartet's man trailing about a half a block behind. She waited until there was space between them. And then she followed.

CHAPTER
TEN

JIMMY COULDN'T get comfortable.

After he and Tess had returned to Rivka's, they'd first gone into the barn to check on Dave, who was sleeping with one hand touching his bucket, as if making sure it stayed within reach.

Murphy had returned and gone back out again, leaving behind a brief note: "No need for exterminators—Rivka's house is exceptionally clean of pests."

Meaning he'd procured an electronic sweeper from somewhere—damn, he was good at doing that—and checked the house for listening devices.

The place was clean—they were free to talk openly.

Still, Tess had been silent as she'd disinfected the cut on the back of his head. After that, she went behind the curtain into her little pantry, to set up her computer and try to get online.

Jimmy stretched out on top of his bedroll on the kitchen floor and tried not to remember the way her eyes had sparkled, up in the tower of the nearby boarded-up Church of the Saints, after they'd gotten that portable sat-dish in place, after she'd opened her phone and discovered that the freaking thing actually worked.

"We're not going to be able to use our phones outside of a certain radius of this dish," she'd informed him, forgetting for a moment that she was angry with him. "This building's just not high enough."

Tess had actually been serious about getting up onto the roof of the much taller, twenty-eight-story Grande Hotel, down in Kazabek's business district. While Jimmy would go into the condemned building if he absolutely had to, he'd sweat bullets the entire time. And this didn't count as an absolutely have-to situation.

Especially since Tess had told him she'd need to go back to the sat-dish regularly to change the power pack.

He closed his eyes, praying for the miracle of sleep.

But his shoulder hurt where part of the roof of that school had fallen in on him today. And his head hurt where that chunk of shingle tile had hit him while he and Tess were in that alley. And his brain hurt from having to be on super high awareness whenever he was around Tess, which was turning out to be every freaking minute of every flipping hour.

And every little noise that Tess made behind that curtain was completely driving him crazy. Reminding him that she was there, mere meters from him. Reminding him that he was still just as attracted to her as he'd been that night she'd invited him into her apartment.

Which was stupid.

Been there, done that.

He knew, when he'd left Tess's apartment that night—that amazing, incredible, terrifying night—that she wasn't the type to mess with. She wouldn't realize that, even if he stuck around for a week or two, what they had going was only a one-night stand.

She would have thought it was something more.

Something special.

Something enormous that scared the crap out of him, and . . .

Shit.

Tess had gotten really quiet tonight after Jimmy had told her that Decker was interested in her. The look in her eyes had been one he couldn't read.

Shit.

The thought of Deck with Tess should have been a good one. Two people he really liked, together and happy. That was a good thing, right?

But instead he was feeling this . . . Christ, was it jealousy? It was. He wasn't just jealous, he was teeth-grittingly jealous.

And he didn't know why.

Okay. He was a lying sack of crap. He knew why. It was because he'd broken his number one rule. He'd slept with a woman—Tess—who actually liked him. Really, honestly liked him. She liked him before, during, and after he slept with her. She also liked him before, during, and even after that conversation in which he'd told her . . . He still couldn't believe the things he told her.

And he was jealous because—and surely this was another sign of the coming apocalypse—he really liked her, too.

In fact, he "liked" her so much, he'd completely lost control when they got it on.

Twenty-five seconds.

Jesus God.

Jimmy still couldn't believe that he'd lasted for only twenty-five seconds that first time.

Tess had been breathing hard beneath him. He could feel her heart pounding.

"Did you really come?" he'd asked, unable to believe that she'd had enough time. "Or were you just being polite?"

Tess had laughed and held him even more tightly, wrapping her legs around him, too. "That was very real," she said. "It was amazing."

Jimmy had lifted his head to look down at her. She was

serious. "You mean I don't need to bother with that four-page apology I was drafting in my head?"

Tess pushed his hair off his face, running her fingers back through it. He had to close his eyes at the sensation—it felt unbelievably good.

"If you're not in a hurry," she said softly, "maybe you could stick around. We could do that again."

Jimmy opened his eyes. "Yeah, and maybe—who knows?—next time I'll take a full thirty seconds. That is, if you can bear it."

She laughed, her eyes dancing.

"You're so beautiful," he whispered. She was back. Tess the angel.

But she rolled her eyes. "Honesty, Nash. Remember?"

He kissed her because he didn't want to argue. He could've kept on kissing her for an hour or even a solid year, but she pulled back.

"Is your leg all right?" she asked, and at first he didn't have a clue as to why she would ask that. His leg?

But when she moved out from under him, he saw blood. He'd bled on her sheets. On *her*.

Jimmy pulled her up and into the bathroom. "Wash," he ordered, turning on the shower and gently pushing her in. He saw her face before he drew the shower curtain shut and added, "I'm negative. I'm tested regularly. But I have no idea where that knife that stuck me has been."

She pulled back the shower curtain to look at him, her eyes wide. "Knife?"

He pulled it closed again, put down the cover to the john, and sat, bringing his leg up so he could get a closer look at his damaged calf. "I get dinged up pretty often. And most people don't give their switchblades a super-sanitary cleaning."

It wasn't long before Tess shut off the water. She opened the curtain, pulled a towel off the rack on the wall, and dried herself. When she got her first good look at his leg, she stopped short. "Oh my God."

"It looks worse than it is," Jimmy said, pushing himself to his feet both to hide it from her and to take a quick turn in the shower.

"I have a first aid kit in the hall closet." She went out of the bathroom, towel around her. But he heard her come back in almost immediately. "I can't believe you call getting stabbed 'dinged up.' "

Jimmy washed all of himself, not just his leg—which definitely looked less awful without all the drying blood.

"Stabbed is stabbed," he told her through the shower curtain as he used some of her sweet-smelling shampoo. "Dinged happens when a knife is pulled, but you *don't* get stabbed. If a blade is brought into a fight, chances are someone's going to bleed. But believe me, there's a big difference between dinged and stabbed."

He finished rinsing himself, turned off the water, and opened the curtain. Tess had put a clean towel on the rack, and he used it.

She'd also set what looked like a tackle box on the sink counter and was rummaging through it. She'd put on a bathrobe, too—one of those thick terry cloth ones, in a deep shade of green.

His leg was oozing, just a little, but he was careful of the towel as he dried around it. "Sorry about your sheets."

Tess threw him a look over her shoulder. "Yeah, that's what *I'm* most concerned about."

He had to laugh. "It's really not that bad."

She found what she was looking for—some kind of antibiotic cleaner. "Sit," she ordered, then got down on the floor in front of him.

It was a double turn-on—being ordered around by a woman who was on her knees.

"This is going to sting," she warned him.

"It'll sting less if you lose the robe—and let me do it." He took the washcloth from her, pressing it against his broken skin. Shit, she wasn't kidding. But it was unmanly to whimper. Besides, she was actually slipping out of that robe.

Oh, yeah. Not a chance of him whimpering now. At least not about his leg.

Still, he scrubbed at it, making sure it was clean, making it really hurt in the process. The pain was hot and sharp and sweet.

"Are you sure you aren't going to need stitches?" Tess asked.

He lifted the washcloth to look underneath. She looked, too.

"You were too stabbed," she accused. "That's definitely a stab."

"No, it's not," he scoffed. "It's a nick. That blade was at least four inches long. He was just swinging wildly. He barely even cut me before I took him—" Out. Christ, what was he saying?

Tess was looking up at him, her eyes wide again as she knelt on the floor, her robe a pool of emerald green behind her.

Jimmy forced his mouth up into a smile. "Hey, you know, we left our beer in the kitchen."

But she didn't move. "You 'cleared the roof,' " she said, and he could see that she finally realized what that meant.

"Yeah." He couldn't hold her gaze, afraid of what he'd see there, deep in her eyes. Afraid of what she might see in *his* eyes—as if the reflection of that last shooter's face still lingered, a face filled with sheer panic as he finally realized just how deadly this game was that he was playing, as he realized instead of killing tonight, he was going to be killed.

Jimmy tried to bring Tess's focus back to his leg. "You

know, I think I could use one of those butterfly Band-Aids. Oh, and a disposable razor if you have one."

His request successfully distracted her.

So he kept that particular tangent alive. "Don't tell Decker, but I'm a total baby when it comes to Band-Aids— you know, the way the adhesive sticks to hair when you try to pull it off?"

Tess laughed and Jimmy knew that she now understood what the razor was for. She didn't even have to get to her feet as she opened the cabinet under the sink and dug one out of its packaging.

He took it from her, took off the little protective cover, and . . . Crap, his hands were shaking again. What was wrong with him?

Tess didn't seem to notice. She was up on her feet, look-ing for that Band-Aid. Except, damn it, she found it before he was done using both hands to shave two little patches on either side of the wound.

She didn't say anything, not even when he dropped the freaking razor. But she unwrapped the bandage herself in-stead of handing it to him in the paper package.

"How many were up there?" she asked as casually as she might've asked how many apples he'd bought at the gro-cery store.

But it was not a casual question. It was very carefully worded. She didn't say *people*. How many *people* were up there? How many *people* had Jimmy sent to the morgue tonight?

"Three," he said as she put the bandage on his leg, her fingers gentle and warm. What was wrong with him? Three was nothing. A mere blip on the body count scale. He knew that. And what was he doing even answering her? This wasn't something he ever talked about.

You don't talk about it, because you don't think about it. He could still hear Vic's voice, playing in his head. It had been almost twenty years, but it was still there, loud and clear. *You do the job, you wash your hands, you go have a good meal, get laid if you're lucky enough. And you get a good night's rest because tomorrow's coming.*

"They were there to kill Decker." Tess didn't ask it as a question.

Because you don't know what new shit's coming at you, with the dawn of that new day. All you know is that it's not your shit. It's not your loose ends. It's not your mistake for saying something that you shouldn't have said to someone you shouldn't have said it to. Capisce?

Jimmy answered it anyway. "Yeah." They were there to kill Deck.

He was clean, he was bandaged, but she was still touching him, her hands solid against his leg, her interest just as palpable.

"You kept them from doing that, you know," she said quietly.

"Doing that and a crapload of other things." Like waking up tomorrow morning.

"You saved Decker's life," she told him. "You got us safely out of there. We all could have been killed."

Jimmy shook his head. "Not really. It wasn't that big a deal. I mean, yeah, if Deck had gone out the front door without knowing they were there. . . . The shooters I took down had training, but not enough. They put one guard at the door to the roof, then assumed they were safe, that they didn't have to watch their backs. They didn't have a clue that I was up there."

He wondered, with a tiny part of his brain that stood off to the side and watched this exchange dispassionately, if she knew that he was talking more about this than he ever had before, with anyone.

Why?

Yes, she was impossibly beautiful in a certain light, at certain times. Like right now. Her eyes took his breath away.

But big fucking deal. He'd taken a whole parade of beautiful women to bed, although never quite like tonight. He'd gotten it on with them and then he'd made his excuses—"Whoops, I'm getting a call from HQ, gotta go save the world"—and left.

So what was he doing, still here?

He didn't have to look far to find an obvious answer. He wanted to make sure she knew that he normally lasted significantly longer than twenty-five seconds. That was freaking embarrassing. He was still here because he had to make it up to her. He had to take her to bed again, to make it good this time.

Had to? What a liar. He *wanted* to.

But that was a lie, too, because, really, sex was just a good excuse to stick around. But it wasn't the real reason he was here.

"I can't imagine what it feels like, to . . ." Tess couldn't even say it.

"It feels too easy." Whoa, where did *that* come from? What does it *feel* like to take another man's life? It feels like nothing. Like just another day that started when the sun rose, and ended the way most of his days ended, with a good night's rest after getting laid.

Except Jimmy couldn't remember the last time he'd been able to sleep.

Maybe that's what was going on here. Sleep deprivation was used as torture in some countries. It was used to break people down, to get them talking. Maybe that was why he was saying things he'd never said to anyone. *It feels too easy.* Shit.

He stood up. "Am I going to freak out your neighbors if I walk into the kitchen like this?"

Tess was still sitting on the floor. She had the strangest

expression on her face. "That's what happened, isn't it? That's how you got stabbed."

"Dinged." He went into the kitchen—the blinds were closed—and found his beer.

"The first two didn't hear you coming."

Jimmy didn't have to turn to know that Tess had come to stand in the doorway. He could see her clearly enough in his peripheral vision. She'd put her robe back on. What a shame.

"So you made sure the third one did," she continued softly. Gently. As if she were talking to a frightened animal or a small child. Or someone she cared about very deeply.

And Jimmy knew the truth. He was here because he liked her. He really, *really* liked her. And she liked him, too.

He was here because his hands had been shaking far too often lately, and he wanted someone to forgive him for all of his sins.

He needed someone to know, instead of just guessing or assuming from all of the rumors that regularly circulated about him.

"It wasn't intentional," he told her. But yeah. He must've made some noise. . . .

"And yet it was still too easy," she whispered.

How did she know that? He didn't even know it himself until she said it.

He couldn't look at her. Not even from the corners of his eyes. He finished his beer and turned to the sink to rinse out the bottle.

He heard her coming toward him. Felt her warmth. And her slight hesitation.

But then she put her arms around him, hugging him from behind, her arms around his chest, her body pressed against his back.

It took him by surprise. He'd been expecting a tentative hand on his shoulder or arm, not this full embrace.

"I'm glad that it's easy," she said fiercely. "I'm glad that you're stronger and smarter and better trained than those men on the roof—than everyone that you go up against. I'm glad that you're the one who walks away. Just . . . oh, Diego, next time give yourself permission to do it without getting . . . dinged."

He didn't know what to do or say in response to that, and when he opened his mouth, "My name's Jimmy" came out.

She was smart, but he didn't wait for her to figure it out. He explained. "Diego's not my real name. Well, it sort of is. It's Spanish for James, but . . ."

"Jimmy," she repeated. She kissed him. Right on his back. Next to his shoulder blade.

He wasn't sure what it was that made him keep talking. It might've been that tiny kiss—a kiss that had nothing to do with sex and everything to do with tenderness and genuine caring. Or maybe it was her arms around him, or the solid warmth of her body against him, or the fact that he could speak to the bottom of the kitchen sink, to the tiny, smiling cartoon cow that looked up at him from the decorative knob of the drain strainer, without risk of the cow turning away in disapproval.

"I get dinged up a lot," he admitted. "Sometimes I think I might . . ." The cow smiled up at him. Tess held him tightly.

But he couldn't say it. He didn't even really know what he was trying to tell her.

Tess spoke then, her voice quiet as that cow smiled on. "Do you think you're somehow trying to, I don't know, punish yourself? For being so good at . . . what you do?"

"No," he said. "It's not that so much as . . ." Oh, Christ. He wanted to leave. Why didn't he? It would take almost no effort to break free from her arms, to pull his clothes back on and walk out the door. He could get into the Agency car and drive until the sun rose, the radio up so loud that he wouldn't have to think.

Instead he stood there as she whispered, "What, Jimmy?" As she struggled to understand.

Which was a pretty freaking enormous task, since he didn't understand any of this himself. "It hurts," he said. It was the best he could give her.

She was smart enough to know that he wasn't referring to his leg, or even how difficult it was talking about this. He could almost hear her thinking. "And . . . that's somehow a good thing?"

"Fuck! I don't know!" He turned to face her. "I'm sorry. Forgive me—"

"It's all right," she said. Her eyes weren't filled with loathing or disgust, just sweet understanding, despite the fact that she couldn't know what he was trying to tell her, couldn't know really why he was angry.

So Jimmy did the only thing he could do. He kissed her. "Tess."

"I'm here," she said.

And she was.

The American, and the Kazbekistani man had both vanished.

They were gone.

Sophia had watched them turn the corner from some distance back—first the American, and then the K-stani. It looked as if the K-stani man had broken into a run, and she'd picked up her own pace.

But now she was at that same corner and the street was empty. She pulled back her veil, hoping that would help her see them. But the entire area was deserted.

It was weird—doubly so because there were no alleys or side streets for someone to duck into to hide.

And this really wasn't so much a street as it was a driveway. Moonlight glinted off the windows of the long, low factory buildings that lined both sides of the narrow passageway. Their entrances were back around on the avenue she'd come from, so there wasn't even a doorway to slip into. She could see loading docks farther down the drive—much farther than the K-stani man could have gotten, even if he'd sprinted at an Olympic gold medalist's speed.

It was a dangerous choice of paths to take while out past curfew. If a police patrol approached, there'd be nowhere for her to hide.

She ventured only a few steps down the driveway before stopping again.

As much as she hated to admit it, she'd lost them. It was far too risky for her to continue. Being stopped by the police would be a death sentence for her. It would mean a swift delivery to Padsha Bashir's nephews.

The American had said he'd go back to Lartet's in a few days. She'd watch for him to return, this time from a nearby alley.

Because she wasn't going into Lartet's again.

Not until she went there to kill him.

Sophia retraced her steps back around the corner and—

She was grabbed, a hand clamped hard over her mouth and nose, her body slammed up against the bricks of the building.

No, that wasn't the building she'd hit. It was a man. He hauled her up and through a window and into the factory before she could fight, before she could think, before she could scream.

But of course she couldn't scream, because his hand was over her face, keeping her from making any noise, keeping her from getting any air.

And she couldn't fight either, or even reach for her gun, because he had her in such a secure hold that struggling got her nowhere.

He pulled her back into the darkness of some kind of office—her leg hit the metal of a desk with a clang—and out a door, down a corridor. Even though it was futile, she was struggling, and her head connected with the doorframe so solidly she saw stars. Or maybe the stars were from the fact that she couldn't breathe.

She couldn't breathe, she couldn't see, she couldn't hear much of anything but her heart pounding and . . .

And then she could see. As she was dragged through yet another doorway, she saw moonlight through the tall factory windows. It was shining on some kind of conveyor belt, on the hard concrete floor, on the crumpled body of the Kazbekistani man who had followed the American out of Lartet's bar.

And now Sophia could think, too, despite the panic that gripped her from the lack of air. She knew she was going to die because, although she'd been careful, she hadn't been careful enough.

It was the story of her life—how fitting that it should be the story of her death as well.

The American—her killer—had realized he was being followed not just by the K-stani man, but by her as well. He'd turned down that particular corner, onto that factory driveway, on purpose. He'd gone up and into this window, and into the factory. She should have seen that that was a possibility. In hindsight, she realized that those windows that lined the drive were all relatively low to the ground. It wasn't an obvious or easy way inside—it would require both strength and skill—but it *was* a way in, and the American had taken it.

And then he'd waited for the K-stani man to come around the corner, to run past, thinking he'd lost the American down by the loading docks. But the American—she'd thought he was little back in Lartet's bar, but he had arms like steel—had gotten behind his pursuer and dragged him here, inside.

When the American had realized she wasn't going to

take any chances and walk down that driveway, he must've quickly found his way to the front of the building and come out of that office window instead, and, heaven help her, she needed air.

And then she got it, as he ripped the burka from her head, as he released his hold on her, yanking her robe from her body as she fell—as he pushed her down onto the hard floor.

And Sophia realized as she lay there, gasping and sucking in precious air, that the K-stani man was only unconscious. His hands were tied behind him with a belt. The American wouldn't have bothered to tie him if he were dead.

"What the hell . . . ?" Incredulity rang in the American's voice, and as she looked up she saw it on his face, too. Pure disbelief on a hard face that belonged to a man who had arms of steel, a face that he quickly tried to hide with that expressionless mask she'd seen him wear while talking to Lartet.

She knew she was not what he'd expected to find beneath that burka, her blond hair gleaming in the moonlight, the white gauze of her gown nearly transparent.

He was not what she'd expected to find either. He was smart, he was strong, he was very good at staying alive. An alpha male in a beta's body. The kind of man who knew how to make money when everyone else was starving, to stay on top when everyone else was going under.

The expressionless mask he wearing, however, didn't completely hide his very male reaction to her very visible female form. She'd seen a similar flash in his eyes back in the bar, and she knew she had a fighting chance.

"Please," Sophia said, reaching up toward him with one hand, her voice thick with the tears she'd been holding back for months. "Oh, please, I need your help!"

CHAPTER
ELEVEN

"WHO ARE you?" Decker asked.

The woman glanced toward the unconscious Kazbeki-stani man lying over by the window, on the cold concrete of the factory floor. "I can't tell you," she whispered. "Not here. Not in front of him."

The tears in her eyes overflowed and poured down her beautiful face.

Deck had lived plenty long enough to know that things were seldom what they appeared to be. Especially when it came to both tears and beautiful faces.

"Who is he?" he asked her, gesturing to the man on the floor.

"I don't know." She was lying. She was also an American. She sat up. Adjusted her dress. Watched him watch her as she sat up and adjusted her dress.

Yeah, those tears were a special effect. As was the dress. Which, despite being torn and bloodstained in places, was one hell of a dress. It was barely a dress at all.

She had a body that worked well with that outfit, despite the fact that she'd obviously been knocked around by someone in the recent past. It was hard not to stare, and she well knew it.

Was this what all K-stani prostitutes wore beneath their robes?

Business should have been booming.

Decker considered himself not easily distracted. And he was definitely . . . distracted.

The tiny revolver that he found in the pocket of her robe helped him focus.

"Keep your hands where I can see them," he ordered as he checked the safety and pocketed the little firearm. She was wearing a ring on her right hand that she'd kept turned inward to her palm at the bar. If it was real, it was worth a small fortune.

Blue eyes flashed up at him. At least he thought they were blue. They might have been green. He couldn't tell for sure in this light. Whatever color they were, she was used to using them to her advantage.

Although, truth be told, when she was wearing that dress, most men weren't going to be looking into her eyes.

"You really think I'm concealing another weapon?" she asked, using her hands to wipe her face. As if her tears were something she was embarrassed by, something she didn't want him to see. It was a nice touch, as was the trace of dark humor in her voice. He liked women who got a kick out of irony. She gestured to her outfit. "In *this*?"

Except for one small piece of limestone, soft and crumbling—a sample for her rock collection?—the robe's other pockets were empty. And as far as Decker could tell, there was nothing sewn into the lining, either.

"I don't suppose you're carrying any ID?" he asked.

She shook her head, wiping her nose with the back of one pale, slender hand. Her nails were bitten down to the quick. "I have no papers, no passport. They were stolen, months ago."

Decker nodded. "You're probably going to think I'm just using this as an opportunity to cop a feel, but I really do need to make sure you're not carrying another weapon."

She gazed up at him with those innocent eyes in that delicate, heart-shaped, porcelain-complexioned face. It was a searching look, as if she were trying to read his mind.

It was times like these he wished he'd bought a carton of those little Oscar award key chains he'd seen in that souvenir shop in Hollywood. They were small enough that he could carry a few with him at all times and hand them out to people when they gave a really outstanding performance. Like this one.

"I understand," she finally said and, keeping her hands clearly in sight, although still trying to hide that ring from him, she pushed herself up and off the ground.

As Decker watched, she faced the wall, put her hands against it, and spread her legs.

Sweet Jesus.

She stood—purposely, he had absolutely no doubt— in the brightest patch of moonlight that was shining in through the window. Lit the way she was, she might as well have been naked.

And standing the way she was . . .

Hello.

He could see through her dress. She had intricate lines— hennaed designs?—on her arms and upper body.

There was no way she had a weapon on her. Except Decker knew that was what she wanted him to think, by standing in the light, by standing in that particular position. It was what she would want him to think if she *were* carrying a knife she could use to slit his throat.

So—what a pity—he had to run his hands over that body.

He started with her outstretched arms, and she immediately winced.

"Sorry," he said. What he was doing shouldn't have hurt.

"Scraped elbows," she explained.

Ah. He tried to make his touch lighter. But she winced again when he reached her shoulders.

"Scraped everything," she amended. "From the quake. I'm lucky I'm alive."

"How long have you been working the street?" he asked, and she glanced back at him, over her shoulder, just as he moved his hands down and across her breasts. Hell of a time to make eye contact. And nope, definitely no Magnum .357 hiding there.

"I haven't been," she told him, but then her eyes filled with tears and she turned away.

Yeah, right.

The muscles in her stomach were tightly tensed, and as he reached between her legs, he tried to make his touch as impersonal as possible. To his surprise, she didn't try to make the contact sexual. In the course of his Agency career, he'd patted down working women a time or two, and they'd sent him a very obvious nonverbal message during that portion of the search.

This blonde stood stone still.

Decker quickly finished, moving his hands down one leg and then the other.

"Done," he told her.

"What, you're not going to check to make sure I don't have a grenade up my ass?" Her voice shook.

"If you do, you can keep it," he said. "Sophia."

She inhaled—he couldn't quite call it a gasp—but he knew he'd guessed correctly. Back in the bar, he'd noticed how carefully she'd watched Lartet as he'd received that note from the burka-clad boy.

As she—Sophia—now turned to look at him, Deck could see her realize both that he'd merely been making a wild guess, and that she, in turn, had given herself away.

She made a choking sound that he first thought was laughter, but quickly realized were more tears. Noisy tears this time. And this time she couldn't seem to make them stop.

"I'm sorry," she kept saying. "I'm sorry."

If this was an act, it was a damn good one. And it got even more dramatic when the K-stani on the floor started to stir. Deck wished he had a miniature Tony award to give her as well.

Sophia lunged for her burka. "He can't see me!" she said. "Don't let him see me!"

He held her robe out of reach. "I thought you didn't know who he was."

"I don't," she said between her sobs. "I only know who he might be, who he might work for." She looked at Decker beseechingly. "Please."

It would have been heart wrenching. If he were fourteen.

"Not Michel Lartet?" Decker asked.

"Besides Lartet." The K-stani man groaned, and she moved so that Decker was standing between them, so that she was at least partially hidden behind him.

"Who, Sophia?" he asked.

"Don't call me that in front of him!"

"Who?"

"The man who killed Dimitri Ghaffari," she whispered. "Padsha Bashir."

Shit. "Ghaffari's dead?" he asked, knowing that he shouldn't trust anything that came from this woman's mouth. Just as he'd noticed her back in the bar, she'd obviously noticed him—and listened in on his conversation with Lartet. Still, his gut instinct was that it was probably true. Ghaffari probably was dead. It would explain why the man had dropped off the face of the earth.

Sophia nodded, fresh tears welling in her eyes. "Bashir's dead, too."

No way. He definitely would have heard about it on the streets tonight if warlord Padsha Bashir had gone to his heavenly reward.

Still, it seemed clear that she believed it to be true.

There was fear and there was feigned fear—and no one was *that* good an actress. This woman was terrified.

But whoever this mysterious Sophia was, unless she was beyond desperate, she wasn't going anywhere without her burka and robe—not in that dress, in this city.

Decker decided to experiment. He kept her outerwear over his arm as he crossed to the man on the floor, as he purposely turned his back on the blonde. With one well-placed tap, not as gentle as a lullaby but as effective, he put the K-stani man back to sleep.

When he turned around again—what do you know? She *was* that desperate—she'd pulled a total ninja.

He would've liked a chance to talk to the K-stani man who was drooling on the dusty floor, but he knew he could always find him at Lartet's.

So Decker took his belt back—no point leaving behind souvenirs—giving Sophia a few more seconds' lead time. Then he followed her out of the factory and into the night.

Tess took her phone and her penlight, and explored Rivka's house.

There was a sitting room off the kitchen on the first floor, and beyond it another room, but when she tried the knob, the door was securely locked.

It didn't really matter—it was obvious she wasn't getting phone coverage anywhere on the ground floor.

She kept her phone open and out in front of her, much in the way Mr. Spock held his tricorder as he and the away team from the USS *Enterprise* investigated a newly discovered Class M planet on *Star Trek*.

She climbed the stairs to the second floor, where there was a hallway and two more of those locked doors. Maybe, during all those episodes, when Spock was checking the gadget's little screen, he was really just looking for intergalactic phone service.

"Searching for service . . ." said the message on her phone's display, ellipses trailing off into infinity. "Searching for service . . ."

Oh, come on. This phone had worked on the roof of that church. And unless a strong wind had already taken out the sat-dish . . .

She went up more stairs to the third floor of the house, refusing to believe her beloved technology could fail her so utterly.

It was there, on the minuscule landing just outside of what looked to be the only real bedroom in the narrow three-story building, that there was a tiny celebration of LED fireworks on the display screen of her phone.

"Who would you like to call?" the text message now cheerfully asked.

Tess went into the quiet of that empty bedroom, the carpeting thick and plush under her feet. This room had a private bathroom—currently sans running water, of course—a huge walk-in closet, and a king-sized bed. It was obviously the room that their host, Rivka, shared with Guldana, his wife of twenty-five years.

It was the only room in the entire house where Tess would have Internet access.

"Shoot," she said. How was she going to manage this?

"It's better than having no communications access at all," Nash said from the doorway, making her jump about three feet into the air and drop her penlight.

When she'd crept past him in the kitchen, he'd been lying with one arm over his eyes, breathing steadily.

"I thought you were asleep." Tess picked her light up off the floor.

"I was just resting," he said. "You *do* have coverage up here, right?"

"Yeah."

"But not downstairs?"

"No."

Nash was silent. They both were, just looking at each other in the shadowy dimness.

Her betrayer of a brain kept flashing pictures of him naked in her bed, of his face above her, his eyes heavy-lidded with desire as he . . . as they . . .

Oh, God.

If she was remembering *that* more times a day than she would ever admit aloud, what must he think about whenever he looked at her?

Although it was quite possibly worse to think that he never thought about their night together at all. It was depressing to consider that it was something that simply never crossed his mind, completely unmemorable and forgotten.

"I'm sorry about before," Nash said, just as she asked, "Is Deck back yet?" They had to stop doing that—both talking at once. People did that when they were uncomfortable with each other, when they had to work to think of things to say.

"No," he said. "He's not. He's . . . You shouldn't worry about him, he's—"

"I'm not worried about him."

"Okay. That's . . . okay."

More silence as he glanced at the bed, at the filmy curtains blowing gently in the breeze from the windows. "I guess we'll have to move into this room then, huh?"

"And what? Rivka and his wife will sleep in the pantry?" Tess snorted. "I don't think so. I know I wouldn't if—"

"They won't have to sleep in the pantry," Nash told her. "There are other rooms in this house—Guldana's law offices."

Rivka's wife was a lawyer? *Had been* a lawyer was more like it—under the current regime, women weren't allowed to practice law.

Unless they did it behind not just closed doors but . . . Suddenly all those locked doors made sense.

God, Tess couldn't imagine having her career—everything she'd worked so hard to achieve—taken from her. Simply because as a woman, she was no longer permitted to do such work.

Like Guldana, she'd probably keep on working, and just pray she didn't get caught.

"It's dangerous for them, isn't it?" she asked. "Having us stay here?"

"They don't know who we are," Nash said, "or what we do. But yeah, it's definitely a risk for them. It's a risk for us, too. If they found out what we're really up to, they might turn us in—to win some look-the-other-way points from the local warlords, you know?"

They might also win some sort of reward money. Like nearly everyone in K-stan, they could probably use it.

"We should clear out of here," Nash continued. "It's one thing if they offer us their room, another entirely if we ask for it. That's just not done. And if they find us in here, that would be thought of as shockingly rude."

Because it *was* rude to be in here without their host's permission. But as far as asking went . . . Tess narrowed her eyes at Nash. "You're somehow going to make them offer us this room?"

"Yeah," Nash said. "Actually, we are."

We. Oh, no. "I'm not going to like this very much, am I?" she asked.

He laughed. It was rueful, and she knew she wasn't just going to dislike his plan, she was going to flat-out hate it. "Definitely not."

Great. Just great.

"I'm guessing Rivka'll get here about twenty minutes after sunup, after the curfew ends," Nash told her as she followed him back down the stairs, back into the kitchen.

"That gives us a couple of hours. But we should probably be ready for him in case he returns earlier."

Tess turned to look at Nash, but he purposely wasn't meeting her gaze.

"So," she said, trying to be brisk and matter-of-fact. And trying to inject a little humor into the situation. "Which side of the bedroll do you like to sleep on? The right or the left?"

Ah. Eye contact. For all of his shortcomings, the man certainly did have pretty eyes. "I'm not going to make you do that," he said. "It'll be enough that I'm in there with you."

"Sleeping where?" she asked. "Have you been in that pantry? Because we're either spooning, or you're sitting up. Which is no way to sleep."

Nash looked behind the curtain and swore softly. "I didn't realize . . ." He turned back to her. "Okay. No problem. I'll be out here until I hear Rivka coming home. But then I'm going to lie down next to you, make it look like we've been together all night, okay? Be aware that's going to happen. Don't be on autopilot and go into self-defense mode on me, all right?" He reached up gingerly to touch the back of his head. "Believe it or not, I've already had enough pain for this entire mission."

"So you're going to just . . . stay awake?" He'd told her they had several hours to wait.

"Don't worry about me."

"I'm not," she countered. "I'm worried that you're going to fall asleep out there and Rivka's going to come back before you wake up. I really need to be upstairs in that room, James. Or I need to figure out a way to get phone service down here. I mean, I could put a sat-dish right on the roof but—"

"No." They both knew that that would be the equivalent of flying an American flag overhead, and then wearing

FBI windbreakers over CIA T-shirts. *Hello! Here we are! Notice us!*

But if she could get a dish way up high, higher than the church down the street, way up on the roof of the Grande Hotel . . . She didn't say it aloud, but Nash certainly knew what she was thinking, because "No," he said again. "Nuh-uh. I'll get you that room. I'm not going to fall asleep."

"But if you do—"

"It's not going to happen."

"But—"

"Look, I don't sleep much when I'm home in my own bed. And after a day like—" He stopped. Swore.

"After an awful day like today," Tess whispered.

Nash—Jimmy—actually looked embarrassed.

"I had nightmares," she told him. "When I fell asleep in the wagon." Her dreams had been a terrible montage of dead and injured children, of grieving and frantic parents, of pain and sorrow and fear, and the persistent, ever present stink of death.

"I'm sorry," he said, and really meant it. Probably because he knew what it was like to wake up sweating, heart pounding . . .

"It's a natural reaction," she said. "Having nightmares, or even being unable to sleep after seeing . . ."

"Yeah," he said. "I know." But it was clear that he believed that while having a nightmare was acceptable for her, such rules didn't apply to him.

"You're allowed to be human, too," Tess told him quietly.

He nodded. "Yeah," he said again, but again she knew he didn't believe it. "I'll be in in a few hours, when Rivka gets home."

He turned his back then, focusing on the contents of his bag.

Tess had worked at the Agency long enough to recognize

when she'd been dismissed, but she still hesitated before going behind the curtain.

Because Jimmy Nash was in trouble. She'd worked at the Agency long enough to recognize that, too.

"I'm here if you need me," she said quietly.

He turned to look at her, one elegant eyebrow raised in a perfect "Oh, really?" look, loaded with innuendo.

"To talk," she repeated, and, cursing him for being a jerk and herself for being a fool, she pushed past the curtain, all but scurrying into the pantry.

Sophia climbed through an open window into a room that was sparsely furnished. It was obvious that the woman living here could ill afford a thief stealing her second-best burka.

But she was trapped in this neighborhood with the sun about to rise, and she didn't have a lot of options. She had to steal this robe and veil—it meant the difference between life and death.

Taking the faded and carefully mended garment from the hook, Sophia dressed quietly, praying that its loss wouldn't create unimaginable hardships for its owner.

She knew she couldn't delay—she still wasn't convinced she'd lost the American. Still, before she went back out the window, she took the ring from her finger—the ring that she'd hoped would help her pay for the falsified papers and passport she'd need to get out of the country—and left it dangling from the hook that had held this robe.

She quietly hit the street, keeping to the shadows, noting the lightening of the sky in the east.

There was no sign of the American. But that was nothing new. Sophia had been running away from him for hours now, and from the very moment she'd left the factory, there had been no hint that he was there—no footsteps behind her, no movement in the shadows. She didn't even have that uneasy sense of being watched.

But it had been so laughably easy to get away from him, she was sure he'd let her go.

And why else would he have done that if not to follow her—to see where she went, whom she was working with, where her loyalties lay.

She was not—*was not*—going back to her hiding place in the Hotel Français until she was certain he was no longer watching her. Having a safe haven with a source of water was beyond valuable. She would keep moving, keep running for days if she had to, before she returned there.

But she wouldn't have to.

She'd led the American in circles in this part of town, moving not just through alleys but also across rooftops, wanting to keep as close as possible to the Saboor Square marketplace.

As dawn approached, the city awoke. With the sun came the end of curfew, and people—mostly women—poured onto the street.

Within minutes the stalls in the square were unlocked and opened, lines already queuing up for bread and fruit.

Sophia stepped out of the alleyway and into the stream of similarly clad women, one of whom nearly knocked her over—blasted veils.

Blasted veils—*blessed* veils. The apprehension she'd been carrying for hours faded as she blended with that crowd, as she became one of many—anonymous and unidentifiable beneath her robe and full veil.

She knew with certainty that she'd finally lost the American.

Because when it came to following someone, no one could possibly be *that* good.

Tess had fallen asleep.

It seemed almost criminal to wake her. Of course, maybe he didn't have to. Maybe all Jimmy had to do was allow himself to be "caught" tippy-toeing out of Tess's pantry, wearing only his boxers and a very satisfied smile on his face.

He'd already stripped out of his clothes—the heat tonight was nearly unbearable. He messed up his hair as he heard the kitchen door open and Rivka and Guldana quietly came inside their house.

"Where are they?" he heard Guldana whisper.

"Maybe up and out, early?" Rivka replied.

"Maybe," Guldana echoed skeptically.

The sheet Tess had used to cover herself had slid down off one arm. She was wearing an oversized T-shirt, and her short hair was neatly arranged.

"Or maybe not yet even gone to sleep," Guldana said, as sharp-eyed as always. "Those pillows over there are un-dented. And look—someone's gone somewhere without his trousers."

Rivka would be fooled if Jimmy stepped out from behind this curtain right now. But Guldana would take one look at Tess—and she would look—and she would *not* see a bride who'd just shared a night of passion with her new husband. She would ask questions, watch them closely, whisper to Rivka, wonder what they were up to. . . .

Tess wanted that upstairs room. Jimmy tried to convince himself that that was his only motive as he stripped off his boxers and crawled beneath that sheet.

She stirred as he tried to nudge her over. There just wasn't enough room for the two of them. He was practically on top of her.

But maybe that wasn't such a bad thing.

And indeed, she reached for him, pulling him closer, warm and sleepy and soft and sweet-smelling and . . .

Oh, yeah.

"Rivka's home," he breathed into her ear, hoping she wouldn't take his expanding response to her too personally, but before he could apologize or even shift back, away from her, she kissed him.

And okay, all right. That was good. It no doubt looked freaking realistic, because it *felt* unbelievably real. Jimmy tried to project himself out of body, to look down and see what Rivka and Guldana would see when they peeked behind the curtain.

They'd see a man who wanted to get laid more than he wanted to keep breathing.

They'd see a woman who had spent all of the night, right up to that point, completely untouched.

He quickly tousled Tess's hair and pulled her T-shirt—not the sexiest of nightwear for a new bride—up to her neck.

She stopped kissing him long enough to yank her shirt up and over her head—after the Gentleman's Den that shouldn't have been such a surprise, yet it still was. Because there she was, the Tess of his dreams, lying naked beneath him, with that slow, sleepy smile and those freckles on a nose that was almost too cute to describe, and he was so totally gone.

He was male, he was human, and it was a classic example of cause and effect. Breasts in the face—Christ, she was even more beautiful than he remembered—caused a definite physical response he could no longer hide.

He'd been mostly holding his own up to that point, but it was the proverbial straw that broke the camel's back. Or rather, it made the camel, so to speak, impossible for either of them to ignore.

And yet Tess didn't seem to mind. She kissed him again, or maybe he kissed her—Jimmy wasn't sure. But either way, she wrapped her arms around him in the most convincing embrace. She even rubbed up against him, making a sound that was unbelievably sexy. It was a sound that even Rivka, who was nearly completely deaf in one ear, had to have heard.

"What was that?" Jimmy heard him ask his wife. He didn't hear Guldana's response because—hey now!—Tess had reached between them, wrapped her fingers around him and . . .

No condom, no condom! What the hell was she doing? The sheet was covering them, they didn't actually need to . . .

But he couldn't pull away from her. Not while Rivka and Guldana were sneaking up to the curtain-covered doorway.

It was right then, as she guided him down and pressed her hips up, as he slid deeply inside of her with nothing between them, groaning aloud at the sensation—soft, wet, hot, it was sex with the volume cranked up to a hundred and eleven—that he realized she was still half asleep.

Or rather, he realized this at the very moment she finally and fully woke up.

"Oh, my *God*!" she said.

From Rivka and Guldana's perspective, as they pushed aside the curtain, it surely seemed as if Tess were reacting to the sudden appearance of an audience.

But Jimmy knew better.

He leapt off her as Rivka roared, "What's going on in my house?"

Jimmy scrambled for his boxers even as Tess yanked the sheet up and around herself. "I'm sorry," he said in both English and the K-stani dialect Rivka and Guldana spoke, as he thrust first one leg and then the other into his shorts. "That wasn't supposed to happen. I just . . . I thought . . ." Come on, Jimbo, stop babbling and stick to the script! But oh, Christ, what *was* the script?

His entire brain was scrambled, and all he could think about was Tess and how badly he wanted to finish what they'd started. What *he'd* started, because, damn it, she wasn't even awake when she, when they . . .

"I'm sorry," he said again, but Tess wasn't looking at him.

"We didn't expect you home so soon," she said to Rivka and Guldana.

Rivka looked at her, looked at Jimmy, his face stony, his eyes cold. "I must ask you to leave my house immediately. All of you."

Guldana touched her husband's arm. "They're American. They're young. Don't you remember being young?"

Tess reached for Jimmy, her fingers warm and solid against his leg, as Guldana murmured, "Besides, we need the money," to her angry husband.

Jimmy looked down into Tess's face, into her eyes.

"James," she said as she squeezed his leg, sending him a silent message with her eyes. *Come on, Nash, get back in the game.* "Honey. I think you better introduce me."

CHAPTER
TWELVE

SHE SENSED him before she saw him, as she was washing the sweat and grime of the night from her face.

Or maybe she smelled him when she turned off the water. Not that he smelled bad. Just different. Warm. Male. American.

There was no way he could have followed her through that market. No way. And yet . . .

Sophia slowly turned from the sink, her face and hands dripping with water, half hoping that fatigue and fear were playing tricks on her, making her sense and smell things that weren't really there. Maybe this old hotel still played host to the spirits of guests from the past. She'd heard once that Leonardo DiCaprio had stayed here, en route to some on-location movie set in the Far East—was it Thailand?

Maybe . . .

But no such luck. He really was standing there. The American from the factory, from Lartet's bar.

He was leaning against the pink-tiled wall of the ladies' room, arms folded casually across his deceptively slight-looking chest.

Fear crashed sharply through her, but she was completely cornered. Even if she could reach the windows before him, even if she could get them open, they were too high up and too narrow to squeeze through. There was nowhere to run—nothing to do but stand there, looking back at him.

He'd somehow gotten through the locked door in the outer room without her hearing him come in.

He'd somehow followed her all the way back here, to the hotel. . . .

"How did you—"

He cut her off. "I'm pretty sure I get to ask the questions first."

It took every ounce of willpower she had to keep her eyes on his face, not to glance toward the pallet she'd made of stolen blankets—her bed—under which she'd hidden that second little gun. What she wouldn't give to have it right now, in her hand.

Instead he handed her the clean rag that she was using as a towel, and she dried her face with shaking hands.

"I'm not going to hurt you," he said.

Sophia nodded, but she didn't—couldn't—believe him.

"All I want is to talk." He had a nice voice, a mellow baritone that had the slightest trace of a Western accent. "Sophia."

She met his eyes—they were light brown, almost exactly the same color as his nondescript hair—but she could see only intelligence and a constant alertness there. There was no recognition, no awareness, no indication he knew he'd hit a giant cash jackpot.

Of course, with this man, this magician who had followed her through that crowded marketplace, that didn't mean anything.

He was much older than she'd thought when she'd seen him both in the bar and in the dimly lit factory—not in his twenties, or even in his early thirties. No, up close, in the hard morning light, she could see that it had been several years since he'd crossed to the other side of forty. He had lines on a face that, from a distance, she never would have described as handsome, although looking at him now, up close, she didn't know why not.

His nose was straight, practically patrician, and the rest of his features were equally even and pleasant-looking, although his mouth was thin, his lips tight. He had lines around his mouth and crow's feet at the outer corners of his eyes. On most people those would be called laughter lines, but she got the sense that this man didn't spend enough time laughing to warrant that label.

"Do you mind if we sit?" he continued. "Out there?" He gestured behind him to the former sitting room, now empty of easy chairs. "I've been on my feet most of the night."

As had she.

Who was he, *what* was he, to have been able to follow her the way he had? And what, exactly, did he want from her?

"Are you CIA?" she couldn't keep from asking, even though she knew that he couldn't possibly be.

His answer was "No," and his amused smile chilled her. He thought it was funny that she might mistake him for a government agent, which meant that he was probably one of those ex-pats who had no loyalty to their former country, or to fellow Americans.

She was *so* dead.

Sophia let him lead her, his fingers firm and his hand warm through the sleeve of her dress. Together they went into the outer room, where her robe and the veil he'd taken from her at the factory lay by the door.

Thoughtful of him to return them. Not that she'd need them for more than the ride to Bashir's palace.

She caught sight of herself in the big wall mirror. Even in the dimness of that windowless space, her dress was exotically sheer—but not too sheer in this light to reveal her collection of cuts and bruises. Because of that, she was better than naked—she was nearly naked and shimmering. Her terror shone around her, too, and she hoped he couldn't see that as clearly as she could in that mirror.

With a quick glance in its direction, she saw that he'd re-locked the door. If she tried to run, it would take some time to throw back the bolt and pull the door open and . . .

No. Best thing to do was figure out a way to get to the gun that was beneath the blankets of her bed.

Her bed.

She could see in the mirror that the American had no-ticed her glance at the door. Good. Let him think she was considering escape in that direction. She looked at the door again, a quick flick of her gaze, just to give him something to focus on.

Because unlike at the factory, he now seemed unaffected by her outfit. Which meant it was going to be more difficult than she'd hoped to get over to her bed.

"You have a last name?" he asked as he gestured for her to sit against the wall that was farthest from both the door and the inner room.

Sophia nodded as she lowered herself to a sitting posi-tion.

He sat on the floor, too, right in the middle of the room, blocking both her route to the door and to that gun.

His eyes were carefully on her face and she shifted, pre-tending to get comfortable, testing him, and . . . Sure enough, his gaze dropped. Only briefly, but it did drop.

Okay. Okay. He was human after all. If she worked this right, she could play out this scenario—bed him, then kill him, then run.

Think. *Think.* What had she already told him? How could she use that best to win his trust—or at least make him close the gap between them?

Back at the factory, she'd told him that Dimitri was dead. Bashir, too. He'd guessed her name—Sophia—but he didn't appear to recognize it, although she also knew that he played his cards close to his vest. He was impossible to read.

If he did know Dimitri, or at least *of* Dimitri, he might also know that Dimitri had a wife named Sophia. And if he knew that, and if she gave him a false last name now, he'd know she was lying and . . .

"Ghaffari," she finally answered him. She couldn't afford to have him think she was lying about anything. "My name is Sophia Ghaffari."

He didn't react. He didn't even blink. "You're Dimitri's wife?" His voice was blank, too—devoid of either skepticism or belief.

"I *was* his wife," she said. "I told you. He's dead."

He was silent for a moment, then, "Yes, you did. I'm sorry for your loss."

She made herself laugh, but didn't say anything more. She had to wait until he asked. If she volunteered too much information, it would come out sounding like a story.

After an eternity, the American spoke again. "I guess you heard me tell Lartet that I have money for Dimitri—money that a mutual friend owed him."

She knew where he was going with this and shook her head. "That's not why I followed you. I don't want your friend's money." Not quite true—she wanted all the money she could get. But it was only a matter of time until everything this man had in his pockets belonged to her.

And if she could manage it, she would kill him after he took off his T-shirt and those cargo pants.

What she wouldn't give to be rid of this awful dress, to have real, Western clothes to wear—pants—even if they were too big. She could cut and color her hair and hide in plain sight among the Western relief workers. . . .

"Why *did* you follow me?" he asked.

She answered that one truthfully. "Because I knew everyone Dimitri knew, and I didn't know you. I wanted to know who you were and who this friend of yours was." Back at Lartet's bar, she had dared to hope that this American might be able to help her—that he really was some do-gooder relief worker who'd be enough of a sucker to lend her a hand. But he'd made it more than clear back at the factory that that wasn't the case. "But there is no friend," she asked him now. "Right?"

He nodded in agreement, watching her with eyes that seemed able to see inside of her head. "Yeah. That's just an easy way to find someone. Free money, you know? People come to the surface, even out of deep hiding, if they think someone's going to hand over some cash."

Sophia made herself hold his gaze, telling herself that he couldn't really read her mind. She tried to make the eye contact something sexual, to infuse it with interest. "So, who are you, then?" She let her gaze wander lazily down his body. He wore his T-shirt loose, size large when in fact he was barely a medium. That was how he managed to look thin when he really wasn't. "You're good, you know," she told him.

He smiled slightly in return and as she looked back into his eyes, she saw it. *Heat.* He *was* attracted to her. Her heart actually skipped and the rush of triumph made her breathing unsteady. But she held his gaze as he shook his head, as instead of answering her he asked, "When did Dimitri die?"

This entire conversation was surreal. That she could sit here and talk about this, as if it had happened to someone else, as if she hadn't really been there at all . . .

She blinked away the echo of her own voice, screaming as Dimitri's head hit the tile and rolled . . .

Keep it together, don't lose it now. Answer his questions, smile at him, keep his interest, do whatever she had to do, and maybe, again, she'd survive.

"Two months ago."

He nodded, and she was glad she'd told the truth. Clearly he'd been asking around, looking for Dimitri, and he may well have spoken to someone who'd seen her husband the night before their lunchtime visit to Bashir's palace. But no one had seen him after that. At least not alive.

Maybe she was reading too much into one little nod, but she could feel the American's trust—and his interest in her—increasing.

"He was . . . executed by Padsha Bashir." That she volunteered. But damn, she hoped he didn't notice that slight hesitation. She was trying to sound nonchalant. As if she didn't give a damn.

"Was there a reason or was it a whim?"

"I don't know for sure," Sophia answered. "I suspect it had something to do with a business deal gone bad. With money that Dimitri owed him."

The American nodded again. "You said before that Bashir's dead, too."

Sophia also nodded. "He died during the earthquake. Part of his palace collapsed."

"Who told you this?"

"No one," she said. "I was there when it happened. I was . . . lucky to get out alive."

"You were there," he repeated. "That was just a few days ago."

"I was living there," she clarified. "In the palace. I had been—for the past two months."

He looked at her, at her hair, at her face. At her dress. Yes, that's right, American, put this dress and those two months together. . . .

She spelled it out for him, allowing her voice to quiver. "I was a prisoner there. Dimitri gave me to Bashir, just before his death."

"Gave you."

"He wasn't the kindest of husbands." Her voice shook even more. Somewhere, Dimitri's headless body was spinning in its grave. Good. Let him spin for all eternity. He deserved it, the fool, for trusting Michel Lartet. "Neither was Bashir."

The American sat very still, just watching her, thinking . . . what? She honestly didn't have a clue.

Sophia let her eyes fill with tears. It wasn't hard to do. "I escaped from the palace right after the first earthquake. That's why I couldn't tell you my name in front of Lartet's man. I didn't know this before last night, but Michel Lartet is working for Bashir. And I'm pretty sure Bashir's nephews are searching for me. That's probably why Lartet had you followed. To get to me. I think he figured if you knew Dimitri, you knew me."

The American actually laughed. He had nice teeth, straight and white. "I don't mean to imply that you won't be missed, but if Bashir's really dead, I think his nephews have other things on their minds right now."

Sophia let a tear escape, and then another. She knew what she looked like when she cried—tears made her seem younger and more vulnerable. Frightened. Alone. This man would have to have ice water running through his veins to keep from reaching for her.

But he didn't move.

"Please," she said, holding out her hand toward him. "They *are* after me. I know it. I need help."

"If you want me to help," he said, still not moving an inch toward her, "you better tell me the truth about why they're after you."

She'd intended to tell him. But she'd expected to be in his arms before she did. This would be so much easier if she were clinging to him, her face pressed against his shoulder.

Instead she was forced to sit there, holding his gaze.

"If you tell me what's going on, Sophia," he said quietly, "I'll help you. But I need the truth."

She nodded, tears streaming down her cheeks, hot rivers of fear and desperation. The truth. What *was* the truth? The truth was she'd say or do anything to stay alive. Anything. .

"I killed him," she admitted with a sob. "Bashir. During the quake."

She let herself fall apart and finally—alleluia—the American moved toward her. Finally she was in his arms, her head tucked beneath his chin, her cheek against the soft cotton of his shirt. He smelled like her yearly childhood visits to her grandparents in New Hampshire, like America—the home of the dryer sheet and the land of the deodorant stick.

Even his breath was sweet.

Sophia let herself cry in earnest.

"Hey," he said. "It's okay. You're okay now."

But she wasn't. Even if she could believe him, she *so* wasn't even close to okay.

"I was with him," she sobbed. "That morning. In his chamber. And then the quake started, and there was chaos. His back was to me, and I picked up his sword—he always kept it nearby. He got such pleasure from other people's fear—and I ran him through." She pulled back to look at him, letting him see the truth of that in her eyes—the horror of taking a life, mixed with the triumphant ferocity of her hatred for Bashir. "I killed him with his own sword."

The American believed her. At least she hoped he did.

"Okay," he said. "You're right. They're definitely after you."

"Please help me." She didn't let him answer. "I have money," she lied. "In a Swiss account. Neither Dimitri nor Bashir knew about it. If you help me get out of Kazbeki-stan, I *will* make it worth your while. Whatever price they're offering for my return—I'll double it."

He was still just looking at her, and from this up-close vantage point, his eyes were extremely disconcerting.

He gave nothing away. Sophia knew with a frightening flash of clarity that all of her interpretations of his responses, his nods, his eye contact, were just that. Her interpretations.

She had absolutely no clue what this man was thinking.

"Please," she said, and her voice shook with fear that was not feigned.

And then, because there was nothing else left to say, she kissed him.

Sophia Ghaffari kissed him so sweetly, it completely caught Decker off guard.

He knew he couldn't trust her. He'd be a fool if he did. Except . . . his instincts were shouting that much of what she'd told him had been the truth. Of course, his instincts were also standing up and cheering about that completely nonhesitant hand she'd already placed upon the fly of his pants.

Sex with a beautiful stranger . . .

It was exactly what he wanted, what he needed.

Except he couldn't do it. She didn't want him—she wanted his protection. This was barter, plain and simple, and he wouldn't play that game. He was better than that.

Wasn't he?

Yes. Although a very large part of him didn't want to push her away. It was the same part of him that was mentally checking the contents of his pockets. Condom—right lower front, along with ibuprofen, bandages, and a Power-Bar: part of a bare essentials health kit he carried in a plastic pouch.

Not that he was intending to use it.

Except, oh, holy shit, he was actually thinking about using it.

But when she went as far as to unbuckle his belt, he finally pulled back, relegating her to arm's length before she managed to completely unfasten his pants. "Hey. I said I was going to help you," he told her. "You don't need to—"

She reached for him. "I want to—"

Yeah, sure. He caught her hands. "Well, I don't."

She actually laughed in his face, tears sparkling on her eyelashes. Jesus, she was sex personified. And impossibly beautiful. Even when she cried. Maybe especially when she cried—and she knew it, too. What had she done to Dimitri to make him willing to pass her off to Padsha Bashir? If that was really what had happened. Decker suspected he wasn't getting the whole story there.

"Liar," she said.

Deck shrugged, knowing that his words were undermined by his physical reaction to her—a reaction she'd already wrapped her fingers around once. He tightened his grip on her hands. Smooth, soft hands . . . "Honey, you can believe whatever you want."

"So you're just going to help me." She was genuinely amused as she pulled one hand free and wiped her nose with the back of it. "Out of the goodness of your generous heart. And you want nothing—whatsoever—from me in return."

Her hair was in her face, a baby-fine blond tangle that would probably slip like silk beneath his fingers. But Decker didn't let himself reach out to push it behind her perfect ear. He focused instead on the impossible—ignoring the fact that her breasts rose and fell with every breath she took, and that she did indeed have hennaed designs on her perfect body beneath that nearly sheer dress. "That's right."

She shook her head. "That doesn't work for me. How do I know I can trust you?"

Decker laughed. "And you think . . . what? That if we have sex, you'll be able to trust me?"

"No," she said. "Bad word choice. Not trust *you*—I'll never trust you. I've learned the hard way not to trust anyone. But if you come into the other room with me and . . . well, I trust myself to make sure that you'll want to keep me around. At least long enough to find out whether or not I'm lying about that Swiss bank account."

She was actually serious. Except there was something in her eyes that Deck couldn't quite get a read on.

"I know what you're thinking," she continued. "You're thinking, Could she really be that good?" She held his gaze. "The answer is yes. But why take my word for it when I'm willing to show you?"

Things like this didn't happen to him. A beautiful woman, wanting to . . .

No, he was deep in Nash's territory. He could hear an echo of his partner's voice. *She begged me to stay. What was I supposed to do? Just walk away . . . ?*

"I think—," Decker started, but Sophia—if that was really her name—leaned forward and kissed him again. He saw it coming, but he didn't back away. He just sat there and let her lick her way into his mouth.

Jesus, he wanted to . . . wanted her . . . wanted . . .

But shit, it was half past late. Decker had to get back to Rivka's house. He had a team to lead, a terrorist's laptop to locate. Tom Paoletti's additional assignment—to find Dimitri Ghaffari—had been secondary. And Ghaffari was dead.

Allegedly. Sometimes he believed Sophia, and sometimes—like right now—he doubted every word she'd ever uttered in her entire life.

That should have been reason enough to not want her giving him those soul-sucking kisses, her cool hands skimming up beneath his T-shirt along the bare skin of his back, her body soft and warm, pressed against him. . . .

It was entirely possible that she worked for Lartet—or even for Padsha Bashir. That she'd been assigned to follow him and find out why he was here, why he was looking for Dimitri Ghaffari, whom he was working for.

The story she'd told him could well be completely fictional, designed to make him say, "Don't worry, I'll help you. I'm with the U.S. government. Your troubles are over—I'm one of the good guys."

And then, after promising to figure out a way to smuggle her safely out of K-stan, he would tell her to stay here, to stay hidden, to wait for him to contact her. But instead of following his instructions, she would wrap herself in that burka and slip out into the streets. She'd take all the information he'd revealed about himself to Lartet or Bashir, and then this entire mission would be in jeopardy. And the lives of his entire team would be in peril.

Decker caught her hands again as she unfastened the top button of his pants—she *was* persistent, wasn't she?—and pulled back to look at her.

She was as short of breath as he was, her mouth wet from kissing him. The look in her eyes was one of pure arousal, but Decker didn't doubt for one second that that was something she'd had a lot of practice faking.

She was a pro, there was no doubt about it.

"Please . . ." She moved to kiss him again, but this time he held her off.

"I can't do this," he said, but even to his own ears, his voice lacked conviction.

"Are you married?" she asked him. "Is that why you don't want to . . . ?"

His cover included a fictional wife in Virginia, but he found himself saying, "No."

"I'm not either. Not anymore." Sophia's eyes welled suddenly with fresh tears that seemed to surprise her more than they surprised him.

As Decker watched, she wiped her eyes with the heel of her hand, as if these were private tears, ones she didn't want him to see.

If this were part of her act, she was damn good.

But then she smiled at him, a smile that was forced and rueful—Sophia the brave, dauntlessly going on despite life's tragedies. "Sorry," she said. He almost applauded her performance.

"Do you have a girlfriend?" she asked, wiping her nose again. "Linda Sue back in Kalamazoo? Trust me, she'll never know."

Even though he had no right to, Deck thought briefly of Tess, who was probably sound asleep not back in Michigan, but in Rivka's pantry. Tess, who really was brave—and honest and true. Tess, who was everything a man could want in a woman, both sweet and sexy, the kind of woman you could take home to Sunday dinner, to meet your parents—after she'd totally rocked your world on Saturday night.

Tess, who couldn't look at James Nash without her heart showing in her eyes.

Decker shook his head. "Look, Sophia, I know you think I'm going to deliver you to Bashir—"

"Yeah, right, but of course you're not. Money means nothing to you." She didn't believe him.

This was where he should stand up and prove it by walking out of there.

Instead he said, "So okay. Say we . . . go into the other room and get to know each other better. Then what? How do you propose I get you out of Kazabek without any papers, without a passport?"

She blinked at that, as if she hadn't really thought too much about that. And wasn't that interesting? It surely meant something, but he just couldn't wrap his mind around what, as she shifted and her gown shimmered.

"I don't know," she admitted. "Don't you have, I don't know, connections?"

He didn't answer that. He just sat and looked at her, hoping she would keep talking.

Maybe some information he could make use of would come out of her mouth.

Yeah, sure. That's why he was still sitting here. It had nothing whatsoever to do with the fact that she'd offered herself to him on a plate.

It had nothing to do with the fact that he wanted—desperately—to take her up on that offer.

No, *want* wasn't the right word for it. What he was feeling was bigger than want, more powerful than need. It was . . .

It was bullshit. That was his dick talking. *Bigger than want,* his ass.

He was beyond horny, she was nearly naked, and he wanted to accept her offer because he was human, he was male, and he had been celibate for too fucking long.

And even though she wasn't a streetwalker as he'd first thought, she obviously saw sex as little more than an intimate handshake. A deal sealer. A way to control her environment and the people around her.

She reached up to touch his face, tracing his lips with her thumb. And again he didn't back away when she leaned in to kiss him.

It felt too damn good.

She was winning and she knew it.

"I need this," she told him, and if he squinted at this entire situation really hard, he could almost talk himself into believing her.

She kissed him again, sliding back onto his lap. And he let her. And he let her and let her, glad he didn't have to worry about her going for that little revolver he'd taken from her at the factory—he'd left it outside—and wondering just how far she was going to take this before she made a break for that door.

Because surely that was her goal here.

Wasn't it?

She'd glanced over at it often enough when they'd first started talking.

"We're both alone in this world," she said, her mouth soft against his throat, her body warm in his hands. "I want to, and I know you want to—"

"You want to, because if I do sleep with you," Deck said, "I'm less likely to return you to Bashir's palace for a lot of reasons, the most compelling being that there's a solid chance they'll stick my head on a pike—" She actually flinched at that—interesting. "—for messing with Bashir's property—never mind the fact that he's dead and they have a date on the execution schedule already reserved for you."

"I want to," she argued, "because I want to. Because I'm alive, and because it's *my* choice—because I finally *have* a choice."

"That's total bullshit," he said, but he wasn't sure she heard him, because she was kissing him on the mouth again, then distracting the hell out of him by slipping her hand down into his pants, and . . .

"Whoa," he said, but she only kissed him more deeply.

She was . . . He was . . . Was he actually going to do this? *Yes.*

And why the hell not? God knows he wanted to.

And, like the lady said, it *was* her choice.

Except Decker knew that it really wasn't.

But she said it was.

And who was he to decide for her, as if she were a child, whether this truly was or wasn't her choice?

If sex really didn't mean that much to her, if she had the mind-set of most of the women that James Nash dated . . .

Except this wasn't a date. And she was selling herself to Decker—there was no question about that.

He was a lowlife, he was scum, because, right at that moment, he was willing to buy.

She slid off him—all that soft warmth suddenly gone—
and here it came. The dash for the door that he'd been more
than half expecting. He had one hand wrapped around her
wrist—an easy enough hold for her to break—but she
clasped his hands and pulled him to his feet with her.

"Let's go to my bed," she said instead. "It's softer than
the tile floor. My knee is pretty bruised."

She lifted her skirt, and he saw that she'd scraped the shit
out of her knee, probably during her escape from Bashir's
palace.

Provided that had really happened.

Yes, let's go to your bed, was what the low-life scum
wanted to say, but there was still some Dudley Do-Right in
his system—and it had control of his vocal cords.

But "I can't—" was all he got out before she kissed him
again, wrapping one leg around him even as she tugged
him with her toward the blankets piled up on the floor in
the other room.

Oh, this was a mistake in so many ways. Too many to
count.

But she somehow had his pants unzipped and when she
slid down to the floor to kneel in front of him and . . .

"Unh," he said as she . . . And then she . . .

Okay. *Okay.* Apparently she wasn't going to make a
break for the door immediately.

Jesus.

Jesus.

He was vulnerable. There was no doubt about the fact
that this was a position of intense vulnerability. If she
wanted to, she could seriously damage him in so many different ways. But if that was her intention, she would have
hurt him already.

And that was not pain he was experiencing.

She tugged him down onto the blankets with her, which
gave her a better angle to . . .

Oh, yeah.

Decker knew that there was a list of reasons he shouldn't be doing this, but the pro side of this particular page sure seemed to cancel out all the cons.

He kept his eyes open, kept track of where she had her hands, aware that although he'd taken a weapon from her back at the factory, he hadn't searched this room.

But ho-kay. All-righty. *This* was not what he'd expected her to do. It was now exceedingly easy to keep track of her right hand as well as her mouth and . . .

Decker reached down and grabbed hold of her left wrist. Keeping his eyes from rolling back in his head was a more serious challenge. He must've made some kind of noise, because she glanced up at him, her own eyes bright.

She'd stayed alive for the past two months, possibly even longer if her story about Ghaffari and Bashir was just a sad tale she'd made up to win his sympathy, by doing this. It was a sobering thought, and yet she managed to distract him—she was that talented.

Skilled.

Practiced.

Jee-*zus.*

It should have been a turnoff—in theory, he would have expected it to be. But Decker had found in life that reality and theory frequently were quite different.

This was . . . surprisingly freeing.

There were no emotional strings attached. It was the first time in a long, long time that he'd had a sexual encounter that wasn't layered with deep meaning, heavy with expectation.

This was . . . what it was.

And apparently she wanted absolutely nothing from him. At all.

This was similar to what Nash did on an almost nightly

basis. Sex with no emotional connection. Sex for the sake of sex. Because it felt good.

And good was one freaking understatement.

Decker knew that he probably should have been ashamed, and sure, if he tried hard enough, he could find part of him that was. Not only should he be back at Rivka's by now, but he was taking advantage of a woman who was in desperate need of help. This poor, frightened, down-on-her-luck woman who—

Holy shit, holy *shit,* whatever she was doing was—

Decker came in a rush that didn't quite blind him enough to keep him from realizing that he'd just lost her right hand. He still held her left wrist, but her entire right arm was hidden . . .

He jerked back, away from her.

. . . with her hand buried beneath them, beneath the blankets . . .

Away from her teeth—fuck!—he rolled hard to his right.

. . . as if she was reaching for a knife or . . .

The sound of a gunshot at close proximity was deafening, as a bullet whizzed past his head.

"Shit!"

. . . a handgun.

Decker rolled back to the left, pinning her arm as well as whatever weapon she had hidden under those blankets.

She cried out—he was hurting her—but too fucking bad! She'd just tried to shoot him in the head.

While she was . . . While he was . . . *Shit.*

Somehow that made her murder attempt unforgivable. Assuming that a murder attempt was something that could be forgiven.

She cried out again as he forced her to let go of the weapon. If she'd been a man, he would have broken her nose because he would've elbowed her far harder in the face while he was at it.

Of course, if she'd been a man, this never would've happened.

Mad as hell—at himself as well as at her—heart still pounding, Deck pushed her back so that she slid on her ass along the tile floor and hit both the pipes and the wall beneath the row of sinks with enough force to knock her off balance.

By the time she scrambled onto her hands and knees, Decker had her weapon, a neat little WWII era Walther PPK, aimed at her forehead. He also had his pants zipped.

"Don't do it," he said.

She looked at the door, at the Walther, at his face, then sat back on her heels. She was crying a river of tears, but this time she didn't make a sound. She just looked at him with eyes that were completely devoid of all hope.

She just sat there and waited—for him to kill her.

CHAPTER
THIRTEEN

TESS GLANCED up as the third-floor bedroom door opened and Jimmy Nash came into the room.

He looked wary and apologetic, and he actually cleared his throat. He didn't even try to force a smile. He was just so damn serious, she had to turn away.

God. Help.

Tess pretended to return her attention to her laptop computer, open in front of her on the bed.

"So." She spoke first, before he did, eyes securely on the monitor. "I once saw this movie where this character—he's supposed to be a Hollywood actor, completely self-absorbed. But he's drunk and he gets into this car accident, like the car flips over but nobody's hurt, and he climbs out and says, 'So. *That* happened,' and I always thought that was just the best line, you know? *So.* That *happened.*"

She glanced up to find him watching her.

"It was never my intention to—," he started, but she cut him off.

"No kidding," she said briskly. She may have been drowsy and confused about where she was and *when* she was, but she remembered, in extremely explicit detail, who had grabbed whom. "That was my handiwork—pardon the pun. I'm the one who owes *you* the apology."

He crossed the room, toward her, toward the bed. "No, Tess, you—"

"Yes," she said. "And it will help quite a bit if you would simply say 'Apology accepted,' and then never mention it again. And don't you dare even *think* about sitting down on this bed."

He stopped himself, straightening back up. He sighed. "Tess . . ."

"From now on, if I'm using the bed, you're not. And vice versa," she told him as matter-of-factly as she could. She even managed to look up at him and flash a polite smile before returning her attention to her computer. "We can work out a schedule for sleeping. Every other night I get the bed and you get the floor, and—"

"Tess—"

" 'Apology accepted,' " she repeated, eyes firmly on that screen. "That's really all I want to hear right now, thanks *so* much."

"What we did—"

"What *I* did," she corrected him sharply.

"What *we* did," he said again, sitting next to her on the bed despite her protests, and folding the computer closed so that she'd have to face him, "was enough to get you pregnant. It doesn't take much, you know."

Of all the things she'd expected Jimmy to say, that wasn't one of them. She blinked at him for a few moments. Pregnant?

"You didn't think about that, did you?" he asked. When he wanted to, he could make his eyes seem so warm, even tender.

Tess shook her head. Her focus had been so completely on the fact that Nash now knew she still wanted him—that he'd found out that if it were up to her subconscious self, they'd be having screaming wild monkey sex every time they had five minutes free. He now knew that her body was at serious odds with her brain when it came to her attraction for him.

He knew that what she wanted was different from what she *wanted*, and that when push came to shove, there was a damn good chance—if she were vulnerable enough—that she'd start pushing and shoving.

With great enthusiasm.

Oh, God.

"I'm not pregnant," she said. "Really, James, the odds of that—"

"But it *is* possible," he pointed out.

"Yeah, but come on, that's worst-case-scenario thinking," Tess said. "It's also possible there'll be another earthquake tonight that'll bring the roof down on top of us."

"Okay," he said. "You're right. But . . . I just wanted you to know that I intend to take responsibility if—"

"What?" She was incredulous. "For something you didn't even do? Don't be ridiculous—"

"Excuse me, I *was* there. I know exactly what I did. And I'm just saying—"

"Well, *don't*. God! Nash! Give me a fricking break." Tess pushed herself farther back on the bed, away from him, all but kicking at him with her feet. "I've told you what I want you to say."

"Apology accepted?" Jimmy stood up.

"Thank you." God.

"No, that was a question," he said. "I didn't say it."

What? "Yes, you did. I heard you—"

He laughed. "No, no, see, I said it, but I didn't *say* it—"

Oh. My. God. "Is this some kind of big hilarious joke to you? Because in case you haven't noticed," she told him through clenched teeth, "I'm not laughing!"

"Yeah." He wasn't laughing anymore either. "Right. I always think it's funny as *shit* when I do something I've never done before—ever. Something that might completely screw up the life of someone I happen to care very much about."

He was standing there, looking about as upset as she'd ever seen him. And if he hadn't run away to Mexico for two months, if he'd bothered to call her to tell her he was okay—even just once, one fifteen-second phone call—she might've actually believed him.

Instead she snorted, trying to push away those pathetic feelings of loss that surfaced every time he said or did something even remotely sweet. *Fool me once, shame on you. Fool me twice* . . . "Oh, you so just want to sleep with me again. Could you *be* any more transparent?"

He closed his eyes and swore softly. Sat down again, this time farther away from her. Sighed. Glanced at her, but then looked at the floor as he said, "The truth is, Tess, that I *don't* want to sleep with you. I really, *really* don't."

Forget transparent. Could he be any more emphatic with that *really*?

"Well. Thanks for clearing that up." Please, please, don't let her start to cry. Dead children were one thing, and certainly worthy of tears, but harsh truths from the mouths of idiots she'd slept with were another thing entirely. "If you don't mind, I have work I need to do . . . ?"

He swore again. Turned to look at her. She now was the one who wouldn't meet his gaze. "Look, I'm sorry if I—"

"Yeah, I get it," she cut him off. "You're worried about your problematic tendency for premature ejaculation, and I'm—" Why, why, *why* did she say that? It was downright cruel and not even truthful. He was being honest and forthright when he'd said he didn't want to sleep with her again, and she, in return, was being a flaming attack-bitch. "I'm such a jerk."

Nash was staring at the floor again, the muscle jumping in the side of his jaw.

"I'm sorry. I really didn't mean that," she continued. And wasn't *this* just perfect. Somehow she'd managed to orchestrate this humiliation-fest so that she was forced to apologize to him about that, too.

"Yeah, I know," he said. He looked up at her. "And even if you did, it's okay. Have at me, please, if it makes you feel any better."

"It doesn't."

There was silence as they sat there, just looking at one other.

They both spoke, then, at once.

Tess said, "We can talk about this for hours and it's not going to—" as Nash told her, "I just want you to know that—" They both stopped.

"What?" she said, wanting nothing more than for him to leave and knowing that he wasn't going anywhere until they had this conversation. "If I'm pregnant, then what? Let's talk about this. Let's run the worst-case scenario. I'm pregnant. What happens then, James?"

He stared at her.

"Are you going to marry me?"

She'd asked it as a bad joke, but he answered as if she were serious. "I don't know," he said. "Maybe. Yeah. If that's what you want."

What? Tess laughed her disbelief. "Yeah, right. What I want is for us to get married and live happily ever after. Happily, except for the fact that you really, *really* don't want to sleep with me. Yeah, that's my idea of a dream relationship. *God.*"

He rubbed his forehead. No doubt she was giving him one hell of a headache. Well, join the club. She had a whopper of her own.

She sighed. "Look, I'm sorry—"

"Your apology isn't necessary," he said, adding when she opened her mouth, "but accepted." He stood up. "Rivka and Guldana are intending to throw a wedding dinner for us. Probably Friday night."

Oh, bloody terrific. Just what Tess wanted—a party to celebrate her relationship with Jimmy Nash. God help her . . . "Please try to talk them out of it."

"I did," he said. "Try, I mean. There's no, um . . . Look, they need something to celebrate right now, and, well, sorry, but we're it."

Oh, joy. "Is Decker back yet?" she asked.

For the briefest of moments, Jimmy actually looked startled. "Oh, shit," he said.

And Tess knew what he was thinking. Last night, he'd been trying to set Tess up with Decker. And this morning, he'd . . . They'd . . . "Look, it's not like anything really happened," she said.

He gave her an incredulous look. "Yeah, except for the part where we had *sex*."

"We didn't have sex!" she said scornfully, even though she knew that by most sane definitions, they had. "We accidentally bumped into each other," she added, knowing how completely stupid she sounded. "Intimately."

Nash laughed at that. "Yeah, it was a real 'whoops' moment."

"It *was*. It didn't mean anything," she persisted. "It wasn't real."

"It was real enough so that you might be pregnant."

Round and round and round they went. "Well, I'm not, so just, God, stop with that, will you?"

"Right. Great." Nash shook his head as he walked out of the room, turning to look back at her from the doorway. "So. *That* happened."

He closed the door behind him, finally leaving her in peace.

Or as close to peace as she was likely to get until they boarded that airplane back home to the States.

* * *

Sophia closed her eyes as the American crossed to the sinks. Her head was ringing and her side was on fire—she'd caught one of those pipes in the ribs.

She heard him turn on the water, heard him splashing, heard the water go off.

The pain was nothing compared to the fear.

She was dead, she was dead, she was dead.

She'd failed to kill him, and now he was going to kill her. *Thy will be done.*

The words echoed in her head even though she hadn't been to church since she was fifteen. Not since she'd decided enough was enough—that her parents' so-called spiritual quest was little more than a combination of a traveling jones and an opium addiction.

Sophia wondered for the first time in years where Cleo and Paul were now, if they were even still alive. If they'd ever even noticed that they'd left her behind in Kathmandu.

She wondered if it would hurt—a bullet to the brain—or if there would suddenly just be nothing.

Nothing.

She tried to tell herself that the nothing would probably be better than this fear—but she feared the nothing.

Still, it didn't come. Her heart still beat. She still breathed, drawing in one ragged, painful breath after another.

Something cold hit her leg, and she flinched. But when she opened her eyes, she saw that the American had wet a cloth and tossed it onto her lap.

He spoke, his voice as chilly as that rag. "Wipe your face."

And, as Sophia did just that, she knew. If it was his intention to kill her here and now, he would have already done so.

No. She looked up at him, into eyes that were flat and empty of all compassion. She was living her worst nightmare. She was going to be dragged to Bashir's palace and beheaded.

She wouldn't go.

When he came closer, she would grab for the gun—her gun—that he'd tucked so casually into the top of his pants. She knew she had no prayer of getting it away from him. But in the struggle, he would shoot her.

She was not going back.

She was *not* going back.

As she watched, heart pounding, the American kept his distance as he dug something out of his pocket. A leather wallet. He opened it.

And he tossed a bill—U.S. currency—at her. It fluttered onto the floor and Abraham Lincoln stared up at her. Five dollars.

"You completely blew your chance for a tip," he told her flatly. "Oh, and if you happen to see Dimitri or his partner, tell 'em I'm looking for 'em."

And he walked out the door.

Khalid had just fallen asleep, curled in a ball on the floor near Murphy, when Decker strolled into the kitchen.

Jimmy grabbed the man and dragged him out into the yard, lowering his voice so it wouldn't carry inside. "About time you got back here."

Deck shook him off. "I'm not that late."

"Yeah, but you *are* late. You're never late. You should have called." As he said it, Jimmy realized they'd had this exact conversation many times in the past, only the words that had just left his lips were usually Decker's.

"We have phones?" Deck asked. Man, he looked exhausted. He was completely wrung out.

"In a limited area, yeah," Jimmy told him. "If you'd checked your messages, you'd know that."

Some life came back into Deck's eyes. "Tess?"

"Yeah," Jimmy said. "She's got the computer up and running, too."

"Good for her."

"Yeah, well, she's probably going to complain to you because I wouldn't let her plant a sat-dish at the top of the Grande Hotel."

Decker nodded and Jimmy realized that he was more than exhausted. He was angry. And upset. Christ, when was the last time he'd seen Decker upset? Angry, yes, and grim, almost always, but . . .

"Everything all right?" Jimmy asked. There was no way Deck could know about what happened this morning, about Jimmy and Tess and . . .

Decker met his gaze only briefly. "Yes." It was an obvious lie. But the real message was also clear. *Back off.* "What do you have for me?" he continued.

Jimmy normally would've gotten on Deck's case, but he was clearly in no mood for anything but efficiently listed facts. So Jimmy gave him just that. "Murph got back a couple of hours ago. He said many of his contacts have gone missing, and the people he did speak to aren't saying much of anything. Rumors are a dime a dozen, though. He was waiting for you to get back before going into details. He's sleeping now. So is Tess. You should probably do the same."

"What about Dave?" Decker asked.

"He spent the night in the barn—with a bag of saline attached to his arm. He went out when Murphy came in—I told him to be back here at oh-eight-hundred so we could regroup. I thought that would give you enough time to take one of your combat naps." Jimmy glanced at his watch. It was 7:20. Of course, he'd expected Deck in much earlier than this.

"That's good," Deck said. "That's perfect. I just need to

close my eyes for a few minutes. How about you—did you get some sleep?"

"I'm fine," Jimmy said. *Larry, what exactly happened out there last night?* He didn't dare ask. Doing so would give Decker permission to ask some decidedly tough questions of his own.

Decker was looking at him, obviously aware that "I'm fine" was not the same as "Yes, I slept." And yet he didn't comment. And he wouldn't comment—as long as Jimmy managed to get his job done.

"Oh, Rivka and Guldana gave their bedroom—third floor—to Tess and me," Jimmy reported as casually as he possibly could. "We set it up so they'd walk in on us, you know, in the pantry, together, when they came home and . . . Because the third floor's the only place the phones work, so . . ."

Decker's reaction was to stand there, just looking at him.

Jimmy kept talking. "I'm going to take advantage of the fact that Tess isn't using the computer right now and get online and—"

Decker finally spoke. "Do me a favor," he said. "See what you can find out about Dimitri Ghaffari—is he married, who's his wife, does he have any business ties to either Michel Lartet or Padsha Bashir, last known street address . . . whatever you can dig up. I currently know jack about the guy." He turned toward the house with a nod. "Thanks."

Jimmy just watched as Deck went into the kitchen. But then Deck turned around and came right back out. "That kid, Khalid, is sleeping in my bed."

"Sorry," Jimmy said. "I told him to lie down on mine—"

"Because you were filled with an overwhelming desire for head lice?" Decker interrupted. He was seriously pissed, practically popping a vein, and Jimmy knew it had nothing to do with the K-stani boy. "Because it's been at least two years since you've had to be dipped in chemicals and—"

"Because he came here straight from the hospital, where he spent the night with his little brother in the ER waiting room," Jimmy said quietly.

This was actually something he'd learned from Decker. Lowering his voice was often more effective than raising it. If someone was loud and in his face, sure, he could shout back, but they'd probably just try to shout over him. But if he got really quiet, they'd have to shut up in order to listen.

It didn't work all the time, but it worked right now. Decker had shut up, but he still looked as if he were seconds from taking Jimmy down into the dirt and pounding the crap out of him.

"Khalid hasn't slept since the quake," Jimmy continued now. He should have said, *Why don't you tell me what you're really angry about? What happened out there to make you late?* But he didn't dare. Decker was his partner, his brother, his friend. He'd die for the man, and he knew Decker would do the same for him. But talking . . . putting voice to deep feelings . . . This was something they never did.

So he kept on discussing Khalid. "He came here to pick up his horse and wagon so he could get to work and earn the money his family's going to need to keep food on the table. In case you haven't noticed, the cost of living in Kazabek has just gone up—dramatically."

Deck may have been silent, but the way he was shaking his head broadcast his disbelief loud and clear. "You hired him, didn't you?" he finally asked.

And told him that his first assignment was to get some sleep so he was fresh when they needed to get moving, yes. "We need transportation," Jimmy pointed out. "Khalid's got a wagon."

"We don't know who this kid is, who he's connected to."

"Like that's anything new," Jimmy countered. "Like Rivka himself wouldn't sell us out to the highest bidder, if he had the—"

Decker's eyes were arctic. "We don't have room on this assignment for you to pick up your usual pack of strays."

"I'm not—"

"And yet you'll do it anyway," Deck cut him off. "You do whatever you fucking want, whenever you fucking want to."

Whoa.

Jimmy wasn't often speechless, but he was grateful he was speechless now, because as soon as his brain clicked back on, he knew that getting defensive wasn't the way to go.

Whatever Decker was pissed off about, it probably didn't have anything to do with Jimmy. Because there was no real reason for Deck to be pissed with him. Well, okay, except for the part, just a few hours ago, where he'd had unprotected sex with the woman that Decker had a thing for.

Of course, Deck didn't know about that. Yet.

Jimmy met his friend's glacial gaze. On the other hand, Deck was a very smart man. He'd no doubt figured it out.

Shit. "I'm sorry," Jimmy said. "But she was all over me. I don't know why I couldn't seem to . . ." Stay away from her.

Now the look on Deck's face was one he'd never seen before—a mix of emotions Jimmy didn't realize Decker ever allowed himself to feel.

And as Deck opened his mouth, Jimmy knew they were about to go where neither of them had gone before. Decker was going to tell him what had happened out there.

But movement over by the house made them both look up. Tess was standing in the doorway, and from her expression, Jimmy knew she'd been there for the past few minutes. Perfect. *Perfect.*

Decker shut his mouth.

"We need transportation, and the kid's got a horse and wagon," Jimmy said again, both disappointed and relieved that Decker wasn't going to spill any of his closely guarded secrets.

"Wake me in forty." Decker nodded curtly to Tess as he went past her into the house.

CHAPTER
FOURTEEN

"WORD ON the street is that Sayid came to Kazabek to meet with one of the local warlords," Murphy reported.

"Padsha Bashir," Dave Malkoff agreed.

After Dave had returned, Jimmy woke Decker and Murphy. Tess had quietly followed them out to the barn to talk, because Khalid, the K-stani boy who owned the cart and horse, was still asleep in the kitchen.

It was a good excuse that also took them out of range of their host's overly attentive ears.

Tess and the others had watched silently as Murphy did a quick but thorough sweep of the brick-and-mud structure, checking to make sure no listening devices had been planted there in the night.

"Yeah," the huge former Marine said now. There was a little bit of California surfer in his otherwise accentless voice. "That's the name I kept hearing, too."

Dude. Tess couldn't help smiling as she silently embellished his sentences for him.

But she stopped smiling when he added, "Bashir's been connected to the GIK for years."

Because the GIK—a group of Kazbekistani religious extremists—had ties to al-Qaeda. Ties that both sides were working on strengthening, apparently. There was nothing even remotely funny about that.

"There's a concerted recovery effort still going on over at

Bashir's palace, where a large portion of the roof collapsed," Dave reported. Although he looked significantly better than he had the day before, he was still pale, and there was a big bruise on the back of his hand from the IV he'd given himself.

While Murphy lounged on a bale of hay, Dave sat up straight, as if he were attending a board meeting. "Sayid's listed as missing," he continued. "Rumor has it he was with Bashir at the time of the quake. They both ran in different directions, and no one's seen Sayid since."

"Bashir's palace is well within our five-kilometer radius of the Cantara hospital, where Sayid allegedly died," Nash said. He was standing, leaning with one shoulder against the wooden wall of the stall, arms casually crossed. "So it fits."

"It's not alleged," Tess volunteered, and they all turned to look at her. Everyone but Jimmy Nash, that is. After this morning, he was probably never going to look at her again. Attempting to talk about their unfortunate . . . encounter had only made things worse.

But it was more than just the flat-out rejection that made her feel so rotten. It was the fact that she'd thought she'd broken the code when it came to reading James Nash. She'd thought she knew him. And she'd actually believed that she'd seen attraction in his eyes when he looked at her.

What a fool.

She'd seen what she wanted to see.

And the truth was, she couldn't read him any better than she could read Decker. Who was looking at her now, his eyes and face relaying only his default nonexpression.

She was all over me, she'd heard Jimmy—Nash—telling Deck.

Tess felt her face start to heat with a blush, but she pushed on. She really hadn't expected Nash to mention anything about their early morning encounter.

Yet he had.

"We received an encrypted email from Tom," she told her team leader briskly. "He said that Sayid's body was successfully extracted from K-stan and that he's been positively IDed. It's him—he's definitely dead. Apparently the White House is eager to release that news bulletin, too—they're going to hold a press conference just short of forty-eight hours from now."

"At which time the entire world will start scrambling to find Sayid's fabled laptop," Nash pointed out. His words were a dire prediction, and he should have looked at least slightly grim, but he didn't. He looked . . . like Diego Nash, superagent, man of mystery. He'd put on a fresh shirt and had even somehow managed to make his hair look good despite the heat and the lack of water for washing. He was calm and cool and so much in control that he seemed unperturbed by the situation. Tess doubted that he'd slept at all last night, but no one would've guessed that from looking at him.

"We need a copy of Sayid's autopsy report," Nash continued.

He, too, was talking to Decker—maybe that was how he was going to communicate with her from now on—but Tess spoke up. "Tom sent one, but I haven't had a chance to download it."

Nash finally looked at her—which turned out to be even worse than his *not* looking at her. "Excuse me?"

Had this man really had his tongue in her mouth just a few short hours ago?

"I said, Tom sent—"

"I heard what you said. You received the autopsy report, and you didn't *down*load it?"

It was hard not to get defensive. She had to work her butt off to keep all sorts of embarrassing emotions from ringing in her voice. "I'm sorry. I thought it was enough to know that he was definitely dead."

Nash started to speak, but stopped himself. When he started again, it was obvious he was keeping himself carefully in control. Or at least she thought that was the case.

But if that really hadn't been attraction she'd seen in Nash's eyes even as recently as last night, then Tess had to doubt every assumption she'd ever drawn from this man's body language, every interpretation she'd made of his words.

"Download everything that Tom Paoletti sends," he told her as if she were his new mentally challenged secretary, "regardless of whether or not *you* think we need it. And let either Decker or me know the moment it comes in."

Tess had had only a limited amount of time on a tenuous connection, so downloading an extensive autopsy report had seemed frivolous. But she didn't attempt to explain. She knew that if she opened her mouth, the demons of hell would come flying out, cackling and screaming. She just clenched her teeth and nodded. "Yes, sir."

Nash's reaction to that may or may not have been disgusted exasperation.

"Right now we're only guessing how far Sayid could have traveled to that hospital," Decker explained to Tess. "The autopsy report will tell us the extent of his injuries and we'll be able to guess a whole lot more accurately. Getting that info's a priority."

Oh, God. "I didn't realize . . ." Tess stood up. "I can go and—"

"As soon as we're done here," Decker said, and she slowly sat back down on the overturned pail she'd claimed as a seat when they'd first come into the barn.

"If Sayid was with Bashir during the quake," Dave said, "and his laptop is somewhere under the rubble at the palace—"

Decker interrupted him. "I spoke to a woman last night who claimed to be with Bashir when the quake hit. Alone with Bashir. She told me that he was dead. Anyone hear any rumors about—"

"No way." Dave was absolute. "Padsha Bashir's not dead. I was outside his palace this morning, and I saw him. He'd been injured, supposedly in the quake, but he was already up and around, surveying the damage, overseeing the recovery effort."

"You're certain it was Bashir and not one of his nephews?" Decker sat forward to ask.

"Yes, sir," Dave said. "He was leaning on a cane, but it was definitely him. At one point, I was only about three feet from him."

"You got that close to Padsha Bashir?" Murphy started to laugh. "Man, if he saw you—"

"He didn't see me."

"He'd have your head, just for being American."

"He didn't see me," Dave repeated.

"You said he was *supposedly* injured in the quake?" Decker asked Dave.

"That's the story they're spinning, sir," Dave replied. "But you know the way the staff always knows what's really going on in a household?"

"You actually have a connection to someone on Bashir's staff?" Murphy said. "Quick, call Tom Paoletti, because this man needs a serious raise."

But Dave shook his head. "I wish I had that kind of connection. I overhead a conversation. Someone who knew someone who worked in the palace laundry. Granted, it's just a rumor, but it fits with some other information I picked up about how Bashir's put a huge price on the head of a palace cleaning woman."

"Hey, I heard that one, too." Murphy sat up. "Yay, me. A mysterious blue-eyed vixen, right? She used the chaos of the quake to steal some heirloom necklace. It's got to be one major necklace though, 'cause the reward's rumored to be fifty thousand dollars. U.S."

"That's no rumor," Dave told them with complete authority. "It's fifty thousand, but she has to be brought back alive. If she's dead, her body's worth only five."

"A mysterious, blue-eyed *cleaning* woman?" Tess repeated skeptically.

"You can pretty much translate that as concubine," Nash informed her. "Padsha Bashir is one of those pious types with lots of rules about how to live—rules that don't apply to him."

"Except, no, see, he marries them," Murphy said. "That makes it okay in his eyes. Of course, he has dozens of quote unquote wives."

"The news that one of his wives stole from him and ran away from the palace would be just as potentially embarrassing to him as calling her what she really is," Dave pointed out.

"You're sure it was a necklace that was stolen?" Decker asked. "Not a ring?"

"I definitely heard necklace," Dave said.

"Did this woman have a name?" Nash asked. "Perhaps . . . Sophia?"

As Tess watched, Decker looked up and briefly met Jimmy Nash's gaze. She knew they'd spent a lot of time in K-stan back when they worked for the Agency. Could this woman be someone they both knew?

"I wasn't paying much attention," Murphy admitted. "Since it didn't seem to pertain to Sayid—"

"Sophia, yes. No last name, though," Dave reported. "Although she was also referred to as Soleil or 'the Frenchwoman.' I *did* pay attention, Murph, because of the size of the price on her head, and because she was Western," he added, almost as if he were apologizing for being so thorough. "It occurred to me, from the size of that reward, that she might not have stolen jewelry from the palace as reported, but that instead she'd taken Sayid's infamous laptop. If Sayid *was* injured when the roof collapsed at the palace, Bashir would care more about saving that laptop. It's no secret that he'd love to get his hands on it—any one of the warlords in K-stan would. I thought maybe he had, only to have it taken from *him*. But then I overheard that conversation about how Bashir didn't get injured in the quake after all, but that he—"

"Was stabbed with his own sword by one of his new wives?" Decker finished for him.

"That's right," Dave said, pleased. "You heard that, too?"

"Yeah," Decker said. "That was . . . Sophia's story. Although she was under the impression that she'd managed to kill Bashir."

"Whoa, boss, you know this woman?" Murphy asked. His eyes were dancing with amusement. He was enjoying this meeting immensely. "Man, you guys are both way better at this spooky stuff than I am. I was out almost all night, and I barely managed to rendezvous with my own ass."

"She didn't." Dave brought the discussion back on track. "Kill Bashir."

"I met her last night," Decker told them. "Or at least I met someone with blue eyes who claimed to be Sophia. She said that she was in Bashir's chamber with him when the quake hit."

"So who is she?" Murphy asked. "Where'd she come from, and what was she doing with Bashir?"

And how was it that Nash—who'd been with Tess instead of out collecting local rumors last night—knew her name?

"I mean, in the bigger sense," Murphy added. "I can guess what she was probably doing with Bashir at that exact moment, but—"

"All that time, she might have been in possession of that

laptop." Decker was completely distracted. It was as if he didn't even hear Murphy, as if he were talking to himself. "It never even occurred to me."

"Yes, well, I'm not so sure about that particular theory anymore, sir," Dave told him. "I mean, about her having the laptop. If she really did try to kill Bashir, that explains the price on her head. She didn't have to take anything from the palace to warrant the size of that reward."

"Is it possible she's working for someone?" Murphy asked.

Tess looked over at Nash as he shook his head, as if, whoever this Sophia was, he knew her well enough to be certain that she wasn't working for the Agency, or even the CIA.

It shouldn't have surprised her one bit that Diego Nash should be on a first-name basis with a concubine. As she watched, he pulled a folded piece of paper from his pocket.

"Whoever she's working for—if she's working for anyone—it's not us," Dave said with finality. "I was one of the last agents pulled out of K-stan three years ago."

"Maybe she's with the French government," Murphy suggested.

"She's American." Nash finally finished unfolding that paper—it was a grainy news photo, from Tess's portable printer. He handed it to Decker. "Sophia Ghaffari. She's married to a man who's part Greek, part French."

Deck stared at the picture with absolutely no change of expression.

"So maybe she *is* working for France," Murphy pointed out cheerfully. "Or Greece. Or maybe even Israel or the U.K.—"

"Ghaffari," Dave repeated. "Ghaffari . . ."

"Is that the woman you met last night?" Nash asked Decker.

He nodded, and when he looked up at Nash, there was a

flash of something in his eyes. Anger. Maybe. Or . . . remorse? "It's her," he said.

"It's got to be hard for a woman that strikingly beautiful to hide," Nash said. "I mean, unless she keeps a burka on at all times. Which, apparently, she didn't do when she was talking to you. . . ."

Another glance up from Decker.

"You don't really think an agent would willingly go undercover as one of Padsha Bashir's wives, do you?" Tess asked Murphy as she sat on her hands to keep from reaching for that picture. She was dying to see Nash's definition of strikingly beautiful. "Reality check, guys—I mean, even if he didn't have a reputation for randomly slicing and dicing his friends and family along with his mortal enemies, there aren't many women on this planet who would be up for that assignment."

"Actually, I know one or two," Nash murmured.

Decker looked up at Nash as he passed the picture . . . in the other direction from Tess. To Murphy. "What else did you find out?"

"Not much," Nash replied. "I lucked out with this picture before I got bounced off-line. I was actually hoping to find an engagement or wedding photo that would provide Sophia's maiden name. This caption reads, 'Dimitri Ghaffari and his American wife, Sophia,' " he told Murphy, who still held the printout.

"You should have asked me for help." Tess looked from Nash to Decker. Especially since research like this was her job. Especially since this was why she was here.

"You have other things to handle—and this woman probably has nothing to do with the missing laptop," Decker told her.

"Yes, but if Padsha Bashir's looking for her, if she *did* try to kill him . . ." Tess looked from Decker to Murphy to

Dave to Nash. "She's in some serious trouble. And there's no embassy here to help her."

"You know, there was a local merchant named Ghaffari." Dave was thinking aloud as he leaned over to get a look at that photograph. "I remember he was doing extremely well. Importing American products—pop culture. T-shirts, blue jeans, videos, books, CDs. Of course, this was a few years back. I never met him. Or his wife. Yes, I definitely would've remembered her."

Murph passed the picture to Tess. The caption was in Arabic, but the photo showed a tall man stiffly posed next to a petite woman. The man was nearly as handsome as Jimmy Nash, with fashion-model high cheekbones and an action-hero jawline, dark hair swept back from his forehead. He was dressed in a tuxedo and smiling down into the eyes of the woman, who was wearing a long-sleeved, high-necked gown.

Tess had been expecting a Lara Croft type, a modern-day Mata Hari—a strikingly beautiful woman who had the guts and smarts to skewer Bashir and escape from the palace during the chaos of the earthquake. But Sophia Ghaffari was one of those ridiculously tiny blond little girls, complete with a porcelain complexion and a face that was fairylike in its ethereal, delicately featured perfection.

She was the kind of woman whom men fell in love with at first sight—the kind of woman men killed to possess. Forget about the fact that she was probably a bitch and a half, spoiled rotten and selfish as all get-out from years of being treated like a little princess.

"She told me Bashir killed her husband—some deal went bad," Decker told them. "She said Ghaffari tried to save himself by giving her to Bashir."

Tess winced. Not even a triple-bitch deserved that.

"Now there's a thoughtful gift that keeps on giving," Nash quipped.

Tess looked up at him in outrage.

"Hey, I was kidding," he told her.

"Yeah, well . . . Not funny."

"Not much in this country is," he countered. "You've got to work with whatever you can find."

"There is nothing even remotely laughable about—"

"I don't know how much of what she told me was true," Decker interrupted them. "She was definitely trying to win my, uh, sympathies, so . . ."

Tess studied the picture again. This woman, Sophia, had been through hell—married to a man who looked like Prince Charming, but who, as soon as trouble made the scene, had proven to be a total invertebrate.

It must have been beyond awful, living in Bashir's palace as one of his "wives." And then to escape with no papers, no passport, only to have a huge reward placed on her head—to become the most hunted person in K-stan. . . .

There was one thing that didn't quite make sense. Tess couldn't imagine that this woman, once having had the good luck to meet up with Decker, would have willingly let him out of her sight.

And yet, apparently, she had.

"Why didn't you bring her back here with you?" Tess asked him now.

"Because she came closer to putting a bullet into my head than anyone's ever done." Delivered in Decker's trademark matter-of-fact manner, it took her a moment to make sense of his words. But across the room, Nash straightened up.

"It was my own fault," Deck continued. "But it seemed like a bad idea to spend any additional time in her company after that."

"Oh, my God, Deck, are you all right?" Tess breathed. He'd nearly been murdered, while she and Nash had been . . .

Decker stood up, as if he were embarrassed by her concern. "I'm going to go back to her hiding place, see if I can find her."

Tess stood, too. "But—"

"I don't think I will," he added. "She was definitely—" He stopped. Ran one hand down his face. "She was scared to death that I was going to turn her over to Bashir. Jesus, I'm an asshole for not seeing that." He was extremely upset, and for once he wasn't trying to hide it—or maybe he simply couldn't hold it inside anymore.

It was actually frightening to see someone like Deck—so solid, so unflappable—looking so totally flapped. Even Dave was wide-eyed.

Deck started to leave, but then turned back. "Tess, get Nash that autopsy report ASAP," he ordered, the team leader to the bitter end.

"Maybe I should go with you instead." Nash had dropped his Mr. Cool act, concern for Decker on his face, in his voice, in the way he was standing there, ready to assist.

But Decker shook his head. "No. I need you here. Figure out a more exact radius around that hospital. Take Tess and walk it."

"Dave can read that report. Probably better than I—"

Deck cut Nash off. "I want Dave out there."

"But—"

"Don't argue with me!" Even Deck seemed surprised by the vehemence in his own voice. He turned to Murphy. "I want you out there, too," he ordered. "Sayid *was* here—and someone knows something. Someone knows why he was here and someone knows where he was staying. Let's find that person, find what we're looking for, and get the hell home."

With that, he turned and slammed the door shut behind him.

"Is it just me," Murphy asked in the silence that followed, "or did anyone else miss the part that explains why Dr. Decker suddenly turned into Mr. Hyde?"

Tess looked at Jimmy Nash. Wasn't he going to follow Deck?

But he just met her eyes and shook his head as he answered Murphy. "You know how you're either really funny or completely silent?" he said as they all started toward the door—all but Tess, who stood there in the middle of the barn with her heart in her throat. "Well, now would be the right time for you to do your silent thing."

"Roger that," Murphy said as he followed Dave out of the barn.

Jimmy stopped at the door. "Come on, Tess," he said quietly. "We've been given our orders."

She had to laugh. "For the first time in your life, you're going to follow orders?"

"Deck's not in danger," Jimmy reassured her. "He was right—wherever this Sophia was hiding, she's not going to be there now. We can help him best by getting you to your computer. After you download that report, I need you to find out everything you possibly can about Dimitri and Sophia Ghaffari."

"Yes, sir." Tess went through the door he was holding for her, and headed swiftly for the house.

Sophia was gone.

Of course she was gone.

Decker hadn't really expected her to still be here, waiting for him to change his mind and return and drag her to Padsha Bashir's palace, where she'd be hideously tortured and executed.

She'd taken everything. Her bedding, her clothes, her small supply of food. The extra burka and robe he'd brought back to her from the factory.

The pair of handguns he'd left, unloaded, outside the

bathroom door were gone, too, along with the two neat little stacks of bullets that he'd set on the floor beside them.

The only thing she'd left behind was the five-dollar bill he'd tossed at her after he'd . . .

Decker went to the sink and splashed water onto his face.

Of course she didn't take the money. She would have no way to exchange it for local bills. And using U.S. dollars in the marketplace would get her looked at, hard, by the shop owners. They might even notice she had blue eyes, guess that she was the woman everyone was looking for, and call the police, eager for a chance at that enormous reward.

Fifty thousand dollars might not seem like a lot by American standards, but here in K-stan, it could set you up for life.

Decker picked up the money from the floor and headed back into the lobby and down the stairs.

He shouldn't have left her.

What had he honestly thought—after she'd tried to fucking *kill* him? That she wasn't telling the truth about Bashir?

But no, he'd been too freaked out to think it through, too pissed off at her—and himself—to realize . . .

Decker had to sit down right there on the stairs. He had to put his head between his knees and force himself to take slow, deep breaths.

Sophia would have done anything to stay alive. And she had, hadn't she? And he'd let her, telling himself that it was her choice.

But it wasn't. She'd thought she had no choice.

And that made it tantamount to rape—what Decker had done with her. *To* her. And he'd double damned himself by leaving her there.

Terrified. Crying. Humiliated.

He was supposed to be one of the good guys. He was supposed to be a hero, fighting on the side of justice.

He should've walked away after she'd first told him about Bashir. He should've given her money—money she could use—with no strings attached. He should've told her to meet him tomorrow or even later tonight. His walking away might've proven to her that she could trust him. And he would've had time to get back to camp and find out if she, in turn, was really who she'd said she was.

Instead he'd fucked this up.

Completely.

There was no way on earth he was going to find Sophia Ghaffari again. Not with Padsha Bashir looking for her. Not a chance.

Decker stood and pushed his way out into the sunlight, relocking the basement door behind him.

He went up the steps and down the alley, out into the crowded marketplace.

He'd followed Sophia through a similar marketplace by wearing the burka she'd left behind when she'd ditched him at the factory. Earlier, he had watched her steal another, watched her climb back out of the window of a rundown apartment building, that nearly transparent dress hidden by this new robe, her face hidden once more by a heavy veil.

People, most of them burka-clad women, too, began leaving their houses as the curfew was lifted, and Decker had pretended to come out of a nearby doorway.

Dressed as he was, his face hidden by a veil, he'd crossed right in front of Sophia. He'd gotten close enough to bump into her, to mark her shoulder and back with a streak of gray dust from the road.

And marked like that, with the added bonus of his own disguise, it had been ridiculously easy to follow her, even through the crowd.

As Decker stood now and gazed out at the busy market,

he saw a veiled figure, dust streaking her robe, standing near a table filled with fruits and vegetables.

Talk about wishful thinking.

It couldn't possibly be Sophia.

Could it?

As he watched, a small hand reached out and pulled an entire melon up into the robe's sleeve. It was artfully done. Poetic, even.

But it couldn't be her. She was miles from here. Had to be. Yet hope sparked in his chest, expanding quickly, as hope was wont to do. After mere seconds he could feel it even in the tips of his fingers. The melon thief was the right height and as close to the right build as he could tell, considering she was dressed in a figure-concealing robe.

The shopkeeper didn't notice the theft. No one noticed. No one but Decker.

Sophia—he was actually daring to think it might be her—moved off. Slowly. Just another shopper who didn't find what she wanted.

Heart damn near pounding out of his chest, Decker followed. Finding one woman in a city of over a million people couldn't possibly be this easy. But, Jesus, he wanted to find her. He needed to . . . what? Apologize?

Sorry about the unnecessary blow job. . . .

The melon thief moved slowly down the aisle of stands and carts, hampered by the crowd. Keeping his eye on that pale streak of dirt, Decker raced to catch up.

He didn't bother to keep his approach covert. She was hampered by her robe and veil—and he knew he could outrun her if she bolted.

He saw the exact instant that she turned and saw him bearing down on her like a heat-seeking missile, because she picked up her skirts and fled.

She was faster than she'd been last night. Faster, and less lucky—as she ducked into an alley he knew was a dead end.

She was smarter than that—smart enough not to leave the safety of the crowd, smart enough not to let him get her alone.

Unless, of course, she was carrying those handguns and wanted the privacy she'd need to blow him away.

Decker stopped at the entrance to the alley, keeping behind the cover provided by a jarringly modern-looking Dumpster.

"I don't want to hurt you," he called out in English, even though the hope had already faded, even though he knew it wasn't Sophia he'd followed. Still, he had to see for himself.

There was nothing, no response. Only the strangest sound. Heavy breathing. Snuffling and . . .

"If you fire your weapon," he called, "the police from the market will be here so quickly, you won't have time to get away."

Again, only that oddly familiar noise. Sniffing and gasping and . . . Was she crying?

"I just want to talk to you," Decker said. "I'm coming back there. . . ."

He stepped out from behind the Dumpster, knowing he made a very clear target, silhouetted against the brightness of the morning sky.

If she rushed him, shooting as she came, she could conceivably escape before the police arrived.

And yet there he went. Right down the middle of that alley.

But even before he saw her huddled in the corner, crouched down on the ground, he recognized what he was hearing—why it sounded so familiar.

This was the same sound his dog—Em's dog now—had made when he ate.

Ranger dove headfirst into his bowl, eating with a gusto that seemed part joie de vivre, part frantic starvation, and part fear that this meal might be his last. It didn't matter what time Deck fed the damn dog, he always wolfed it down in record time, chomping and slurping and gasping.

Just the way the melon thief was devouring the entire melon she'd stolen from the marketplace—seeds and rind and all.

Decker realized instantly that she was destroying the evidence. The theory being that if there was no melon, then she couldn't have stolen it.

He realized a fraction of a second later—as the last of his hopes were dashed—that not only wasn't she Sophia, but she also wasn't even a woman.

"She" was a boy. Barely a teenager, he'd taken off the veil to have better access to that melon. He was skinny, with dark hair and pale skin—as if he didn't often get out into the sun.

He was also missing his right hand. He'd been marked—most cruelly, and some years ago, from the look of it—as a thief.

"I thought you were someone else," Decker told the kid, using the local dialect, hoping to alleviate his fear. "It's okay—I'm not going to turn you in."

The boy's entire burka was a mess, with streaks of dirt and dust and melon down the front of it.

Deck backed out of the alley, glad that Nash hadn't come with him. If he were here, Khalid would no doubt have a new assistant.

Decker went back to the marketplace, knowing what he'd known even before he'd left Rivka's barn.

That he wasn't going to find Sophia Ghaffari unless she wanted to be found.

And she didn't want to be found.

CHAPTER
FIFTEEN

"WHERE IS he?" Tess leaned close to ask, and Jimmy saw that she was perspiring beneath the scarf she was required to wear—at least in this part of town—whenever she stepped outside of the house.

The temperature was already two million degrees, and the sun was still climbing into the sky. They stood in Rivka's yard and sweated as they watched young Khalid harness his horse to his wagon.

Jimmy was grateful for his cargo shorts and short-sleeved shirt—the back of which was already soaked. Tess must've been dying.

"Other side of the neighbor's wall," he told her now, his back carefully to that wall in question. "Across the street and east. Don't look."

She gave him an exasperated roll of her eyes. "I wasn't going to."

"You know, if you don't want to do this—"

Tess cut him off. "I do."

He was the one having serious doubts. "I'm not so sure—," he started.

She stepped even closer. "I am. I can do this."

To someone, like, for instance, *Boston Globe* reporter Will Schroeder, who might've been watching them, like, for instance, from behind the neighbor's stone wall where he was too far away to hear their hushed voices, it would look very much as if Tess were gazing up at Jimmy with eyes that were filled with affection and concern.

Of course, her concern was only that Jimmy was going to change his mind and make her stay behind.

"This isn't hard," she said, "or dangerous."

"You're kidding, right?" he countered. "Because there's not a moment that passes here in K-stan that *isn't* dangerous."

"I *meant*, it's not *more* dangerous than staying behind while you go off and play James Bond." She winced. "Sorry—that came out wrong. I know that this isn't any kind of a game."

Damn straight it wasn't. "Decker isn't going to like the idea of your being alone out there," he told her. It was easier to say *Decker* instead of *I. I don't like the idea of you alone out there.* Damn it, this was a mistake, sending her out so that Schroeder would follow her instead of Jimmy. If something happened to her . . .

But Schroeder was a persistent prick. Jimmy could shake him—no doubt about that. But it would take effort. And then Schroeder would wonder why Jimmy had gone to such effort to shake him. He'd lurk in the neighbors' yards night and day and night in hopes of finding out.

"I won't be alone," Tess assured him. "I'll be with Khalid."

"Whom we don't really know," Jimmy countered.

"Who thinks you're God's nicer brother," Tess told him. "He's so completely ready to worship at the altar of Nash. You own him. Totally. I don't know all of what you said to him—"

Jimmy shrugged. "I just offered him this job."

"You're really great with kids, you know."

Okay. Now he was starting to get embarrassed. "It's not that big a deal. It's not that hard to do. You listen when they talk. Most kids spend their entire lives being ignored or used as punching bags. Conversation can be a real pattern interrupt."

Tess wasn't so willing to shrug it off. "Khalid told me you cleared it with Rivka—that he can keep his horse and wagon here for as long as he needs to. Do you have any idea what that means to him?"

Yeah, actually he did. "His own barn is a pile of stones." Jimmy kept his voice even. "As long as Rivka doesn't mind . . ."

It wouldn't take a lot of effort to make sure that Khalid continued to treat him like a hero. And more important, he was going to treat Tess like a hero's wife.

Khalid, like Rivka and Guldana, thought Tess really was Jimmy's wife. And how weird was that?

"He adores you," Tess said, smiling up at him. "If I wasn't afraid you'd take it the wrong way, I'd tell you I do, too. You're the very nicest jerk I know."

Jimmy laughed. "Yeah, and you're too forgiving."

"You want me to stay mad at you?" she asked. "That could cause real problems, considering we're sharing a bedroom."

But not a bed.

Jimmy cleared his throat. "Well, it's one thing to forgive, but . . ."

"I think it's useful," she said. "My not completely hating your guts. I mean, communication could be a hassle."

"You don't just not hate me, Tess, you actually like me," he said, and it wasn't until the words were out of his mouth that he realized they sounded like an accusation.

Tess adjusted her head scarf. "I'm sorry if that makes you uncomfortable. I'll try harder to hate you. Does it help that I think you're relationship challenged and a socially pathetic loser?"

Jimmy laughed. "Yeah," he said. "It does. Thanks."

She smiled back at him. "Good." She stood on her toes

to plant a chaste kiss on his cheek. "Have a nice day, dear. I'll make sure Khalid brings me back by curfew."

He caught her arm. "Yeah, whoa, he better have you back way before that." Jimmy had told the kid to find the nearest work party and to get Mrs. Nash signed on to help doing something relatively safe. Like handing out aid packages. He'd told Khalid to stay away—far away—from the Grande Hotel. "I need you back here, this afternoon at the latest, finding out everything there is to find out about Sophia Ghaffari."

Because, Sainted Mary, Mother of God, *what* was up with this Sophia woman and Decker? Jimmy had never seen his partner so completely rattled.

And by a recently escaped palace concubine? A woman Decker had been with for at least part of last night? A significantly lengthy part of last night. Deck had returned to Rivka's well after the sun was up.

Add into the bizarre equation the fact that said recently escaped palace concubine had very nearly managed to kill Decker. Which meant that, at some point, Deck's guard had been down.

Or at least lowered.

And didn't *that* make Jimmy's imagination run wild.

Except for the fact that this was Decker. Put him alone in a room with a palace concubine, and Deck would probably end up helping her do her taxes.

Across the yard, the horse sneezed and shook its head, making the bridle jingle. Jimmy looked up to find Tess watching him. He was still holding on to her arm. Too tightly.

He let her go.

"You all right?" she asked softly.

"I'm worried about Deck." Okay. His honesty surprised her almost as much as it did him. "Killing me when he finds out I let you go out with only Khalid," he added.

And she so didn't buy it. But being Tess, she played along. "It's not like we have a choice. Besides, we'll probably both be back long before Decker is."

Over by the wagon, Khalid gave Jimmy a thumbs-up—horse, boy, and wagon were all almost ready to go. To take Tess out of the safety of this yard and into the city.

Shit.

"If you're stopped by a patrol of any kind, either official police or one of Bashir's goon squads, let Khalid do the talking," Jimmy told Tess. "And if you're in doubt, keep your head covered."

She was smiling at him. "No eye contact, even if I'm directly addressed. Especially if I'm directly addressed. It's not always easy to tell Bashir's men apart from the police, although depending on the precinct, the police might be even more difficult to deal with than Bashir's squads of murderers, so don't let my guard down. When I come back to the house, don't forget to check that that piece of rope is hanging on both the gate and by the door. If it's not, don't go in the house, don't slow down, just walk on past. Check inside that old shed down the street for messages. You know, if you talk really fast, James, you may have time to tell me all this for a third or even a fourth time before the wagon clears the gate."

Shit. "Sorry, I'm just . . ."

Tess touched his hand. Her fingers were actually cool. In this heat. How did she manage that? "I'll be careful."

"Yeah, I know you will."

She squeezed his hand. "You be careful, too."

While Tess distracted Will Schroeder, Jimmy was going to walk the perimeter of the newly modified target area around the hospital.

The information from Sayid's autopsy report had made him significantly revise his estimate of how far the terrorist

...ader might have been able to walk after being injured in the quake.

And he had been able to walk.

His ribs, his shoulder, and his right arm had been badly broken, but the damage to his legs was minimal.

He'd had a head injury, but cause of death was internal injuries.

Tom Paoletti had reported that Sayid's hospital files listed him as conscious but extremely confused at check-in. He was unable even to ID himself, yet he'd told the triage medic that he'd walked there. That medic had probably assumed anyone ambulatory to that degree could wait to see a doctor. He'd blown it big-time by sticking Sayid into a makeshift bed in the lobby without checking his blood pressure—which by then was probably dropping fast.

According to hospital records, Sayid had bled to death within a matter of hours.

With his injuries, he simply could not have made it to the hospital under his own steam from more than a few very short kilometers away. And that was assuming he had a giant S on his T-shirt.

Jimmy had checked a map and noted that Padsha Bashir's palace was still well inside the revised target area.

In addition to walking that newly outlined perimeter, he was intending to find the most severely damaged part of the palace and walk the most obvious route from there to the Cantara hospital.

While Tess led Will Schroeder on a wild goose chase.

Putting herself in danger, god damn it.

Tess broke into his thoughts. "Seriously, Jimmy. I know this thing with Decker is distracting you. Be extra careful out there today."

And now, from Will Schroeder's point of view, it looked as if she were gazing at him with concern in her eyes—

because she *was* gazing at him with concern in her eyes. Because she thought *Decker* was distracting him.

"I'll be fine," he told her. "I'm not the one who's pregnant."

"Yeah, well, I'm not either," she said, but she dropped his hand and took a step back, just as he'd intended. But she knew that, too. She shook her head as she looked at him and laughed. "Congratulations—right now I honestly hate you."

She wasn't supposed to be amused. And yet he couldn't keep from smiling back at her. Damn, she was cute when she smiled like that. Cute, and smart, and . . . "Try to find out what Will Schroeder knows," Jimmy ordered her, mostly because smart women hated being ordered around.

"You're that certain he's going to follow me. Instead of you."

"Yes, I am." There were many reasons why, when forced to choose between following Jimmy or following Tess, Will Schroeder, ace reporter, would choose Tess.

Because she was a woman, because she was young, because Will didn't know her and would assume he had a better chance at wheedling information from her, because Will had surely noticed the way Jimmy looked at her. Because . . . "Will's good at what he does," he told her. He glanced over at the neighbor's yard. And there he was. Will Schroeder. Trying to hide. And failing. Christ. "Good at some things."

"Apparently he was good enough to find us here at Rivka's. You know, we should just go over there, tell him about Sayid and the laptop, and offer him an exclusive on the story if he works with us."

Jimmy laughed. "Yeah, right."

Tess adjusted her scarf, trying to get air underneath it. "What exactly do you have against him?"

"He's a reporter. Isn't that enough?"

"The members of the Fourth Estate *can* be our friends," she told him. "Valuable friends."

"Ready, sir and ma'am," Khalid called.

Jimmy started for the wagon.

"Did you really sleep with his wife?"

"What?" Jimmy turned and looked at Tess. "Where did you hear that?"

"It was just something he said—implied really—when he got off the bus yesterday."

He could tell from her eyes that she believed it, believed that Jimmy was not just capable of, but highly likely to.

"It's a long story," he said, which was stupid because number one, he didn't owe anyone an explanation for anything he ever did, and number two, they were both better off if she judged him and found him less-than. "That's synthetic." At her blank look, he added, "Your scarf. You need to get one that's made of cotton."

Tess nodded. "And, hmmm, he changes the subject."

"Cotton breathes. You'll be much cooler. I'll pick one up for you."

"You know, really, all you have to say is 'None of your business.' "

"None of your business," Jimmy said.

"Unless, of course, it *is* my business. Unless it's something that I need to know because I'm going to be dealing with this guy and—"

"Yes," Jimmy told her. "The short answer is yes, I slept with his wife. He hates my guts—you two can start a club—but be careful. He'll probably try to charm your pants off. Literally. Don't let him get too close."

And now he could tell that she'd changed her mind. Now she *didn't* think he was capable of . . . How the hell had that happened?

"She didn't tell you she was married, did she?" Tess guessed. "That must've hurt."

"None of your business."

"What was her name?"

"I don't remember anymore."

She laughed. "You're such a liar. It was Jacqueline—Jackie—Bennett, wasn't it?"

How the hell did she know that? "Did Decker tell you—" He cut himself off. Of course Decker hadn't said a word. Tess was a comspesh. No doubt she'd done some homework on Will Schroeder. With her hacking skills, she probably knew more than Tom Paoletti did about all of them. Except Jimmy. His records had been deleted.

Except, of course, that one file that the Agency kept buried so deep that not even Tess would be able to find it.

Good thing.

He could just imagine the information it contained.

James Nash, aka Diego Nash, aka Jimmy the Kid Santucci, b. 11 August 1969, White Plains Hospital, New York. Mother: Marianna Santucci, b. 1950, d. 1987. Father: unknown.

It would include all kinds of lists.

Periods of incarceration. February 1982 through January 1986, Bedford Juvenile Center. August 1988 through January 1989, Sing-Sing Correctional Facility, Ossining, New York.

Felonies committed. Grand larceny. Assault with a deadly weapon. Conspiracy to commit murder—a trumped-up charge added to his record when he'd refused to turn state's evidence on Victor Dimassiano, the man who'd been the closest thing he'd ever had to a father.

Assignments he'd taken while at the Agency.

Deletions he'd performed for his country.

That particular list alone would make her back off for good. After fifteen years, it was several pages long.

No, if she knew more about him than other people did, it was only because he'd made the mistake of telling her about himself on that crazy night he'd gone to her apartment.

"What do you want me to say, Tess?" Jimmy asked her now. He got closer to her, too close, and lowered his voice. "That I loved her and she broke my heart?"

She was looking up at him, those big eyes wide, ready to believe that bullshit, ready to make him out to be some kind of romantic hero. Ready to . . . How had she put it when talking about Khalid? Ready to worship at the altar of Nash.

God help them both.

He was having a hard enough time keeping his hands off of her, and when she looked at him like that . . .

"I fucked her," Jimmy said flatly. "And the only heart that was broken was Will's."

Once again, he was holding her elbow much too tightly. He let her go, disgusted with himself for too many reasons to list.

She didn't say anything as she followed him over to the wagon. And then she couldn't say anything because Khalid was sitting there. She just looked at Jimmy as he helped her onto the wagon, as she made herself as comfortable as possible on the hard wooden seat next to the K-stani boy.

Jimmy couldn't bring himself to meet her gaze more than briefly. "Sorry," he said. He wondered if she knew that his apology was for more than his rude words. He was sorry for so much—all the way back to his inconvenient birth.

"I'm sorry, too, James," she said, and freaking meant it.

He stood there, like an idiot, watching as the wagon cleared the gate, because she was looking back at him.

"Be careful," she called. "No dings today, okay?"

It was lunchtime before the reporter came close enough to talk to her.

Tess sat in the minuscule amount of shade thrown by

Khalid's wagon and cut open the corner of the military-issue meal-in-a-pouch that Jimmy Nash had put in her bag back at Rivka's.

Spaghetti and meatballs was written in no-frills default computer print on the outside of the plastic, but whatever was inside had the consistency of pudding. Or baby food.

"It helps if you put it inside your shirt for a few minutes," Will Schroeder said as he approached. He was smiling at the look of horror and disbelief she was sure she was wearing. "That way it'll heat up—at least to body temperature."

"I've already opened it," she said. "No way am I putting it in my shirt now."

Will Schroeder had a nice, friendly smile in a pleasant enough face, although his sunglasses kept her from seeing his eyes. With the fair skin of a redhead, he also wore a hat to help protect himself against the sun. Tess could see traces of sunblock along his hairline and beneath his ear. Even using an SPF 30, he probably had to reapply it frequently to keep from doing a total lobster.

As the official spokeswoman for the Freckle League, she could relate.

"It's actually kind of nice that this stuff is slightly cool," she said, shading her eyes to look up at him. "Although I think it'll help if I stop thinking of it as spaghetti and meatballs. If I gave it a French name, maybe I could pretend it's gourmet soup, served chilled, from a four-star restaurant."

He laughed and motioned to the remaining patch of shade. "May I?"

"Of course. It's Will, right?"

He nodded as he sat down. Held out a hand. "Schroeder. From Boston."

They shook. Between their two right hands, they were wearing five different Band-Aids. It made Tess think of Jimmy Nash and his dings. Of course, there wasn't much that didn't make her think of Nash. She'd done little else all morning long, in between praying that she'd get her period and praying for a freak snowstorm.

"Tess Nash," she said. "From . . ." She laughed. "I don't know where I'm from anymore." Certainly not Iowa, where she'd been born. Or even San Francisco where she'd moved with her mother after her parents' divorce. "I lived in D.C. for the past few years, but Jimmy, my husband— we were just married—is from Boston, too. He's with People First."

"Yeah," Will said. His smile didn't fade, not a bit. "I had the pleasure of meeting *Jimmy* in Bali a few years back."

Pleasure? "Yes, he told me," Tess said, just as pleasantly. "I met Larry there, too."

It took her a moment to realize that by Larry he meant Decker. Jimmy and Larry. Larry and Jimmy. Just a coupla American guys.

Right.

"Let's cut the crap," Will said, still smiling. "Shall we? I know you're not a relief worker—none of you are."

Tess calmly ate her lunch. "Soupe glacée de tomate au boeuf," she said. "It actually does taste better if you think of it that way."

"Don't worry," Will said. "Your secret's safe—for now."

Did he actually think she was worried about right now? She glanced up, certain of what she'd find—that no one was within earshot. He'd have made sure of that—he had secrets to hide, too.

Tess tried to catch Khalid's eye from across the yard. If he came toward her, this conversation would have to be postponed. But Khalid was deep in discussion with several other young K-stani men, no doubt still talking about this morning's explosion and the ensuing column of smoke that still rose from a street just blocks away.

Rumors of a suicide bomber spread faster than the fire

that had been caused, in fact, by a relatively small-sized gas leak.

It was dangerous enough here in this earthquake-battered city without bringing suicide bombers into the equation.

Vague threats from low-level reporters didn't even rate a mention.

"I want answers to some questions," Will said, and his threats got a little less vague. "Or I'll start pointing fingers and naming names—and you'll all be on the next flight out of here so fast . . ."

"You will, too," Tess pointed out. There was probably a way to eat gracefully from this type of plastic pouch packaging. Practice would no doubt help.

He shrugged. "I already finished the job I came for—last night I filed a story about the quake."

Shit.

Will was grinning, because he was sure he'd won.

Which he had. Unless she spun this situation on its side. Tess calmly finished her MRE. Working from the support office at the Agency, she'd handled media manipulation plenty of times in the past. Leaking information to the press was part of psychological operations. Psyops was an invaluable tool to a team in the field.

Because these days the bad guys got their news from CNN, too.

But although Tess had been the "unnamed source" in too many news reports to count, she'd always contacted those reporters and leaked the story under her precise conditions. She'd always been completely in control.

The trick here was to somehow trump Will Schroeder's threats and end up on top. Tess knew what she had to do, but first she'd try to rattle him. "Jimmy told me what happened in Bali. You know, with your wife."

He was good—his surprise was limited to a two-second

freeze that he covered with laughter. "Ex-wife," he corrected her—but it was just a tad too casually. And if that weren't a clue, his body language all but screamed how very little he cared. Which of course, meant that he did care. Very much.

But Tess just nodded. "That's probably for the best, considering—"

"That Jackie was a lying whore?"

Tess was fascinated and couldn't keep from asking more, despite the fact that she had a limited amount of time to deal with Will's threat. Their lunch break was almost over. "She's an investigative reporter, too, isn't she?"

Will's bio on the newspaper's Web site mentioned that he'd spent a number of years teamed with photojournalist Jacqueline Bennett, who'd recently won a whole slew of awards for her pictures from inside an Indonesian terrorist training camp, taken in the aftermath of the bombing in Bali—pictures printed not in the *Boston Globe*, but rather in *Time* magazine.

Those photos had enabled the local government, who was working with both the U.S. and Australia, to send in a task force of SEALs and SAS to shut down the camp. The Agency had used the photos, too, to apprehend more than a half-dozen high-ranking al-Qaeda leaders who'd left the country before the camp's takedown.

"Yeah, if by investigative you mean she fucked the right people to get photo ops." Will laughed. "I saw her on Jay Leno, talking about how dangerous it was getting those photos. How risky. Yeah, the biggest risk she took was that the condom might break. And now she's the media's darling. Queen of the fucking decade."

Which was he more pissed about—the fact that his wife had been unfaithful, or that she'd scooped a huge story and kept his name off the byline?

"Marriages don't last long in either of our two businesses," Tess said diplomatically.

Will laughed again. "Yeah, like you and *Jimmy* are really married."

"We are."

He didn't believe her—not a good sign. "My condolences."

Enough was enough. "How long have you been with the *Globe*?" Tess asked. "Seven years? And then three before that with the *Middlesex News*?"

He looked at her over the top of his sunglasses, his eyes very blue. "Am I supposed to be impressed that you know—"

She didn't let him finish. "More about you than you know about us? Yes."

"That's going to change right now. Who exactly do you work for?"

Tess shook her head. "You don't get to ask questions. You get to sit there silently and listen."

He laughed. "I've got to hand it to you, babe, you've got balls, but—"

"We're here because al-Qaeda has eight different training camps in Kazbekistan—and those are just the ones we know about. We're here because, for the first time in years, the borders are open to the West, and we won't create an international incident if we're caught going someplace unauthorized. We're here because there's been lots of Internet chatter similar to right before 9/11, and we will not—*will not*—allow a terrorist attack of that magnitude to happen on U.S. soil—or anywhere else—ever again. We're here because Ma'awiya Talal Sayid died in Kazabek, in the Cantara hospital, from injuries sustained in the quake. Do you need me to spell *Ma'awiya* for you?"

Will shook his head. "No. *Shit,* this is . . . What proof do you have that—"

"The White House is going to hold a press conference announcing Sayid's death tomorrow at 11:30 a.m. U.S. eastern time," Tess said. "You will not release any information about Sayid to the *Boston Globe*—or any other news organization—before 11:30 a.m. U.S. eastern time."

He sputtered. "You're kidding, right? You just hand me the biggest story of the year—"

Tess spoke over him. "You will not identify me or anyone I work with at any time."

"—and you think I'm not going to use it?"

"Sayid's death is not the biggest story of the year," she interrupted herself to tell him. "Not even close."

That shut him up pretty quick.

"You will not even so much as speculate on the presence of U.S.-sanctioned counterterrorist teams currently in K-stan," she continued. "You will stop staking out our house, you'll stop following us. In fact, you won't draw any attention to us in any way. If you have information for me, you'll contact me discreetly. Otherwise, you'll wait for me to contact you."

"Lots of rules," Will said.

"Yes," she agreed.

He shook his head. "I don't think—"

"This agreement is nonnegotiable," she told him.

Will was silent for several long moments, just watching her.

"So you give me this information about Sayid's death," he finally said, "information that I'm not supposed to use, and I get . . . ?"

"You get proof that I'm a solid source of accurate information," Tess told him.

"Suppose I refuse? Suppose I tell you to take your rules and stick 'em where the sun don't shine, and go call CNN—"

"Then my associates and I will be out of the country and

you'll be minus a source," she told him. "A very valuable source."

He thought about that. Good boy, Will. Think hard. Realize exactly what all this means.

"You're here because you're looking for Sayid's laptop," he finally theorized.

Tess clenched her teeth to keep from smiling. She had him. Locked in. Thank God.

"Yes, we are," she told him. "And you will not include that information in any of your news reports. Not until after we find it. At which point, you'll get an in-depth exclusive—but it will be on *my* timetable, is that understood?"

"Yeah." He was silent again, no doubt realizing that that exclusive would get him a whole lot of attention. Maybe even more than Jackie got from her pictures.

Will leaned closer. "Can you at least tell me if there's any weight to the rumors that Sayid was in Kazabek to meet with Padsha Bashir?"

"Tess!"

She looked up to see Nash crossing the yard. He was breathing hard and dripping with sweat, as if he'd run hard for several miles.

She was on her feet and heading toward him before she even knew it. "Jimmy! What happened? Are you all right? Is Decker . . . ?"

Something had to have happened to Decker to make Jimmy this upset. He pulled her, hard, into his arms, and she held him tightly, bracing herself for the bad news.

Which didn't come. "Deck's okay—and you are, too—thank God. Thank *God*." He pulled away. "Sorry. I'm sorry. Christ, I stink. . . ."

"I don't care," she told him. The entire front of her shirt was now damp, but that didn't matter. "Are you all right?" she asked him again. "What happened?"

He looked around—at Will Schroeder and Khalid, at the dozen or so other relief workers who were watching them, curiosity on their faces.

It was then that Tess saw something that looked an awful lot like realization flash in Jimmy's eyes. Realization, along with a little bit of *Oh, crap, what have I done?*

He laughed weakly, ran a hand—and she could have sworn it was shaking—through his hair, pushing it back, out of his eyes. "Well . . ."

"This is James Nash," Tess announced as she went to get him something to drink before he suffered heatstroke. "My husband."

She handed her water to Jimmy, who nearly emptied the bottle in one long swallow. Khalid was right there with more for him.

"Thanks," Jimmy said.

The group had begun to disperse when it was clear he wasn't some random madman off the street. But Will Schroeder and Khalid both remained nearby.

"Do you want to sit down?" Tess asked.

Jimmy shook his head. "No, I'm . . . Look, this is so stupid. I was . . ." He looked from Tess to Will and Khalid and back, and the smile he gave her was rueful. And terribly sweet. "I'm embarrassed to admit it, but . . ."

Tess turned to Will and Khalid. "Will you give us a minute please?"

But Jimmy stopped them from moving out of earshot. "No, it's okay. It's just . . . I freaked out. I was across town and I started hearing these rumors about an explosion. And then people starting saying how some kid strapped TNT around his waist and walked into a relief aid station and blew himself up along with twenty people—all Westerners. And then I heard that it was here, in this same neighborhood that Khalid told me he was going to bring you to today, and . . ."

And he'd run, all the way here, to make sure she hadn't been hurt. Tess's heart was in her throat as she reached for him. "I'm okay."

He held her tightly. "I know. I see. I'm"—his laughter was shaky—"a total fool."

Will Schroeder was staring at them, openmouthed.

Jimmy ignored him as he pulled back to look at her. "I shouldn't have let you go out without me. That's not going to happen again. In fact, pack up your stuff. Khalid, get the wagon. We're calling it a day."

"It's barely half past noon," Tess protested. "We promised to stay for a six-hour shift."

But Jimmy pulled her close again and spoke into her ear. "I need to contact Tom, stat." More loudly, he said, "Our phones are out again, or I would've called you. I ran all that way, in this heat. . . ." He swayed. "Wow. Maybe I should sit down. . . ."

Tess wrapped his arm around her shoulder. "Help me get him into the wagon," she ordered Will. Her voice shook, and she hoped it came across as worry for Jimmy, rather than disappointment. This was all an act, a way to get her back to Rivka's—to her computers.

And she'd actually thought . . .

Well, on the bright side, if she'd been fooled, everyone else surely had, too.

Jimmy's knees gave out—he really was a brilliant actor—just after he was up and in the back of the wagon. Without Will's help, and without Tess throwing all of her weight into keeping him from falling, he would have landed face-first on the wooden boards. As it was, it was quite a struggle to set him down gently. It somehow ended with Tess sitting in the wagon bed, with Jimmy's head solidly in her lap, his eyes closed.

Khalid tossed her backpack in next to her and scrambled up onto the driver's seat. He called out an order to his tired horse, some magic command to give the beast new life, and they lurched forward. Will had to jump back to keep the wheel from rolling over his foot.

"Thank you," Tess called to him.

"I'll see you," he said.

"Yeah, he'll be following you around in earnest now," Jimmy murmured. His eyes were open, now, and when she looked down at him, he winked. *Winked,* damn it.

"No, he won't, and when did we lose phones?" she asked instead of pulling back and letting his head bounce on the hard wood of the wagon bed, the way she wanted to. Khalid was still watching and listening.

"I don't know when the system went down," Jimmy told her. "All I know is that when I tried to use it, it kept cutting out."

Tess leaned across him to reach her pack. Pulling it closer, she unzipped the side pocket that held her phone. She opened it and nothing happened.

Troubleshooting 101's first rule was to always check the power button. Oops. It was off. She turned the phone on, and it immediately beeped.

"Mine's still working," she told him.

There was a message waiting, but Jimmy reached up and took her phone out of her hands. "Let me see that."

"The signal's not strong," she said, "but the system's definitely still up. Maybe you've got a hardware problem."

He was pushing an array of buttons, clicking on the menu and . . . He handed it back to her.

"Aren't you going to call Tom?" she asked. She looked at her phone. "Hey." He'd deleted that message. "What if that was important?"

"It wasn't," Jimmy said. "I'm going to wait and send Tom email." He looked pointedly up at Khalid and back. "Encrypted," he mouthed silently.

"You didn't even listen to it. How do you know . . ." . . . *it wasn't important?* She figured it out before the words left her mouth.

He knew because he'd left that message. He'd called her when he'd heard those rumors about the suicide bomber, and her phone hadn't been on. He honestly hadn't known if she was dead or just an idiot.

He'd deleted the message, but he hadn't been able to erase the phone's list of missed calls—a record of the times that he'd called but hadn't left a message. She quickly flipped over to that menu and . . . Whoa. He'd called her seventeen times in a forty-eight-minute period. While running through the debris-cluttered streets of Kazabek.

His freak-out hadn't been an act. The act had come *after* he'd found her, safe and sound.

Jimmy was watching her from his vantage point, down in her lap. His expression was unreadable, but he was a very intelligent man. He had to know that she now knew . . .

"I'm sorry I had my phone off," she told him.

"Wake me when we get to Rivka's," he said, and closed his eyes.

CHAPTER
SIXTEEN

"YOU DID *what*?" Jimmy stopped right there in the doorway to Rivka's barn, staring at Tess. What she had just told him was un-fucking-believable.

She, however, was maddeningly calm as she went inside and made herself comfortable on the overturned bucket that she'd claimed as her spot during their meetings. "I think you probably heard me perfectly well the first time."

" 'Scuse us." Murphy attempted to squeeze past, Dave right behind him, and since squeezing wasn't one of Murphy's talents, Jimmy was forced to step farther into the barn.

"Will Schroeder?" he asked Tess.

"Yes. Will Schroeder." She pretended to look over some notes she'd made on a yellow legal pad.

The early evening sun streamed in through the cracks in the battered wooden door, illuminating the dust that hung in the air.

It should have been soothingly pastoral.

But Jimmy was on the verge of meltdown, and Tess knew it, too. He could see wariness in her eyes as she risked another quick glance in his direction.

He cleared his throat. "You actually told him about . . . ?" He couldn't say it. He probably could've screamed it, but he was trying his goddamnedest not to have a complete nutty. Especially since it would be his second for the day, and his policy was one nutty per millennium. If that.

"I told him we're here to find Sayid's laptop." She finally met his gaze. "I had no choice."

"No choice?" His voice sounded tight. "Are you trying to get me killed? Is this some kind of twisted revenge?"

Dave had just sat down, but now he stood. "Maybe we should give them a few minutes alone," he said to Murphy.

But Murph settled back on his favorite bale of hay. "Are you kidding? This is just starting to get good. Revenge for what?"

Tess held her ground. "Of course I'm not trying to get you killed! Don't be ridiculous."

Jimmy couldn't stop himself from pacing. "You don't understand how much that prick hates me."

"This wasn't about you." Tess put down her legal pad. "Look. If you could get past your childish bias against Will Schroeder for just half a second—"

"Don't you god damn get condescending with me!" As he spun to face her, he lowered his voice instead of raising it, which was probably a mistake, because he knew from experience that doing so made him sound and look dangerous as hell.

Dave and Murphy apparently thought so, too, because they were both on their feet.

Ready to protect Tess.

From him.

"Jesus Christ," he said to them. "What do you think? That I would actually . . . ?" He could see from their faces that they did, indeed, think exactly that. "God damn it."

Tess was on her feet now, too, still talking. "—you'd realize this was the perfect way to deal with him. The *only* way. He's ambitious, he's smart, he's eager to prove to Jackie Bennett just what she gave up by dumping him—and God, Jimmy, he knows who we are. He could blow our cover at any given moment. Now it's in his best interest to keep quiet."

"He didn't know about Sayid." He turned to Dave and Murphy. "Sit."

They sat, but not without exchanging a look. Silently communicating exactly how they were going to take him down if he lost it and went for Tess's throat.

Christ. Give him a break. He wasn't a freaking animal.

"So I gave him a heads-up on a story that's going to break big in twenty-two hours." Tess was no longer trying to keep her annoyance from ringing in her voice. "Do you honestly think that after he heard the White House news bulletin that Sayid was dead he wouldn't know exactly what we were doing here? This way, he's on our side. Under our control."

"*Our* control? *Your* control."

"Yeah. *My* control." Anger flashed in her eyes. "Is that what's bothering you? The fact that I might have actually done something that you couldn't manage to do? You know, you can be so *fucking* immature."

He laughed. He couldn't help it. The tough talk simply didn't work well with that nose and those freckles. Pollyanna from the 'hood.

He must've sounded as if he were on the verge of madness—and maybe he was—because Fred and Ginger rose to their feet again, obviously eager to dance.

But this time it was Tess who glared at them. "You can't be serious! You actually think you're going to have to defend me—from *James*?"

Murphy shrugged. "Shit happens."

Dave was less succinct. "The pressures in the field sometimes trigger volatile behavior. And in this particular group of personnel, there's a greater degree of unfamiliarity among teammates—"

"Yeah, well, hello, Dave, meet James Nash. You, too,

Murph. Shame on you. I happen to know that one of Jimmy's goals on this mission—possibly even his primary one, despite the fact that it shouldn't be"—that was a not so subtle message aimed with a flash of her eyes at him—"is to keep me safe. So in the future, please don't insult him by implying otherwise."

Tess was fiercely indignant—for him.

He'd treated her like shit more than once, including this afternoon when he'd refused to talk to her at all on the ride back to Rivka's house. And he'd thrown a bona fide freakout today, imagining the absolute worst-case scenario—Tess, torn to pieces by some zealot with a bomb.

In his mind, as he'd run all that way—seven miles—he'd sifted through the rubble and dust and blood, collecting all that was left of her.

And when he'd seen her sitting there, alive and unharmed, he'd nearly fallen to his knees and wept.

That reaction had scared him almost as much as thinking she was dead.

So he'd made up that story about needing to get in touch with Tom Paoletti. And he'd erased the frantic message he'd left on her voice mail.

But she was Tess. Smart and sensitive and clever enough to put seventeen missed calls and one wild-eyed son of a bitch together, to figure out the truth.

And instead of looking her in the eye and admitting he was in uncharted territory and quite possibly losing his mind, he'd closed his eyes and pretended to go to sleep.

He could practically feel her frustration, her questions, her need to talk to him on that ride home.

But he'd kept his eyes tightly closed.

Then she did it. "Sleep," she whispered. "Really go to sleep, Jimmy, as long as your eyes are closed." And she'd started running her fingers through his hair. "My mom used to do this when I was little," she told him softly, "when I had trouble relaxing."

And somewhere between wherever they were and Rivka's, Jimmy had actually done it. He'd fallen asleep.

So completely that he didn't wake up when they went through the gate into Rivka's yard. And he didn't wake up when Tess lifted his head and replaced her lap with a mere pillow.

He'd slept for nearly six hours in that wagon, shaded by an umbrella that Guldana had dug out of the storage shed and watched over by Khalid, who sat nearby.

Tess, on the other hand, had spent all of those hours hard at work, tracking Dimitri and Sophia Ghaffari through cyberspace.

He'd woken up with a headache and a sense of panic— not a good combination.

Khalid had informed him that Decker had checked in and set up a meeting—this meeting—for seven o'clock. It was now 6:58 and the motherfucker was on the verge of being late. Again.

Jimmy himself had had just enough time to splash water on his face and go looking for Tess—to apologize for failing to assist her, for sleeping the entire day away. Christ, when was the last time he'd done that?

But she had already been on her way out to the barn. And before he could even open his mouth, she'd dropped that bomb about Will Schroeder.

"Sit down," she told Dave and Murphy now in that elementary schoolteacher tone that some women could do so well.

They sat, their inner eight-year-olds unable to defy her.

"They probably heard about that time in Istanbul when I threw Camilla Riccardo off the hotel roof," Jimmy volunteered.

Tess turned her ferocious glare on him. "Why do you say things like that?"

He was trying to regain control by being flip. It usually worked. He tried again, adding the smile that usually got him laid. "Because I love it when steam comes out of your ears."

She was unmoved. "You're just perpetuating the nasty rumors," she said as sternly as she'd spoken to Dave and Murph.

But schoolteachers had never frightened him, even as an eight-year-old. "Maybe I like the nasty rumors," he countered.

"Maybe you do," she threw back at him. "God forbid you ever allow yourself to feel too happy."

Jimmy laughed his disgust. "Don't even begin to psychoanalyze me, babe. You don't know me at all."

"I know," she said quietly. "You've made certain of that."

Decker closed the barn door behind him, and they all turned to look at him. Dave, Murphy, Nash, and Tess.

Sweet Tess.

Who, seconds earlier, had been standing there, looking at Nash with her heart in her eyes.

The tension in the barn was so thick it had practically formed a thunderhead churning in the rafters above them.

Nash was as close to becoming unglued as Decker had ever seen him. And Tess now looked as if she were about to break her own knuckles, she was clenching her fists so tightly. Anything to keep from bursting into tears.

Decker sighed.

She looked bone weary and miserable, as if the stress from the past few days was sucking the very life out of her.

It was entirely his fault.

For bringing her here.

And for leaving her alone with Nash last night. Nash,

who hadn't been able to keep his hands off of her despite Decker's threats. He'd confessed as much this morning.

She was all over me.

Jesus, blame it all on *her,* you weak-willed son of a bitch.

No doubt about it, he was going to kick Nash's ass, first chance he got. And get his own ass kicked right back, which was fine. He deserved it, fool that he was for thinking his warning would keep Nash away from Tess.

Decker had been too deep in his own misery this morning to register exactly how big of a goatfuck this entire mission had become, from every possible angle. Shit, where Nash and Tess were concerned, it had been a goatfuck before the word *go*.

Everything about this situation underlined the inherent wisdom of his policy to keep work and sex absolutely separate. If he ever had the chance to work for Tom Paoletti again—and as each hour slipped past, that seemed less and less likely—he was going to insist on leading only all-male teams.

That would handle the work part.

As for the sex . . .

Maybe in a year or two, Tess would be over her infatuation with Nash.

And maybe by then, Decker would have forgiven himself for taking advantage of Sophia Ghaffari.

Yeah. Maybe.

It would sure as hell help if he could find her and get her safely out of Kazbekistan.

"So my day sucked ass, too," he said, breaking the silence, and Murphy, bless him, laughed.

"Who's got good news for me?" Decker came farther into the barn. "What do you say, Dave? Can we pack it up and get the hell out of Dodge? Tell me please, sweet Jesus, that you found Sayid's laptop this afternoon."

Dave Malkoff shook his head. "Sorry, sir. I have nothing

concrete—just a whole lot of public opinion that seems to imply Sayid was, indeed, staying with Bashir for an undetermined amount of time before the quake."

Decker looked at Murphy. "Murph? You sitting on that missing laptop over there?"

"I wish. I'm still working on locating most of my contacts, boss. Although if you want some good news, Angel called. The caterer's agreed to do the wedding lunch for only twenty bucks a plate." He laughed. "I think she went into the negotiations flashing a few tattoos and packing some major heat. You can take the girl out of the gang, but you can never really take the gang out of the girl."

"Why do I get the sense that you wouldn't dare call Angelina a girl if you weren't halfway around the world from her?" Decker asked, glancing over at Nash, who had folded his arms across his chest and was leaning against the barn wall, pretending to relax.

"You got that right," Murphy agreed.

It was remarkable, really, how awful Nash looked. His clothes were stained with sweat and dirt. He was rumpled, as if he'd wrestled wild dogs in the dusty road before taking a long nap. Deck could see the line dividing clean from dirty near his partner's ears and around his jawline. Nash had splashed water on his face rather haphazardly, as if the intention had been to wake himself up rather than to wash.

Which meant that it was possible that Nash had actually slept for part of the afternoon.

Which might explain the current friction—current additional friction—between him and Tess. If she had let him sleep for more than the three and a half minutes that he usually allowed for a combat nap . . .

"I was approached by Will Schroeder today," Tess reported, her voice carefully void of all emotion as she sat on an overturned bucket. "Since he already knew that you and James weren't your average relief aid workers and threatened to make that public knowledge, I made a deal with him."

And so much for Decker's theory about the too-long nap. She'd made a deal with Will Schroeder. Jesus. He didn't dare look at Nash.

"I told him the truth—about Sayid. I thought our not getting kicked out of K-stán was more important than any one member of our group's . . . discomfort at the idea of working with Schroeder," Tess continued, carefully not looking at Nash either. "The pros seemed to outweigh the cons. He gets an exclusive story—but only when we're ready to give it to him. We get his silence—and an extra set of eyes and ears out there. As long as he follows our rules—"

Nash couldn't keep silent another second. "What makes you think he's going to follow *your* rules, when he's never followed anyone's rules before?" he asked, pretending to laugh, pretending he was merely amused. But then he shook his head. "Never mind. It's too late. We'll just have to clean up this mess *after* the shit hits the fan." He turned to Decker, still trying to play it übercool.

Although Deck knew his partner well enough to know that beneath that oh-so-casual attitude, Nash was beyond pissed off. He was, as Nash himself so aptly described it, on the verge of shitting monkeys.

"Unless you want me to make a preemptive strike," Nash continued, now speaking directly to Deck. "I could find Schroeder and take him out of the equation."

Tess made a disgusted sound as she looked at Nash for the first time since Decker came into the barn. "Right. Decker's going to tell you to go and *kill* Will Schroeder—"

Nash turned and smiled at her. His smile didn't quite hide the fact that the muscle in his jaw was jumping. "I wasn't talking about killing him, although now that you mention it, that does sound appealing," he countered. "But no, I was thinking more in terms of a back alley ambush. A concussion and a broken jaw'll get him sent back to the States. Although I better give him a broken leg, too, don't you think? He's a persistent prick. A nice rap with a length of pipe, right beneath his knee'll keep him from doing any international traveling for a good long—"

"Stop," Tess said, her eyes looking very large in a face that was far too drawn and pale. "No one here thinks you're even remotely funny."

Murphy shifted his weight, but wisely kept his mouth shut.

Again Decker broke the silence. And changed the subject. Taking sides was not going to help the team dynamic right now—although he was securely with Tess on this one. Will was a potential threat that she'd done her best to keep contained. "Needless to say, I didn't locate Sophia Ghaffari. Any luck finding info we can use to track her? Tess?"

His comspesh stopped glaring at Nash and turned her attention to a pad of paper that she pulled up off the floor and onto her lap. "I don't know, sir. I've got what seems like a lot of useless details. Hers and Dimitri's last known address and phone number." She looked up at him. "I tried calling, but the entire landline system's down.

"I've got Ghaffari's business address—same as his home." She pulled some loose pages from the back of the pad and stood up, heading toward him as she continued to speak. "I did a cross-reference, and found that Furkat Nariman and his family are currently residing at chez Ghaffari, and that a transfer of property ownership was put into his name five weeks ago. Nariman is one of Padsha Bashir's closest advisors. He also happens to be an outspoken advocate of GIK support of al-Qaeda."

She handed Decker three pages, copies of documents printed out from her computer, then stood close enough to point to the signature line on the first.

She smelled like Emily. Well, okay, not exactly like Em, just similar enough. Like a clean American woman—like sweet shampoos and fresh-scented deodorant.

Sophia Ghaffari had smelled like a soap scented with herbs and spices that were more exotic, more like the musky aroma of incense—at least to his American nose. Whatever it was, it hadn't completely masked the sharper smell of heat and sweat.

Of fear.

"Here's where the document should have been signed by the previous owner—Ghaffari," Tess pointed out.

Decker focused on the paper before him. It had been signed in a loopy and distinctive hand, the name quite clear—Padsha Bashir.

"Shit," Decker said.

Nash came over to look, too. Dave and Murphy were right behind him.

"And check *this* out." Tess pulled the second sheet onto the top. "I hacked into Ghaffari's bank records. His accounts, both business and personal, to the tune of over a half million U.S. dollars—" Murph let out a low whistle as Tess pointed to the line that read U.S. $537,680.58. "—were emptied and closed on the exact same date as that property transfer," she told them.

"And lookie who signed the withdrawal slip," Murphy said, tapping the page with a finger that was twice the size of Tess's.

"Padsha Bashir," Tess said. "Again."

Dimitri Ghaffari was dead. Sophia had told Decker the truth, at least about that. This was proof enough. In order for those finances to be transferred the way they had, Dimitri Ghaffari had to be dead.

"He just signed both of these documents as if the house and that money were his. And look at this." Tess flipped to the third page. "Across town, just an hour later that same day, there's a neat little deposit into Bashir's account. Same exact dollar amount. He didn't try to alter it or hide it or—"

"Why should he?" Nash cut in. "The money, the house— it *was* his."

Tess still didn't get it. She looked at Nash as if he were speaking Dutch.

"He married her," Nash said tersely.

Dave was more exact. "Padsha Bashir married Sophia Ghaffari. At which point everything she owned became his."

Tess shook her head. "But there was no marriage certificate."

"There wouldn't be," Dave told her, "at least not one documented in computer records. Not if it was done in a religious ceremony."

"And from what we know of Bashir," Nash added, "it was a religious ceremony. Probably done within minutes of Mrs. Ghaffari achieving her widowhood."

"Minutes? My God," Tess realized. "Are you saying that Bashir killed Dimitri Ghaffari and then . . . ?"

Instead of being indicted for murder, he'd married Sophia— and gained complete possession of Dimitri's home, Dimitri's money.

Dimitri's wife.

Sophia had told Decker she'd been a prisoner in Bashir's palace for two months.

Two *months*.

She'd *told* him. She'd asked for help, and he treated her with suspicion and mistrust.

"Did you find any information that might help me locate Sophia now?" Decker asked Tess.

She looked down at her notepad, shaking her head. "It doesn't look good. I found two previous addresses. Various shipping and import permits—records of fees paid, that sort of thing. A long list of mentions in the weekly English-language newspaper—gossip column stuff. Lots of background on Ghaffari. He went to school in France, worked for a few years at an uncle's import business in Athens, spent five years in the Greek islands, running some kind of windjammer-type cruise business—you know, high-class cruises on sailboats for tourists? That was right before he came to Kazabek."

"Oh, man," Murphy said. "You ever been to Greece? It's gorgeous. All blues and greens and white sand. To willingly leave that for the Pit . . . You'd have to be crazy. Or running from the law."

"Or in love," Dave suggested.

Murphy and Nash turned and looked at him. Decker, too. It was such a non-Dave thing to say.

"What?" Dave said defensively.

Tess was the only one who took it in stride. "Yes," she agreed. "That's my guess, too. Especially since shortly after his arrival in Kazabek, when Ghaffari makes his first appearance in the newspaper gossip column, he's accompanied by his, quote, beautiful American wife, unquote."

She looked at Decker then, and he knew from her hesitation that she was about to hit him with bad news.

"This is already more information than I'd hoped for," he said.

"Yeah, well . . . I found very little mention of Sophia at all," she reported. "There's no record of their wedding, no engagement announcement, nothing like that—and I searched Greek, French, and U.S. databases as well. Almost any time her name appears on Kazbekistani documents, she's Sophia Ghaffari. Without knowing her maiden name, there's no way I can find out where she came from—and I'm having no luck finding it. I mean, someone knows it. Someone *has* to know it."

"Yeah, well, there's no guarantee that knowing her maiden

name would provide us with any information we could use to locate her right now," Decker tried to reassure her.

"I actually attempted to run a search for Sophia, born in the United States between 1965 and 1980, and came up with just under a trillion possible matches." She made a noise of intense disgust. "Of course, that's assuming both that she was born in the States, *and* that Sophia was the name her parents put on her birth certificate."

"Let me see that first list of addresses," Nash ordered. "Maybe we can get a sense of the Kazabek neighborhoods she's familiar with."

"It's not a list." Tess handed it to him. "There're only two."

"Two's better than none," Nash told her.

"I'm sorry," Tess told Decker as Nash opened a map of the city, spreading it on Murphy's bale of hay. "I wish I had better news for you. You know, I thought I was onto something with the gossip columns—one week the newspaper ran a photo and called them 'Dimitri and Miles Ghaffari.' I thought that might've been a typo—you know, that somehow her maiden name got used instead of her given name. But I got nothing from searching for Sophia Miles—I even tried alternate spellings. And another week they were called 'Mr. and Mrs. Farrell Ghaffari.' But Sophia Farrell came up blank, too—"

"What?" Dave cut her off. "Wait, I was only half listening."

"I said Sophia Farrell came up—"

"No," he said. "Before that. You said . . . Did you say *Miles*?"

"Yeah," she said. "But I got nothing from it. I think it was just, you know, editorial brain farts on the part of the typesetters. This newspaper obviously didn't spend a lot of money paying proofreaders. It was amazing how many

times they misspelled both Dimitri and Ghaffari. And
sometimes she was Sophia, sometimes Sophie, sometimes
Saphia—"

"Did you run Miles Farrell?" Dave asked her. He had
such a peculiar expression on his face that hope sparked inside Decker.

Tess blinked at him. "No."

"I mean, you did say it was possible that Sophia wasn't
her given name," Dave said. "And although I didn't know
a Sophia Farrell or a Sophia Miles, I did know a Miles Farrell a few years ago. She'd be about the right age. And she
was definitely American."

Murphy laughed, clearly tickled. "Davey, Davey. You are
determined to win MVP for this op, aren't you, dog?"

Across the room, Nash stopped looking at the map. "You
said you didn't recognize that newspaper photo of Sophia
Ghaffari."

"I didn't. But I wouldn't have. I never actually saw Miles,"
Dave said. "When I dealt with her, she always wore a full
burka. Never took off her veil. I think it made her feel more
secure. I didn't blame her—God forbid she's seen talking to
someone who's later IDed as CIA, you know?"

Jesus, that hope that had started as a tiny spark now
filled Decker's chest and damn near clogged his throat. He
had to keep himself from grabbing Dave by the shirt and
shaking him. "So she worked for you?"

"She provided information, yes. But she never accepted
any kind of payment," Dave said. "Which was very un-
usual. On top of that, everything she ever gave me was
golden. She apparently had access to people and places. . . .
She was the first person to tell me that the American embassy was pulling out. I'm telling you, she knew about it
before I did. I'm sure it must've felt to her like we were deserting her—deserting all the Americans in K-stan. Which,
of course, we were. A few weeks later the K-stan govern-

ment was overthrown, and the U.N. just sat back and let it happen. Most of the people who'd been working with us—working for democracy and freedom—were killed. I tried to contact her before I left Kazabek. I waited at the rendezvous point for three hours, but she never showed."

Contact. Rendezvous point. Holy fuck. Holy, holy fuck. Maybe there was a God, and maybe Decker was going to get a chance to make things right.

More right than the current fucked-up tangle of wrong he had wrapped around his throat.

"Because I never heard from her, I was afraid she was a casualty," Dave continued. "But maybe she's still alive. Maybe she and this Sophia are one and the same. It makes sense. Someone in Sophia Ghaffari's social and business circle would have had access to the right people, to the kind of information Miles gave me—"

Nash was thinking the same thing Decker was, only Nash had retained his ability to speak. And somehow he knew that Decker needed help.

"How did you contact her?" Nash interrupted Dave, who was just starting to warm up to his new theory. "Did she have a way to contact you?"

Dave blinked at Nash in total surprise. Flap, flap, with eyelashes that were ridiculously long for a man. Decker had never noticed that before, or the fact that Dave's eyes were green, not brown. Each blink seemed to take an eternity. Flap, flap, flap. Five lifetime-long blinks before Dave turned to Decker. And spoke two of the sweetest words he'd ever heard in his entire life.

"Of course."

The shopkeepers in the marketplace confirmed what Sophia had overheard last night from Michel Lartet—that the Grande Hotel had been structurally damaged.

Access to Kazabek's tallest building had been cut off

from the street. In fact, that entire part of the downtown area was off-limits to both the general population and peacekeeping troops alike.

It wasn't so much a matter of *if* the building would fall, but rather *when*.

Aftershocks still shook the city, and everyone Sophia spoke to seemed confident that the hotel was a death trap, waiting to topple.

As she sat outside a shelter that was opening for the night in one of the most conservative mosques in City Center, she adjusted her veil so that she could gaze up at the Grande Hotel. It gleamed in the distance, its windows reflecting the golds and reds of the setting sun.

From here, it looked no different than it had the first time she'd seen it, on her first visit to Kazabek with her parents, all those years ago. It had been shining and pristine, with room service inside and limousines out front, and she'd gazed at it wide-eyed from the backseat of the taxi as they'd driven past.

Years later, she and Dimitri had spent their wedding night in the bridal suite. The circular driveway had been partitioned off from the street with concrete dividers to keep car bombers at bay, and the limos were few and far between. The fact that the power went out regularly in rolling blackouts helped hide the shabbiness and decay—not that she'd cared.

Dizzy with the knowledge that Dimitri had followed her to Kazabek, that he was willing to give up everything—everything—just to be with her, she'd been hopelessly in love.

Foolishly in love.

Much like the Kazabek Grande Hotel, Sophia would look the same now, too, to someone who had known her seven years or even two months ago. Prettier than she had a right to be for a woman with a brain, as Michel Lartet had so often told her.

But inside, she was structurally damaged.

Had she escaped certain death this morning thanks to the whim of that American? Or had she survived only because he didn't fully comprehend the enormity of the reward Bashir's nephews had surely posted for her return?

Or had his intention all along been to help her—help he would have given regardless of whether she serviced him, help he no longer cared to provide after she'd tried to put a bullet in his brain?

Had she lost her chance to be rescued because she'd forgotten what it was like to live in a world where heroes still existed, where help came for free?

Oh, how she wanted to go home.

But her home was inhabited by strangers.

And Dimitri was dead.

She'd come the closest she'd ever come today to her own death. All day, as she alternately ran through the city or hid, sleeping only in brief snatches, she thought about that moment in the hotel bathroom, where she had been ready to choose immediate death over return to Bashir's palace.

Right now, that choice was hers to make any time, at any given moment.

She had a handful of bullets for each of those two guns the American had returned to her. But she'd need only one.

Well, two, actually.

One for Michel Lartet.

Killing him would be easy enough to do.

In theory, at least.

Sophia sat and watched the volunteers at the mosque set up a sign bidding all in need to enter.

She knew that inside the walls of this mosque, her desire to spend the night covered by her robe and veil would be respected.

But the thought of spending the night completely covered—in this suffocating heat—was unpleasant.

Still, she needed water. Food.

She would have both of those things here.

What she wouldn't find was a place to lay her head where her heart wasn't filled with fear.

It was only a matter of time before Bashir's men started searching these shelters, looking for her. And unlike the Muslim clerics, they would not hesitate before tearing off a woman's veil.

If she went to the Grande, she could sleep undisturbed—provided the building didn't fall.

She'd have access to Western clothes there—assuming the boutique in the lobby hadn't gone out of business in the past two months. The hotel also had a store that sold bottled water, so she'd have plenty to drink, as well as sundries.

She'd always loved that American word—sundries.

Aspirin and cold medicine and toothpaste. Things travelers might've forgotten to pack. Makeup and breath mints and hair care products. Shampoo and blow dryers.

Hair dye.

Sophia got up slowly, careful not to jar her side, to aggravate her most recent collection of bruises, and started to walk. Away from the mosque's promised sanctuary. Toward the Grande Hotel. She could get inside easily, despite the guards and the area's restrictions.

She knew a way in through an underground tunnel that began in the basement of the Sulayman Bank Building, seven blocks to the south. The bank owner's son, Uqbah, had visited Minneapolis during a trip to the United States and had come home raving over the underground system that allowed people to get around the city, untouched by inclement weather. He'd built a private route, traversable via golf cart, from his office to his favorite lunchtime spot at the Kazabek Grande Hotel.

Because it just wouldn't do for a sandstorm to keep him from his afternoon dalliance with his mistress.

They'd lunched together many times. Dimitri, Sophia, Uqbah, and his beautiful friend, Gennivive LeDuc, who lived in a suite right there at the hotel.

A devoted People's Party member whose message was diluted by his failure to cease his wasteful personal overspending, Uqbah had been killed in the days following the overthrow of the government and the warlords' return to power.

Weeks earlier, Genny LeDuc had packed her bags and left Kazabek on the same flight that took the American ambassadors to safety. She'd sent Sophia a postcard from the south of France.

Some people had all the luck.

With Sophia's current string of bad luck, the Kazabek Grande would fall the moment she set foot in the formerly opulent lobby.

Still, as far as death went, she preferred that to a beheading.

And it was far less definite in terms of being life-ending than a bullet from the barrel of her own gun. There was a chance that the hotel wouldn't fall at all, that she'd get in and out while the building still stood, that she would survive.

Even though she had to hurry to get to the financial district before curfew, she chose not to take a shortcut, going instead through Saboor Square.

Automatically checking the wall where she'd made her mark with a piece of limestone and . . .

Sophia stopped.

She wasn't supposed to stop. She knew that. It brought attention both to her and to the mark on the wall—to this

entire method of covert communication. To follow proce-
dure, she should walk right past. Circle around and walk
past again if she needed to, never giving the code on the
wall more than a cursory glance.

But she was out of breath from hurrying, pain burning
her side, and she bent down, pretending to adjust her san-
dal.

She had to count bricks, make sure she was checking the
right one. It had been so long, and of course the brick she
was supposed to use for her message changed, depending
on the date.

But that was indeed the mark she'd left several days
ago—a vertical line on the twelfth brick from the end, seventh up from the ground.

And that was definitely a horizontal line, bisecting hers.

An answering mark.

In years past, before the United States government and
the U.N. had pulled out of Kazbekistan, leaving the people
at the mercy of the warlords, that answering mark had
meant she should check the side of the butcher's shop. Made
of wood rather than bricks or stone, this was the neighborhood's bulletin board. In a society where most people still
didn't have telephones, everything from legal notices to birth
announcements to scribbled reminders to pick up fresh vegetables on the way home from work was posted there.

Sophia would look for a message tacked to that wall that
started with the words "Lost dog. Answers to the name
Spot." The message would contain a time and location—a
place where she and her unnamed CIA contact would meet.

She'd scribble an answering note right on the sheet. "I
have found your dog," meant she'd be there. "American,
go home!" meant she couldn't risk meeting him then.

But in the aftermath of the earthquake, the butcher's
wall was covered with flyers posted by people who were
searching for missing family members. A message about a

lost dog wouldn't last long. It would be pulled down to make room for more important matters.

Which was no doubt why, two bricks over, written in chalk on today's brick in fact, was a small Arabic numeral nine and the letter T, with a square around both of them.

Nine o'clock. At the Tea Room, here in Saboor Square.

They'd met there many times, she and her CIA friend.

Sophia made herself start walking again. She forced herself to keep breathing. She was feeling light-headed from lack of food, from fatigue, from pain. And from sudden overabundance of hope.

It was entirely possible that her worthless, battered ass was about to be saved.

CHAPTER
SEVENTEEN

Jimmy was lying on a bale of hay, arm thrown up and over his eyes, when Tess brought three cups of coffee into Rivka's barn. She set one down nearby, careful not to disturb him, and he didn't let on that he wasn't asleep.

"You okay?" she asked Decker quietly as she handed him a cup.

Deck smiled. Shook his head. Laughed. He was obviously still embarrassed as hell. "I don't know. I hate waiting. I'm not very good at it. And I'm . . . pretty nervous."

Tess glanced over at Jimmy again before she sat down cross-legged next to Decker, right there on the dusty floor. "Maybe I should've made decaf."

"No, this is great," Deck said. "This is . . ." Jimmy could see the muscle in his jaw jump as he made himself meet her gaze. "Very nice of you. Thank you."

"Dave'll find Sophia and bring her back here," Tess reassured him.

Deck forced another smile and said, "I know. He's been a valuable asset to this team."

They were both so freaking unbelievably nice. In fact, they were *the* top two genuinely nicest human beings Jimmy had ever met, and had this been another time and another place, he might've given in to the urge to shout at the pair of them to give up and just go get married, for the love of God.

How could Tess not see that Decker was crazy about her?

But now was probably not the time to put that topic of discussion out on the table.

Not after Decker had announced, right smack during a meeting no less, that he'd had a sexual encounter—holy shit—with Sophia Ghaffari that very morning, during a power struggle that had gotten out of hand.

And sainted Mary, Mother of God, how hard had *that* been to do? To stand there in front of an audience that included Tess Bailey and . . .

He'd told an almost no-detail version of what had happened, putting the blame on himself.

"I'm sorry if I've embarrassed you," Deck had said, "but Tess had to know why I need her to be in the room with me when Dave brings Sophia back here tonight. I didn't want there to be any surprises. What I did was stupid and wrong—"

Tess cut him off. Her cheeks had been tinged with pink that Jimmy had first thought was from embarrassment. "What *she* did was wrong. You said no."

Decker shook his head. "Apparently not with enough conviction."

Tess was unconvinced. And very fierce. That was anger coloring her cheeks. Anger at Sophia. "No means no. Why should the rules be different for women than they are for men?"

"I should have walked away," Decker said, refusing to forgive himself.

"Yes," Tess agreed. "You should have. But she shouldn't have—"

Decker cut her off. "She did what she did because she felt threatened. I should have figured that out. She's not the bad guy here."

"You aren't either," Jimmy had told him, but it was pretty obvious that Deck didn't believe him.

"He told me he's hoping to get a permanent assignment as part of your team," Tess told Decker now. They were still talking about Dave Malkoff.

"He should be leading his own team," Decker countered.

"He doesn't want to," Tess said. "And he's vehement about it." She laughed. "You would have thought I was suggesting he stick needles in his eyes. I was, like, 'Keep breathing, Dave—no one's going to force you to be a team leader if you don't want to be one.' "

The barn started to shake. Aftershock.

"I guess he doesn't want the responsibility." Deck laughed, but it was without humor. "Right about now, I can't say I blame him."

They were all getting blasé about the aftershocks that regularly rocked the city. Jimmy didn't bother to move as Decker stood and hung the kerosene lantern from a hook on one of the overhead beams. It could hang there and swing without any danger of being knocked over.

"I think it's because he knows his own strengths and weaknesses," Tess told Deck as the world stopped shaking. "Dave's very good at some things, but his people skills really do need work. He doesn't inspire supreme confidence across the board—the way you do."

Decker was silent, just looking at her, rubbing his forehead as if he had one bitch of a headache. He glanced over at Jimmy, as if trying to decide whether he really was asleep.

So Jimmy moved his foot. Just a little. Just enough to let Decker know that he was conscious and listening.

"What happened this morning was, um—," Decker started, but then stopped and swore softly.

Tess was holding her own mug of coffee with both hands. "You don't owe anyone an explana—"

"I don't do that," he said. "I don't want you to think that I make a habit of—"

"I don't," she said. "Deck, believe me, no one does. But even if you did, so what? If it was Jimmy who . . . Well, does anyone think less of James because he *does* make a habit of—"

"Yes," Decker said. "There are definitely people who think less of him. *I* think less of him for the way he treated you."

Tess was silent.

Jimmy had his eyes closed—he was barely even breathing at this point. He knew that Deck was disappointed in him, but it was still remarkable how much it stung to hear him speak those words. *I think less of him. . . .*

He sensed more than saw Tess glance over at him. When she finally spoke, she'd lowered her voice.

"I knew exactly who he was when I invited him in that night," she told Decker. "Don't you dare think that he took advantage of me, because he didn't. If anything, I took advantage of him. It's just . . . things don't always work out the way you plan, you know? Sophia—she did what she did because she wanted to get her gun in her hand. But she didn't factor shooting and missing into her plan. There were things about my night with James that I didn't factor in either. I didn't expect to like him so much—to keep on liking him after we, you know, hooked up. I thought there'd be an ick factor—like, he'd be all fake and, I don't know, smarmy, I guess. And then I'd be kind of relieved when he left in the morning. But . . ." She laughed. "I liked him. I still like him. He's . . ."

Jimmy held his breath.

"Sweet," she said.

What? It took everything he had not to laugh out loud. That was like calling an alligator cuddly.

"It sounds stupid," Tess continued, "but he is. He tries

to hide it but . . . he's a good person, a good man. And he's in bigger trouble than you know, by the way."

"Actually," Decker said, "he's way better off than I thought."

Jimmy had expected him to question her. Trouble? What the fuck? He wasn't in *trouble*. But saying that he was better off than Decker thought? What did *that* mean?

Shit.

"But talk about things I didn't factor in," Tess said. "I never in a million years expected to be working so closely with him again. With either of you."

They fell silent then, just sipping their coffee. Jimmy could smell the cup Tess had brought out for him. He wanted it, but he couldn't possibly sit up now.

"I'm sorry I agreed to let you come here," Decker said quietly.

"I'm not," she said. No hesitation. But again she laughed. "Jimmy probably is, though."

She was right. Jimmy was very, *very* sorry. About too many things to count.

"I pretty much threw myself at him this morning," she told Decker. "He's not . . . He didn't want to, but we were trying to make it look like . . . and I took it too far. God." She laughed. Or maybe this time it was a sigh. "You're not the only one capable of making stupid mistakes, you know. We didn't even have a condom. It was beyond stupid, and now he's completely freaked out. About everything."

How could she sit there and tell Deck about that? Did she get off on twisting him totally into a knot? God *damn*, Jimmy had told her that Deck had a thing for her and . . .

But, of course, she now assumed Jimmy had been wrong. It wouldn't occur to her that Deck was nuts about her despite the fact that he'd gone and let Padsha Bashir's runaway bride give him a face dance. It wouldn't occur to her that it was, in fact—in Jimmy's mind at least—proof positive of Decker's deep affection for Tess.

Decker was silent. Probably drawing and quartering Jimmy in his mind.

"Will you do me a favor?" Tess asked him. "When he wakes up, will you reassure him that it's never going to happen again? I was half asleep and . . . He's made it really clear that he's not interested, so . . ."

"Yeah," Decker said. "I'll make sure he knows."

"Thanks. We're all under a lot of stress—you even more than the rest of us. I just . . . I wanted you to know that you're not the only one who's had a lapse in judgment."

"Yeah," he said. "I am aware of that. It seems to be contagious."

Jimmy heard her stand up. "I'm going to get more coffee. Want anything from the kitchen?"

"No," he said. "I'm good. Thanks."

Jimmy heard Tess walk across the barn, heard the door open and then close behind her.

"You know," Decker told him, before he, too, stood up and walked away, "you're an even bigger asshole than I am."

There was a light burning in the barn.

Sophia saw it from the yard and hesitated just inside the gate. If she could see it, the police patrols could, too.

But then she realized that it was okay. These people weren't hiding. They were allowed to be here. They could have the lights on.

The man behind her touched her arm. Until he'd spoken to her after materializing like a sudden apparition in the Tea Room's outdoor garden, she hadn't recognized him as the short-haired CIA agent in the ill-fitting dark suits she'd dealt with all those years ago. But the sound of his voice

had erased her doubt that the two radically different looking men were one and the same.

"I'd like to introduce you to our Kazbekistani hosts only
after we get you cleaned up and dressed in American clothing," he—Dave—said now.

Yes. That was smart. Sophia saw that there was a light
coming from the house, too. The door to the kitchen was
open, and she could see people moving around inside.

Their hosts. As in K-stani citizens. Did they support Padsha Bashir? They probably did. Most Kazbekistanis kept
their heads down and supported whoever was currently in
power. Supporting the opposition could get a person killed.

There was a lot in Kazabek that could get a person
killed. Like standing in a yard and catching the attention of
people with an allegiance only to keeping their families
alive. People whose lives would be changed by the blood
money from a warlord's hefty reward.

She had to keep alert. She wasn't out of danger, not by
any means.

"I'll need to color my hair before I meet anyone." Sophia
spoke just as softly as he had.

"We've already thought of that," he told her. "We've got
everything we need to darken your hair right in the barn."

We.

"Who's we?" she asked. She should have asked before
this. But she had been so relieved to see him, she'd actually
fallen into his arms and hugged him like a long-lost brother.
And when he'd told her they needed to get to safety, that he
had a place they could go to talk, she'd followed.

"We'll talk inside," he said, gesturing toward the barn
with his head.

So she followed Dave again—he'd actually told her his
name, which either meant the CIA had had a policy change,
or he was no longer with that particular alphabet agency—
silently across the yard.

The barn door opened, and an American woman was there to help hurry her inside. Through her heavy veil, Sophia caught only a glimpse of a round female face, a face that looked as if it could belong to Shirley Temple's even sweeter granddaughter.

A quick glance around revealed that they were sharing this barn with a tired-looking horse. It was a rustic building, part wood, mostly stone and clay. A lamp hung from one of the beams, and the light didn't shine into the far reaches of the barn. Still, she could see that there was someone—a man—sitting back in the shadows.

"Who's we?" she asked again. She sensed more than saw someone else behind her, someone besides Dave, hidden from her view by the folds of her burka and this blasted veil.

"Friends," Dave told her. "We're friends."

"My name is Tess," the woman told her. "The first thing I'd like to do is take you into one of the horse stalls, sit you down, and see if you need medical attention. Is that all right with you?"

"You're safe here." Dave's familiar voice came from behind her again. "You can take off your veil."

"She's probably a little overwhelmed," Tess told him—understatement of the century. She moved directly in front of Sophia, making sure she could be seen. "I'm sure you'll take it off when you're ready." She smiled. "It's very warm in here, and I apologize for that, but all the doors and windows are shut so no one can see in. No one can see you. You *are* safe now."

Sophia realized she was clinging to her veil with one hand. Her other was hidden in the folds of her robe, wrapped around the larger of her two guns, finger on the trigger.

Tess kept on talking, her voice musical and reassuring. "I'm not a medic, unfortunately. I can really only handle basic first aid. Scrapes and the like. Murphy's our medicine man. He's very good. A former Marine—"

"No such thing," a new voice, a man's voice interrupted, not from behind her, where Dave still was, but from the side. She hadn't seen anyone over there. He, too, moved so that she could see him. He was racially mixed, very tall and wide, with a smile that was nearly as friendly as Tess's. "Once a Marine, always a Marine."

"My bad," Tess said with a conspiratorial smile for Sophia. "Murph's a Marine. I know you're probably not thrilled at the idea of a male medic—I wouldn't be—but I'll stay with you. Okay? You're safe here. In every way."

Sophia found her voice. "I don't need medical attention."

Tess stepped to the side to start leading her toward the back of the barn, but Sophia could hear the smile in the younger woman's voice. "Good. That's good to hear. We don't have a lot of water to spare, so we can't offer you more than a sponge bath, but I do have some clothes I can lend you. They'll be a little large—I'm bigger than you—but they're clean."

"How many of you are there?" Sophia asked. She couldn't get a sense. And she wasn't going to take off this veil—or let go of her gun—until she had a better explanation for "Who's 'we'?" than "Friends."

"There are five of us," Tess told her.

Michel Lartet had been Dimitri's friend.

Sophia stopped walking, and Tess, no doubt astute enough to realize she needed more reassurance, moved in front of her again.

"You've met me," Tess said, "and Dave, and there's Murphy and Nash and . . ."

The ghost of an odd look crossed her face. It was little more than a hesitation, but it was enough to push Sophia over the edge and into deep suspicion. Especially since Dave's words from out in the yard came back to her with a rush—*We've got everything we need to darken your hair. . . .*

How did he know she was blond? He'd never seen her— not even once—without her burka and veil. And Tess spoke to her as if she knew who she was, yet Dave had never known her as anything but Miles Farrell.

"And Decker," Tess was saying, but Sophia spoke right over her.

"Tell your *friends* not to touch me—tell them to move back!" Her voice came out sounding very sharp.

Tess looked behind Sophia. "Give her space," she warned whoever was back there, before speaking to Sophia. "No one's going to hurt you."

"Yeah, but if I don't get some answers, I'm going to hurt *you*," Sophia told her, bringing her gun up and out. It flashed—a reflection from the lamp overhead—as she aimed it at Tess.

"Nash—don't!" Tess barked. She looked back at Sophia, her hands held out slightly in front of her but down low, re-assuringly. She completely ignored the gun. "Sophia, what questions do you want answered?"

Screw this veil. It made it impossible to see—and this Tess woman had just answered one of her biggest questions: Did they know who she really was?

Apparently, yes.

"Tell your *friends* to move—slowly!—to where I can see them," Sophia ordered as she pulled off her veil with one swift yank. "Tell them if they get too close, I *will* shoot you. Tell them to keep their hands in sight."

She'd been sweating beneath her burka, and her hair was soaked and sticking to the sides of her head, to her face.

"No one's going to hurt you," Tess was repeating.

"Shit, Dave," she heard one of the men say—not Murphy, but another. "You didn't check her for weapons?"

"Sophia, listen to me," Tess said, her smile long gone. "We're not officially connected to any government organization—U.S. government, that is. We're civilians."

Dave and Murphy and another man—movie-star handsome, with dark, wavy hair—moved into view. They were carefully keeping their hands where she could see them.

"I was rescuing her," Dave said. "I didn't think I had to—"

The movie star let loose a string of unprintable words. "Tess, for Christ's sake, at least move back!"

"We're Americans," Tess continued, moving not at all, "who work for a private company which is, in turn, contracted by the U.S. government. We want to help you, Sophia. We're going to get you out of Kazbekistan."

It sounded good. It sounded better than good. But how did she know it wasn't just a story they'd made up? An attempt to get her to go—compliantly—to Bashir's palace.

The movie star kept his hands in sight, and still moving slowly, he stepped directly in front of Tess, putting his body between her and Sophia's gun. Some of the tension left his handsome face. "Decker *said* she was armed."

"Decker," Sophia repeated. Tess had said the fifth member of their group was named Decker.

"What was I supposed to do, Nash?" Dave was pissed. "Force her to surrender her weapons? Or maybe you think I should have knocked her onto the concrete and cuffed her there at the Tea Room? Heck of a way to reassure her she was safe."

"If you're going to stand in front of me, don't talk *about* her, talk *to* her." Now Tess was angry, too.

But only four people stood in front of Sophia. "Where's this Decker?" She looked toward the corner, where she'd caught a glimpse of that man when she'd first come in. He'd moved closer, his hands up, but he was still in shadow.

"I'm Decker," he said, in a voice she'd heard before. It was . . . No, it couldn't be.

But he stepped into the light, and it most certainly was. "If you have to aim that weapon at someone, Sophia, aim it at me."

"You," she breathed. It was indeed the American. From Lartet's bar.

From this morning at the Français.

Oh, God.

Ah, God.

During their scuffle this morning, Decker had given Sophia Ghaffari a black eye.

And, from the way she was standing, left arm wrapped around her torso as if holding herself together, he'd probably also broken one or two of her ribs.

"Remember this morning, when I said that I wanted to help you?" he asked her now.

She didn't move. She just stared at him.

"I meant it," he told her. "I still mean it. I'm going to help you. But you've got to help me a little here, too— you've got to start by lowering your weapon before you accidentally hurt one of my friends."

Sophia glanced over at Nash, who was still shielding Tess—bless him.

Decker wanted that sidearm pointed in a different direction *now*. It was a small enough caliber, but at close range it could really do some damage.

But Sophia didn't lower the damn thing, and Nash didn't back off. In fact, if Decker knew Nash—and Decker did— he was about to move *toward* both Sophia and that little handgun.

Decker held up one hand, a silent order to Nash and the rest of the team to keep back. Wrestling Sophia to the floor of the barn would certainly give them possession of her weapon. But there definitely was a better way to do this.

One that didn't include Murphy sewing shut the latest extra hole in Nash's body.

"Think, Sophia," Deck told her. "If we were going to hand you over to Bashir, we would have done it already. I mean, why bring you back here? Why not just have Bashir's men pick you up at the Tea Room?"

It was a damn good question.

"I don't know." As she looked up at him again, he saw what most people would think were mere tears in her eyes. But he recognized it for what it really was.

Hope.

Thank God.

He kept talking. "You know, I busted my ass trying to find you again." He nodded at the questions he could read on her face. "Yeah, I did. We all did. Tess, in particular, deserves some serious overtime pay. But truth is, it was dumb luck—Dave knowing you. You knowing Dave." He paused, letting that sink in, then pushed it. "You never had reason to mistrust him before, did you?"

She shook her head.

Come on, Sophia, lower that weapon. . . . "Dave, tell her we're not going to let Padsha Bashir anywhere near her," Decker ordered, his eyes never leaving her face.

"Bashir will never so much as *touch* you again, so help me God." Dave's normally flat voice rang with emotion, and Decker realized that the former CIA operative must have had detailed knowledge of what the rest of them could only imagine—just what it had been like for Sophia to live in Bashir's palace for all those weeks.

"You're safe now," Tess said softly.

The tears in Sophia's eyes were dangerously close to the overflow point.

"Lower your weapon," Deck told her. "And please put the

safety back on. Keep it holstered—both of your weapons—
will you? At least while you're here with my team."

And with that—the fact that he wasn't asking her to surrender her weapons—he won.

As she lowered the damn thing, tears slid down her face.
He wanted to cry, too.

Instead he kept on talking. "I have no idea if you've had
any training in the handling of this type of weapon," he
told her. "But it's been my experience that ignorance—or
even lack of experience—plus firearms often results in accidents of the very fatal kind."

"I'm good," she said, using one hand to quickly wipe her
face. "I usually don't miss." She squared her shoulders and
lifted her chin. "I guess I owe you an apology."

She really knew how to deliver a convincingly brilliant
Brave Little Soldier.

Decker shook his head. "No," he said. "I'm the one who
should apologize to you."

What was it about this woman that pushed all his warning buttons? Before they'd located her, he'd been worried
damn near sick. How could he have mistrusted her? How
could he have missed reading what must've been pure fear?
What was wrong with him? And how the fuck had he let
things get so completely out of hand between them?

But now that she was here, he was picking up all kinds
of weird vibes. She was still afraid—maybe of him, of them
all, of being caught. He wasn't sure of exactly what. But he
was sure that she was playacting again.

She was presenting herself to him—to them all—as the
person she thought they wanted her to be.

Jesus, she fascinated him.

Which was the answer to the question, *How the fuck
had he let things get so completely out of hand?*

"I didn't know who you were," Decker told her now.
"This morning. I couldn't be sure that you didn't work for

Bashir or one of the other warlords. I apologize for . . . hurting you, but I'm sure you can understand my need for caution."

As far as apologies went, that one was completely lame. An apology shouldn't include a "but."

Decker tried again. "Sophia, I am truly sorry for—"

She crumpled. She just went down, onto the floor. Decker didn't see it coming—he'd been watching her, and there was no indication at all that she was going to faint.

Before he could so much as blink, Murphy had scooped her into his arms.

"Bring her back this way," Tess ordered, reaching up to take the lamp down from the hook.

When Decker moved to follow, Nash blocked him.

"Let Tess," he said.

Tess saw Sophia's eyelids flutter as Murphy set her down on several bales of hay they'd dragged into the empty stall. The wooden half walls made it slightly more private than the rest of the barn. They'd brought in the team's first aid kit and a bucket of rainwater for washing. It was part medical examination room, part bathing area.

"I can do it," Sophia said, pushing Murphy's hands away from her robe. She looked up at Tess. "I don't want you in here."

"I think you should let Murphy stay and look you over, especially since you fainted," Tess pointed out, ignoring the fact that the other woman obviously meant that as a plural *you*.

But Sophia sat up. She didn't seem at all dizzy or groggy. If anything, it was her side that was hurting her. Her ribs. It was as if simply breathing hurt her.

Poor Deck. He'd surely noticed that, too. And the look in his eyes when he saw that bruise on Sophia's face . . .

He seemed to have forgotten the fact that Sophia had tried to kill him. Avoiding a bullet in the head seemed justification for a bruise or two.

"I didn't faint," Sophia said to Tess. "Not really. It just seemed like the easiest way to end the conversation. I was afraid he was going to apologize right in front of everyone for—" She cut herself off, shaking her head. "Clothes, water, antibacterial ointment," she said instead, gesturing to the supplies that were laid out. "I've got everything I need—I don't need help."

"What's best for a broken rib?" Tess asked Murphy.

"Really," Sophia said.

He shrugged. "Time and rest," he told Tess. "And a definite ban on Farrelly brothers movies. Laughing hurts like a bitch."

"I'll keep the jokes to a minimum," Tess said.

"Although some people claim it feels a little better with an Ace bandage wrap," he told her. "It's worth a try. Not too tight, though."

She nodded. "I'll call you if we need you."

"You sure?" he asked, his worry for her in his eyes. Sophia was still carrying a weapon. Or two.

Tess smiled at him. "Go."

"I don't want either of you to stay," Sophia said as Tess rummaged through the first aid kit, searching for the Ace bandages.

Her back to Sophia, Tess waited until Murphy was out of earshot before turning to face the other woman. "You could probably use help bandaging your feet," she said. "And I know you can't wrap that rib by yourself."

Despite the sweat and grime, Sophia Ghaffari was remarkably beautiful. It was her nose that completely made her face. It was slightly too large and somewhat uniquely shaped—just enough to change her from girlishly sweet to regal Queen of the Faeries. Heart-shaped face, clear blue eyes, baby-smooth skin, delicately graceful mouth . . .

Okay, don't think about where Sophia Ghaffari's mouth had been.

Sophia was examining Tess's face just as intently. "You have quite the little fan club," she said.

Tess smiled. "They do tend to be overprotective."

"For good reason. They don't call Kazbekistan 'the Pit' for nothing," Sophia told her. "Is that ring you're wearing for real? Because a wedding ring doesn't offer the same amount of protection here that it used to. In fact, you might be safer taking it off."

"It's real," Tess told her. Decker had thought it best not to share all their secrets with Sophia. "And it's crazy, really. I just got married—I'm in way over my head."

"Not to Dave, I hope. He's just too cute. I've got him at the very top of my short list of second husbands—third. Third husbands." Sophia laughed. "Although maybe he'd rather wait to be number five or six. Maybe by then I'll get it right—figure out a way to keep 'em from dying on me."

How could she make a joke about that? "No, not Dave," Tess said.

"And it's definitely not Murphy. The vibe I got from him was more devoted friend." Sophia said. "That leaves Decker and what's his name. Mr. I'm Too Sexy for My Shirt."

"Jim. It's Jimmy," Tess told her, even as Sophia continued to talk.

"Can you believe that out of all of the great music produced each year in the U.S., that song, along with 'YMCA' and 'Achy Breaky Heart,' continued to be the top requested karaoke CDs right up until the bars were shut down? My husband owned an import business—music, books, movies, clothes. Pretty much anything American. Pop-Tarts. He brought in a shipment of Pop-Tarts once, made a killing. A real killing."

Sophia fell silent, just shaking her head. She'd zoned out, staring at nothing, temporarily caught in the past.

And Tess knew. It was all an act. The breezy conversation, the big smiles—Sophia Ghaffari was as big a poser as James Nash.

"Do you need help getting those sandals off?" Tess asked her briskly.

"Oh. Thanks. No." They were loose enough so that Sophia could slip them off without bending over to unfasten them. They hit the floor, one at a time. "I'm not going to get rid of you, am I?" she asked, looking up at Tess with her very blue eyes.

Tess moved the sandals aside. "Nope. Sorry."

"This is really strange, you know. Being here. Talking to you. In English. I haven't seen another American woman in years, and . . . here you are. So . . . friendly. So . . . normal. You look like you might've stepped out of *Survivor*."

Tess laughed. "Is that what normal looks like these days?"

Sophia shook her head. "I don't know. I lost normal years ago. But I do know that normal American women don't look like the cast of *Friends*." She smiled and it didn't seem forced.

You do. Tess kept herself from saying it.

"Dimitri loved both of those shows." Sophia could really keep up both ends of a conversation. "Right up until satellite TV was outlawed. So, when exactly did you get married? You and . . . Jim, is it? Jim . . . Decker?"

Oh, dear. Sophia apparently thought that—

"Jimmy Nash," Tess quickly corrected her. "Decker's first name is Lawrence—although I don't think I've ever heard anyone call him that. At least not to his face. He's Decker. Or Deck. Or sir."

Sophia covered her face with her hands.

She wasn't crying—at least Tess didn't think she was. She just sat there, bent over, absolutely still. Tess wasn't even sure if she was breathing.

It was such a total contrast to her Kelly Ripa impersonation. "Are you all right?" Tess started to say.

And Sophia sat up, pulling her hands down so that she could look at Tess over her fingers, her mouth and nose still covered. "Thank goodness," she said, her voice muffled. "I thought . . ." She closed her eyes, shook her head. "Never mind."

"I know what you thought," Tess told her. "Decker told me what happened this morning—not to embarrass you," she added quickly, when Sophia looked up, aghast. "It was so I could reassure you that . . . I think he wanted you to know that you were as safe as possible here—from more than just Padsha Bashir."

Sophia—the real Sophia—looked back at her, her eyes haunted. "Why didn't he tell me who he was?" she whispered.

"How could he?" Tess said. It wasn't meant to be at all chiding, just an explanation. Complete trust was a rare and valuable commodity here in Kazbekistan. Surely Sophia knew that better than most. "You didn't believe him when he said he'd help you."

"You have no idea where I've been these past months, what I've—" Sophia's voice shook—no act. "The thought of going back there . . ."

"Actually, I do know where you've been." Tess thought of exactly what that property transfer meant, along with that withdrawal of funds from Dimitri Ghaffari's account, both signed by Padsha Bashir. Decker had said that it was likely Bashir had killed Sophia's husband in front of her. "I can imagine what it must've been like, living at Bashir's palace."

Sophia began unfastening her robe. Without a word, she took it off, along with the flimsy gauze dress she wore underneath.

And Tess knew that she was wrong. Before this moment, she absolutely could not have imagined what it had been like to be a prisoner—a possession—of Padsha Bashir.

The expression on Tess's face must have been more than Sophia could stand, because she tried to bring the poser back.

"I think we should cut my hair before we dye it," Sophia said, but her voice shook. "Don't you?"

Tess couldn't keep the tears from her eyes as she brought the water closer. "You really are safe now," she told the other woman.

"Yeah," Sophia said, but Tess knew that she didn't believe it.

Jimmy was just about to give up and go when Tess emerged from behind the pantry curtain.

"She's finally asleep." She looked from Decker to Jimmy. "I promised her one of us would be out in the kitchen all night."

Decker nodded. "I'll be here," he told her, speaking just as quietly.

Sophia wasn't the only one sleeping. Rivka and his wife had turned in hours ago and were fast asleep in the office up on the second floor.

"I'm heading out in just a few minutes," Jimmy told Tess. "Alone."

She barely even glanced at him. "Sophia is certain that Sayid wasn't staying at Bashir's palace."

Decker, however, looked at Jimmy long enough to send him a clear message. *You are the world's biggest idiot.*

Jimmy felt compelled to defend himself. "I'm just saying that I slept all day so I'm going out."

"She took the news pretty hard," Tess told Decker. "You know, that Bashir's still alive."

Deck nodded. Sighed.

"That palace is huge," Jimmy pointed out. "How can she be *certain*—"

"She is." This time he got a look from Tess that was hot with anger.

And okay, maybe Deck was right. Because only an idiot wouldn't have known that now was not the time to argue with the woman, let alone allow his words to drip with disbelief. "You're telling us that someone who was little more than a palace concubine *knew* what was going on in every corner of that—"

Tess cut him off again. "A palace concubine who was used—repeatedly—to *entertain* Bashir's important guests. Apparently the son of a bitch got off on debasing and humiliating some of his so-called wives—Sophia in particular. She said that out of all Bashir's guests, Sayid was . . ." Her voice shook. "He was a very religious man. Unlike the others, *he* never cut her."

"What?" Decker swore softly.

This time, even Jimmy managed to keep his big mouth shut.

Tears brimmed in Tess's eyes, and he realized that the look she'd shot him before wasn't anger—at least not anger at him.

Please, Jesus, don't let her cry. If she broke down and cried, he'd have to put his arms around her—how could he not? And once he had her in his arms, he wouldn't want to let her go. Self-indulgent prick that he was, he'd hang on to her way too long—long enough for her to realize that everything he'd said this morning was fiction.

The truth is, Tess, I don't want to sleep with you.

Yeah. Right. He didn't want to sleep with her, the world was flat, and Elvis was his father.

Although, considering his cheekbones and the fact that the King had surely visited New York City in 1968, the Elvis thing actually might've been true.

"Bashir essentially pimped her out," Tess told them, "but it wasn't just for sex. If they wanted to, any one of his esteemed guests could have killed her—and the only person who would've cared was the woman who came in to mop the blood off the floor. Imagine living like that. Never knowing, day to day, if you were going to be killed for sport—or just *merely* forced to . . . She told me Sayid didn't touch her, that he was deeply religious. A fanatic, sure, but . . . He *did* order her death, though. But even then, she said it had shades of a mercy killing. It was only because he and Bashir had a falling out that she wasn't executed. *God.* Can you imagine?"

It was truly sick and twisted, but Jimmy could imagine. The world he lived in was harsh and dark. People like Tess didn't belong in it.

He turned away, because damn it, she *was* starting to cry.

"Most of Bashir's guests didn't beat the shit out of her." She spoke in fits and gasps. "Although some of them did. Most of them were satisfied with just . . . God, Deck, with just carving their initials into her skin."

Damn it. Jimmy closed his eyes. He didn't dare look at her. Didn't dare turn back to her.

"I'm so sorry," Decker whispered.

Jimmy could tell from Tess's breathing that she was trying to keep from crying too loudly.

"Honey, it's okay to cry," Deck murmured.

Honey?

He turned around, and sure enough, the son of a bitch bastard had Tess securely in his arms.

Which was exactly what Jimmy had wanted, wasn't it?

Yes.

No.

Shit.

Tess lifted her head and looked up at Deck, her face wet with tears.

Her expression was heartbreaking, but it was her eyes that got him. Her eyes actually held hope.

"I promised her that we were going to keep her safe," Tess told Decker. "But we need to get her out of Kazbeki-stan. We'll need help from the Agency to do that."

Decker shook his head. "We're on our own for this," he admitted, stepping back from her, the team leader once again. "We've already contacted both the Agency and the CIA. They say they can't have anything to do with an extraction—you know, pulling Sophia out. And it's not going to be easy smuggling her over the border."

Goddamn idiot. Jimmy would've lied to her. Anything would've been better than that brutal honesty shit.

She was, of course, aghast. "After all the information she gave them as Miles Farrell . . . ?" She wiped her face with her shirtsleeve.

"Yeah, Dave's pretty steamed, too," Decker told her. "But they're afraid that any falsified documents they send over here might be intercepted. Or traced. As for providing financial help . . ." He rubbed the back of his neck, sighed, and continued to shovel the bad news directly onto her head. "We're not hopeful. The current administration at the Agency has a policy that other groups are trying out. It's meant to discourage people from staying behind in dangerous countries postevacuation. It's a bottom-line deci-sion—rescue attempts cost big bucks. And failed rescue attempts . . ." He shook his head. "The policy says 'Get out when we tell you to get out or good luck—you're on your own.' And they told Sophia to get out years ago."

Tess got even more mad. "What?"

"Yeah, well, even though I'm loath to say I agree with Doug Brendon, on this one I do agree," Decker said. "Sophia and her husband stayed in Kazbekistan too long. Probably out of greed—it was a chance to make a fast buck. No one's perfect, Tess," he added, when she started to interrupt. "It doesn't mean the price they ended up paying was fair or just. Because it's not. But the fact remains that Sophia took a gamble and lost."

"Well, I'm not going to leave her here." Tess was pissed.

"Yeah, I'm not either," Decker said. "I never said that."

"She could use my passport," Tess suggested. "We could put a cast on her arm, pretend she's me and she's hurt and has to go back home."

"No way," Jimmy said. They both looked over at him as if they'd forgotten he was there. "Bad idea."

"Yeah. Bashir's men are going to be watching for that," Decker said.

"But if she pretended to be zoned out on painkillers, or sick—yeah, sitting in a wheelchair, yakking her guts out—and Jimmy went, too, you know, as Mr. James Nash and his vomiting wife—"

"And how do *you* get out of the country without a passport?" Jimmy couldn't believe she'd think for a minute that he would be willing to leave her here. Even with Decker, who, with his special tear-absorbent T-shirts, would clearly take very good care of her.

"I'll wait a few days, then report mine stolen." She had an answer for everything.

Except, "I'm supposed to be doing a job here," Jimmy pointed out. "Not babysitting an ex-pat who's changed her mind and wants to go home."

But Tess even had a solution for that. "Then we'll wait until we're done here, and Sophia can go with you then."

Which would mean leaving Tess here, in Terrorist Central, all by her lonesome. "No way," Jimmy said again.

"But—"

"No fucking way. I veto that idea."

Tess laughed in derision. "Like you have the power to veto—"

Decker stepped between them. "Look, we're all tired."

"I'm not," Jimmy said. "I slept all day."

"Which is my fault, too, right?" It came out of Tess sounding defeated instead of challenging. Damn it, she was going to start to cry again.

"Maybe you should go, Nash," Decker suggested.

Jimmy felt awful. "It's not your fault," he told Tess.

Decker practically pushed him toward the door. "Go."

It was an order this time.

And suddenly the last thing Jimmy felt like doing was leaving Tess here to cry out her frustration and grief in Decker's capable arms.

As he went out the door, he couldn't keep himself from giving Deck a hard look.

Like he had any right at all to be proprietary.

As he stepped into the yard, he heard Decker's laughter, soft and faintly mocking, then his voice, saying gently, "Come here, honey. It's okay."

Honey.

Motherfucker.

Gritting his teeth, Jimmy didn't look back.

CHAPTER
EIGHTEEN

LAWRENCE DECKER was obviously determined never to spend even a single second alone with her.

It was almost amusing, the way he choreographed it. When he was around, Sophia had a continuous tag team of chaperones.

When she first woke up, it was Murphy. She had breakfast with him and Decker.

Murphy fed an artfully believable story about why she was in their kitchen to Rivka and Guldana, their K-stani hosts.

She was Julie Erdman, an old friend of Dave's from his days at World Relief. She'd been staying north of the city in a tent that hadn't been properly anchored. A strong wind pushed it over. Not only had it knocked her down, making her look as if she'd gone a round or two with the local heavyweight champ, but it landed right in the middle of the camp's dinner. Which was cooking on an open fire. When it came to tent fabric, flame resistant and flame retardant were, apparently, two very different things. Particularly when water was in low supply.

Not only did the tent burn, but so did Julie's sleeping bag and all of her clothing and other belongings.

Murphy managed to tell the tale with a hint of an amused wink aimed at their hosts. Like, "Can you believe how silly we Americans can be?"

He was a masterful liar. He didn't spend a whole lot of time on her story. He just explained why she was going to be sleeping in their pantry, and then moved on to a funny account of his fiancée's attempt to find the perfect wedding dress.

Sophia was tempted to pull him aside and ask him if his Angelina was pure fabrication, too.

After breakfast, Tess appeared exactly when Murphy went outside to pump water from the well in the yard—one of the small chores they did to help their hosts. Tess looked tired, as if she hadn't slept much last night.

With Decker, she walked Sophia out to the barn. This morning Tess was going with Khalid to help with the relief effort. Someone had to—it was, after all, the alleged reason they were in Kazabek.

James Nash was already in the barn, tall and handsome and charming and well-groomed—like Dimitri, he was one of those men who managed even to sweat with style. He was another *alleged,* as far as Sophia was concerned. It was hard to imagine him married to Tess. Men like him just weren't that smart.

He was with the K-stani boy who worked with them.

There was a lot of eye contact, but nobody said much of anything until the boy, Khalid, led the world's ugliest gelding out into the yard.

It was then Tess turned to Decker, who was flipping through a stack of papers—reading some kind of computer printed report—his mug of coffee in his other hand.

"This is a total waste of manpower," she said.

"No, it's not." Nash stepped closer.

Decker only glanced up very briefly as she turned to do battle with Nash.

"Yes, it is," Tess countered. "If Murphy's coming, too—"

"There's no *if,*" Nash told her.

"Excuse me, are *you* team leader?"

"You're not going to win this one," Nash said. "You're just not, so—"

Tess pointedly turned away from her husband—Sophia was starting to believe they really were married—and toward Decker. "I can guarantee that before we go two blocks, Will Schroeder will be sitting in that wagon with me. Sir, I don't need Murphy. He's got other things to do."

Nash didn't give up. "Oh, *Will Schroeder*'s going to keep you safe. That makes me feel *so* much better."

Who was Will Schroeder?

Tess ignored him. "We might as well make use of Will," she told Decker. "And yes, between him and Khalid, I'm sure I'll be very safe."

"Yeah," Nash said. "Because if you run into any trouble, Schroeder can give everyone paper cuts."

Decker looked up from the documents he'd been trying to read, and directly at Sophia. It was probably quite by accident, since along with avoiding being alone with her, he'd also made a point never to meet her gaze.

"Does this sound as childish to you as it does to me?" he asked her, amused resignation pushing the edges of his mouth up into what almost could be called a smile.

Sophia froze. It was stupid. She'd never been shy, but here she was, suddenly tongue-tied as she looked into this man's eyes.

For the second time in two days, Dave saved her. "Sorry I'm late, sir." He breezed in, filling the sudden, uncomfortable silence.

Murphy, too, stuck his head in the barn. "Excuse me, boss. Almost ready to go," he called.

Everyone addressed Lawrence Decker as *sir* or *boss*.

Everyone but James Nash. "I'm not the one being unreasonable here, Deck."

"I'm sorry, sir." Tess backed off. "We'll handle this, of

course." She raised her voice. "Murph, you don't need to come with me."

"You get into that wagon, Murphy," Nash called, "and you stay there. Or I will make you sorry you were born."

"Oh, *that's* nice." Tess looked at Nash as if he were scum.

"Do you have plans to meet Will?" Decker asked Tess.

The answer was no. Sophia could see it clearly in Tess's eyes, but she obviously didn't want to say it. "I'm sure he's nearby, waiting—"

"No specific time and place?" Decker interrupted Tess.

"No, but he made it quite clear—"

"Take Murphy," Deck ordered.

"Hah!" Nash said.

"This time," Decker continued, with an exasperated look at Nash. "And set something up with Schroeder for tomorrow. Using him and freeing up Murph is a good idea."

Tess looked at Nash. She didn't say, "Hah!" But Sophia knew she was thinking it.

"Is there coffee?" Dave asked, eyeing Decker's still nearly full mug. He was wearing a Pink Floyd concert T-shirt with his jeans.

"Inside," Tess told him.

Decker had already returned his attention to that print-out, but now he glanced up. At Sophia. And then at Dave. "Be quick."

"You want some?" Dave asked Sophia.

She shook her head as she watched Tess put bottles of water into her backpack. "No, thanks."

"Do you have your scarf?" Nash asked Tess.

"Yes, I do." She shouldered the pack, and as she straightened up, she looked hard at him, as if taking inventory of all of his bandages and scratches. "How's your arm?"

"Better," he told her.

"Your head?"

"Fine."

Tess nodded. "Good."

She turned to go, but he caught her arm. "Tess, I'm, um, sorry about being late."

"I was just worried about you," she said. "It's frustrating, Jimmy, because I can't insist that Murphy goes along whenever *you* leave. And if you don't check in . . ."

"I can take care of myself. I don't need anyone's help."

She nodded. "Yeah, I get that. Loud and clear." She looked over, as if she felt Sophia watching, and smiled. It was forced. "I've got to go. See you later."

"Be careful."

"Right."

Nash watched her as she went toward the door without looking back.

Decker cleared his throat. "What did you find out last night?"

Nash didn't look over until Tess closed the barn door behind her. "Fifty K'll do it."

Decker swore. "That much?"

Nash looked from Decker to Sophia and back. "It's going to be a match pot situation," he said, and she realized they were talking about money. Fifty thousand dollars, U.S.

Same as the reward Bashir had put on her head.

Bashir, not his nephews, as she'd believed. She hadn't managed to kill the bastard. Tess had broken that news to her last night.

Which meant that if Sophia was caught, Padsha Bashir would hand-deliver her punishment.

And it was going to cost fifty thousand dollars to smuggle her out of the country.

She sat down heavily on the nearest bale of hay.

She looked up to find Decker gazing at her.

Not only would it cost fifty thousand dollars, but she would have to trust whomever she paid that fifty thousand dollars not to turn around and sell her to Bashir for an additional fifty thousand dollars.

Assuming, of course, that she'd be able to get her hands on fifty thousand dollars.

Decker knew what she was thinking. "I guess there's no Swiss bank account," he said.

Sophia shook her head. "No."

He nodded. "Okay."

"Is that actually lamb stew that Guldana's cooking?" Dave asked, coming back into the barn.

"Yup," Nash said.

"What's the occasion?" Dave asked. "I mean, *is* there an occasion?"

"I got married," Nash said flatly. "Rivka and Guldana wanted to throw a party to celebrate."

"Oh, that's tonight?" Dave turned to Sophia. "You better plan to stay out of sight. Frankly, the dyed hair isn't that good of a disguise. Rivka and Guldana used to run with the university crowd, and I don't know who all's likely to attend their party, but God forbid someone comes who used to know you. If they see you, they'll definitely recognize you."

"I'll stay here in the barn," she said.

"You need me to stick around?" Nash asked Decker.

"No," Decker said. Dave was here, making himself comfortable on a second bale of hay. But Decker turned to Dave. "Look, I have to run out, too. Can you get started without me? I should be back in about an hour."

Get started?

"We'll be fine. We have some questions that you might be able to help us with," Dave told Sophia. "About Bashir—his palace, his organization—as well as Ma'awiya Talal Sayid.

You're one of the few Westerners who's ever actually met both of those two, uh, gentlemen."

"Where are you going?" she heard Nash ask Decker as they headed out of the barn.

Deck glanced back at her before he went out the door, but she didn't hear his reply.

This was ridiculous.

That there should be gridlock in downtown Kazabek was completely absurd.

"I'm going to go see if I can't find out what the problem is," Murphy told Tess as he climbed out of Khalid's wagon.

"What problem?" Will Schroeder asked. "Things are back to normal in the Pit."

Just as Tess had expected, the redhaired reporter had waved them down not a half mile from Rivka's house. He'd hopped into the back of the wagon. What a coincidence. He was heading over to the relief coordination headquarters for this sector of the city, too.

The people at the sector HQ had sent them—volunteers with a horse and wagon, a real rarity—over to the main HQ, in City Center. There were supplies that needed to be picked up and distributed.

Will, of course, stuck around to help.

Which meant that he sat there in the wagon with her, hogging the shade from the umbrella, much cooler than she was, dressed in his short-sleeved T-shirt and shorts.

City Center wasn't really that much farther downtown, but considering they couldn't move faster than the herd of sheep being driven along the road in front of them . . . It had been a solid two hours since they'd left Rivka's.

It was doubly frustrating for Tess, since the appearance of Will meant that Murphy didn't have to babysit her anymore. But Murph wasn't going anywhere until he found out exactly where Tess would end up.

"I have my phone," she'd argued.

"Will it work when you're over at City Center?" he asked.

"It might."

"And it might not," he said cheerfully. "I'll wait and find out where you're going. A few more minutes won't matter either way."

That had been an hour ago.

"I heard the BBC broadcast this morning," Will told her now. "The news about Sayid's death is still their top story. There's lots of speculation about whether or not the U.S. has possession of his infamous laptop. Fox News says we have it, Aljazeera says no way. Of course, they're getting ready to release a video that will prove Sayid's still alive."

Tess leaned forward to address Khalid. "How close are we?"

"It's just another block," he told her.

"Okay," she decided. "Let's just start loading the wagon from here. Will, you're with me. Khalid, when Murphy gets back—"

"Here he is now."

And there Murphy was, indeed. He was half a block away, heading back toward them, a full head taller than everyone around him.

Boom. The sudden loud noise—an explosion—was incredible. And just as stunning was the pickup truck that seemed to launch into the air just behind Murphy.

Tess grabbed Khalid around the waist, pulling the boy off the bench seat and down into the wagon bed as the shock from the blast hit them.

It pushed them back, and they bounced and scraped along the wood. Will must've slammed against the rickety boards at the wagon's end, breaking through them. Because Tess, still clinging to Khalid, hit the road so hard that she saw stars, her head bouncing in the dirt.

Murphy.

Dear God.

Debris was raining down—chunks of metal and wood, some pieces burning. Tess pushed both Will and Khalid beneath the wagon.

What looked like a hubcap landed on the sidewalk, but oddly, she couldn't hear it hit.

"Are you all right?" Tess tried to shout over the ringing in her ears. She had to get out there—she had to find Murphy.

Khalid said something she couldn't hear. He had a scrape on his face, but other than that looked to be in one piece.

Will was saying something, too, cradling one arm against his chest. "Think I broke my fucking wrist," she read his lips more than heard him. Would her ears never clear? "Are you okay?" he asked her.

She nodded. Was she? Everything seemed to be still attached. She'd hit her head, scraped an elbow and a knee. . . .

Khalid was gesturing. Above them, the cart was lurching and rocking. And then she could make out his words, very distantly, as if he were speaking over a transistor radio from far, far away.

"My horse!"

She let the boy go since the worst of the debris seemed to have fallen. He scrambled out into the street to calm the animal and to push burning embers off its back.

She followed, Will behind her.

"Car bomb," she heard him say in that AM radio voice. No shit, Sherlock.

The smoke was thick and greasy, rolling up into the sky from the flaming skeletons of two different vehicles. The truck she'd seen in the air had landed wheels up and was burning. The other looked like some kind of cargo van.

Most of the crowd had scattered, rushing to cover. But now the injured and bleeding were picking themselves up off the ground if they could, dragging themselves away from the fire.

From where she was, Tess could see no sign of Murphy. "Stay with Khalid," she ordered Will.

Nearly everyone was moving in the other direction—away from the blast site. Some people just sat in the street. Some would never get back up again.

The smoke was chokingly thick. Tess had lost her scarf, so she pulled the front of her shirt up over her mouth and nose and headed to where she'd last seen Murphy.

"He rules with fear," Sophia said. "I didn't meet anyone in that palace who wasn't scared to death of him. Even his nephews." She laughed as she shook her head. "He plays them off of each other, in a constant competition. It would have been funny to watch if, um . . ."

If she hadn't lived every moment wondering if she'd be executed now or later.

Deck sat in the barn and just let Dave run the interview with Sophia. His trip into the city had taken a little longer than he'd expected, and she'd already answered most of Dave's questions about Bashir's palace, about the layout of the place and the security there—the number of guards, any patterns and routines they might fall into.

Dave had a legal pad upon which he was taking notes, and when Decker had come in, he'd already filled dozens of pages with his spidery scrawl.

"Keep going," Deck had said. Dave could catch him up later. No need to make Sophia answer these difficult questions twice.

"A rumor that I've heard," Dave said now, "is that Bashir's sterile. Some late childhood illness . . . ?"

"Yeah," Sophia told him. "I'm pretty sure that's true. I don't think he believed it at first. That's probably what got him started with his vast collection of wives—you know, it must be the woman's fault that there are no children, so find another wife. That and the fact that he stood to gain financially from killing his enemies and marrying their wives. Neat little trick, huh?"

She shifted in her seat, glancing briefly at Decker. He could see that she was trying to be nonchalant. She was trying to pretend that talking about this wasn't hard as hell.

The porcelain paleness of Sophia's face—the part that wasn't bruised—was accentuated by her hair, now dyed a dark shade of brown. The short cut that Tess had given her made her look young and fragile. It was an effect enhanced by the clothes that Tess—who was much taller—had given her. On Sophia, Tess's shirt hung loosely from her shoulders, and her pants had to be cinched with a belt around her waist.

"That was a power thing, too," she added. "His marriages to the wives of the men he wanted to best. I don't think he enjoyed sex even half as much as he liked winning. It wasn't about pleasure for him, it was about inflicting pain and humiliation. Half the time, he didn't . . ." She cleared her throat. "You know, ejaculate." She forced a laugh, but she didn't meet either of their eyes. "I don't know, maybe he was saving that for one of the wives that he liked—assuming he was even capable of liking anyone—and . . . Is this going to show up in some Agency report?" Now she did speak directly to Dave. "Make sure you include the fact that he has terrible halitosis. Terrible. And flatulence."

Now it was Dave's turn to clear his throat. Come on, Dave. Say something comforting, something kind. *That must have been awful—what you went through. To have your entire life just . . . stolen from you. To have to fight to stay alive, to endure, even while knowing it was possible your life could end instantly, on the whim of a man who hated you. . . .*

"It's important, Sophia, that the information we include

in our reports doesn't come off sounding, well, as if it was provided by someone with a definite agenda. You know, in terms of wanting to make Bashir look bad," Dave said.

Oh, Dave.

Sophia laughed. And laughed. "I don't have to make things up so Bashir looks bad. All anyone has to do is go into the wing of his palace where he keeps his wives and count their scars. Do you know that he gives his new brides a special gift upon their marriage—" She cut herself off, her hand up over her mouth. "No. No one will ever believe that."

There were tears in her eyes now—real tears. Decker wanted to push this, to ask her what it was that no one would believe. He wanted her to stick around for a while—this seemingly honest version of Sophia. But if he'd thought she looked fragile before, well, this Sophia looked as if she might break into a million pieces.

So instead he asked her, "Do you want to take a break?"

"No." She wouldn't look at him. She straightened up, quickly wiping her eyes. "Let's get something in this report that will make a difference, that'll make people understand who and what Bashir is. He's always been described as a religious man," she told them. "But that's total bullshit. He uses some of the beliefs of Islam to his advantage, but he is in no way the devout Muslim that most people think. He plays the part in public. He even had some top-level al-Qaeda leaders fooled for a while—including Sayid. But they caught on, and they wanted nothing to do with Bashir.

"The falling out was mutual," Sophia continued. "That's one of the reasons I knew Sayid wasn't staying at the palace. He was no longer welcome. But you know what? I thought of a way that you can double-check me if you want."

Dave looked up from his notepad. Glanced at Decker, before giving his full attention to Sophia. "Double-check you?" he asked. "How do you mean?"

"Ma'awiya Talal Sayid had some kind of serious medical condition," Sophia told them. "Did you know that?"

"No," Dave said.

Decker sat up. Shit, no.

"I don't know exactly what it was," she continued, "but he needed some kind of treatment that I think involved, I don't know, maybe blood transfusions? Once when I saw him he had these tubes—they looked like they were filled with blood—attached to his arm."

Decker looked at Dave. "Why would someone need blood transfusions?"

"Maybe Murphy would know. Sophia, please, go on."

"Both times he stayed at Bashir's palace, there was a shipment of medical equipment from the hospital. I'm not sure exactly which hospital is closest to Bashir's palace—"

"L'Hôpital Cantara," Decker said, exchanging a look with Dave. There would no doubt be records of such a shipment.

"This," Dave said, "is exactly the break we needed." He flipped back several pages in his notepad. "I have Sophia's estimate of the dates Sayid visited Bashir over the past two months."

Excellent. "Can you describe the equipment you saw?" Decker asked Sophia.

"I think there was an IV stand in his room. You know, one of those metal hook things, like a coat stand on wheels? And a tall machine—a box with tubes . . . maybe it was some kind of monitor." Sophia looked from Decker to Dave and back. "This helps?"

"Yes," they said in unison.

"We know Sayid was in Kazabek at the time of the quake," Dave told her. "We don't know where he was staying. But if he needed medical equipment supplied by a local hospital . . . Well, we'll find out exactly what equipment was shipped to Bashir's palace in the past and see if there was a similar shipment made elsewhere in the city several days before the quake. If we can get that address, we'll more than likely know where Sayid was staying."

But what were the chances that his laptop was still there?

"Dave," Decker asked, "do you have a contact at—"

"The Cantara hospital?" Dave finished for him as he stood up. "Not yet, but I'm about to make one." But then he stopped, obviously remembering Decker's request that he not be left alone with Sophia. "That is, unless you want me to—"

"Go," Decker said, and Dave went out the door.

Jimmy Nash was playing a game of 'If I Were Sayid' when his phone vibrated.

He'd heard the distant explosion, heard the rumors that had immediately started. *Car bomb. In City Center.*

He'd stayed seated. He'd even kept himself from reaching for his phone. Murphy was with Tess. They were both safe—over at the north sector relief aid headquarters. He was not going to freak. Not this time. She was doing her job, he was doing his.

It might've looked to some as if he were simply sitting in an open-air café, enjoying a cup of coffee, but he was, in fact, hard at work, running different scenarios.

Option one. He was Sayid, and he was in town to meet with Padsha Bashir. Where would he stay? Bashir's palace, of course. The only other place that came close to the kind of comfort that could be found at the warlord's palace was the Kazabek Grande Hotel—and that was the last place Sayid would stay. He wouldn't be caught dead in that testament to Western culture and capitalism.

Option two. He was Sayid, and he was in town, but he wasn't staying at Bashir's palace because . . .

There was no reason Sayid wouldn't stay at the palace. It

was secure, it was comfortable, it was safe—from all of Bashir's enemies.

Of course, it wasn't safe from Bashir. Hmmm.

He was Sayid, and he was in town, but he wasn't staying at Bashir's palace because he *wasn't* meeting with Bashir.

And if he wasn't meeting with Bashir, it was possible there had been a falling-out. In which case Sayid would need to be careful while he was in town, to hide his presence *from* Bashir.

He was Sayid, and he was in town, and he needed to be sure Bashir didn't find him while he was in town. Where would he stay?

If *he* were Sayid, he'd stay the last place on earth Bashir—or anyone—would expect him to stay.

The Kazabek Grande Hotel.

Jimmy could see it from his table here in the café—a structurally damaged time bomb, the late morning light reflecting off its windows.

Shit.

He was going to have to go in there. Before this was over, before they got on that plane that would take them back home, he was goddamn going to have to go into that motherfucking about-to-fall building. He just knew it.

It was immediately after this most unhappy realization that his phone started to shake.

The rumors about that car bomb were flying fast and furious in the street outside the café. Even the waiters were talking about it now. A hundred people killed, dozens injured. A cargo van had been driven right up to the front of the main relief headquarters.

Jimmy flipped open his phone and saw that Tess's number was on the display. Thank God. She *was* safe.

He stood up, aware that he was getting curious glances from simply having a phone. Who in this city could possi-

bly have a working phone? He tossed several bills on the
table and went out into the street as he took the call.

"Hey," he said, working to make sure his voice sounded
completely unworried. "What's up?"

"Jimmy!" she said, her voice shaking, little more than a
exhaled sob.

Instant adrenaline flood. The connection was bad, she
kept cutting out. His heart nearly stopped. "Tess! What's
the matter?"

". . . can't believe . . . actually got you!"

"Where are you? Are you all right?"

"I'm fine," she said. "I'm . . ." It was garbled, but then
he heard, ". . . Murphy! We were with Khalid, in the cart,
just outside main . . . Q . . . City Cent . . ."

No fucking way.

"Shit, Tess, I can't hear you very well!" He moved back
several steps, searching for better reception, until . . .

". . . car bomb," he heard, and he stood still. His heart
was beating again, though. It was pounding, as if he were
running a six-minute mile.

"at the hospital . . ." she said. "Servant of the . . .
Guided. . . . dul-Rasheed."

Jimmy forced himself not to start running, to start
searching for a map.

"Are you hurt?" he asked her. "Is that where you are? At
that hospital? Repeat the hospital's name, Tess. God damn
it, I'm having trouble hearing you!"

"Abdul-Rasheed." He could barely make her out. ". . . Murphy's inj . . ." He strained to make sense of her words, but
then part of it leapt out, clear again. ". . . wouldn't let me
in with him."

"Are you hurt?" he asked again.

"I'm fine," she said.

Fuck. As the king of evasive answers, he knew damn well
that "I'm fine" was not the same as "No, I'm not hurt."

"Please, Jimmy," she said. ". . . got to make sh . . . Murph's getting . . . care of . . . urt bad . . . can't reach Deck . . . an't believe . . . got you. This . . . nection's bad. I'm gon . . . peat the . . . pital. Abdul-Rasheed Hospital. Abdul-Rasheed Hospital."

She repeated the hospital's name over and over and over, with bits and pieces of it cutting out, until he was convinced he got it.

He did the same, repeating it back to her, then repeating, "I'm on my way."

"Thank . . ." he heard her say.

The connection was cut, and Jimmy started to run.

Tess hung up her phone and punched in Decker's number again.

Again, there wasn't even an automated message telling her that the "customer you are trying to reach is out of range." Even though she was standing on the room's only piece of furniture—a hard wooden bench—with her phone up as close to the narrow slit of a window as she could get it, she still got nothing.

She tried Dave's number.

Zilch.

Okay. Okay. Jimmy was on his way to Murphy. That was good. That was very good.

Tess wiped the last of her tears from her face as she climbed down from the bench and started to pace, aware that for the first time since she'd gotten off the plane in northern Kazbekistan, she was actually chilly.

The irony of that was profound, and she rubbed her bare arms as she examined the inside of the tiny prison cell into which the police patrol had thrown her.

The walls, floor, and ceiling were solid stone. The bench was bolted down and the window—far too narrow for even a child to slip through—was way up, close to the ceiling.

It was obvious that there was only one way out of this cell, and that was through the ancient wooden door.

Tess ran her hand across it—the wood was thick and smooth, made even harder with age. There was a small barred window in the center, with some kind of apparatus on the outside that would allow it to be opened and shut.

She heard footsteps coming down the stairs—boots on stone—and tucked her phone back into her pocket. She sat down on the bench, knees and ankles together, wiping her eyes one more time.

The window screeched opened and a man addressed her in the local K-stani dialect. She couldn't see his face.

"I'm sorry. I'm American," she said. "I don't speak—"

"Of course not," he interrupted. "You expect everyone to speak English, wherever you go."

That wasn't what she would call the best of starts. She politely shook her head. Everything she did had to be polite. "No, sir. I'm in your country with my husband and my friends—all Americans—who speak your language. What I expected was never to be separated from them."

"Do you consider your apparel to be appropriate for the streets of Kazabek?"

She was wearing a running bra with her bloodstained pants. It was the type of top that women in America frequently wore when they worked out, or even just worked in the yard.

"I respect your culture and customs, and was dressed quite appropriately," she told him, "before I used my over-shirt as a tourniquet on my friend Vinh Murphy's leg. I thought keeping him from bleeding to death was more important than keeping my arms covered."

There had been so much blood, and Murphy's leg probably wasn't the worst of his injuries. He'd been burned on his arm and chest, his skin raw.

Get Decker! she'd shouted at Khalid over the sound of

sirens as she'd yanked off her shirt. Deck was back at Rivka's, with Dave and Sophia. The boy had turned and run as she'd . . .

You're okay, she'd told Murphy. Oh, God, he was in such pain. *You're going to be okay, Vinh. Stay with me.*

Didn't see it, he'd gasped. *Should've seen it coming. . . .*

"Surely there was something else you could have used, besides your shirt," the man now admonished her. "Surely someone else could have helped him."

Tess's hands—Murphy's blood still caked around her fingernails—were trembling. She tucked them now beneath her arms. Don't cry, don't cry . . .

"There wasn't," she said. "His own shirt was burned onto his body. There was no one else around. Your police were far more interested in harassing me than helping the injured. . . ."

I am warning you for the final time to get inside!

Tess didn't even look at the police guard. *I'm not leaving him. How're you doing, Murph?* They were next in line for the ambulance. A paramedic had come by, dispensing morphine, and she could tell from Murphy's slackening grip on her hand that he was starting to float.

Angelina, don't leave me, he mumbled.

She didn't see it coming, either, when the police guard backhanded her across the jaw. . . .

"What kind of country is this?" Tess demanded now. She was standing up, she realized, her hands tightened in fists at her sides as she glared at that little window.

It closed with a thunk, and Tess breathed a shaky sigh of relief.

But it was short-lived because the key turned in the lock and the door swung open. Shit. This wasn't good.

She sat back down. Relaxed her hands.

"We have some questions for you," the man said. He gestured to the open door. "Please."

She didn't move. Shit. She could hear Jimmy's voice chastising her. *For God's sake, don't look directly at him. Eyes down, Tess. Come on, you know you're not going to win a debate with these people.* Eyes down—*shit,* that was hard to do. She closed her eyes instead. "Questions?" she asked.

"About the incident," he said.

Tess shook her head. "I don't know anything about . . . anything. I just happened to be there."

"And yet you *were* there, causing trouble."

"No," she said, quickly adding, "sir."

"The police report says otherwise," he said. He paused. She didn't dare look at him. "Shall I have the guards escort you upstairs?"

Out in the hall, she heard weaponry being locked and loaded. *Ca-chunk.*

Tess stood up. "No, sir," she said.

"Please," he said again with another sweeping gesture. He had such a pleasant voice, a pleasant accent, a pleasant face.

Don't look at his face.

Head down, eyes lowered—damn it, this was hard to do—Tess went out into the hall and up the stairs, toward the Kazbekistani police interrogation room.

CHAPTER
NINETEEN

WHEN THE door closed behind Dave, Sophia was completely alone with Lawrence Decker.

She closed her eyes briefly, knowing he was as uncomfortable as she was. Maybe even more so.

Okay. Come on. She could do this. She'd had sex with men she'd despised. Surely she could have a conversation with this one.

She forced a smile, forced herself to look at him. "You probably have things to do—"

He spoke over her. "I got hold of the money we'll need to buy you safe passage out of here."

Good thing she was sitting down. As it was, she had to steady herself with both hands on that bale of hay. James Nash had said it would cost *fifty thousand* dollars.

Decker wasn't done with his mind-blowing news flash. "I had it put into a Swiss bank account—it'll be easier to transfer from there. We'll figure out some way to put it into escrow—maybe held by one of the local clerics. That way we don't pay it until you're free, and the . . . businessmen we hire to smuggle you into Afghanistan don't have an opportunity to collect from both us and Bashir."

She had to ask. "Did you talk the Agency into ponying up the funds to—"

"No, they, uh . . . No."

Now he was the one who wouldn't look at her.

311

"So to whom am I going to owe fifty thousand dollars?" she asked, even though part of her already knew. "And what's the interest rate?"

"Zero percent," he said, finally meeting her eyes.

She was gaping at him, she knew it.

"I wasn't getting much more than that anyway." He shrugged. "The bank rates suck these days, you know."

"You had fifty thousand dollars just . . . sitting in the bank?" She couldn't believe it.

Of course now she'd gone and insulted him. "Yeah, and *you* had over half a million before Bashir stole it."

"But I ran an import business. That was working capital. You're . . ." A mercenary? That's what Sophia had thought. That they were hired by the Agency, but . . . "What *are* you?"

Decker actually laughed at that. "You mean, besides crazy?" His smile erased some of the lines of fatigue on his face.

But Sophia couldn't smile back at him. She couldn't even look at him again. She wanted to cover her face with her hands. Who would risk fifty thousand dollars on a stranger who had tried to kill him, a stranger who was obviously little more than a whore?

"Hey," he said gently. "Just so there's no question in your mind—I don't expect anything from you, Sophia. I'm not looking for . . ." He cleared his throat. "If you someday get to the place where you can pay me back—"

She looked up at that. "I will," she said.

"Well, good." He nodded, taking her words at face value. Which was amazing, too. "Good."

Sophia couldn't help it. She started to cry. "I'm sorry," she sobbed. "I'm sorry, I don't mean to . . ." Now that she'd started, she might never stop.

"Ah, God," he said. "Honey, you know, it's okay to cry.

You don't have to apologize." His words were gentle, but he didn't move any closer.

She knew without a doubt that this man was never going to touch her again—never. It was another thing she could add to that long list of all she'd lost.

"Awful people did terrible things to you," Decker continued softly. "You don't have to pretend it's okay anymore. In fact, it's been my experience that you heal a little faster if you—" But then he stood up and took hold of her arm. "Get down." His voice was suddenly sharp, his words an order.

Even through her tears, Sophia realized that there was some kind of ruckus out in the yard. Just as he pushed her down behind that bale of hay, the door burst open.

"Sir! Sir! Are you here, sir?"

It was only Khalid, thank goodness.

But it was a quite distraught Khalid. His cheek was badly scraped—it had bled down his neck and stained the collar of his shirt. His clothes were torn and streaked with soot, too. He looked as if he'd been used, rather violently, to clean out a chimney.

He was crying. Poor Decker. Everyone around him today was in tears.

"I'm right here," he told Khalid, who let out a stream of rapid-fire K-stani.

"Slow down," Deck said right back at the boy in the same dialect. "Breathe, son. Start back at the beginning. There was a car bomb. Where?"

"City Center."

"Who's been hurt?"

"Murphy," the boy sobbed. "He's bad. He went in an ambulance to the hospital."

"Tess?"

"They arrested her," he told Decker.

The muscle was jumping in his jaw. "Who did? Was she injured?"

"No," Khalid said. "But she was shouting at them because she wanted to go to the hospital with Murphy, and they wouldn't let her, and they told her she had to get inside, that she was indecent, and she still wouldn't let go of Murphy, he was bleeding so badly, so they hit her and they threw her into this truck and I don't know where they took her but Mr. Schroeder said he'd make sure Murphy got to see the American doctor, and then he'd go find out where they took Tess, and he gave me this"—he handed Murphy's phone to Deck—"and told me to call you, but I couldn't get it to work, so I unhooked Marge from the cart and rode over here as fast as I could."

"Who took Tess?" Decker asked the boy again.

The look on Deck's face was terrible, and Sophia knew that whoever had taken Tess had better not hurt her or they would not live to see another day.

"Was it Bashir's men or the police?" he asked.

"I think it was the police, but I don't know. I'm sorry, sir." Khalid's face crumpled.

"That's all right," Decker said. "It's okay. We'll find out where she is. You did a good job, son. A *good* job. Get something to drink—for yourself and Marge." He turned to Sophia. "Where would they have taken her? From City Center?"

She wiped her face, her own tears a thing of the past. Why had she been crying? She couldn't even remember now. "The biggest police station in Kazabek isn't far from there. Chances are, even if it was one of Bashir's patrols, they'd bring her there."

With one quick motion, Decker flipped open the street map. "Show me."

It took her a moment to find City Center. "Even if she *is* there, you won't be able to help her. Only her husband will be able to pay the fines and sign the forms for her release. Here." She pointed to the police station on the map.

She could see that Decker knew what she was saying was true, but he didn't like it one bit.

"Give me Murphy's phone," Sophia told him. "I'll reach Nash—his number's programmed in, isn't it?"

Decker nodded, hesitating only slightly before handing it to her, an apology in his eyes. He'd tried to wipe it clean, but blood had a way of creeping into little crevasses and cracks. She knew that far too well.

She pretended it didn't bother her as she opened it, and it came to life. "Searching for service . . . ," it said.

"You'll be all right here by yourself?" he asked. As if he were going to stay behind if she said no.

"Yes," she lied, scrolling through Murphy's electronic phonebook until she found Nash, James. She glanced up at him. "Just—before you go—ask Khalid which hospital Murphy's been taken to. So I can tell Nash. I'm sure he'll want to know."

Deck nodded. He pointed to the phone. "Go up onto the third floor of the house with that. You should be able to get through up there. Don't use your real name when you speak to him. This is important—there's no telling who might be listening in."

She never would have thought of that. "Yes, sir."

He met her gaze. "It's *chief*," he said. "Not *sir*. I wasn't an officer—I don't know why they all call me that."

He was serious. He honestly didn't know.

But he went out of the barn without another word.

Sophia followed and watched from the shadows just inside the door as he spoke to Khalid, who held a bucket of water so his horse could drink.

Decker looked over at her. "Hospital Abdul-Rasheed."

She nodded, gave him a brief wave. She'd once thought of him as little—it seemed ridiculous now. He was compact, yes, but he was pure, radiant energy. And there was no such thing as a "little" lightning bolt.

As she watched, he helped Khalid onto the horse, then, using the stone wall that lined Rivka's yard as something of a gymnastic stepping stone, he leapt up behind the boy, like the hero in a cowboy movie. He reached around Khalid for the reins and, as he dug his heels into the horse's sides, they went out the gate with a clatter of hooves.

The only thing Decker was missing was a white ten-gallon hat.

Sophia pulled her scarf up, and ducking her head so her face was covered, she scurried across the open yard and into the house, so she could try to call Nash.

Jimmy was on the verge of putting his fist through a wall.

No one he'd spoken to—nurses, doctors, cleanup crew—had seen Tess. And his phone was useless this far south.

Murphy was in intensive care. He was stabilized, but just barely. He'd need extensive and delicate state-of-the-art surgery to save his leg. But he wasn't going to get it in K-stan.

The American doctor, one of the Doctors Without Borders team that had come in following the quake, was harried and impossibly young. There had been no American woman asking about Murphy, not that he'd seen, no. Although he did tell Jimmy that he, like Murphy, was a former Marine.

When? Back when he was freaking twelve?

The doctor took several of his precious minutes to step closer and tell Jimmy that there was a relief aid helicopter coming in very shortly. It had been given special permission to deliver a shipment of desperately needed antibiotics to this hospital. The doctors were not permitted to ship any patients out, but if, in the chaos of this delivery—chaos caused by their additional need for extra haste in light of an approaching sandstorm—if Murphy were to make his way up to the roof . . .

What the doctor was saying was more than clear. Murphy's best chance of survival lay in getting to a real hospital, outside of this armpit of a country.

Getting him to the roof, however, was going to be a challenge.

And Jimmy still hadn't found Tess.

He was getting Murphy ready to travel when Decker appeared.

"What are *you* doing here?"

Hell of a greeting. "Nice to see you, too," Jimmy told him. "Tess called me. Told me Murph was hurt."

"Tess?" Decker asked. "Not . . ." He stopped himself. "Miles?"

Huh?

Oh, yeah, Miles was what Dave had called Sophia back when she'd been an informant for the CIA. "Why would *she* call me? *How* could she call me?"

"Khalid brought us Murph's phone. I left it with her."

"Yeah, well, welcome to Snafu-land, where equipment malfunctions and nothing goes as planned." Jimmy quickly filled him in about the impending chopper delivery.

"We need to get word to Miles," Decker said, opening his phone and glancing at it—it was lifeless—before putting it back in his pocket. "She needs to get over here so we can put her on that helo. She can pretend to be Murph's wife, and . . . Look, James, Khalid's got his horse out front. I need you to get back to Rivka's and—"

"Shit, Deck," Jimmy interrupted him. "I've still got to find Tess."

Decker looked up, frowning slightly. "*Find* her? Tess isn't out?"

Out? "What?"

"Didn't you tell me she called you?" Decker said.

"Yeah. She asked me to come here to the hospital, pronto. She was freaking out about Murphy," Jimmy told him. "But I don't know where she is. And nobody's seen her."

Now the look on Deck's face was not a good one.

Jimmy felt himself get very still. "You said Tess isn't out," he repeated. "Out of what?"

"Of police custody."

"Police custody?" He managed to speak but his voice cracked like a fourteen-year-old's. "Are you telling me that Tess is sitting somewhere in some Kazbekistani *prison*?" He didn't wait for Decker to answer that. Christ, he could not believe this. "What the hell happened?"

"Khalid told me she used her shirt to keep Murphy from bleeding to death, and got taken in for being underdressed."

"Fuck! *Fuck!*" It was entirely possibly that he was now foaming at the mouth. "If they so much as lay one fucking finger on her—"

"Are you going to be able to get her out?" Decker interrupted sharply. "Because if you're going to go over there and get yourself arrested, too, that doesn't do me—or Tess—any good."

"I'll get her out. Where is she?" Jimmy asked from between gritted teeth. Yeah, he'd get her out of there, and *then* he'd fucking kill them all.

"Best guess is the main police station," Decker told him.

"Best *guess?*" God *damn* it . . .

"If you find when you get out there that your phone works," Decker told him evenly, "call Murphy's number. Tell her—Miles—to get over here as quickly as possible. I want her on that helo."

"Where the fuck is the main fucking station?"

Deck gave him the address. It wasn't far. If he ran, he'd be there in five minutes.

"That's not where Tess is."

They both looked up to see Will Schroeder standing in the doorway. The reporter was holding one arm against his chest as if it were broken.

It was only because Schroeder looked as if he were in enough pain that Jimmy didn't grab him and slam him against the wall. "Where is she?"

"There's a smaller police station over on Rue de Palms," Schroeder told them. "Number 68. She's there."

"She's there?" Jimmy asked. "Or you guess she's there?"

"She's there," he repeated. "I've been working on a story about . . . well, according to whispers from the locals, sometimes people who go into number 68 don't come out. Easy there, Jim, I doubt they'd do that to an American. My guess is they just wanted to make her very hard for us to find. Extend the incarceration period. Because really, all she needs to get free is for her husband to come and pay a fine, sign a paper saying he'll punish her properly."

Breathe. What Jimmy had to do was breathe.

"And you're certain . . . ?" Decker asked.

Schroeder nodded his red head. "I've been paying people to watch the place. They definitely saw her taken inside."

Decker looked at Jimmy. "Go. I'll send Khalid to get Miles."

Jimmy nodded. "If I have phone access, I'll—"

"Yeah. Go."

"I love you," Jimmy told Schroeder and, grabbing his ugly face, kissed him—right on the mouth.

"Jeezus! Why does he do things like that?" he heard the reporter complain as he ran toward the stairs.

Murphy's phone rang.

Yes! The number on the screen was Nash's.

Sophia answered. "Nash! I've been trying to—"

"Do you trust Deck?" he asked, no greeting, just point-blank.

It was a hell of a question.

She stalled, unwilling to admit to a near stranger something that she'd only recently admitted to herself. "Decker asked me to call you to tell you—"

"I'm up to speed," Nash interrupted. "Can you hear me as well as I can hear you? This is one freaking great connection."

"Yes, I—"

"I'm on my way to get Tess. I don't have time to explain. If you trust Decker—and you should—get dressed. Fast. Full burka and robe. Get over to the Hospital Abdul-Rasheed. Run if you have to. Murphy's on the fourth floor. If he's not there, head for the roof. Decker's with him, he'll explain. Did you get all that?"

"Yes—"

"Do it," he said, and hung up.

Sophia ran down the stairs, out of the kitchen, dressing as she went.

"Is everything all right?" Guldana called after her, but she didn't stop to explain.

She had to slow her pace when she hit the street—a burka-clad woman running would have drawn too much attention. But she walked swiftly—as swiftly as she dared—toward City Center.

Toward Decker—whom she apparently trusted with her life.

The American doctor stuck his head in the door. "Time," he said to Deck. "Chopper'll be here in thirty minutes. It's going to take you that long to get upstairs."

"Thanks." Decker nodded at Khalid, and together they began wheeling Murphy's bed out the door.

He glanced at the clock on the wall. Will Schroeder had left twenty minutes ago, riding Khalid's horse, broken wrist clutched to his chest. He'd volunteered to get Sophia, so Khalid could help carry Murphy to the roof. If Will could reach her in time, he could bring her back, so she could be smuggled out of the country aboard that helicopter, with Murphy.

There were no guarantees—that Will would make it to Rivka's without getting lost, that Sophia would trust Will and go with him, that they would get back here before that helo took off.

But sometimes everything in the universe lined up just right.

Sometimes it wasn't necessary to do every goddamn thing the hard way.

Maybe, just maybe, this was going to be one of those times.

Wouldn't *that* be nice?

"Mrs. Nash, your husband has come for you."

Inside the cell, Tess closed her eyes, preparing for this to be another round in this relentless and frightening mind game.

She'd stand up, heart pounding, ready to throw herself into Jimmy's waiting arms when the door swung open. Only he wouldn't be there. Her captors would laugh, telling her again that it was going to be days, maybe even weeks, before her husband tracked her down.

Of course, they'd say, maybe he'd be so glad to be rid of such a troublesome wife, he wouldn't even bother to look. He'd just go home without her.

Tess knew Jimmy would never do that. But finding her was a different story. Even if she managed to connect with him again—her guards hadn't searched her and didn't know about her phone—she had no clue where she was.

So she didn't move. She just sat there, daring to hope, but not to hope so much that she would cry if Jimmy weren't truly out there.

But the door opened and, dear God, there he was. He'd found her. Tess leapt to her feet, opening her mouth to greet him, to thank him for coming so quickly, but he spoke first.

"Not a word out of you." His voice was sharp, stern.

He met her eyes only briefly, and then he almost pointedly looked away, letting the police officer do all the talking.

"Put this on." Tess was handed a burka and robe.

She looked at Jimmy as she fastened the front of the robe. But she read nothing—*nothing*—on his face.

She knew she shouldn't speak, not after his admonition, but she couldn't keep from asking, "Is Murphy . . . ?"

"Silence" came Jimmy's terse reply, but he met her eyes and nodded once.

Murph was alive. Thank God. She put on the burka, and Jimmy reached over and lowered the heaviest screen. Okay. Now it was really dark.

He moved to her other side so he could take her by the elbow—the one that wasn't badly scraped.

"Watch your step," the policeman told her.

Yeah, no kidding. It wasn't easy going up those stairs with a bag on her head. But Jimmy held on to her.

"We hope never to see you back here again."

The feeling was definitely mutual.

She felt the warm blast of air as the door to the police station was opened. Freedom!

Jimmy kept his hold on her elbow going down the front stairs of the narrow little building and out into the street.

The wind was really starting to kick up—a storm was brewing—and it tugged at her burka, making it even harder to see.

And still Jimmy didn't say a word to her. He just led her down the street, walking much too quickly. He didn't slow until they turned first one corner and then another.

And then he stopped.

Tess peeked out from under the edge of the burka. They were in an alleyway, well off the main street, so she pulled it off entirely. It was hard to believe that just minutes ago she'd been cold.

Jimmy had his phone out and was dialing. He glanced at her, but still didn't speak, and then slightly turned away.

"Dave," he said into his phone. "Nash. Wow, another good connection. Yeah, I'm over near Rue de Palms, South. I'm not sure why, but my phone works over here." He paused. "No, I can't reach Decker either. If you talk to him, tell him I've got Tess—it's a long story, I'm not going into it now." Another pause. "Shit, you don't know about this, do you? Murph's been injured. Deck is with him—he's going to be all right, Deck's making sure of it. Just, if you talk to him, tell him Tess is safe." He glanced up at the sky as another ovenlike burst of wind tugged at Tess's robe. "I know he's going to be anxious to hear that, and I doubt he'll get back to Rivka's before this storm hits. We're going to be hard-pressed to make it ourselves." Another pause, then, "Yeah, thanks."

Jimmy flipped his phone shut, turning his full attention to Tess, taking in her sweat-matted hair and the collection of scrapes and bruises on her soot-smeared face.

He could probably tell from the tracks of clean on her cheeks just how much time she'd spent crying, just how frightened she'd been.

And still he showed no sign of emotion at all.

Until he spoke.

"I'm fine?" he said, throwing her words from their phone conversation back at her. "I'm *fine*?"

He actually shouted it, and Tess could now see on his face and in his eyes that he was furious—with her, at her, because of her. And he was finally letting it show.

She reminded herself that this was a good thing—far better than his keeping it all inside. She bumped the bricks of a building—a two-story house—with her back, but he still kept coming.

"You don't think it might be a good idea to mention that—oh, yeah—you're in a freaking prison cell in a country where civil rights means they only whip you within an inch of your life instead of killing you outright?" he asked her.

Tess was trapped against the building, penned in on one side by a stack of crates and on the other by a set of stairs leading down to what looked like a basement door. She lifted her chin. "I was fine. I am fine. They didn't hurt me."

He touched her jaw, no doubt checking to see if the darkness there was dirt or— She flinched. She was bruised from being hit when she wouldn't leave Murphy's side.

"They didn't hurt me much," she amended.

"God damn it, Tess." His voice broke and he pulled her into his arms and held her so tightly, she almost couldn't breathe. "I walked past this room," he told her, his voice muffled, his face buried against her, "an interrogation room. And I almost . . . Jesus Christ, I almost killed the motherfucker. He was lecturing me on how I should punish you. Fifteen lashes and four days of bread and water and God *damn* it! All I could think was if he'd hurt you, if he'd taken you in there and . . . Please tell me I got there in time."

Oh, Jimmy . . . "You did," Tess told him, holding him just as tightly. "You did. They just asked me questions and bullied me—they tried to scare me. They said you wouldn't find me—"

"You knew that was a lie, right?" he pulled back to ask, to gaze searchingly at her. "That I'd do whatever it took to find you?"

She nodded, her heart in her throat. "Yeah," she said. "I knew."

She also knew that he didn't mean it the way it sounded.

It wasn't meant to be romantic—he'd do whatever it took to find Decker or Dave or Murphy, if they were missing, too.

Although look at her. She couldn't even manage a friendly thank-you-for-saving-me embrace without playing with the man's hair with one hand and running the other down the broad expanse of his back. What was it about Jimmy Nash that made it so hard for her to keep her hands off him? She'd cried on Decker's shoulder last night and hadn't thought once of grabbing *his* ass.

"Sorry," she said. "I—"

But she couldn't apologize, because he kissed her.

He kissed her, hard, and—oh, God, she couldn't help it—she kissed him back.

Sophia hurried toward the hospital.

There was a storm coming, the wind kicking up whirling devils of dust—which was a good thing. It meant that she wasn't the only woman moving swiftly along the streets, as if trying to get home before the air got too thick with sand and dirt to see.

She heard what had to be a horse, hooves drumming, and she pulled back the heavy screen of her burka. Sure enough, a horse was charging down the middle of the street.

It looked a lot like Khalid's horse—it was the same shade of dirty white, and indeed, the rider was bareback. But that wasn't Decker up there playing cowboy. This man was taller, broader. He rode awkwardly, as if he'd never been on a horse before in his life.

Sophia lowered her veil as he went past, and pressed on. It couldn't be much more than another mile now.

Afterward—mere minutes after that first frantic kiss in the alleyway—Tess's first thought was, God, she was an idiot.

Could she *be* any more of an idiot?

And she was a weak-willed, totally predictable idiot, to boot.

Jimmy's head was down, and he was still catching his breath, but eventually—like within the next twenty seconds—he was going to open his eyes and look at her. It would sure help if she knew what she was going to say.

Sorry would make it sound as if she thought this was entirely her fault. But she had definitely not been alone in that mad scramble down those steps and through that rickety door into this dusty basement. Jimmy, after all, was the one who'd picked her up as if she weighed next to nothing and pressed her back up against this wall so she could wrap her legs around him and . . .

Oh, God, she'd wanted him so much and it had felt so good. . . .

But *thank you* was entirely too pathetic—as if he'd thrown her a bone. Which wasn't the case. Because he'd wanted her. Even if he hadn't told her—succinctly, albeit somewhat crudely—she would've caught on from his extreme sense of urgency.

No, what had just happened here wasn't about him rewarding or even comforting her. Once again, he'd been so quick on the trigger that if she hadn't been equally revved up, he would have left her in the dust.

This had been about taking, not giving. On both of their parts.

Maybe she should just say, *Excuse me.* As if the sex they'd just had was nothing more than a biological accident, like burping or farting. Whoops. Excuse me. Couldn't help *that.*

"Shit," Jimmy said. "*Shit.*"

Of course, *shit* was an option she hadn't considered. But, wow, it really did seem to say it all, didn't it?

And there it was, in his eyes as he pulled back to look at her. Total remorse.

"Shit," Tess echoed softly, because it certainly seemed to fit this situation.

There wasn't time for either of them to say anything more, because she heard it at the exact second Jimmy did—footsteps on the floorboards above them. Whoever's basement this was, they had just come home.

He quickly pulled out of her—all that solid, thick warmth suddenly gone—and helped her pull her pants back on, somehow putting himself back together, getting rid of the condom they'd used, all at the same time.

Thank God they'd used a condom. Thank God he'd had one to use.

Jimmy grabbed her hand and pulled her out the basement door and up the stairs, into the alley.

"Shit," he said again as a strong wind hit them. Apparently this was also a good comment to use after getting a faceful of sand.

Tess tried to spit with her mouth closed. God, she now had sand in her teeth. She felt it crunch just from tightening her jaw.

Overhead a helicopter thrummed—where did *that* come from? But talking meant opening her mouth again and there was no telling when another blast of sand was going to hit them.

Jimmy jammed her burka down onto her head, and for once she was grateful for it.

He pulled a bandanna from the same pocket that had held that lucky condom and tied it around his face, covering his mouth and nose. "It won't be so bad," he said to her then, "when the wind's at our back. Do you think you can run?"

Did he mean, *Do you think you can run in that robe?* or

Do you think you can run after that wobbly-knee-making sex we just had?

Either way, her answer was yes.

When Sophia arrived, Decker was standing in the lobby of the Hospital of the Servant of the Rightly Guided—the Hospital Abdul-Rasheed.

She knew from the look on his face as she approached him that something bad had happened.

"Murphy?" she asked.

He pulled her away from the other people waiting there. It was especially crowded because of the storm that was coming. Most people were choosing to wait it out here, in the relative comfort of the hospital lobby. "He's gone."

"Oh, no," she said, sickened by the senseless loss. Poor Angelina, making wedding plans back in California. "I'm so sorry. I didn't know him that well, but—"

"No." Decker stepped closer, lowered his voice. "He's alive. But we got him out of here on a Red Cross helo—"

"Helo?" she asked.

"Helicopter, chopper."

Ah. She'd seen one pass over her head just minutes ago. And she understood, instantly, why Decker had wanted her to come down here. Murphy was gone—and if she'd been here on time, she'd be gone, too.

"I'm sorry," she said again. "I hurried. . . ."

"It was worth the try," he told her with the same calm he'd used to reassure Khalid back in the barn. "We do the best we can—sometimes it works. Sometimes it doesn't. But now the million-dollar question is whether we should stay here to wait out the storm or—" He swore sharply.

Sophia peered from the screen of her burka, following his gaze out the front windows.

Two open trucks, each filled with a dozen members of

Bashir's patrols, were pulling up. It was clear the soldiers were intending to take shelter from the sandstorm here in the hospital lobby.

"I need to leave," Sophia told him. "Right now."

It was amazing how cool and collected her voice sounded to her own ears, considering the panic that was rising inside her.

Decker didn't hesitate. He took her by the elbow and headed for the side door.

Where—no!—another truck filled with soldiers was pulling up.

"Don't stop," he told her. "If you stop suddenly, it'll draw attention to us. Come on, we can do this. We're just going to walk right on past them."

She was safe, she was safe, she was safe. Decker would not let anything happen to her.

"Hold on to your burka," he told her as they approached the door, and he even managed to smile, as if he thought that was funny. "I mean that literally, hon. The wind's picking up."

He wasn't kidding. As they went outside, Sophia was glad for his steadying grip on her elbow. Without it, she felt as if she might've blown away.

But coming out that side door, she realized where they were. "The Hotel Français is only a few blocks from here."

"Which way?" he asked.

"Left."

Either way they had to walk right past the soldiers. Sophia kept her head down, her feet moving. . . .

"Hey, American . . ."

Don't stop, don't stop, whoever it was, they weren't talking to them.

"Hey!" It was louder now, and Decker did stop. "Where are you going in this weather?"

"Is there a problem, sir?" Decker answered. It was a different dialect than the one Khalid spoke, but once again his grammar was perfect.

The soldier laughed. "The problem is crazy Americans who don't appreciate how deadly a storm like this can be."

"We've got a few more minutes before it gets bad, Lieutenant," Decker told him, as calm as can be. "And we don't have far to go."

They started walking again.

"Hey!"

Sophia withdrew her arm from the spacious sleeve of her robe, reaching to take her gun from the pocket of the jeans Tess had lent to her.

Decker spoke to her in a low voice. "Easy. There's still plenty of talking left to do." He turned back to the lieutenant. "Yes, sir?"

"Here, crazy American," the man said. "Catch."

And he threw something at Decker. It was a scarf to tie around his face, to keep the blowing dust and dirt from his mouth and nose.

"It'll be useful," the lieutenant said, "even though you don't have far to go."

"Thank you, Lieutenant," Decker said. "You're too kind." He wrapped it around his face.

"Go with God," the lieutenant told them as he followed his men into the hospital lobby.

They walked on, Decker's hand still on her elbow, Sophia's heart still pounding.

CHAPTER
TWENTY

"I LIVED here off and on for about five years," Sophia told Decker, "starting the summer I turned ten."

The hotel was dark, the storm outside making the late afternoon seem more like night.

Decker shook sand and dirt from his clothes and hair. He'd need two weeks of showers to get the last of it out of his ears.

He followed Sophia up the stairs, thinking, *Shit*. This was the perfect end to one total goatfuck of a day. Murphy injured, Tess locked up . . . And now here he was, back at the scene of the crime, so to speak, where he'd let Sophia . . .

Oh, yeah. This boarded-up hotel could be made into a memorial to Deck's bad judgment.

He should have known that Sophia wouldn't be able to make it over to the hospital in time. Instead he'd risked it, which resulted in her being in danger of being discovered by Bashir's men, which resulted in the two of them—tah dah da dah, sound the official Fuckup's Fanfare!—right back here. Thank you *very* much. Alone together until the storm ended.

Which could easily be until morning.

Decker opened his phone. Nothing happening there. Not that he'd expected it. With this wind, their sat-dish was in Pakistan.

"Nash called me," Sophia said as she led him down the

hall. "On Murphy's phone. He said he was on his way to Tess. He seemed to know where she was."

"Yeah," Decker said. "I'm sure he arranged for her release. He was, uh, pretty upset."

"I know that they're not really married," she told him.

"No, actually, they are."

She gave him such a disbelieving look that he couldn't help it, he laughed. "Okay," he admitted. "They aren't. Who gave it away?"

"You did," she told him.

Now it was his turn to look at her quizzically.

"You're kidding, right?" she said. "I mean, it's pretty obvious that you're in love with her."

Decker stopped short. "You're wrong. I'm not."

"My mistake." Sophia opened a pair of French doors into an enormous room with big windows. There was slightly more light in there, and Decker slowly followed her in. "This was my favorite room in the hotel. The grand ballroom. This was where Yousef, the eldest son of Prince Zevket, first met Madeleine Lewis. Do you know that story?"

"No." The windows looked out on the hotel's center courtyard. It was dusty and neglected, with a center fountain that had broken in two. Did Sophia really think he was in love with Tess?

But she had gone into tour guide mode, ultrasmooth and extra fake. She sure could tap dance when she thought she needed to. He wished she didn't think she needed to when she was around him.

They'd been on the verge of some kind of breakthrough this morning, before Khalid had burst in. She'd actually started to cry—real tears, not those crocodile ones she did so well.

"It was June 1920," she was telling him now, as if he gave a good goddamn about Prince Whosis and Madeleine . . . Albright? No, that wasn't right.

"Madeleine was the daughter of a famous nature photographer—Reginald Lewis."

Lewis, that was the name.

"Yousef gave up his kingdom to be with her, and Madeleine, well, her father disowned her, too," Sophia continued. "But they didn't care. They went to America together and lived happily ever after. Until Hitler invaded Poland and started World War Two. Madeleine lost her husband and both of her sons in the war." She sighed dramatically. "I used to wonder, what if, when she stood in this room, at the very moment that she fell in love with Prince Yousef, what if she had the power to know what was to come? All that heartache and loss . . . Would she have taken that same path anyway?"

She fell silent, staring out the window, down at the courtyard, at a dried piece of brush that was being tossed about in the wind.

"I used to think no. If she knew, how could she bear to . . . ," she said softly as Decker held his breath, as the real Sophia peeked out. "But now . . . I don't know."

She looked up and laughed much too brightly—an attempt to slam the door shut that didn't quite work. "I mean, twenty-two years of happiness—that's more than most people get, don't you think?"

It was a rhetorical question, but Decker answered it anyway. "I think life is hard," he told her. "I think sometimes some people get lucky, and then it's less hard for them, for a while. I think twenty-two years of happiness is a gift. If that's really what they shared. And you're assuming a lot there, because a lot can happen in twenty-two years."

She turned again to look at him. "She's really nice, you know—Tess. Sometimes you can say that about people and it's not meant to be a compliment, like nice is something bad, but I don't mean it that way. Tess really *is* genuinely nice. Except she's in love with Nash. That must be fun, huh?" She laughed again, more fake merriment. Being here with him like this must really be making her nervous. He didn't blame her. He was on edge, too. "Although she'll get over *that* soon enough."

"No, she won't."

"Trust me, she will."

Decker smiled and shook his head. "I don't think so."

"Time will tell."

"Yes, it will," he agreed.

"You could just kind of hang out, you know, underneath the basket, ready for the rebound. . . ."

"You play basketball?" he asked, desperate to change the subject.

"Yeah, right." She laughed, far too gaily. He wished she would cut that out. "I'm the star center of the Kazabek women's basketball league. Can't you just see us running down the court, burkas on?" Her smile weakened, but then came back, brighter than ever. "Seriously though, Dimitri was a big Lakers fan. He lived in Los Angeles for a couple of years and got hooked. Thank goodness for satellite TV."

Maybe she'd begin to relax if he wasn't looming over her. Decker didn't often loom—he just wasn't that tall—but she was on the short side of average. He sat down on the floor, leaning back against the wall beneath the windows.

"I know I make you nervous," he said, figuring why the fuck not simply grab the proverbial bull by the horns. "I hope you're not afraid of me."

He'd managed to surprise her. "No," she said. "I'm not."

She slowly sat down, not quite beside him, but not on the other side of the room either. And he could see in the dim light from the windows that she'd stopped with the fake smiles.

"What happened between us—," he started.

"I don't want to talk about that." Damn it, now she was on her feet again.

"What *do* you want to talk about?" he asked, looking up at her. "Dimitri?"

It was obvious that was the last thing she'd expected him to suggest. "*You* want to talk about Tess?"

"Okay," he said, because he knew an affirmative reply would keep her off balance. He didn't particularly want to share his feelings about Tess with her, but what the hell. He'd already shared physical intimacies with this woman, and being honest about this might do him good. "I'll tell you this—you're partly right. I probably could love her—it wouldn't take a lot. You said it yourself—she's genuine all the time, and I like that about her. I like her—I admire her—very much."

The expression on Sophia's face made him keep going.

"I'm also attracted to her," Decker confessed. "She's, uh . . ." How should he say this? "She's got a body type that I happen to appreciate. I mean, I like women with women's bodies and she's got one of those. *And* a brain to match. Smart women do it for me. I just don't get why some women think they need to pretend they're stupid to be attractive to men." He laughed. "Maybe so they're attractive to the stupid men, but . . . I also happen to think that Tess is the best thing that ever happened to Nash, if you'll excuse the clichéd expression. I'm okay with that—really—because to be honest, I don't know if I could handle two years of happiness, let alone twenty-two."

Sophia slowly sat down next to him. "Why not?" she asked softly.

She was finally here with him. The real Sophia. The strangely shy Sophia, who didn't quite know what to say to him without putting on her big fake act. The one who'd been forced, for months, to give sexual favors to strangers.

The one who'd probably seen her husband murdered right in front of her eyes.

"Because, like I said, life is hard," Decker said slowly. "And sometimes it can be brutally harsh. I've seen some terrible things that . . ." He shook his head. "It's hard to explain, Sophia. I'm not keeping secrets from you, I just can't . . . Maybe what I feel is like survivor's guilt. How can I let myself be that happy when . . . I had friends on the *Cole,* and in Khobar Towers. Friends who died on 9/11. They don't get even one more day of happiness, you know?"

She nodded, her face pale in the fading light.

"But then I come to places like Kazabek, and I think what the hell am I doing here? I'm fighting terrorism, but I'm only fighting the symptoms. I'm not getting anywhere close to the cause." Decker was silent for a moment. "In the end, I just do the best I can. That's all I can do. That's all anyone can do, I guess."

They sat for many long minutes in silence, as it got darker and darker in the room, as the wind howled outside.

"I can't talk about Dimitri," Sophia finally whispered. "I . . ."

"That's okay," Decker said quietly.

He could barely see her in the dimness. She was sitting with her back against the wall, knees up, arms folded around them. As he watched, she rested her forehead on her arms.

"I loved him," she admitted. "And he loved me. I lied about that . . . the other day."

"Yeah," he said. "I pretty much knew that."

"We were working—*I* was working—with this group that was trying to restore democracy to Kazbekistan," she said softly. "It was so stupid. I should have known Bashir would find out that we were involved. It was a death sentence if we were caught, but I never thought . . . We'd done business with him in the past, gone right into the palace. A lunchtime meeting didn't seem out of the ordinary. But I trusted the wrong people. Michel Lartet—he was Dimitri's friend, and . . . I trusted him because it was so obvious that we'd all make more money with Bashir out of power. It never occurred to me that Lartet would sell us out."

"You helped your husband run his business?" Decker asked her.

"It was my business," she told him, lifting her head to look in his direction. But Decker knew she couldn't see his face any more clearly than he could see hers, and hers was a pale blur. "My company. Dimitri only pretended to run it. He wanted to go to France, to safety, when the government fell. But I thought we'd turn a bigger profit by sticking around. So we stayed."

They sat in silence again, and Decker knew from the sound of her breathing that she was holding back her tears.

He waited, but she wasn't going to say it.

So Decker said it for her. "You think he died because of you."

That did the trick. She finally started to cry. "I know he did. And then I . . . I betrayed him."

"No," he said. "You survived. I think he'd be glad about that."

Decker didn't touch her. He didn't dare. He just sat beside Sophia Ghaffari as she let herself grieve.

Jimmy had been out in the barn with Tess, getting an updated situation report about Ma'awiya Talal Sayid from Dave. They still didn't know what medical condition he'd had, or what kind of treatment he'd needed, but Dave *had* found out that there were no records of any shipments of medical equipment from the Cantara Hospital to Bashir's palace during the week immediately preceding the earthquake.

There were, however, records of deliveries to the palace that corresponded with Sayid's previous visits.

Dave was in the process of telling them that he was working on getting an exact list of the medical equipment when Guldana had come in, shutting down their conversation.

The Kazbekistani woman had informed them that due to the bad weather, the party she and Rivka had planned to celebrate Jimmy and Tess's recent wedding was canceled.

What a shame. Jimmy had tried to look disappointed.

However. She was not going to let her good meal go to waste. Dinner would be in an hour. In her best public defender's voice, Guldana ordered Jimmy to wash up and change before coming inside. And then, refusing to hear Tess's arguments—helped by the fact that Tess didn't speak K-stani and Guldana didn't speak English—Guldana took Tess with her back into the house.

Tess had met Jimmy's gaze before Guldana wrapped a blanket around her as protection against the wind and sand. Her unspoken message was clear. Sooner or later they had to talk.

About the fact that they'd had sex.

Again.

Despite his resolve to stay away from her.

Damn it, he'd come freaking close to doing her right there in an alleyway. Engaging in a public act of lasciviousness was an offense that was punishable by death.

Hers, not his.

And, just to put the icing on the cake, there was the Decker thing. Decker pretended it didn't matter, but Jimmy knew better. In a perfect world, Tess should have been Deck's girlfriend. So okay. The world was less than perfect, and accidents happened.

But nailing Tess to the wall in some strangers' basement could not be passed off as an accident.

Although it had been there, in the aftermath, that Jimmy had had a eureka moment.

This was how he was going to do it. It was a win-win situation. He was going to have the instant gratification of a sexual relationship with Tess, which would, in turn, be the impetus of his split from Decker.

Deck would be so disgusted with him that he'd be glad when Jimmy made some lame excuse not to be part of the next assignment he got from Tom Paoletti. And without Jimmy around, weighing him down, making people eye him suspiciously, Decker would have the career he deserved.

"Tough day," Dave commented as the door closed behind Tess.

"Yeah," Jimmy agreed. He'd've thought that figuring out a win-win plan would make him feel less like a giant loser.

Although the day had not been without good news. Murphy had made it onto that chopper and gotten out before the sandstorm hit. Khalid had ridden Marge back to the barn to share that information with them.

The kid had also reported that Will Schroeder, hero of the hour, had finally gone into the ER to get his broken wrist treated. Deck was still in City Center, too, with Sophia.

All in all, things could've been a whole helluva lot worse.

He and Tess could've been caught in the midst of their joyride. Tess could've pushed him away, for that matter, instead of damn near igniting in his arms as she hungrily kissed him back.

God damn, the woman could kiss.

"The storm should abate around four a.m.," Dave said.

Jimmy's heart did a curious dance. It should have been sinking because he wouldn't be able to avoid that impending conversation with Tess by going out into the night. *Sorry, babe, can't talk now—have to go save the world.*

Instead he'd be forced to go into that upstairs bedroom with her and lock the door behind them and . . .

"You sure about that?" Jimmy asked Dave.

And admit that he could no longer keep his hands off of her, drop to his knees, and beg for more.

Please . . .

Tess had done some begging just a few hours ago. She'd begged for him to hurry as he'd fumbled to cover himself and then . . . *God* . . .

"Yup."

It took Jimmy a moment or two to remember what Dave was agreeing to. Storm. End. Four. Tonight.

Right.

Although it wasn't as if Dave had access to the K-stani version of the Weather Channel. But then again, Dave was currently in the middle of a record-winning streak when it came to providing accurate information. If he said the storm would freaking abate by four, Jimmy should probably take it as gospel.

"I'll make sure Tess knows," Jimmy told him. She was going to want to get out there and set up another of those portable sat-dishes as soon as possible—get their feeble communications system up and limping along again.

But first they had to endure Guldana's dinner.

And then . . .

"James, are you all right?" Dave asked.

"I'm fine," he said, and went to get washed up for dinner.

Sophia awoke with a start, sitting bolt upright, her heart pounding. Where was she?

"It's all right." Lawrence Decker's evenly modulated voice came out of the darkness. "I'm on watch."

And she remembered. She was in the ballroom of the Hotel Français. Outside the window, a sandstorm raged.

Padsha Bashir had a price on her head—literally. And Dimitri was dead.

"Go back to sleep," Decker told her.

The way he said it made her think of *Star Wars*. Of Obi-Wan Kenobi and his Jedi mind tricks.

You will now go back to sleep.

"Put your head down," Decker told her.

She wasn't sure how he could see her in this darkness, but she obeyed him, settling back on the coolness of the floor, wishing she had a pillow or two.

"No one's going to be out on a night like tonight," he told her quietly. "You're safe here."

She was safe. She knew that she was. This man wasn't going to let anyone hurt her. She actually believed that to be true.

It was quite a remarkable feeling.

"Close your eyes. Go to sleep," he told her again.

So she did.

Tess was sitting at the card table that Guldana had set up right there in the third-floor bedroom when Jimmy Nash came in.

He looked confused as he closed the door behind him—she didn't blame him.

"I'm sorry about this," she told him, gesturing to all of it. The table covered with the ornately decorated cloth, the festive meal for two laid out upon it, the romantic candles that made their shadows jump intimately around the room, even herself. She'd been transformed, too.

"Stopping Guldana wasn't . . ." Tess tried to laugh. "Well, the words 'more powerful than a locomotive' come to mind."

He was looking at her, at the dress Guldana had made for her. Well, Guldana had said *dress*—it was one of the few K-stani words Tess recognized—but this thing was a nightgown, really. It wasn't something that could be worn in public, unless maybe you were Lil' Kim.

It was sort of funny to think about—all those K-stani women, so chastely covered in their full-length robes, wearing the equivalent of Victoria's Secret lingerie beneath.

Funny. Right. As if anything having to do with women in K-stan could be considered at all funny. Tess still got a lump in her throat whenever she came face-to-face with Guldana—a still young, very vibrant woman, despite the fact that her dark hair was prematurely streaked with gray.

Guldana was—had been—a lawyer before the regime change. She'd worked hard to get an education, to build a career and all that came with it—not just a sizable income, but also the respect of her peers.

But according to the current laws, under the warlords' rule, men and women could not be peers. Women were not allowed to work. Guldana was forbidden from practicing law.

Tess could not imagine what it had been like—to lose everything, practically overnight. To wake up to find herself suddenly in a world where merely speaking up could be punishable by a severe beating.

"She brought me up here," Tess told Jimmy, "and she'd already filled the bathtub with water that she heated in the kitchen. I mean, she carried it up all those stairs in buckets, and what was I supposed to say? No, I don't want to take a bath? I was dying to. Then once I took the bath, it seemed rude to not put on the dress—I mean, she went to all that trouble to make it and to cook this dinner, too, and she was already disappointed about having to cancel the party and . . . I'm sorry, but I just couldn't tell her no."

Jimmy didn't say anything, he just sat down across from her.

He looked good in candlelight. His hair was wet and slicked back from his face, which, along with the dancing shadows in the room, really accentuated his movie-star cheekbones and eyes.

"I have no idea what she put in my hair," Tess told him, since it seemed clear that he wasn't going to say anything at all, and the silence was freaking her out, "but it's kind of slippery. It smells good, so I guess it could be worse. She went really heavy with the eyeliner, and you know me, I don't normally wear a lot of makeup, so . . . Yikes. I look kind of, you know, 1989 Goth. . . ."

Jimmy smiled at that. And finally spoke. "It works," he said. But his smile faded much too soon, and he sighed as he looked at all the food laid out in front of them. "This smells amazing."

"Yes," she said. "Yes, it does." She was so completely not hungry at all. She wasn't going to be able to eat, not even a single bite.

He met her eyes again, but only briefly. "So . . . do we eat? Do we talk? Eat and talk? Talk, then eat? Eat, then talk?"

Tess couldn't keep from laughing. "If I didn't know better, I'd think you were nervous."

He laughed, too. "Yeah, well, I am. Nervous. I'm *beyond* nervous. I'm . . ."

He was serious. As she watched, he seemed to brace himself. He looked directly at her and said, "I owe you an apology."

Tess looked down at her plate—anything to keep from maintaining eye contact—and sighed. *And here we go. . . .* "No, Jimmy, you don't."

"Yeah, I do."

Okay. She just had to do this. Get it over with. It was her turn to brace herself, after which she forced herself to look up and steadily hold his gaze. She was blushing, though. She knew she was. "What happened this afternoon wasn't—"

"That's not what—" he interrupted but then cut himself off. Frowned slightly. "What happened this afternoon wasn't what?"

"Your fault," she finished.

"Oh. Well, I guess that's probably a matter of interpretation, but—"

She had to know. She had an idea, but . . . "What did you think I was going to say?"

That stopped him cold. His eyes shifted, very slightly. "I don't know."

Yeah, he was *so* lying. Tess laughed her outrage. "You thought I was going to say, 'What happened this afternoon really wasn't that big a deal, I mean, it doesn't even count as real sex because it was over so soon, and as far as orgasms went it only rated about a point oh five on a scale from one to ten,' and you are *such* a loser, Nash, because you can't even go into your 'That Was a Mistake, Tess' speech until you run 'Was It Good for You, Too?' and reassure yourself that yes, you are a sex god."

She was good and mad at him now—which sure beat embarrassed—and she pushed her chair back from the table and stood. "Screw you, Nash. You've got the floor tonight, I've got the bed. I don't care whose turn it really is. I'm exhausted, I'm sore, I've got scrapes in places I didn't know it was possible to scrape—"

"Are you all right?" He actually sounded concerned.

Compared to Murphy, she was ready to run a marathon. But compared to the way she'd felt a week ago as she'd gotten ready for bed in her own apartment . . .

"Everything hurts," she told him. "My toenails hurt, all right? So just let me get some sleep."

She heard him sigh as she crossed to the bed and pulled back the covers. Damn it, she had this slimy stuff on her hair. She could either wash it out now, with the tepid water still in the bathtub, or wash it out in the morning, when the water was cold.

"Do I get a chance to talk?" Jimmy asked. "Or would you just prefer to go with the script you wrote?"

Washing it out meant she'd have to walk right past him.

Cold water in the morning might be nice, but not washing it out now meant she'd slime up the sheets, which she'd surely regret tomorrow night.

"Okay," he said. "Now you're not talking to me. Nice."

Tess sighed as she set the alarm on her watch. "I'm *not* not talking to you, Nash. I'm just not talking. I'm tired. I've had something of an eventful day."

"Don't set it for any earlier than four a.m.," Jimmy told her.

"I have to replace that sat-dish under cover of darkness," she reminded him. "Four a.m. is cutting it a little close."

"You can't replace it until the wind stops," he pointed out. "That's not going to happen until about four."

Still . . . "I'll check the weather around midnight," she told him.

"*Dave* says the storm's not going to end until about four."

She reset her watch to two a.m.

"So Dave's information is good, while mine is suspect," he said.

"Dave is happy to let everyone do their share, while it wouldn't surprise me one bit if I woke up at four to find out that while we mere mortals were sleeping, you single-handedly replaced the damaged equipment, led Sophia— on foot—over the mountains and across the border to safety, *and* rebuilt Khalid's house and barn."

"Damn," Jimmy said. "You really think I'm that good, huh?"

"That wasn't a compliment," she told him as she rummaged in her bag for the T-shirt she slept in. "You're a lousy team player, Nash. The part I left out was where your brain explodes from lack of sleep—and then we're left short-handed."

"I've slept more on this assignment than I ever have before," Jimmy told her. "I think I've got at least, oh, four or five solid days before my brain explodes."

God. "Is everything a joke to you?"

His response was immediate. "No, which is why I want you to sit back down so we can talk."

"So you can apologize," she clarified.

"I'm sorry *is* one of the things I'd like to say, yeah. Because I am. I'm sorry. I'm really sorry. I shouldn't have lied to you."

What? She turned to look at him. Did he just say . . . ?

"Although, you know, it really wasn't a complete lie when I said it," he continued. "Even though I *did* really want to, I also didn't. Because, well, Deck's my friend, and I thought maybe if I was out of the picture he'd have a chance with you and—"

"What are you talking about?" Tess asked.

He stared at her. "What?"

"You lost me," she said. "You're sorry because you *lied* to me? Which lie, exactly, are you referring to, Nash? I want to make sure we're talking about the same one."

He made one of those wounded, offended sounds that liars could make so well.

"You lie so often, you don't even recognize when you're doing it anymore." She held out her hand, pretending to be him, lowering her voice to say, "Hi, how're you doing? I'm Nash. Diego Nash." She switched back to her own voice. "Truth or lie?"

He laughed. "It's not that simple."

And again, she'd had enough. "You want to apologize to me?" she started, as he spoke over her.

"Okay. You're right," he said. "I lie. All the time because, yes, that's not the name I was born with. But you're wrong, too. It also happens to be the truth, because it's who I am right now. Like most things, it's more yin and yang than truth or lie."

"Oh, just cut the crap and apologize, Confucius, so we can get this over with!"

He must've known she was seconds from losing it, because he obviously reined himself in. "I'm sorry for—," he started.

"Apology accepted." She turned away.

He was on his feet. "God damn it—"

"I think you should sleep in the barn," she told him, praying he would leave the room before all her frustration and anger and upset from this awful, awful day took its toll and she started to cry.

"—you don't even know what I'm apologizing for!"

"I don't care," she whispered. "I just want you to go."

"Well, tough shit," he said. "Because I do care, and I'm not going until you hear me out. Jesus Christ, Tess, what happened this afternoon in that basement was *the* most honest interchange we've had since I got back from Mexico."

Mexico. That made her turn around to look at him. He'd actually dared to mention *Mexico*?

"I lied when I said I didn't want to sleep with you again," he told her, his voice softer now, barely more than a whisper. "Same way you lied when you said you didn't want to sleep with me."

Oh, God. "But I don't want to sleep with you," Tess whispered back. "What happened today was—"

But he was shaking his head. "I'm not talking about this kind of want." Jimmy tapped his temple with his finger. He had such long, elegant, graceful fingers. "I'm talking about *this* want." He covered his heart with his hand. "*This* want." His hand went lower, cupping his crotch.

"There are all these reasons up here"—he tapped his head again—"for staying apart. The head goes, *No no no, don't do that because dot dot dot,* but the body goes, *Yeah, but I WANT to.*" He laughed. "It's kind of crazy, actually. I'm out in the barn, and there's Sophia, and I look at her, and up here"—he tapped his head again—"I'm thinking— Okay, look, it's a man thing. Men just think this way, and I apologize for it in advance. But I'm thinking, Wow, there's a woman who's extremely attractive—she's got everything in the right place, nicely proportioned, pretty hair, pretty face—wouldn't *that* be a truly enjoyable fuck— No, don't turn away, Tess, because down here . . . Look at me," he commanded, and she saw he had his hand on his heart. "Down here, there's nothing. Down here I'm thinking, Hey Blondie, move out of the way so I can look at Tess. I'm thinking, Where's Tess, because even though I can't make her come ten different ways the way I *want* to, at least I can look at her and imagine it."

She had to sit down. She felt behind her for the bed and sank down onto it.

He moved toward her. "Tell me you don't think about it 24/7. You and me."

Dear God. Tess wasn't sure she could speak, so she nodded. Yes. Yes, she thought about it. About him. All the time.

And there they were, in the candlelight, gazing at each other. Thinking about that afternoon, in the basement. The sound Jimmy had made as he'd entered her, first with his fingers and then . . .

At least that was what Tess was thinking about. She swallowed, and it seemed to echo in the quiet of the room.

Jimmy cleared his throat. "Yeah," he said. "So, I pretty much knew you felt that way from the start, and that was, um, scary, because if you weren't going to be sending out slow-down signals, that left it up to me, which basically meant we were going to spend this entire mission fucking like bunnies." He laughed as he said it, but he looked at her sitting there on the bed, then lifted one eyebrow very slightly. "I don't suppose you want to . . . ?"

Tess laughed, and she knew he'd done that on purpose. He'd made an effort to lighten up this conversation, to break the mood. Still, she stood up. Moved away from the bed.

"No. Because we're not . . . We're people, Jimmy." God, he was right—it had been much easier when she thought he didn't want her. "So what's your deal? You just decided this afternoon that, hey, this not having sex with Tess really isn't working. Why don't I try *having* sex with her for a while?"

He actually thought about that for a few moments, then nodded. "Yeah, I guess so. I guess maybe because we both seemed to reach our limit—"

"Temporarily," she interjected.

He thought about that, too. "Is that really what you think? Because I don't. I admit that this isn't the most comfortable place to be, because it means I'm going to have to have a conversation with Decker and that's going to blow. But I think we've crossed the line too many times, and I for one am not interested in going back."

Oh, God. "Then I guess I'm the one who's going to have to give the mistake speech," Tess said. "Because this afternoon *was* a mistake—"

"You want to have a relationship?" Jimmy interrupted her. "Because if you want, you could give me the hard relationship speech instead."

Tess looked at him, hard. "Are you mocking me?"

"No," he said, but then he smiled. "Well, maybe a little. Look, I'll save you the trouble and get right to the bottom line. People aren't bunnies, right? Right. People—particularly female people—have relationships. So . . . you want to have a relationship? Because I do. I want to have a relationship with you. I want it very much."

It was so bizarre. It was as if Tess were living one of her wildest fantasies. Jimmy Nash standing in front of her, telling her that he wanted . . .

This was surreal. This man was a born liar. What did he *really* want? "What kind of relationship?" she asked.

He frowned slightly. "I don't know. A regular one. What do you mean?"

"Exclusive?" she asked.

"Yeah, isn't that what makes it a real relationship?" he asked. "Sure, I know some people have open ones, but that's kind of like having a sky roof. Pointless. I mean, you can say it exists, but whenever you look up, nothing's there."

"Some people can make it work," she argued. "A relationship can be anything you want it to be. It's an individual thing—custom made. Everyone gets to set their own rules, define their own boundaries. What do *you* want this relationship to be? I mean, I have to know before I can even consider agreeing to it. And you have to know what I would want from you, too."

"Okay," he said slowly. "I guess I want this to be a relationship where I would always go along with you if you were going someplace dangerous, and, um, one where you could make me laugh and maybe, hopefully, I could make you laugh, too, and . . ." He shrugged. "The rest of the time we'd, you know."

"Yeah." She *did* know. And was this his true goal here? "We'd fuck like bunnies."

Jimmy smiled. For some reason, he always smiled like that when she used adult language. "Yeah," he agreed. And then he stood there and watched her, and waited.

He'd left out an awful lot. Like a need for honesty and openness, a need for communication, for sharing secrets, for trust.

But those were her rules.

God, she'd be crazy to trust this man.

"I don't know if I can do this," she admitted. "I don't know if I want to do this."

"You do." He was completely serious. "I don't really know why, but you definitely do. I'm not a nice person. I've done things that would shock and offend you, and . . . you still like me. And it has nothing to do with the fact that I'm good in bed, probably because I haven't managed to convince you of that yet."

"How do I know," Tess said, "that as soon as we get back to the States, you won't run away to Mexico again?"

"Okay," he said, starting to pace, but stopping himself mid-stride. "Good. Yeah. I prepared for this one."

She laughed in disbelief. "Prepared . . . ?"

"Oh, yeah. You think I didn't know I was going to have to work to talk you into this?" he asked her. "To be honest, I don't know why I ran like that. I just . . . I had to book it out of town. I don't . . . Bottom line, I have no real excuse."

Tess waited, but he didn't say anything more. "That's your prepared answer?" she finally asked. "That you have no real excuse?"

He nodded. "Yeah."

"You couldn't come up with something better than that?"

"Well, yeah," Jimmy said. "I could, but . . . it wouldn't be the truth."

Ding. If this conversation had had a scoreboard, Jimmy would've just made another point. But he didn't need a tally to know that. He just had to look at her. Which he was doing from across the room.

Although, little by little, he just kept getting closer.

"So what happens now?" Tess asked. "I say okay, and you give me your class ring, and that means we're . . . what? Going steady?"

"I don't have a class ring to give you. Probably because I never went to class. Although if you really want a token of my affection, you could tell me who you want killed, and I could take care of it for you." He smiled.

"That's not funny," she said.

"Yes, it is," he said, and he was finally close enough, so he kissed her.

And it happened again. Tess closed her eyes and kissed him, too, but she couldn't just kiss him without touching him. And she couldn't touch him without wanting him closer, and suddenly she opened her eyes, and they were on the bed, bodies pressed together, legs entwined, hearts pounding.

"God *damn*," Jimmy breathed as he lifted his head to look down at her. "Don't you maybe want to take it slowly for a change?"

She didn't take the time to answer. She just pulled his head down for another kiss. Slowly meant there'd be time to think, and right now she didn't want to do anything but feel.

The first kiss had gotten them over to the bed, and this second went a long way toward getting them naked. Which, with all that skin against skin, felt almost unbearably good.

Jimmy—who had probably never gone anywhere without a supply of prophylactics in his pocket from the time he turned sixteen—seemed to pluck a condom from thin air and somehow covered himself. And by their third kiss, he was inside of her.

Which was just what she wanted. She wanted no-frills, missionary-position sex—full penetration, no imagination, hard and fast and deep.

But Jimmy not only stopped kissing her, he held himself still and kept her from moving, too. Well, at least he kept her from moving the way she wanted to be moving.

"Hey . . ." She opened her eyes.

"How do you do?" he said from his vantage point directly above her. "I'm the guy you're having sex with. I was feeling just a little anonymous, so I thought I'd call a time-out."

Anonymous? Was he kidding? "Jimmy," she said, and she pulled his head down so she could kiss him.

But he pulled back. Somehow he caught her wrists with only one of his hands, and held them above her head. Of course, that made it more difficult for him to hold her hips still. But despite that, he managed to keep himself just too far away from her, which was driving her crazy.

"This also gives me the opportunity to not come within twenty-five seconds of the time we start having sex," he told her. His eyes were half-closed now and it was getting harder for him to talk—he clearly liked the way she was moving beneath him. "Which could go a long way in my attempt to convince you to have sex with me again."

Smart man, he'd noticed that she hadn't actually said yes to any kind of a relationship.

Stupid man, he didn't realize that they already had a relationship.

"Despite evidence to the contrary," he continued, "I don't always lose control."

Didn't he realize . . . ?

"But I love it when you do," she told him breathlessly. "It's amazing. It's . . . It's like when you kiss me." She could see from his eyes that he was trying to understand, but he just didn't get it. This wasn't a particularly good time to attempt a complicated explanation but she gave it a try. She wanted him to know. "When you kiss me, the world disappears. I lose track of everything but you, and . . ." She knew what to do. "Kiss me."

He did—a little ridiculous smack on her lips.

She looked at him.

He smiled. And kissed her properly.

Total meltdown. And it wasn't just on her end. Suddenly her hands were free—Jimmy must've let her go. And he even forgot whatever game it was he was playing, because he pushed himself deeply inside of her.

It was enough, in turn, to push her right over the edge. Which was all it took—didn't he know how thrilling that was?—to make him follow.

Nevertheless, Jimmy didn't stop kissing her for a good long time.

CHAPTER
TWENTY-ONE

"GOT A minute?" Nash asked, his voice lowered.

Decker glanced up from the papers and maps spread out on the bale of hay. "What's up?"

Nash looked over to where Sophia was curled up, sleeping on a blanket, right on the barn floor.

After the storm, the walk back from the Hotel Français had been uneventful. Upon their return, Decker had told Sophia that she'd be perfectly safe—and far more comfortable—sleeping in the pantry, in the house. But she'd told him she felt more secure in the barn.

With him.

"Not in here," Nash said now. "Can we step outside?"

"One second," Decker said. He had to cross the St. James Hospital off the list. That was kind of funny. St. *James.*

Tess had printed out a list of every hospital and health clinic in Kazabek and the immediate suburbs, and he was marking each of them on the map. If he, Dave, and Nash each visited two per day, checking to see if they'd made a delivery of the medical equipment Sayid had needed, they'd be here for at least another week and a half.

And that was only this list.

Across the room, Dave had a similar list of hospitals and clinics in all the outlying suburbs and villages within a few dozen miles.

Tess was now upstairs, on her computer, attempting to

get a message out to Tom Paoletti. She and Nash had gone out early and replaced their sat-dish, but this new system wasn't running as well as the old one had. Which was one of those incredible hindsight revelations. Deck hadn't realized how well their communication system *had* been running—until it was gone.

Tess was trying to send an email request for additional autopsy information on Sayid. There had been no mention of a medical condition—a blood disorder or other chronic disease—in the original autopsy report. If the client still had access to Sayid's body, she'd told Decker, perhaps they could run additional tests, find out exactly what ailment he'd had. With that info, they would then know if his need for medical care was constant or merely occasional—an important piece of the puzzle.

It would be nice to know if they were futilely searching for a delivery that had never been made.

Decker followed Nash out into the yard. "Is there a problem?" he asked.

"Make the word plural," Nash said. He laughed at Decker's eye roll. "Let's start with the easiest first. Sophia."

Uh-oh.

"She mentioned that you got the fifty K needed to get her out of the country."

Decker nodded. "Yeah." The morning was already hot, last night's wind a thing of the past. Too bad—he could use a breeze right about now.

Nash crossed his arms. "I thought Paoletti said the client wouldn't cough it up."

"The money's mine," Deck said, telling him what he obviously already knew.

Nash was silent.

"What's next?" Deck asked.

Nash finally spoke. "You don't really think she's going to pay you back, do you?"

"She says she will."

"Oh, well, then, if she *says* so . . ."

"What's the problem, Nash? It's not your money."

The muscle in the side of Nash's jaw was jumping. "Are you prepared to lose it? Because you're going to lose it all."

"Yeah," Decker told him. "Yes, I'm prepared to lose it all. Is that all right with you? What's next?"

"Christ, Larry . . ."

"What's next?"

"Are you screwing her?" Nash asked.

Deck just looked at him.

"I don't particularly like her," Nash told him—no big surprise. "I certainly don't trust her. She's spent at least two months using sex to stay alive, and suddenly you're just giving her a huge amount of money? I'm sorry, *sir,* but it's a legitimate question. As XO of this team— What the fuck am I doing as any team's XO? But here I am, and hey, what do you know? I have the right to question any team member—any—who appears to have 'fallen under the influence of an outsider with unknown allegiances.' And fuck you for bringing me to a place in my life where I'm forced to quote regulations from a rule book."

Poor Nash. He was actually right.

"No, I am not engaged in any inappropriate activity whatsoever with Sophia," Decker answered. "What's next?"

"So is this guilt talking?" Nash wouldn't let it drop. "Or was this just a fifty-thousand-dollar blow job? No wonder you have sex only once every decade." He laughed—he had this bad habit of thinking that he was the funniest man alive. "Some men need Viagra to have sex more often. You need an economics class—a refresher course in supply and demand. You have a serious decimal point problem, my friend. You need to move it about three zeroes to the left. These days, fifty bucks and/or a nice dinner covers most kinds of fellatio-induced guilt."

"What's. Next."

Nash didn't notice that Decker was getting pissed. He was too busy laughing at his own pathetic joke.

"And on we move to problem number two," Nash said. "Also a woman. What a coincidence."

Decker knew what was coming and closed his eyes. Thank the Lord, Nash had finally given in.

Nash laughed softly. "Shit. This is harder than I thought it would be."

"Look," Decker said. "I know what you're trying to tell me, and it's all right—"

"No, it's not."

"It's all right with me," Decker specified.

"Well, shit," Nash said again. "It shouldn't be. You like this girl."

"Tess is a woman," Deck pointed out. "And yeah, I like her. She's terrific. She's smart and she's funny and loyal and sweet . . . and sexy as hell. I'm genuinely happy for you." And it was true, he really was.

So much so that he gave Nash a hug.

Nash stared at him as if he'd lost it. Maybe he had.

"Congratulations," Deck said, a little embarrassed.

And still his partner just stood there.

"This is a woman you could spend your life with." Decker hoped Nash was thinking long term.

"Who are you? Jesus?" Nash backed away from Deck. "You don't freaking hug me and say *congratulations*! You punch me in the face and curse me out and . . . listen to what you're saying! Listen to the way you talk about her— you're in love with her! *This is a woman* you *could spend your life with!* Not me. I'm not looking for someone to spend my life with. Damn it, Deck, you should be mad at me for stealing her out from under you, not hugging me. And when the fuck did we start hugging, anyway?"

"You didn't steal her," Decker said.

"Yes, I did. I was with her, and I wanted her, so I took her. I'm a total asshole," Nash said. "I knew how you felt about her, and I still couldn't keep my hands to myself."

What was it Nash had said before about guilt talking? "If you want," Decker said, "you could give me fifty thousand dollars. It does wonders, you know, in relieving feelings of guilt."

Nash stared at him. "You're joking," he said. "I'm standing here, trying to have a serious conversation about some extremely serious shit, and you're joking."

"We have work to do," Decker reminded him. He started back inside. "Was there anything else?"

"Yeah, you got any extra condoms? I'm almost out. Three last night and one this morning—the woman sure loves to fuck."

Deck stopped short and turned back to look at Nash. What the hell? It was as if Nash were trying to make him angry, as if he were disappointed in Decker's reaction to his earth-shattering news.

Except Decker had seen the way Tess looked at Nash. The fact that they were involved not only was not a surprise, it was a relief. He'd been hoping it would happen, and his earth hadn't come anywhere close to shattering when it had.

Nash, however, looked as if he were standing on shaky ground. He managed to look both defiant and embarrassed. And he glanced around them to make sure no one else had overheard that crude and very personal statement he'd made about Tess.

And *here* was an interesting thought. Did Nash actually *want* Decker to kick his ass?

Would it make him feel better, less terrified and out of control perhaps, if Decker rang his bell a few times and knocked him to the ground?

Maybe just the threat of violence would do the trick.

Deck was tired—it had been one hell of a long night. He couldn't remember the last time he'd slept. Was it yesterday or the day before?

"You better be treating this woman with the respect that she deserves," Deck said, his voice as hard as the look he gave Nash.

Nash said nothing. He just stood there, working hard—from the look of him—on grinding his teeth into little stubs.

So Deck gave him some more of the same. "Not just when you're with her, but all the time," he continued. He'd always hated locker-room talk, and Nash knew it—which made this whole thing even weirder. "Or I'll kick your ass."

"How could she want me when she could have you?" Nash shook his head, his eyes haunted. "I can't figure that out."

This was . . . unique. Them talking like this. Decker had to wonder if Nash found it as strange and wonderful as he did.

Or just plain terrifying.

And was Nash really serious? Because from Deck's point of view, Nash got it completely backwards. How could she want Deck when she could have Nash?

Either way . . .

"It doesn't have to make sense," Decker said to his friend. "You just . . . roll with it, and thank God for your good fortune."

"What if . . . ," Nash started. He couldn't seem to look Decker in the eye anymore. "What if I don't want her?" he finally said. "You know, the same way she wants me? What if I just can't resist the sex?"

Decker wanted to cry for his friend. He wanted to urge him not to run away from Tess just because he was scared of everything he was feeling. But to acknowledge both of those things—that Nash was scared, that he had feelings . . .

He couldn't do it.

"Then you better tell her that now," Deck said instead. "Right? Don't make her think you're on the same page and then ditch her after the assignment's over."

That muscle jumped in Nash's jaw again. "It's impossible to know what the future will bring."

Decker got in his face. "It'll bring some serious trouble if you string her along and then ditch her after this assignment is over. Do you hear me?"

Nash didn't respond. Not to that, anyway. He just said, "Condoms?"

"There's a small supply in the medical kit, in the kitchen," Decker told him before going back into the barn. "You're going to have to ration."

Tess and Nash were late to the meeting.

Nash had gone up to get her, and it took them at least fifteen minutes to find their way downstairs and over to the barn.

Tess's cheeks turned pink when she realized they were all there and waiting—Decker, Dave, and even Sophia.

"Sorry," Tess said. "I was, um, researching kidney failure." Sure she was.

She looked directly at Sophia. "It suddenly occurred to me that what you might've seen in Sayid's room was a dialyzer—a tall machine, kind of narrow, with tubes coming in and going out?"

Sophia glanced at Decker. She'd just had this exact conversation with him.

"Understandably, Sophia didn't spend much time looking at it," he answered for her.

"It was some kind of medical machine," she told Tess, "and yes, it was tall, but other than that . . ." She shrugged.

Tess handed Deck a printout from her computer. "I'd bet the farm that three times a week Sayid needed something called—"

"Hemodialysis," he finished for her. "You'd win that bet. I just spoke to Tom Paoletti, who, long story short, found out that the autopsy team was having a deadline crisis, so they rushed the report—including only information about the injuries that pertained to Sayid's death. The fact that he had something called a"—he consulted a piece of paper upon which he'd handwritten some notes—"PTFE graft in his arm—access for hemodialysis—was considered unimportant." Deck laughed his disgust. "File that under information we could have used a week ago. Which reminds me," he interrupted himself. "Paoletti let me know that Vinh Murphy's doing well."

"Thank God," Tess breathed, the only one of them brave enough to give voice to her relief. She turned to look up at Nash, who was standing close enough to touch her—just a hand briefly on her back—without anyone but Sophia noticing.

"He's been medevaced all the way to Germany," Decker told them, "and he's already had the first round of surgery on his leg. Commander Paoletti also gave me a heads-up— Murph's name is going to be released on a list of Americans killed from that car bomb, so if you happen to catch the news and hear he's dead, don't get upset. It's being done to protect the helo crew and the hospital staff who helped smuggle him out."

"Angelina's been told he's all right, hasn't she?" Tess asked.

"I'm sure Tom's taken care of that," Decker said. "But when I talk to him again, I'll double-check."

"Any news on who's behind the car bomb?" Tess asked.

"GIK extremists," Dave answered. "There's lots of talk on the streets—rumors that there'll be more attacks. We need to keep our eyes open when we're out there, and stay away from potential targets."

"Like hospitals?" Nash asked.

Decker handed a piece of paper to Nash and to Dave. Sophia leaned closer and saw that it was a list of names and addresses of hospitals. "Here's what we need to look for," he started, but Tess interrupted him.

"Where's mine?" she asked.

Decker glanced at Nash. "We decided the risks of sending you out alone were too—"

"*We* decided?" she said.

"I decided," he told her, taking the bullet for Nash, whose idea it clearly had been. "The police have been known to keep tabs on people who've been in custody. If you were seen going from hospital to hospital asking questions about dialysis equipment, you could put this entire mission in jeopardy."

Tess backed down. What could she say to that? But it was clear from the look she gave Nash that he was going to hear more about this later.

"Let's get to it," Decker said.

It was well after four a.m. when Jimmy returned. Tess was still up, obviously waiting for him, and he was so overwhelmingly glad about that, he almost turned around and ran right back down the stairs.

Instead he closed the door behind him and carried the bucket of water he'd brought up from the kitchen into the bathroom.

He heard the click as she closed her computer. "How did it go?"

As he came back out of the bathroom, he was sure he let nothing show on his face, but somehow, just by looking at him, she knew there'd been trouble. She scrambled to her feet. "What happened?"

It seemed pointless to lie or even to soften it. "I was set up. My contact—Leo—figured out that it was Sophia Ghaffari I wanted smuggled across the border. I guess his plan was to grab me and, uh, convince me to tell them where she was hiding." That part he *did* soften by not using the T-word—torture. No point in upsetting her—Deck hadn't let it get that far.

Tess was at his side instantly. "Are you hurt?"

"I'm fine." Jimmy met her eyes and knew she was remembering that that was what she'd told him, while sitting in a K-stani prison. He corrected himself. "I'm not hurt. Deck came in, got me out of there."

The lump on the back of his head where they hit him didn't show—she didn't have to know about that. But he'd scraped the heel of his right hand when he'd fallen, and she found that now.

"You need to clean this out," she said.

"Yeah, I'm going to. I brought up some water."

"Any other 'dings'?" she asked, looking at him hard.

"I don't think so." He allowed himself only the briefest of embraces before he pulled away from her. She was warm and soft and he knew that all he had to do was kiss her and she'd fall back with him onto the bed. He desperately wanted to take advantage of this adrenaline-induced hard-on he was still packing, but right now he smelled bad.

Cold sweat always made him stink.

Of course, he hadn't started to sweat until he and Deck were on their way back here. It wasn't until he started thinking about how bad it would be if one of Leo's men managed to follow them to Rivka's that he got good and scared. If he and Decker let that happen, Sophia wouldn't be the only one in danger.

Tess would be at risk, too.

Someone coming in to grab up Sophia might take Tess instead. Or they might simply take both women to Padsha Bashir, not knowing or even caring which one would win them that hefty reward.

Jimmy didn't want Tess anywhere near the sadistic warlord. Even being in the same city with the son of a bitch was bad enough.

He sat down in the chair so he could take off his boots. Damn, his feet hurt. He and Deck had clocked about seven miles tonight at hyperspeed, and these boots weren't made for running.

Tess was hovering, ready to help him out of his jacket, and then his shirt. She was checking him for more dings.

"I didn't realize Deck was going with you tonight," she said, pulling him up and out of the chair so he could take off his pants.

"He tagged along, hid in the shadows. . . ."

Clearly his erection wasn't as much of a distraction to her as it was to him. But it wasn't as if she didn't notice— how could she not? She was just more interested in taking inventory of his injuries.

"That must hurt."

She was talking about his knee. It was rug-burned. He'd scraped it right through his jeans, or maybe because of his jeans. And he was going to have a bruise there, too. It was already starting to turn purple.

"I've had worse," Jimmy said. "You know, sometimes I think Deck's got some kind of sixth sense—like he knows there's going to be trouble before it happens." He shook his head. "All the nights he didn't come, I didn't need him. Tonight I did, and he was there." It was doubly freaky, because it had happened before.

"Maybe he picks up something from you," she suggested. "Maybe you give off some kind of signal that something's wrong and—"

"Tonight I didn't know," Jimmy said. "Tonight, I was caught completely off guard." That was what shook him up so much—the fact that he hadn't spotted the setup going in. That was the kind of careless mistake that could get him killed. Or worse, it could get Decker or Tess killed.

God damn it, he hated that he'd put them both in danger.

"Maybe it's subconscious on your part," Tess said. "Maybe it's subconscious on his part, too. Whatever, it is, I'm glad for it. It's what makes you guys such a good team."

"Yeah, I don't know," Jimmy said. "Decker would be good with anyone—and maybe even unstoppable with a better partner. You said yourself I'm not a team player."

"What? Jimmy, I was mad at you at the time."

"That doesn't make it any less true."

She led him into the bathroom, taking one of the candles in with them and setting it on the back of the toilet. "You and Deck *are* unstoppable. You're legendary."

"Notorious," he corrected her as she splashed some of the water from the bucket into the plugged sink.

"That's bullshit, and you know it." She wet a washcloth and got to work cleaning all the bits of dirt and cement from his hand.

"Ow!"

"Better find a bullet to bite, because this is going to take a while."

"This would hurt less if you were naked," he told her, and she glanced up at him.

"You've used a variation of that line on me before."

Crap. "Sorry."

"I bet." She glanced up again. "Now might be a really good time to tell me what happened tonight."

What was there to tell? Leo had made the mistake of using force, of instigating violence, of putting the death card into play. *Tell me where Sophia's hiding, or we'll kill you.* Once Leo did that, the game became deadly. And when Decker burst through the window and threw Jimmy that weapon . . .

"Leo the Claw made a big mistake," he told Tess now.

She laughed. "Leo the *what*?"

"Yeah," he said. "That's what he calls himself. Leo the Claw. What the hell does that mean? And oh, by the way, never trust a man who gives himself his own nickname."

Tess laughed again.

That was good. He was entertaining her.

"I did some business with him a few years ago, before he became 'the Claw.' He was bipartisan back then—you know, he worked for the highest bidder. I actually liked the guy. . . ."

Jimmy realized that he'd fallen silent and that Tess was looking at him, concern in her eyes. He forced a smile. "But apparently he'd had one run-in too many with Padsha Bashir and discovered he liked staying alive so much, he was willing to make less money and pledge allegiance to Bashir.

"So fast-forward to a couple of days ago. I contacted him, not knowing about his new connection to Bashir, and told him I was looking to smuggle a friend across the border, how much would it cost?

"I think that's where I gave it away—you know, that my 'friend' was Sophia. Because Leo said fifty thousand dollars U.S. and I didn't leap out of my chair and say the K-stani equivalent to *Are you out of your freaking mind?* I just sat there and nodded, because I was thinking that it would probably end up being at least that much—the same as the price Bashir had put on her head.

"So okay," Jimmy continued. "I don't realize it, but I've given it away. I come back here"—thank God Leo's men hadn't followed him then—"and Leo the freaking Claw toddles off to see his business partner and says, 'Yo, yo, yo, I think I've found Bashir's missing girl, but I'm a little understaffed.' So the partner gives him a half a dozen more men—" All amateur soldiers with lousy aim. All no longer of this earth, poor bastards. "And they wait for me to return. Which I obligingly did tonight.

"Like I said, when I arrive, my guard's down . . . And so

they bring me into this little room, and they've got me in this chair, and Leo's doing his Nazi interrogator routine. And Deck comes through the window, Leo dives for cover, and . . . Off we go, running six-minute miles in work boots through a disaster zone. It took us a long time to get here because we had to make sure we weren't followed."

They had been.

At first.

But Jimmy had gone around behind the man trailing them, in a move Decker called "circling back on their own six." He'd taken the tracker out silently and left him there as a warning to anyone who might come after. As a warning to Leo. *Don't ever fuck with me again.* . . .

"I think this is as clean as it's going to get," Tess told him.

He looked at his hand. *Out, damned spot.* . . . "Thanks. It's . . . Thank you."

"So . . . are you going to tell me what happened?" she asked.

Jimmy laughed, but it was obvious she wasn't being funny, and he felt his smile fade away.

She was just standing there, waiting.

So he said, "Okay, I left out where they hit me on the head and I fell. I mean, I figured you knew that because . . ." He held up his scraped hand as exhibit A. "But other than that . . ."

She nodded, folding her arms across her chest, as if she were cold. "Okay." She pointed over her shoulder at the bedroom. "I'll, um, be out here while you finish getting washed up."

He'd disappointed her. He knew he'd disappointed her. But what was he supposed to say?

There were more of them and they had superior fire-power, but it still felt like slaughter, like shooting fish in a barrel.

Or, *That last man didn't hear it coming. One second, as far as he was concerned, he was alone. The next he was in a headlock, and then he was dead. He barely had time to struggle, didn't have time to reach for a weapon.*

It had helped that he had been one of the ones in the room—laughing—while Leo had described the effect of a full electrical current attached to a man's gonads.

But the truth was, Jimmy had seen too much death, too much bad for the alleged sake of good.

"I'm doing the best I can," he told Tess now.

She looked so sad. "Yes," she said. "I know."

She closed the bathroom door behind her.

He washed quickly, stripping off his briefs and soaping himself up all over. He rinsed by stepping into the bathtub and pouring the remaining water from the bucket over himself, his head included. He dried himself in the flickering light, hung the towel on the rack, and blew out the candle.

And it was dark.

Tess had doused the candle in the other room, and had gotten into bed. That darkness and silence were far from welcoming, and he nearly went back into the bathroom.

But she'd left his side of the bed turned down—amazing how fast that had happened. One night and he already had a side of the bed.

Jimmy slipped between the sheets and she turned to him, soft and warm and already drowsy.

And naked.

With an unwrapped condom in her hands. He nearly cried. Thank you, Gods of the Universe, for sending him this woman who somehow knew exactly what he needed.

She covered him as he kissed her, and then she covered him even more completely, straddling him and pressing him deeply inside of her.

"Tess," he said.

And she kissed him.

CHAPTER
TWENTY-TWO

TESS LOOKED exhausted as she poured herself a cup of coffee.

"Have you seen Khalid?" she asked, looking from Sophia to Decker.

"He's in the yard," he told her, finishing up the last of the rice cereal in his bowl. Guldana had added just the right spices to the gluey mixture. It looked awful, but tasted heavenly. Of course, breakfast always tasted particularly good on a morning after. After a life-or-death experience, that is.

Some people had sex to get their blood moving. Others risked their lives.

Some—like Nash, who apparently didn't give a damn how late he kept Tess up—did both.

Last night, Decker had taken on twelve-to-one odds—well, twelve-to-two after he got a weapon back into Nash's capable hands. He'd gone in not knowing how hard Nash had been hit—he'd seen his friend take that blow to the back of the head and go down hard. It could have been bad.

Instead it was merely half bad.

And yet here Deck was. Alive. Having breakfast. And enjoying every bite.

"What's up?" he asked Tess.

She had stopped in the door to the yard, the bright sunlight making her look even more weary. "I haven't heard from Will Schroeder since the bombing. He hasn't contacted you, has he?"

"No." Decker took his bowl to the sink.

"If it's okay with you, I'm going to send Khalid out to find him—to set up a meeting in the square for this afternoon."

He crossed toward her, aware that Sophia was tracking him. It would have made him self-conscious—the woman watched his every move and followed him if he strayed too far from her—if he hadn't known a great deal about the psychological strains and stresses of prisoners. And although Sophia was no longer trapped in Bashir's palace, the price on her head made her still very much a prisoner.

The way the woman watched him wasn't personal—she perceived him as holding the key to her freedom.

"That's not a good idea," he told Tess.

Frustration rang in her voice. "Just because Jimmy doesn't want me going out alone—"

Decker cut her off. "*I* don't want you going out alone."

"But if I can get in touch with Will," Tess argued, "then he can come with me. We can go out together—help check out that list of hospitals." She lowered her voice. "Every day that passes, we have less of a chance of recovering that laptop."

"Yeah," he said. "I'm clear on that. But . . ." He glanced over at Sophia, who was—big surprise—watching him. "If you go into the city with Will that'll leave Miles . . ."

"I'd be all right," Sophia said. "I can stay here alone."

"Excuse us for a minute," Tess said to the other woman, and pulled Decker with her out of the house. She took him clear over to the gate before she stopped and faced him. "She's always listening in, and I'm sorry, but I think we need to be more careful around her. I'm not really looking to contact Will so I can visit hospitals with him. I just used that to prove that she really does pay attention to everything anyone says.

"We got an email from Tom this morning, Deck," she continued. "He wasn't able to call—something's funky with our phones again—but he just received important information from the client. They got access to a cell phone belonging to Faik Nizami, an al-Qaeda operative based in Afghanistan. This is a man who's known to have been in contact with Sayid repeatedly since 2001. On the evening before the quake, Nizami took a phone call originating from the Kazabek Grande Hotel."

Decker must've reacted, because she said, "Yeah. Jimmy said that was the last place he would have expected Sayid to stay—which made it high on his personal list of possibilities, even before Tom's email."

Decker sighed. "Still, it's just one phone call. It may not have been from Sayid."

"How about three?" Tess asked. "An outgoing call to Sayid's personal cell on the morning of the quake, duration one minute seven seconds. Then another call, just a few minutes later, to the Kazabek Grande, duration twelve minutes. Check out this scenario: Nizami calls Sayid's cell, they're cut off. He tries calling back, can't get through. So he finally calls using the landline at the hotel."

"Or," Deck suggested, "Nizami is long-distance brokering some kind of meeting in Kazabek between Sayid and a third party. That third party—unknown—is staying at the Grande, and he calls Nizami the night before the quake. In the morning, Nizami contacts Sayid, gets the location for the meeting. Then he calls back that third party at the hotel, and passes that information on."

Tess looked at him. "Gee," she said. "Way to burst my bubble."

"Your scenario might be right," he told her. "And even if it's not, that potential third party might've left some information in his hotel room that'll lead us to Sayid's accommodations." He pushed himself up so that he was sitting on the fence—just a guy having a chat with a pretty young woman in the sunlight on another cloudless day in Kazbekistan. "I assume whatever plan you have in mind doesn't involve us doing a room by room search of the Kazabek Grande Hotel—which, I feel compelled to point out, has been structurally damaged and is in danger of collapse."

Tess smiled, and it made her look far less tired. "Jimmy mentioned that, too. Do you know, is he claustrophobic?"

"I don't think so," Decker said.

"He hates the idea of having to go in there."

"He was in New York City on 9/11," Decker told her. "I'm pretty certain he watched the Towers come down from a close proximity."

"Oh, my God."

"I don't really know for sure, though. He never talked about it. Not with me, anyway."

She gaped at him. "Everyone talked about 9/11. Where they were, what they did . . ."

"He didn't," Decker said. "He doesn't. Talk about things like that. I know him better than anyone—I know what he's going to say and do before he does it. But I don't have a clue where he came from, where he's been, what he's seen and done, and . . . I know the things that matter, though. I know I can trust him—and I do. With my life. I also happen to know that he loves you—"

"That's really funny, because he insists *you* love me."

Well, *here* was a conversation he'd never thought he'd be having, Decker had to laugh. "I really do admire the hell out of you. If I didn't love you before, I love you now—just for having the balls to say that."

She was not amused. Her cheeks were turning pink, too. She'd embarrassed herself. Or maybe she just felt embarrassed for him. "I'm sorry, let's not go there. I know that . . . I didn't mean to—"

"I love you as a friend," he clarified. "You're good for him, you know."

"My plan"—she cleared her throat—"is to get inside the hotel, access the computers, and search the guest records for Nizami's cell phone number. That outgoing international call would definitely show up as an additional charge to the room. When we find a record of that call, we'll have Sayid's room number. Assuming scenario number one."

Decker gazed at her. With her long sleeves and her long pants, she was starting to perspire in the heat. Or maybe it was the prior topic of their conversation that had her sweating.

"Can you hack into the hotel records from here?" he asked. "If we have to go in, I'd prefer knowing the room number in advance—spend the least amount of time possible in a building that's about to fall."

She nodded. "I'll try." She glanced back at the house, where Sophia was standing just inside the door, in the shadows, watching them. She lowered her voice even more. "Excuse me for being out of line, sir, but you and Jimmy were nearly killed last night and I think we need to be more careful."

"He told you about it?" He couldn't keep the surprise from his voice.

But she just laughed. "Yeah, he told me all about it. Right. He told me the Disney version, without a body count. Deck, come on, I want to help Sophia, you know that, but not at that kind of price. I don't know what happened last night, but Jimmy was really upset when he got back. I think we also have to consider the fact that we don't know this woman—"

"You honestly think she had something to do with last night's setup?" Decker asked. "They're looking *for* her. They want to bring her back to Bashir. She's not in league with them."

"What I think is that we've got five people—besides our team—who know she's here," Tess told him. "Rivka and Guldana, Khalid, Will, and Sophia herself." She counted them off on her fingers. "Getting back in Bashir's favor seems to be a Kazbekistani national pastime. What are the two things he wants most? Sophia and Sayid's laptop. We really only have Sophia's story of why Bashir's after her. And again, I'm sorry, I like her, I do, but I pick up a heavy stench of pants on fire whenever she opens her mouth."

"A . . . what?"

"Pants on fire," she said. "As in, *Liar, liar* . . . ?"

"Got it. And yeah, she's good at spinning."

"Yes, she is," Tess agreed.

"So let me see if I've got this straight. You think Sophia's going to try to get back in Bashir's good graces by—"

"Delivering Sayid's laptop to him," Tess finished for him. "And I'm not saying I think that's what's going on. I just think we should be aware of the possibility."

"We don't have his laptop," Decker pointed out.

"Not yet," she said, "but we *are* going to get it."

"Shit."

"Anything I can do to help?"

Tess glanced up from her computer and over at the bed where Jimmy was stretched out. "I'm sorry. I didn't mean to wake you."

"You didn't," he said. "I've been awake for a while. Hoping you'd notice me over here."

He smiled at her and it was too much. Combined with those eyes and cheekbones, and with the golden tan, gleaming muscles . . . She forced her attention back to her computer screen. "No sex while I'm working," she said.

"Two minutes," he said. "That's all I need."

She looked at him again and he wiggled his eyebrows.

"Come on, admit it," he said. "You're considering it."

"No, I'm marveling at the fact that I'm sleeping with a man who attempts to entice me back to bed with the promise of getting made in two minutes. That's less time than it takes to cook a soft-boiled egg, I'd like to point out."

"How's twenty minutes sound?" he asked. "That's the length of most people's coffee breaks."

"I can hack into Kazbekistani bank records," she said. "Why can't I even *find* the blasted Grande Hotel? Is it possible they don't have computer records?" As she said it, she knew that was absurd. A modern hotel with all those rooms? Their billing system had to be computerized. *Had* to be.

"Imagine if you smoked." Jimmy was still working on getting some. "You'd spend at least ten minutes every few hours having a cigarette. It's actually more like fifteen, because not only do you have to get outside, but then you have to get to wherever it is they allow people to pollute the air. I remember back when I was a smoker, I spent some time at the Agency office in San Francisco."

It took everything Tess had in her not to look up. Jimmy had been a smoker who worked out of the San Francisco office?

"They had this little sundeck on the twentieth floor where the smokers could huddle, out of the rain, under this one little awning," he continued.

She could see him from her peripheral vision—he had both hands behind his head and was gazing up at the ceiling.

"The elevators were so busy it never took me less than ten minutes to get there from the ninth floor, and only slightly less, maybe eight minutes, to get back. Factor in the hike from my office to the elevator and the five and a half minutes I'm out there frantically sucking in the nicotine, and it's practically a thirty-minute production number.

Needless to say, ~~didn't work in that~~ ~~HPOINT~~

Tess's heart was in her ~~tually, that she could be so~~ that Jimmy Nash had actually volu~~.~~ himself. *I remember back when I was.* ~~Fortunately, I~~

"Why'd you quit smoking?" she ask~~.~~ on her computer. Maybe this was the secret ~~.~~ to talk about himself. Pretend she wasn't really ~~p~~ tention.

"I started working with Deck," he told her. "He was ~~s~~ freaking fit. It was definitely an ego thing—I wanted to be able to keep up with the big bad Navy SEAL." He laughed. "Like that was ever going to happen. But by the time I realized it was hopeless, I'd already quit smoking, so . . ." He shrugged.

"When were you in San Francisco?" she asked. "You know, my mother lives there."

"Yeah, I do know," Jimmy said. "You mentioned that in your interview with Tom."

She looked up, startled. "You remember that?"

"Your mom's a sculptor, your dad's a librarian, your parents divorced, and you bounced between the two of them. And spent too much quality time with your computer. You still feel safest when you're plugged in. Tom was impressed that you had that good a read on yourself. I was, too."

Tess dragged her gaze back to her computer. There was no reason to feel anything but admiration for the fact that he had a good memory. "No fair," she said. "I didn't get to sit in on *your* interview."

He laughed. "I don't do interviews. I just grab on to Deck's coattails and glide on in."

Did he seriously think that or was he just trying to be modest? "What did your parents do?" she asked, eyes on her computer screen.

ool in Kent,
the housewife
er about ten years
ng with the cancer.
n two different towns."
"Dad was a professor at a priv
Connecticut," he told her. Nash's parents. It reeked of
thing. She, uh, did ba cy support staff had dubbed
ago and she ? abricated—and as false—as his
They're murmured, But really, what had she expected?
mother had cancer." because it was the expected
but was his inability to But what she was
open up and tell her

Last night, when he gave her that PG-13 version of his run-in with Leo the Claw, she knew.

She couldn't do this.

Oh, she could do *this*. She could have a couple of days—or even weeks, if this assignment dragged on that long—of great sex with a man she was attracted to. But as for a relationship . . .

No, this was definitely temporary. She needed trust, not watered-down half-truths and fictionalized parents.

"Don't you think it's just a little creepy that you'll sleep with me, and even claim to want a relationship, yet you can't even tell me—really—about your parents?" Tess asked.

He was silent, and she looked up at him.

"I would love to know who you are," she told him. Why did she bother? She should just close her computer, leap into bed with him, and redefine "coffee break." But instead she sat there and talked at him. Did he hear *any* of this? "Skip your parents. Parents can suck. Parents are hard. Tell me a secret. Tell me something that you've never told anyone. You want to have a relationship, James? Talk to me. Otherwise, all we're doing here is having sex."

He opened his mouth, and she had a moment of pure, shimmering hope. He was going to do it, and she was a big, fat liar, lying to herself about how this was only temporary, and she was only in this for the great sex. Right.

She was so crazy in love with this man, her heart skipped a beat when he told her he used to be a smoker, for the love of God.

But then he spoke. "Actually, right now we're *not* having sex. I couldn't help but notice."

At first his words didn't make sense. And then she realized that he had made a joke.

Correction. He'd *tried* to make a joke.

One day she'd look back on this and laugh. She'd be on the phone with Peggy, her roommate from her first year of college, and she'd say, "Remember that total dickhead super-agent type I had that fling with, first time I went out of the country on assignment?"

And Peggy'd say, "Oh yeah, the James Bond wannabe. What a jerk."

And she'd say, "There I was, pouring my heart out, begging him just to talk to me, and he makes some stupid joke."

And Peggy'd say, "Because he was probably feeling really vulnerable—thinking that if he told you who he really was, you'd reject him, and like most idiot men, he was scared to death."

Tess closed her computer and stood up. She had to get out of here before she went over to that bed to comfort Jimmy for feeling so *vulnerable*. "Vulnerable, my ass," she told him crossly.

"What?" He sat up, his hair charmingly rumpled. "Time for a break?" he asked hopefully.

Yeah, right. At the top of her agenda for all she had to do today was have two minutes of great sex with Mr. Vulnerable. It was right up there with hooking her computer

battery up to that awful generator so it could recharge and
lugging water up from the well, because until the power
came back on—

"Holy shit," she said. She slapped her forehead. "The
power's still out. The banks all have generators—their computers are running. But the Grande Hotel's been evacuated.
The place is probably dark, the computer's got no power,
and any backup batteries are long gone. We're going to have
to go there with a power source, reboot their system . . ."

Like Jimmy and Decker and Dave, she now had suddenly been dumped into wait mode. Wait for cover of darkness so they could go, undetected, into that hotel.

They had about two hours until sunset.

Two hours to . . . *No. Put your libido down and step
away from the man in the bed. . . .*

They had two hours to gather all the equipment they
were going to need.

"That generator we've been using to recharge our
phones and my computer battery," she said to Jimmy. "Is it
portable?"

"Yeah," he answered. "Well, *portable* is subjective. Murph
called it portable, but it's heavy as hell. We can move it if
we have to."

"All the way to the Grande Hotel?"

He winced. "That's going to hurt. But maybe if we got a
baby stroller . . ." He thought about that. "Yeah, that
would do it. Although God help us if we're stopped by a
police patrol."

Tess threw him his pants. "Get dressed. We need to go
get a baby stroller."

Jimmy laughed. "Words that make a man's blood freeze
in his—"

He froze, and she inwardly cringed, because she knew
what he was thinking. Back when they weren't having sex,
they'd slipped and had sex. Without proper protection.

It was quite the foundation for a solid, lasting relationship—small talk, sex, sex, more sex, and sheer terror.

Yeah, they'd get far.

"I'll be downstairs," she said, and escaped out the door.

Sophia was in the barn, in the stall next to the horse named Marge, cleaning off the baby stroller that Nash had found in the shed.

Decker's latest news—that they may not be able to find someone willing or trustworthy enough to smuggle her out of Kazbekistan, even for fifty thousand dollars—had been devastating.

It was good to have something to do with her hands, to keep her busy as she tried to figure out her next move.

She was going to have to get out of Kazabek, that much was clear. Maybe she could go up into the mountains, well outside of Padsha Bashir's territory. There'd be other dangers, other warlords, but none who had put a price on her head. She'd have to keep her face concealed, but that wouldn't be too hard to do. She could make her way north, and maybe eventually find someone to guide her over the border.

She'd been on her own like this before, with little resources. At age fifteen, she'd returned to Kazabek without her parents. Of course, back then she'd worn her hair cut short and had dressed like a boy. She'd pretended to be French. It was possible to get away with quite a lot simply by pretending to be French.

She was going to need money to survive—lots of it.

It was one thing for Decker to loan her thousands of dollars with the knowledge she would be out of Kazbekistan and working to pay him back. It was another entirely for him to give it to her knowing she could well be trapped in the mountains for years. Or captured and killed.

"We'll figure out an alternative," Decker had promised her after dropping his bomb.

She'd wanted to cry. Instead, she'd volunteered to wipe cobwebs and rust from a twenty-year-old baby stroller.

Deck was clearly exhausted from whatever he'd been up to the night before—Sophia didn't know what, no one had told her. But he lay down and took a nap, right there, on the floor of the barn.

She'd positioned herself as close as she could without fear of waking him.

The door now opened with a bang, and Nash came in.

"Shhh," Sophia started to say, but then ducked down so that she was out of sight, her heart pounding. James Nash had been followed not just by Tess and Dave, but by a stranger. A tall man with red hair.

"Deck," Nash said.

"Yeah. Over here." Decker sounded wiped, but he sat up. "Hey," he greeted the redhead. "How's the wrist?"

"Broken. Hurts like hell."

"I bet. Thanks for your help with Murphy."

"He's a good man."

"If it had been me," Nash said, "you would've let me die, right?"

Sophia relaxed a little. Whoever this was, Decker and Nash knew him enough to joke with him. Except no one was laughing.

"Schroeder's been busy," Nash told Decker.

Will Schroeder—she'd heard that name before.

"I was digging around," Schroeder said, "asking people if they knew Sayid, if they'd seen Sayid, and lo and behold, I found someone who did and had. A taxi driver. Said he'd picked Sayid up, the afternoon before the quake, from—get this—the Grande Hotel."

From her hiding place, Sophia saw Decker exchange a look with Nash.

"That's great," Decker said. "We already had reason to believe he'd been staying there—this is a good confirmation."

"When are you going over to the hotel?" Schroeder asked.

No one answered him.

"Dumb question. It's going to be tonight, as soon as it's dark. Well, good. I'm coming with you."

Nash opened his mouth, but Tess put her hand on his arm, stopping him.

"Actually, I haven't decided yet who's going," Decker said. "It's not going to be easy getting in there undetected, and it's certainly not going to be any safer once inside. For both of those reasons, I don't want to go in with a crowd."

This time it was Tess who couldn't keep from speaking. "I have to go."

"No, you don't," Nash said.

"Yeah," Tess said earnestly. "Jimmy, I do. First I have to get the computer running, then I'll need to access the telephone records, and—"

"If you get caught out after curfew . . ." Nash said.

"If *you* get caught out after curfew, it'll be bad for you, too," she argued.

"Did you *like* it there, in jail?" Nash asked. "You already had your one strike, Tess. In Kazbekistan, you don't get another."

They had faced off again. Sophia looked over at Decker, who rubbed his forehead and sighed.

"Okay, you tell me," Tess challenged Nash. "How are you going to do it? How are you going to reboot the hotel's computer system? Huh?"

"Easy," Nash shot back. "If I get there and my phone doesn't work, I'm going to put that sat-dish you wanted so badly up on the Grande Hotel's roof. And then I'm going to call you and you're going to walk me through it."

Tess swore. "That's *so* unfair." She turned toward Decker.

"What?" Nash countered. "It's unfair to want to keep you safe?"

Tess saw the way Decker was looking at them, and she shut her mouth, no doubt realizing that, once again, their quibbling made them sound like arguing children.

"Will that do the trick?" Decker asked her. "If we get there and don't have phone access, if we put a dish on the roof of the Grande . . . ?"

Tess gritted her teeth. She hated to admit it, but, "Yes," she said. "Yeah. Yup." She swore again.

"If it's just you and me," Nash told Decker, "we'll be able to move that much faster."

"Hey, Tess, looks like I'm not going either," Dave said mildly. "Don't take it personally, okay?"

"But it *is* personal. It's all about what Jimmy wants. Why did I even bother to come here if no one's going to let me do my job?" Tess fumed.

"You'll be doing your job," Nash said sharply. "You'll just be doing it back here, where the risk of being gang-raped during a so-called police interrogation is considerably less."

"What about the risks *you* face?" Tess countered hotly. "I'd like to put in a bid that Dave goes instead of Jim. Let's not forget that Leo the Claw is out there, no doubt eager for *his* revenge."

"Okay," Decker said. "I think we know where we all stand."

"That's absurd!" Nash spoke right over him.

Tess turned to Decker. "This is just an oh-oh-seven power trip, you know. Nash, James Nash, has got to be the one to save the day—"

"The fuck I do!" Nash exploded. "If I thought I was James fucking Bond, I wouldn't be wasting time with *you*."

Tess jerked back as if he had hit her.

And there was silence.

Decker sighed.

"No," Nash said. "No, that came out wrong. I meant, I wouldn't be wasting time *arguing* with you."

But Tess didn't look as if she believed him.

"This is my decision," Decker said. "*My* decision. Just so we're all clear on this." He looked at Dave, then Tess, then Nash, one at a time, waiting until he got eye contact. Then he said, "I'm going. With Nash. Tess, you're going to have to do your job—your important job—from back here, because not only does that mean you'll be safer, it means *we'll* be safer, too."

"Yes, sir. I'm sorry, sir. I have no excuse for—"

"Dave, you're here with Tess and Sophia."

"Yes, sir."

Decker turned to Will, who looked as if he were about to speak. "No, you cannot come. And if you argue, I'll shoot you."

Will shut his mouth.

"We'll head out immediately after curfew," Decker announced. "Dave, come talk to me and Nash about the best way to get inside that hotel."

Sophia stood up. "The best way into the Kazabek Grande is through a tunnel—an underground walkway—from the basement of the Sulayman Bank Building over in the financial district."

Everyone stared at her, but she looked only at Decker.

"You don't have to wait for dark," Sophia told him. "If you want, I could show you. We could go right now."

CHAPTER
TWENTY-THREE

THERE WAS an elevator at the end of the tunnel that led directly into the Kazabek Grande Hotel.

It was the only access leading up—there were no stairs.

Decker, of course, didn't see it as a problem, despite the lack of electricity. He and Dave set to work, prying the doors open.

Jimmy made sure both the portable sat-dish and the battery pack were secure in their packs. They'd decided to take the battery instead of the noisy generator. It was slightly lighter, which was a plus. On the negative side, it had a limited amount of juice. They'd have to work fast.

The baby stroller had done the trick, carrying the heavy equipment through the street. A couple of lightweight blankets kept the hot afternoon sun from "the baby's" face.

But now they had to climb an elevator shaft—oh, joy—with all those extra pounds on their backs.

And if Jimmy complained, Deck would make some mild comment about how, when he was in the SEAL teams, they used to jump out of planes with over a hundred pounds of gear and weaponry strapped onto them.

Yeah, well, Jimmy *wasn't* a SEAL. He wasn't James Bond, either.

Damn it, he could still see that look on Tess's face when he'd said what he'd said out in the barn. *I wouldn't be wasting time with you.*

At worst, it sounded as if he was making a crack about her obvious lack of Bond Girl attributes.

At best, it sounded as if he thought the time he'd spent with her was a waste.

Jimmy opened his phone. No service. Big surprise.

"How many access points into the hotel does this elevator have?" Decker was asking Sophia.

"Three," she told him. "One in the parking garage, one in the lobby, and one that opens directly into a suite on the seventeenth floor. Uqbah Sulayman's mistress lived there."

"You know the suite number?" Deck asked. He always collected as much information as possible, which was usually nice, but not when they were standing directly underneath a building that everyone and their engineer brother expected to fall at any moment.

Fall, as in, down.

With a roar that sounded as if the gates of hell had opened up.

"Suite 1712," she told him. "North Tower."

Finally the doors screeched open.

Dave helped them on with their packs. "Are you sure you don't want me to stick around?" he asked. "This tunnel is secure—Sophia's safe. I could take care of setting up the sat-dish on the roof."

As Jimmy watched, Deck glanced at Sophia.

"I'd be fine with that," she obviously lied.

But he shook his head. "No, I want you back at Rivka's as soon as possible. As it is, you'll be hard-pressed to make it before curfew. Let's not tempt fate."

Besides, Tess was back there, with only Will Schroeder and Khalid to protect her. Which was a joke. Because if there was trouble, Tess would take charge and protect *them*.

Khalid had told Jimmy the way she'd gotten him and Will beneath the wagon when that bomb exploded in City

Center. Then she'd charged *toward* the explosion, searching for Murphy. Khalid had also brought another little detail to light—apparently Will had found another shirt for Tess to wear after she'd used her own to successfully control Murphy's bleeding. But instead of covering herself, she'd used it to play Florence freaking Nightingale, to stanch other people's wounds.

"You coming?"

Jimmy realized that Decker was poised at the entrance to the elevator shaft. Sophia and Dave were already heading back down the tunnel.

"Yeah," Jimmy said, looking up into the dimly lit shaft that stretched as far as he could see. "I'm right behind you." He took out his penlight, turned it on, clamped it in his teeth, and began his ascent into a building that was on the verge of collapse.

Tess's phone rang. The number on the display was Jimmy's. "Yeah," she said as greeting, while she got her own computer connected to the Internet.

"We're in," he told her. The connection was bad but not awful.

"That was fast," she said, entering her password. Of course *fast* was relative. It had, in fact, been 112 of the longest minutes of her life.

"Yeah," he said. "There was some kind of a balcony thing up on the eleventh floor. Deck set up the dish out there. I'm hooking the system up to the battery pack here in the hotel office. Holy Christ, this place stinks. I think the quake made the sewers back up. You should be glad you're not here."

"Right," she said. "I'm really glad I'm not allowed to participate the way I want to. You sure know exactly the right thing to say to make me feel better."

"Sorry. I—"

"Describe the hotel's computer system, please."

"It's just a PC, nothing much to brag about. And I am sorry. About what I said before, too. I hope you know I didn't mean it the way it sounded. I was talking about right then. That moment."

"Yeah, actually, Nash," she said, "when it comes down to you, I don't know anything. I don't really know you—I mean, other than your favorite sexual position and the fact that you actually like anchovies—so I kind of have to go on the face value of the few things that do come out of your mouth."

"What, just because I don't want to talk about my parents—one of whose names I never even knew . . . ?"

Tess had to laugh. "Oh, that's just perfect, Jimmy. Throw me a bone. That'll make up for everything."

"Look," he said. "I honestly didn't mean—"

"But you *did* mean to make sure that I stayed back here, nice and safe. God, even in the field, I'm stuck working support. Do you know how frustrating that is?"

"You're the one who's always shouting about the importance of being a team player," he said. "Suck it up, and be part of this team."

"This is hardly the time or place for this conversation," she said stiffly, because deep down—about this, anyway—she knew he was right. *She* was the James Bond wannabe. *She* wanted to be the one to save the day.

"Yeah, I know." He said something, but he wasn't speaking into the phone, and she realized he was talking to Decker. He came back. "Okay, everything's connected. Tell me how to do this."

"Turn on the battery, and the system should reboot automatically," she told him.

That made him laugh. "How am I going to reboot the hotel's computer system, huh?" he said, tossing her words back at her. "Like it's something only the genius comspesh can do . . . Okay, here we go. They use Windows. Hail, Bill Gates. Oops, I'm getting a scan disk message and being chastised for shutting off the computer improperly. In French no less, which makes it sound naughty."

"It's going to take a few minutes," she told him. "That's a fairly old system, huh?"

"Yeah, I'd say circa 1995, without a whole lot of whistles and bells. Which is lucky—it uses less battery power."

"Just so you know," Tess said, "after this is over, if the Agency offers me a field position, I'm taking it."

He was silent, and she thought she'd lost the connection.

"Are you still there?" she asked.

"Yeah. I'm . . . just surprised."

"I thought that would be easier. For all of us—including Decker, who's probably got a big black X next to my name, under the heading that says 'Bickers and Whines Too Much.' "

There was a pause, and then Jimmy said, "So much for us going steady, huh?"

"You know it wasn't working," she told him.

"Actually, I thought it was working rather well. At least until I publicly insulted you."

"That's not what this is about," she told him. "It's about me wanting you to be someone you're not. I love you, Jimmy, but I want to change you, and that's . . . it's just plain stupid. And so is being in a relationship with someone that I know—I *know*—will hammer me emotionally, someone who can't—not won't, *can't*—give me what I need."

"Okay," he said. "I'm in."

"Good," she said, completely unsurprised at his total lack of response to her heartfelt words. It was nothing more than she'd expected.

But then he did surprise her. He lowered his voice. "Don't take the Agency field position. The bureaucracy will drive you nuts. Stay with Tom's team. I know it's where you really want to be, Tess, and . . . I was already planning on leaving. This assignment—it was really just one last favor to Deck."

"But . . ." Tess knew she shouldn't ask, she *couldn't* ask. That battery was going to run out far too quickly, and Jimmy and Deck were sitting in a twenty-eight-story death trap.

"Tell me what to do," Jimmy said, and they got to work.

The Kazabek Grande used good old-fashioned locks to ensure their guests' privacy. As Nash acted as the channel between Tess and the hotel computer, Decker located a master key.

And a map of the hotel.

It was enormous, four connected buildings constructed in a classic K-stani style, around a completely enclosed and private center courtyard.

Back when Decker first came to Kazbekistan, that courtyard had been luxurious, with a swimming pool and lounge chairs and even a bar serving tropical drinks. There had been palm trees and lush greenery, flowers everywhere.

Now the pool was bone dry, the trees brown, the lounge chairs broken and bent, their bright colors long since faded.

"Suite 933, West Tower," Nash announced, snapping his phone shut.

They immediately headed through the eerily empty lobby to the stairs marked WEST in seven different languages. Nash wanted to get up there and get out as quickly as possible.

"Not only was the call to Nizami's cell phone billed to 933, but the hotel also received a special delivery from the Kazabek Kidney Center. The room was being used by one

Mr. Ifran Aklamash Umarah. Tess is passing that name along to Tom Paoletti and the client."

"Good." It was possible Sayid had used that alias before. Even though the terrorist leader was dead, it would still be useful to find out where he'd been and whom he'd talked to recently.

As they took the stairs up and up and up, penlights out, Nash was quiet, almost pensive.

He said some rather choice words though, when, upon hitting the ninth floor, a sign on the wall indicated that 933 was all the way down at the end of the dark hallway.

The key did the trick. The suite was as dark as the hall, but at least there were windows.

Jimmy went in first, flashing his light quickly around the sitting room and stepping briefly into the bedroom, making sure they truly were alone. He crossed to the windows, peeked out, then opened the curtains only a fraction of an inch.

"Room faces the street," he told Decker as he went back into the bedroom to do the same thing at that window.

It wouldn't do to have someone standing down on the street—one of Bashir's men, for example—notice that a pair of rooms on the ninth floor suddenly had their curtains open.

Still, the last rays of the setting sun streamed in through that narrow slit, providing just enough light for them to see.

Decker quickly found the room's safe in the bedroom. It was unoriginally placed behind an oil painting of an ocean sunset.

He set to work as Nash methodically searched the room, sticking any papers he found into his pack.

Murphy—bless his many talents—had managed to scrounge up some C4 before he was injured. There wasn't much of the explosive, but Deck didn't need a lot. With proper placement, like on the hinges—"This thing has its hinges on the outside," he called to Nash, who laughed at the design flaw—it would pop open this safe. He cut a fuse, lit a match.

"Fire in the hole," he warned Nash as he stepped back.

Bang. It hardly made more noise than a popped brown-paper lunch bag.

And the safe hung open.

"Shit," he said.

Nash came to look. "Whoa."

A laptop—probably *the* laptop, thank you, Jesus—sat on top of stacks and stacks of neatly packaged, crisply new United States currency. Hundreds and twenties. Mostly twenties. Old style—all green.

"Is it real?" Nash grabbed a pack, pulled out a bill, and held it up to the light. "Not even close. A ten-year-old would know this is a fake."

Decker stashed the laptop in his pack. It was an older model and nearly as heavy as that battery they'd lugged from Rivka's. "What if that ten-year-old—or forty-year-old—hadn't seen U.S. currency in years?" he asked. As was the case for a large portion of the population of K-stan.

"Then it might look pretty damn real. What do you think Sayid was here to buy?" Nash helped him pull the counterfeit money out of the safe and jam it into their bags.

"If we're lucky, he's kept some sort of diary or log on his laptop," Decker said.

"Dear Diary," Nash said. "Today I came to Kazabek to purchase a rocket launcher. It's only slightly used, and at twenty thousand dollars it's quite a good deal. Especially considering the money I'm using cost only fifty dollars to make. Although, gosh darn it, I sure use up that green ink in my printer cartridge awfully fast."

Nash's phone rang. "Hey," he said, answering it. He stuck it between his ear and shoulder as they continued searching the room. "Good timing. Guess what Deck just put in his backpack?"

It would be bad form to assume the laptop in the safe was the laptop they wanted, and walk away without checking carefully beneath the king-sized bed.

"Shit."

Deck looked up. He didn't like the sound of that.

"Schroeder's gone," Nash reported to Decker. He paused, listening again. "Tess went down to check on him and Khalid, found Khalid in the barn. The kid was tied up and gagged so he wouldn't run and tell Tess that Schroeder was leaving. She thinks the prick's probably on his way over here. Khalid said *he* said something about wanting to get photos here at the hotel." He paused.

Photos. Decker rolled his eyes. God save them from reporters.

"Yeah, well, you're not the only one who didn't anticipate it, Tess. Dave should be back soon, and we will, too. Really, don't beat yourself up over this. We're not in any danger. There's no way he'll find the tunnel. Just . . . Yeah. Stay cool. We're on our way."

And they were. Nash pocketed his phone as they shouldered their bags and went out into the hall. "I am so ready to be out of here."

Decker followed him into the stairwell.

Eighth floor, seventh floor, sixth floor, fifth. As they hit the fourth, approaching the lobby, they both slowed slightly, just enough to be sure they were moving soundlessly.

Nash covered his penlight so it was little more than a glow in his hand. Decker turned his off, slipped it into his pocket.

As they drew closer to the door leading out into the lobby, Nash held up his hand. *Stop.* His light went off, too, since the door was ajar and the dim twilight from the lobby windows came in through the crack.

He looked back at Deck, who nodded. Yeah, he'd noticed it, too. It wasn't so much that he'd heard something as felt it.

A microscopic change in atmospheric pressure due to additional bodies within an enclosed space.

Or the invisible, soundless wake that continued to disrupt the air molecules long after someone had stopped moving.

Or an electrical current that came from another living being. Or lots of other living beings.

Nash already had his sidearm out and held at ready.

And then they heard it. *Snick.*

Most people, even when trying to be silent, just couldn't hold completely still for very long.

There was definitely someone out there.

Again a *snick,* followed by an absolutely unmistakable rustle.

Deck signaled to Nash—slowly, carefully, so as to disturb as few oxygen molecules as possible. *Fall back.*

They went up the stairs, touching as little of the steps with the soles of their shoes as humanly possible.

They had barely gone a half a floor when it happened.

Decker gave Nash a *What the fuck?* look, but then instantly realized what it was.

Aftershock.

It started as a low rumble and worked its way up to a definite brain-rattling shake.

Oh, boy. Hell of a time to be in a building that was on the verge of collapse.

Apparently whoever was waiting for them in the lobby felt the same way. They all started talking—a babble of voices, a variety of dialects, but the same general message. *We have to get the hell out of here.*

Decker knew Nash was thinking the same thing. But, *Up,* Deck signaled. He grabbed his penlight and switched it on, covering the bulb the way Nash had before, making sure there was enough light to be seen. He signaled again. *Go up.*

Nash went, but he didn't want to. "They're about to clear out," he whispered. "If we wait . . ."

In the lobby, whoever was in charge spoke over the voices. "Hold steady! This will bring them down to us."

Something crashed—it sounded like one of the smaller chandeliers breaking free and hitting the tile floor—and there was a shout. "Here they come! From the South Tower!"

And then a voice speaking English: "It's an ambush—they've been following me for days—Decker, look out!"

There was a ripping sound—an automatic weapon being fired. Who the hell were they shooting at?

"That was Will Schroeder," Nash realized. "Shit, did they kill him? If they didn't, I'm fucking gonna. I can't believe he led them here."

Another shout in the local dialect. "That wasn't them, idiot! There's no one over there!"

"Six-man squads, each stairwell, now! Go!" Deck heard the command, and he and Nash broke into a full run, light bobbing. No need to be quiet any longer.

Nash, however, had his phone out. "Come on," he said as he attempted to dial. "Ah, Christ, don't fuck with me now."

It was slowing him down. "Come on, Nash, *move.*"

"God damn it! Deck! Check your phone!" Nash was the closest to wild-eyed that Decker had ever seen him. "Is it working?"

And he knew what Nash was thinking. Tess. If what Will had shouted was true—that he'd been under surveillance for days—then he'd probably been followed when he went to see them at Rivka's house.

Where Tess was now.

Alone.

Decker checked his phone. "No."

"We have to get back there, and we're going *up*!"

Decker knew what Nash was thinking. Up, with no chance of a helo waiting there to pull them off the roof.

"Dave's probably back by now," Decker told him. Dave— and Sophia. Jesus. If Rivka's house was being watched— or worse, if everyone in there was brought in for questioning . . .

"Yeah," Nash said. "Yeah. Dave's probably . . ."

He'd pocketed his phone and was using his arms to help pull himself more quickly up the stairs. Which was good, because Decker could hear the sound of a squad of soldiers following not more than five or six flights below.

The aftershock was over and the hotel still stood.

Someone shouted. "Here, they're in here!"

Good, draw 'em all into this stairwell.

"What's Dave going to be able to do?" Nash asked Decker.

"I don't know," Deck said. "But he's Dave, he'll do something."

"Where the hell are we going?"

That Decker *did* know. "Seventeenth floor."

Nash knew instantly why they were going there. "Suite 1712," he said. "North. *North*. We're in the wrong freaking tower!"

Back in the early 1970s, when the Grande was brand-new, you could make a full circuit of the hotel on each floor, passing from the corridor in the West Tower to the one in the North Tower to the East Tower to the South, and then finally back again to the West.

Each tower had its own elevator, as well as a stairwell, but if you were staying, say, in 1712 in the North Tower, you could take any elevator—North, South, East, or West— and still find your way to your room. Eventually.

But in the late '80s, trouble came to town and often visited the Grande in the form of armed robberies and kidnappings of its wealthy guests. The hotel management erected walls on each floor between the towers, to restrict movement inside the hotel. It was an attempt to eliminate the vast array of escape routes.

The walls that were built to separate the towers were little more than plasterboard over a cheap frame made of two-by-fours.

Of course all the walls in this formerly four-star hotel were ridiculously thin.

"Deck," Nash said again. "We're in West—not North! We're in the wrong tower!"

"No such thing," Decker told him, "when you've got C4 in your pocket."

Jimmy hated this.

But as much as he hated this, as frightened as he was about Tess's safety, as freaked out as he was by the thought of this building coming down on his head, he loved watching Decker work.

The man was relentlessly cool under pressure.

They came out of the stairwell on the seventeenth floor, and Decker shone his penlight to the left without hesitation. "This way."

Was it . . . ? Yes.

They ran to the end of the hall, but Decker didn't blow a hole in that flimsy wall that had been constructed directly on top of the diamond-patterned corridor carpeting.

Instead he used the pass key he'd lifted from the front desk to unlock the door to the last room on the right.

They went inside and closed the door behind them.

The goons giving chase wouldn't realize they'd lost them until they hit the roof.

At that point, they'd probably start a room-to-room search, but they'd restrict it to the West Tower.

Of course, by the time they got down to the seventeenth floor, Decker and Jimmy would be long gone.

By the time the soldiers got to the seventeenth floor, Jimmy would be back at Rivka's, where Tess would be waiting, safe and sound.

Tess, who loved him, but who recognized that he was poison and thus didn't want to be with him.

Jimmy didn't blame her. If he could have, he would have run away from himself a long time ago.

Damn it, wasn't that what he had done when he joined the Agency?

No. They'd changed his name, but they hadn't changed who he was.

Decker was standing on the bed, tapping on the wall behind it, searching for the studs. He seemed satisfied as he stepped back onto the floor. "Help me move this."

Jimmy grabbed one side of the metal bedframe, and together they pulled the mattress and box spring away from the wall.

Deck knelt on the floor, tapped the walls one more time to make sure he'd gotten it right. He took from his pocket the remainder of the C4 explosives he'd used to blow the safe in Sayid's room and went to work.

If there was one thing Deck was good at, it was blowing shit up. It was one of those special Navy SEAL skills.

Jimmy took out his phone. Nothing. "Fuck."

"Aftershock probably knocked over the dish I put upstairs," Decker said, lighting the fuse. "We'll be out of here soon." He stood up, moved back. "Fire in the hole."

Pop.

Only a SEAL could blow something up relatively quietly.

Decker had blown a neat little hole in the wall, near the baseboard. Using his foot, he kicked out more of the plasterboard, making it big enough for them to squeeze through.

"Help me," he said again, and Jimmy grabbed one side of the bed, moving it back in place, against the wall.

Talk about brilliant.

Someone coming in to give the room a cursory look would never see the hole.

Jimmy went first, under the bed, through the hole, and into the adjoining room—which was in the North Tower. As was suite 1712, which held the elevator shaft leading down into the tunnel that would take them safely back to the financial district.

And then back to Rivka's.

And Tess.

CHAPTER
TWENTY-FOUR

TESS WAS in the kitchen with Khalid when the earth started to shake.

It was worse than usual, so she grabbed the boy, pulling him with her into the doorway to the yard, praying that this was just an aftershock, that this wasn't another massive quake.

Please, dear God, don't let the Grande Hotel fall. . . .

She'd spoken to Jimmy a matter of minutes ago. There was no way they could already have moved out of the hotel complex. Not yet.

Shaken off the kitchen table, a pan fell with a clatter, and the glasses clinked in the cabinet.

Thankfully, whatever it was, it didn't last long.

"Are you all right?" Tess asked Khalid, who nodded.

She grabbed one of the lanterns, still swinging from its hook, and ran swiftly upstairs, passing Rivka on the landing.

Guldana was spending the night with their eldest daughter, whose husband had broken his leg in the quake and was still in the hospital, in traction.

"Are you okay?" she asked him as she went by.

"Sadly, I'm growing used to being shaken about."

Cr-r-r-ack! It started with a single explosion in the distance, but didn't stop there. It kept going, rumbling and roaring like thunder gone mad.

It was the kind of sound the Kazabek Grande Hotel might make as it collapsed.

Tess couldn't tell which direction it was coming from. "Is that from the south or north?" she asked, her heart in her throat. *Please, God, no . . .*

Rivka only shook his head.

She ran for the bedroom. "Searching for service . . ." her phone told her.

She grabbed the robe and burka she'd been given at the police station, grabbed the bag that held the last portable sat-dish they'd brought with them.

She rushed down the stairs and through the kitchen and out into the yard where it was—shit!—dark, of course. Curfew had just begun.

She could see the sky glowing in the distance—something was on fire, and occasionally still exploding. Which direction was that? She was all turned around.

Okay, Bailey, slow it down. Don't panic.

First things first. She had to go to that abandoned church, get the communications system up and working. Once she could use her phone, she could try to call Jimmy.

Please, don't let him be dead.

"You aren't intending to go out, are you?" The slightly accented, deep male voice came out of the darkness.

Startled, Tess looked over at the gate. Who was out there? She dropped the bag with the sat-dish and tried to kick it behind the wheel of Khalid's battered wagon before an enormous flashlight clicked on and was shone right in her face.

She squinted at the shadowy shape of a man. Shapes. Was there an entire police patrol right there at the edge of Rivka's yard?

"No, sir," she said. "Of course not. I . . . heard the noise and came out to see . . . Do you know what's burning? I have friends who were working—relief work—down near the Grande Hotel. I'm worried about them."

"I'm afraid I don't know. I suppose it could be the hotel. Do you mind if we come in?" Whoever he was, he'd already opened the gate.

Tess backed up. "Forgive my lack of hospitality, sir, but my husband—he's with People First. He didn't make it back before curfew. I'm afraid it would be considered improper—"

"Oh, but you're American. Surely you don't follow such quaint customs in your own home?"

As he moved closer to the house, the light from the kitchen door and windows fell on him. He was a large man with a full beard, dressed in a uniform that wasn't police. He held that flashlight in one hand, and a cane to support himself in the other.

And it wasn't a police patrol that he had with him, but rather a veritable army—submachine guns held at ready by men with harshly featured faces and stone cold eyes.

"As I said, sir," Tess told him, forcing a smile. "This isn't my home."

"No, it's not, is it?" The man with the cane looked past her, toward the kitchen door. "Good evening to you, sir."

She turned to see Rivka standing there, astonishment on his broad face. He fell to his knees and spoke in the K-stani dialect that Tess had made up her mind to try to learn. It was such a lilting, pretty language. But she recognized only a few of the words that Rivka spoke—the title "great sir," which could be translated to "lord" or even "king"—and then a name: Bashir.

Oh, *shit*.

As Sophia watched, the armored trucks rolled away.

Padsha Bashir was returning to his palace, taking Tess with him.

"This is bad," Dave admitted. "This is very bad. Nash is going to freak."

They hadn't made it back to Rivka's before curfew—thank goodness. If they had, Sophia would be on her way to the palace, too. The thought made her stomach hurt and her mouth dry.

Because of the curfew, they'd had to move slowly.

Or rather, Dave—beautiful, wonderful Dave—had made sure they took the absolute safest routes, moving from one secure hiding place to another, taking their time. He hadn't pushed her to hurry; instead he'd waited, again and again, while she'd caught her breath.

They'd been hiding here in an old storage shed just down the street from Rivka's when the trucks had pulled up.

There had been a terrible explosion. Even Dave, who knew everything, didn't know what that was. Even Dave was afraid that the Grande Hotel had finally come down.

With Decker and Nash inside.

Sure, why not? Sophia had learned that God could, indeed, be that cruel.

Shocked by that explosion, stunned by the sight of Padsha Bashir standing in Rivka's yard, Sophia had watched in silence as the warlord went into the kitchen.

She'd sat in that kitchen, just hours earlier.

Dave put his arm around her—not for comfort, but because she was shaking so hard he was afraid the shed would start rattling.

Bashir was in there for quite some time, and there was nothing they could do. He had an army of men with him, some of them standing lookout in the street, not far from their hiding place.

"Don't let them take me," Sophia had whispered.

"I won't," Dave had promised, but she could see from his eyes that he didn't really understand what she meant. *Don't let them take me alive.*

Although she clutched her littlest gun, she knew she didn't have the ability to turn it on herself. A few days ago, she would've, but now—even now, even after Decker had told her they couldn't risk smuggling her out of K-stan, even after she'd heard that explosion that well may have taken the lives of both Decker and his friend, Nash . . . she couldn't do it.

Because she'd had a taste of goodness, a reminder that truth and light were out there, counterbalancing the world's ugliness and evil.

And it sparked something to life inside of her, something that had been waiting, lying silently dormant.

But once awakened, it grew ferociously, filling her with . . .

Hope.

She didn't just not want to die—she wanted to live.

Sophia sat with Dave in that tumbledown shed, and watched as Bashir left with Tess. He'd left some of his troops behind. Hidden. In the house. In the barn.

Waiting for the rest of them to come home.

"First thing to do is to get you someplace where you'll feel safe," Dave said now.

"No," Sophia said. "The first thing is to make sure Decker doesn't walk into an ambush." Assuming, of course, that he was still able to walk.

"Shh," Dave said almost silently, his finger against her lips.

Outside the shed, a shadow moved.

A voice whispered, "Dave, sir? Is that you?"

"Khalid?" Dave pushed open the door and hauled the boy inside. They had to squeeze tightly together to stay hidden, but Sophia didn't mind. "Where did you come from?"

"I was in the house, sir, but they didn't see me when they came in. Did you know . . . ? That was Padsha Bashir!"

"Shh," Dave said. "We know."

"I went out the window, but I stayed close and listened. He asked Mrs. Nash about that man—her friend, Will. And he asked her all kinds of questions about a computer, and she said she didn't know what they were talking about, but then Rivka told Bashir everything."

Dave swore, and Sophia realized that before this, she'd never heard him utter such words.

"He told him Tess had a computer upstairs," Khalid continued, "and that she and Mr. Nash and Mr. Decker and you, too, sir, didn't seem to spend all that much time on the relief effort. He told him you had telephones that worked, and that Murphy had died, but no one was sad and still talked of him as if he were alive. He said he thought you were spies for the American government, always whispering together out in the barn." The boy looked at Sophia. "Rivka told him about you, too, miss."

She couldn't help it, she drew in a breath. Dave's arm tightened around her shoulders.

"He said he believed you were Mr. Decker's girlfriend, even though he already had a wife. He said he was tired of that shameless behavior going on in his house and he was planning on telling you to leave—but I know he didn't mean that because just earlier today he told me how sad he would be when you had to go back home."

"Did Bashir ask a lot of questions?" Dave asked. "Tell us everything—as much as you can remember."

"There were lots of questions," Khalid told them. "What is this girlfriend's name? Julie Something. Rivka said he didn't know—didn't care to know—her last name. Had he seen her passport? Yes, yes, of course . . ."

Sophia looked at Dave. What? Rivka hadn't seen her passport because she had no passport.

"What does she look like?" Khalid paused. "Begging your pardon, miss, but he said you were scrawny and plain. He said he'd walked in on you in the bathroom, while you were washing up and . . . he said . . ." He leaned close to Dave and whispered in his ear.

Dave laughed softly. He looked at Sophia. "Rivka was protecting you. I think he probably knew he couldn't lie about everything. If they searched the house—and they were going to search, that was a given—they'd find Tess's computer setup. They'd see all our equipment and know we aren't your average relief workers. But he *did* lie about you. He told Bashir that you were, uh, built like a boy. He used, um, slightly different language. He also said you had a pierced, uh, well, nipple. Which, in his opinion, was the equivalent of decorating a hovel with gold paint and lanterns in hopes that people would be blinded by the glitter and not notice the disrepair." He laughed again. "I do love Rivka."

"After that," Khalid said, "Bashir had no more questions about you."

Rivka had managed to protect Sophia.

But not Tess. Heaven help her.

"Okay," Dave said. "Let's assume Decker and Nash are out there, they're alive, and they're heading back here. They're not going to go into the house. They're not going to get close. Tess, bless her heart, managed to put out a warning."

What?

He pointed toward Rivka's gate. "We have a warning system. A short piece of rope, both on the front gate as well as the kitchen door. We set up two, because the side door's not so easy to see from the street. If either piece of rope is not where it's supposed to be, that means trouble. Tess managed to grab the rope from the gate, drop it into the street, and kick it beneath the truck without anyone seeing. Deck and Nash will check for the rope, see that it's gone, and check this shed, actually, for messages. What we've got to do is figure where we can go—someplace safe to regroup and plan our next move. Which, I assume, is going to be getting Tess away from Bashir."

"I know where to go," Sophia said.

Tess tried to pay attention as she was led through a labyrinth of palace hallways. She tried to orient herself. Part of the palace's roof had fallen in during the quake and was in the process of being repaired.

If she were going to attempt an escape, the construction zone would be the route to take. She focused on visualizing where she was in relation to that front lobby.

She tried not to think about what Padsha Bashir had told her shortly after they'd arrived at the palace, after she'd been led through the ornate doors and past the sentry's station into that busy lobby. Even at this time of night it was hopping, with guards and other people coming and going, phones ringing.

It appeared to double as both prisoner- and equipment-holding area. It was there that Bashir's men had unloaded everything they'd taken from Rikva's house, all the bags and boxes and packs.

Including the one Tess had tried to kick behind the wheel of Khalid's wagon—the one that held that sat-dish and power pack. It sat off to the side, with stacks of crates and bundles—loot Bashir's army had taken from other unfortunates.

"We'll set up a trade with your husband," Bashir had said. "You for him—and the laptop."

"I honestly don't know what you're talking about." Tess had stuck to her story, the way Jimmy told her to. She was a relief worker, recently married to a man she didn't know all that well. It felt like a betrayal, but it was the cover Jimmy had told her to use if something like this happened. He could, he'd reassured her, take care of himself.

She hoped so.

The captain of the guard stood courteously to the side as Bashir took a phone call, only speaking when the warlord turned to acknowledge him. The two men spoke softly, and Tess realized they didn't know she couldn't speak their language.

There was a lot they didn't know about her.

Whatever that phone call had been about, it hadn't made Bashir very happy. He turned to leave, but then he turned back to Tess. "The Grande Hotel *has* fallen," he told her.

Her heart stopped beating.

The son of a bitch was lying.

Please let him be lying.

It *was* possible that he was lying, because after he'd spoken, he'd then watched her closely for her reaction.

Tess had channeled Jimmy and managed—she hoped— to look only slightly disappointed. "I guess it's a good thing that area's been evacuated," she'd said, her voice even. Unconcerned.

He'd laughed, and she was led away.

On the stairs going down, she passed Will Schroeder, in handcuffs, being led up.

He'd been badly beaten, and he peered at her through swollen eyes. "Tess, I'm so sorry," he said. "This is all my fault." He was shoved hard, and he fell to his knees.

The guards who were leading Tess pulled her down the stone stairs much too quickly, and she stumbled and slipped, falling and sliding down six or seven steps on her rear and scraping her elbow all over again.

"Don't hurt her," she could hear Will shouting as they were dragged in two different directions. "Don't you bastards hurt her!"

Jimmy followed Decker past the posted signs announcing intent to demolish, through a basement door, and into the boarded-up old Hotel Français.

H.F. was all that the message said, the message that was stuck to the inside wall of the shed. *H.F.* scribbled on a scrap of paper had meant nothing to Jimmy. All he'd known for sure—to his growing despair—was that Tess hadn't written it.

"This doesn't mean she's not okay," Decker had said to him.

Deck knew his way around the decrepit hotel without turning on his penlight. Apparently this was where he and Sophia had come that night that he . . . hadn't done her taxes.

They went up a flight of stairs, and then up another, and . . .

Tess wasn't here. Jimmy knew she wasn't here. And yet, when they went into a dusty old ballroom and Sophia appeared from the shadows with another slightly taller, slender figure beside her, his heart had leapt.

But it was only Khalid.

"Thank goodness," Sophia said, hands clasped tightly in front of her. "We heard the explosion, thought the hotel might've—"

"We didn't hear anything inside the hotel," Decker told her. "But after we were on the street, we saw the fire. Where's Dave and—"

"Fuck Dave. Where's Tess?" Jimmy asked.

"Dave went out to get something," Sophia told Decker. "I don't know what. And Tess . . ."

She looked at Jimmy, and even though he couldn't see her face clearly in the pale moonlight, he knew. Something bad had happened. He just never imagined exactly how bad until Sophia put it into words: "Padsha Bashir came out to Rivka's house. Somehow he knew you were looking for Sayid's laptop. He took Tess."

Padsha Bashir.

Took.

Jimmy didn't realize he needed support until Decker had his arm around him, until Deck helped him to the floor and pushed his head between his legs.

Jesus Christ, when had he turned into a freaking little fainting girl?

But God, oh God, Bashir had Tess. . . .

Dave chose that moment to return with a clatter. But he gave Jimmy little more than a curious look as he set a large canvas bag on the floor.

"Weapons Are Us," he announced. "Murph told me where he kept something called his Worst-Case Scenario Bag. Anyone need some C4 or a grenade launcher?"

Jimmy reached for the bag, ready to cowboy up and, with a 9mm room broom in one hand, and yes, thanks, an AK-47 with attached grenade launcher in the other, kick down the door to Bashir's palace, shouting Tess's name, like a bad mix of Rambo and Rocky.

Decker, always able to read his mind with great accuracy, pulled the bag out of Jimmy's reach.

"We've got the laptop," he told Dave and Sophia. "But we're going to need to revise my extraction plan."

The guards laughed as Tess cowered, crying, in the corner of the tiny cell.

Play the part, play the part, play the part. Jimmy's voice echoed in her head.

There were five of them.

One or maybe two, she could've taken. But not five.

It wasn't hard to call forth the emotion that brought tears streaming down her cheeks.

The Grande Hotel has fallen.

The door—modern, compared to this ancient cell—closed with a clang that Tess welcomed, because along with locking her in, it locked those five guards out.

She crouched there, crying, as she took a silent inventory of her latest injuries. Elbow—burned. Tailbone—bruised. Ankle—slightly twisted, but the pain was nothing she wouldn't be able to work through.

But it made her think of Jimmy and his dings, and her sobbing sounded even more authentic.

I'll do whatever it takes to find you.

She didn't doubt that for one second. The only thing that would keep Jimmy Nash from kicking in the palace doors was death.

If he was still alive, he was already on his way over here. Tess knew that for a fact. She had to plan for that, be ready for him.

But how?

Step one, get out of this cell.

The last of the guards finally got bored with watching her and went back down the hall.

Coming in, Tess had seen a small table and—good news—a single chair at the entrance to this long row of cells. A stack of books, some papers, the remains of an unpleasant-looking dinner on a tray. There was some kind of light switch on the wall, along with a telephone.

A telephone? A *telephone*.

Her own phone had been confiscated, which was moot because their communications system was completely down. The last undamaged sat-dish was in Decker's backpack, sitting on the tile floor of this palace lobby, with the other equipment Bashir's men had taken from Rivka's house.

And yet, upstairs, Bashir had spoken to someone on a telephone.

Yes, it was possible that phone was little more than a palace intercom system, confined to this building. But maybe . . .

Step two, retrace her steps back to that lobby in hopes that that pile of equipment hadn't yet been moved. Help herself to Decker's backpack. Head for the roof, find a deserted spot, and set up the sat-dish, so that when Jimmy came after her, his phone would work.

Step three, access one of Bashir's phones and . . .

It wasn't as impossible as it sounded. Tess had noticed coming in that security in the lobby, as well as the rest of the palace, was lax. It was a common enough mistake. There were so many guards around the outside of the palace and at each of the gates, it was assumed that anyone inside was supposed to be here. They'd passed quite a few servants on their trip to this cell, and none of them had been so much as acknowledged—let alone challenged—by Tess's guards.

But first, step one.

Head still down as she pretended to cry, Tess peeked out from beneath her arm. The hallway was empty. She quietly stood, making those weeping sounds more softly now, and looked around.

The cell was barely twelve feet by six feet. It had the same type of stone walls and floors as the cell in the police station, but the door was modern—a set of metal bars that slid open along a mechanized track.

The ceiling was high—the largest dimension of the cell was from floor to ceiling, at about fifteen feet—and it wasn't stone, but rather wood. It was made of rows of what looked like two-by-fours, set side by side by side.

Tess went to the door and peered down at the end of the hall. She was right about that single chair. All but one of the guards had left.

He was the one who'd had his hands all over her on the walk downstairs, copping a feel every chance he got. Good. He deserved a gonad displacement.

Moving back into the cell, Tess looked up at the ceiling and spit on her hands, rubbing them together.

She placed both hands on the wall in front of her, then reached back with one foot and then the other, bracing them against the opposite wall. She was just the right height. With her arms pressing against the one wall, her feet against the other, she could walk backwards, shuffling her hands, up and up and up and up.

In his movies, Jackie Chan always made it look so easy, but it wasn't. Her arms and legs trembled from the effort. Afraid to exhaust herself on her trial run, she came back down.

Tess then took off her jeans and shirt, putting her boots and the robe back on.

She took her time, artfully arranging her clothes on the floor in the farthest corner from the door. She stepped back, satisfied.

It looked as if she'd made like the Wicked Witch of the West and melted, melted away, leaving only her clothes behind.

She spit on her hands again and climbed, this time all the way to the top, where she wouldn't be seen by a guard standing in the hall.

Taking a deep breath, Tess let out a blood-chilling scream.

Decker sat, listening to Dave and Nash arguing about the best way into—and out of—Padsha Bashir's palace, where Tess was being held.

In the glow of a penlight, Sophia had drawn a layout of the place, marking the location in the basement where she believed Tess would be held. She called it a dungeon, for lack of a better name, since it was underground and apparently very unpleasant. Dave had taken a turn with the handmade little map and put Xs over the parts of the building that had been damaged in the quake.

Sophia was silent now. She'd been lost in her own thoughts ever since Decker had told her that, before discovering Tess had been taken, his plan had been to head north. Decker would take Sophia and Sayid's laptop and hide with them in the mountains.

Dave, Nash, and Tess would stay behind to clean up and discard their extra equipment, and pack their clothes. They'd leave aboard a commercial airliner. Their luggage would undergo an extensive search, but the police and Bashir's men would, of course, find nothing. Once out of the country, they would contact Tom Paoletti and arrange for an air extraction.

A Seahawk helicopter, probably filled with SEALs from Team Sixteen, who were "training" in nearby Pakistan, would race into K-stani airspace to some desolate mountain location, and pull aboard the laptop—and Sophia and Deck—and race back to safety.

It was the perfect solution to getting Sophia out of this hellhole of a country. Put her in possession of the laptop— No, why take chances? Handcuff her to the damn thing so they couldn't take it without her.

Decker couldn't imagine getting the laptop out of K-stan any other way, not with Bashir and the police and every major and minor warlord in the region hunting for it.

And while the U.S. government wouldn't make the effort to pull Sophia out, they would provide—and pay for—a military extraction to get their hands on al-Qaeda's future plans.

But now they were in a bind. Their cover was blown— none of them would be able to leave via airliner. Not now. And communications were down. Getting any kind of message to Tom Paoletti was going to be a real challenge.

Nash had gone out to retrieve the sat-dish Tess had put on the church tower, but the last aftershock had knocked the power pack loose. It had ripped free from the dish, tumbling to the ground.

Even if they could find an alternative power source, their comspesh—the one person who had even the slightest chance of patching it together and getting it running—was a prisoner in Bashir's palace.

Thanks, Nash pointed out, to Will Schroeder.

Which wasn't really that much of an exaggeration.

Best Decker could figure was that the reporter had attracted Bashir's attention by his investigation of the secret police compound at 68 Rue de Palms. If the police had started following Will, who'd stumbled upon that taxi driver who'd picked up Sayid at the Grande Hotel, and the police had then questioned the taxi driver and found out that Will was asking for information about Sayid . . . Well, they would certainly have brought that to Bashir's attention. And Bashir would have insisted Will continue to be followed, and when Will had come to their home base at Rivka's this afternoon . . .

Well, it was done now.

Nash was running out of patience, pacing in and out of the candlelight. He was ready to walk up to the palace gate, ring the bell, and kill everyone who got between him and Tess.

Dave, however, wanted it all choreographed exactly. "How are you going to get in?" he asked, including Decker in the conversation. "That place is a fortress—don't underestimate their ability to keep you out. And that damaged area is going to be heavily guarded. You're going to have one heck of a body count, and that's going to result in discovery—they'll know you're there within minutes. You're going to have to know where Tess is, free her, and then you're going to need some kind of vehicle to get you out of there."

The plan now was to send Dave into the mountains with Sophia and the laptop. Decker and Nash would enter Bashir's palace, find Tess, grab her, and run. They'd all attempt to meet in several days and make the long, dangerous hike across the mountains and out of Kazbekistan together.

Nash and Dave had started arguing over the pros and cons of taking one of Bashir's own humvees to muscle their way out of the palace.

Sophia spoke right over them. "Deck."

"Yeah."

She had her arms wrapped around herself as if she were cold—which couldn't be the case in this heat.

"I can get us inside," she said.

Dave and Nash both fell silent.

Decker couldn't believe what she was offering. "Are you suggesting—"

"That you walk up to the front gate," Sophia said. "All three of you. You'll need other clothes—traditional K-stani robes. But you'll be able to carry as many weapons in with you as you want. No one's going to challenge you, because you'll be there to collect the reward—and to deliver me to Bashir."

"Dear God, Sophia," Dave breathed, speaking for all of them. Well, except maybe Nash, who was nodding.

"There's a holding area just inside the main door," she told them. "A lobby, if you will. The captain of the guard will have us wait there while he tries to figure out what to do with me—and with you. Because when we get there, Bashir will be asleep."

"Sophia," Decker started. How could she suggest this?

"This is good," Nash interrupted. "This is really good. While you're waiting there, I'll slip away, find Tess. We'll meet over here." He tapped the area on the penciled map where Dave said Bashir's armored trucks were garaged.

She was sitting there, scared to death at the idea of coming face-to-face with Bashir again, and yet offering . . .

"It's likely that the captain of the guard will try to take me downstairs," Sophia said. "He'll probably offer you rooms for the night so you can meet with Bashir and collect your reward tomorrow. If you insisted on staying with me, though, he might just go ahead and put us all in one room until morning."

"Yeah," Nash said. He really liked this plan. "Who's going to guard Sophia better than the men who want to collect that reward? The captain would save himself a hassle."

"And if the captain goes and wakes up Bashir?" Decker asked.

"Then we improvise," Nash said.

"Don't look at me like that," Sophia told Decker. "I'm not doing this for free. I want that fifty thousand dollars—but I want it free and clear."

"Done," Nash said.

She turned to him. "Yeah, well, I'm not," she said. "I want a promise from you, too."

"Name it," he said. "You've got it."

"If something goes wrong," Sophia said. "And I'm . . . not able to collect that money . . ."

"We don't have to do this," Decker interrupted her. "There are other ways inside without putting you at risk."

"Other ways to get all three of us inside?" Nash countered. He wanted to get into that palace, to find Tess, so badly that he didn't realize what he was asking of Sophia. "Armed?"

"Jimmy, think about this," Decker implored him, purposely using the nickname Tess used. All it got him was a dark look.

"What do you need?" Nash asked Sophia, obviously ready to promise her anything.

"Michel Lartet," she said. "He gave me up to Bashir, and if I die, I want him dead, too. The same way Dimitri died."

Nash was silent. They all were.

"I want him to know what's coming," Sophia whispered,

"the same way Dimitri knew—the same way I'll know. I want him to kneel on the floor and wonder what it will feel like when his head rolls. And I want him to know that it's me doing this to him, reaching back, even from death, to strike him down."

She was looking at Nash, who looked unswervingly back at her.

Somehow she knew that, out of all of them, Nash was the one she should ask to do this terrible thing.

"Consider it done," he told her quietly.

"I can help."

"No, you can't." Jimmy didn't have time for this, but Khalid wouldn't back down.

"Yes," the boy insisted, "I can."

"Your little brother needs you alive." Jimmy emptied his wallet, pressing the bills—both K-stani and American—into Khalid's hand. He couldn't give the kid his wristwatch—he still needed that. But he pulled off the gold ring he wore on his left hand and gave that to him, too. "Dave, you have any cash left?"

"You need me more," Khalid said.

"Hide this," Jimmy instructed him as Dave handed over another wad of bills—probably more than the kid had earned in his entire life. "When you get home, hide it somewhere outside of your house. Dig a hole and bury it, do you understand?"

"Thank you, sir—"

"If they come to question you—*when* they come to question you—start by shouting about how we left without paying you and how badly we mistreated you. Then you show them the bruises on your face to prove it."

"These were from the bomb in City Center," Khalid said.

"They won't know that." Jimmy saw that Sophia was finally ready to go.

He also saw that Khalid was only pretending to acquiesce. The kid stood with his gaze lowered, pretending he had no intention of following them out the door. Yeah, sure.

Jimmy looked at Decker in despair. "Don't make me be the one to do this," he said.

Decker had mercy on them both and gave the kid what looked to be an almost gentle tap. It was amazing how effective that could be—like pushing an on-off switch. Khalid's legs buckled, and Deck lowered him to the floor as Jimmy pushed Sophia's rolled up jeans beneath the boy's head.

He'd wake up tomorrow morning with one hell of a headache. No doubt he'd be pissed, but he'd be alive. Of course, unlike the rest of them, he'd still be here, in Kazbekistan.

Sophia and Dave had already gone out the door, and Jimmy and Decker hurried to catch up.

CHAPTER
TWENTY-FIVE

IT WENT according to plan, considering that the plan was for fifteen armed guards to step down from the front gate of Bashir's palace, their semiautomatics locked and loaded and aimed directly at them.

Decker stood back and let Dave talk.

Nash wore an M16, grenade launcher attached, slung over his shoulder, as if he didn't have a care in the world. He yawned, completing the effect of fatigue and boredom, squinting from the searchlights that were shining in their dirt-smudged faces.

Deck knew better. Beneath his hooded robe, Nash was a virtual arsenal of weaponry and ammunition.

Yes, they'd heard rumors of a curfew. Dave spoke in the dialect used up in the mountains, in Firyal. It was spooky how authentic he sounded.

But they'd gotten tied up on the road from Ikrimah. Transportation was spotty and they'd had to walk most of the way.

Yes, they knew it was very late, but they'd thought His Excellency and Lord Most High Padsha Bashir would appreciate them taking care to have the thief he'd been searching for locked inside his own gates tonight.

Decker was holding Sophia's arm. He'd felt her trembling start when they'd begun their approach to the palace. Covered completely by her robe and burka, it was surely hard for her to see or hear any of this. Still, she knew what was happening.

"She's changed her hair, of course," Dave told the guards who glared at them. "But it's the woman Bashir's been searching for."

At Dave's nod, Deck yanked the burka off her head, jerked the robe from her body, pushing her down onto the street.

Naked.

She'd insisted on being naked beneath her robe, saying that if they were going to do this, they should do it right.

Her scars would convince the guards that she was, indeed, the woman Bashir was looking for.

And her nakedness would prove that she wasn't armed beneath her robe, that this wasn't a trick or a trap.

"Push me down hard," she'd told Decker back at the Hotel Français. "We have to make this look real."

So, yeah, okay, it looked real.

The light gleamed off her body, all that skin, all those angry-looking wounds that were finally starting to heal—wounds he'd thought were hennaed designs, or maybe even tattoos, put there by choice, when he'd first met her.

She lay in the street, head down in defeat, eyes tightly closed.

"It's not a big deal," she'd told him back at the hotel. "Being naked like that. It's not like I haven't . . ." She'd shaken her head. "Being naked is nothing."

It wasn't nothing. She was as vulnerable lying there as she could possibly be.

Decker threw her robe down beside her—which was also part of the plan. She would cling to it, as if trying to cover herself. In reality, they'd quickly stitched her little handguns into the sleeves. If she needed to, she could grab them and fire right through the fabric.

The highest-ranking guard, a lieutenant, nodded, his eyes

wide. "Bring her inside," he told them. He turned to his
sergeant. "Get the captain."

Jimmy Nash used the spectacle of a naked woman being
dragged into the palace to slip out of the lobby and down
the corridor.

No one saw him go—all eyes were on Sophia.

Jesus Christ, Bashir was one sick bastard. Tess had told
him and Decker about the cuts on Sophia's body. Seeing
them was . . . It was the farthest thing from a turn-on he
could imagine.

Bashir, apparently, got extra happy at the sight of blood.

Jimmy smiled grimly. He'd love a chance to give the
fucker a postmortem boner.

He was halfway down a flight of stairs when his phone
vibrated and nearly made him discharge his weapon into a
row of potted plants.

What the hell?

He opened it. The number was one he didn't recognize.
"This better not be a sales call."

"Jimmy? Is that really you?"

Holy Mother of God in heaven above, he nearly couldn't
squeak out a single sound. "Tess!" He sounded like Mickey
freaking Mouse. He tried to move back even farther into
the shadows, tried to keep from speaking too loudly.
"Yeah, it's me." Holy Christ! "Where *are* you?"

"Oh, thank God," she said. The connection was awful,
her voice tinny and distant, as if she were calling from
Mars. But at least she didn't keep cutting out. "Thank
God. Bashir told me the Grande Hotel came down, and
I've—" She broke off, whispering, "Wait, wait, shhh!"

After what seemed forever, she said, "Okay, they went
past. I'm on a land line—my phone was confiscated—
and it's a little inconvenient. Not to mention how pissed

Bashir's going to be when he gets his phone bill. Jimmy, please tell me, are you really all right?"

"Yes! Where the fuck are you?"

"I am—the fuck—near the roof of the palace, about four—no, five—chimneys to the west of what looks like some kind of helicopter landing pad. I set up our last sat-dish here, near what looks like a guard outpost—currently unmanned. I was hoping you'd be close enough for your phone to work. I haven't been able to get through to Decker."

"Are you all right?" he asked as he turned around and headed up instead of down. She sounded all right. Please Jesus God, let her be all right. He took the stairs two at a time to the first floor, the second . . .

"I'm a little scared," she admitted. "Okay, yeah, I'm a lot scared. You should see Will Schroeder—they beat the crap out of him. He's in one of the cells on the lowest level. There was a guard posted and he looked unconscious, so I didn't do more than make note of his location. But I'm worried he's—"

"Are *you* hurt?" he interrupted her as he passed the third floor. "You."

"I'm fine—honest. You know, Bashir's got so much security on the gate, it's assumed if you're in the palace, you're supposed to be here. I've been walking around for a while—I went all the way to the lobby to get the bag with the sat-dish, and then back up here. I found a tray with a couple of coffee mugs. I've been carrying it around and people—servants, I think—have walked right past me. I haven't been challenged yet. Which is good, because I don't exactly speak the language."

She paused just as Jimmy reached the top floor and looked for the stairs that would lead to the roof.

When she spoke again, her voice sounded even smaller. "I'm not exactly sure yet how I'm going to get out of here.

I don't know when the guards change shifts, but I'm pretty sure I don't have a lot of time before they realize I'm not in my cell. I was thinking if you could create some kind of diversion—" She cut herself off as he found a door, opened it.

"Shit," Tess said. "Someone's really coming this time. Jimmy, I'll call you b—"

"It's me," he said. God *damn,* this was lucky. He was assuming he'd have to head up to the roof, stick his head out the door to get his bearings. But she'd already hung up. "Tess," he hissed. "Tess!"

And there she was.

In the shadows at the top of the stairs. "Jimmy?" she breathed. "Oh my God! You're inside the palace . . . ?"

Jimmy pocketed his phone as he went up the stairs, as Tess came toward him, and then, oh my God, indeed, because he had her in his arms. She clung to him, and he just wrapped himself around her and held her as tightly as he possibly could.

"I knew you'd come," she said, her faith in him ringing in her voice. "I knew it."

Sophia knelt on the cool tile floor just inside the front doors to Padsha Bashir's palace.

She kept her head down and her eyes closed as voices babbled around her.

She held her robe in both hands, keeping her guns nearby, but she was careful not to cover herself too much. She was well aware that her nakedness was the cause of much of the excitement and confusion.

Decker was standing near her, behind her. She couldn't see him—even if she opened her eyes—but she could feel him there.

She hadn't been able to look at him when she'd first stripped off her clothes back in the Hotel Français. That had been hard for her to do, hard for him, too. But she knew he would get angry at the sight of her, at her mementos of Bashir's abuse. And once they were at the palace, he could not react.

He had to know what to expect.

She, for once, hadn't been able to chatter away. She'd just stood there, eyes down and silent.

"I don't want you to do this," Deck had said quietly. "I don't want you to have to go back there."

She'd looked at him then. "I want the money. So unless you can think of another way for me to earn it . . ."

Now she heard the footsteps, heard Decker shift his weight behind her.

She opened her eyes just a little and saw a dark brown pair of boots before her. She didn't let herself look any higher.

The boots' owner put his hand beneath her chin, pulling her face up. "Look at me," he commanded.

She opened her eyes. It was the captain of the guard—a large man with a full beard, eyes that seemed almost to twinkle, and ruddy, round cheeks. Friendly cheeks. If his beard had been white, he would've looked like Santa. Santa of the guard. She'd seen him often, standing in the hall, waiting to speak with Bashir.

"Hah!" he'd said to her once, coming out as she went in to Bashir's chamber. "This time you wait for me."

"Ah, yes," he said now. "I remember you. Such pretty eyes." His hand was warm, his touch oddly gentle, even as he reached down to cup her breast, his thumb tracing one of her nearly healed cuts. "Such a shame."

Decker stepped into her peripheral vision, close enough for her to feel his body heat. "Don't touch," he muttered as if there were a real difference between being looked at and being touched. As if it mattered at all.

"She's already dead," the captain told Decker. He looked

past him to Dave, who'd taken on the role of leader so Decker could stay as close as possible to Sophia.

None of the guards had seemed to notice that the third man who had brought her in—Nash—had vanished.

"The reward won't be ready until morning," the captain said. "My sergeant will escort you to a room where you'll be quite comfortable. As for the girl, I myself will see that she's properly confined."

Sure he would.

"We didn't bring her all this way only to lose her now," Dave said. "If we wait, she waits with us."

The captain took several steps back, and the dozen or so of his guards in the room raised their guns. As did Decker and Dave—aiming theirs directly at the captain. They all froze there. No one moved, no one spoke.

It seemed absurd that they were going to die protecting her virtue.

But if they died, they'd surely take the captain with them.

Seconds ticked by, interminably slowly, and still no one moved.

Finally the captain laughed. "If that's what you want, you may as well wait right here," he said, then turned and walked away.

Jimmy closed his phone. "Tom's going to try," he told Tess, who was sitting at the top of the stairs, near the roof of Bashir's palace.

As in try to get a military helicopter to fly over the border into a hostile country, all the way to the capital city of Kazabek, to pick up a team of civilians who did not work, officially, for the U.S. government?

Jimmy smiled at the look of obvious disbelief that was surely on her face. "They won't be coming in to save *us*," he told her. "Their single objective will be to pick up that laptop."

He touched her hair, his hand warm against her cheek, and for the six thousandth time in the past few minutes, Tess said a silent prayer of thanks that the Grande Hotel hadn't fallen.

Jimmy had told her that, to the best of their knowledge, the explosion she'd heard had been the result of a gas leak in the proximity of one of Bashir's ammo dumps. All it would have taken was one person, lighting a cigarette. . . .

"Good job getting communications up." Jimmy laughed, shaking his head. "How the hell did you get out of the dungeon? Sophia described it to us and—"

"Shouldn't we get moving?"

He sat down next to her. "No. Tom asked us to wait a few minutes. He's going to call right back. If he can't get a chopper heading out here ASAP, we'll have to extract according to Deck's plan—hot-wire one of Bashir's armored cars and blast out through the side gate. Head for the hills. If we dismantle this sat-dish and take it with us . . ."

They'd be able to set up an air extraction from their location in the mountains. Save themselves the long, dangerous hike across the border.

But once Tess dismantled the dish, they'd lose contact with Tom. For not the first time this trip, she wished their sat-com radios, with their long, mobile antennas, had survived their journey, wished they'd been able to replace them when they reached Kazabek. But not even Murphy, the king of scroungers, had been able to get his hands on that kind of equipment.

Jimmy was looking at her as if he still couldn't quite believe that she was here and she was safe. He couldn't believe she'd gotten out of her prison cell and then gone all the way to the front gate, back to where she'd seen Bashir's men drop the equipment stolen from Rivka's house.

"I've done field training," she reminded him. "And I've passed the PT requirements. I know you're always going to think of me as 'Tess from support,' but I paid attention in class. I know how to fight. And I noticed right away that most of Bashir's security is on his outside perimeter. After they stashed me in my cell, only one man stood guard."

"You got past a posted guard?" he said in surprise, which was a little annoying.

"Yeah," she said. "I did. Remember that the next time you get the urge to mess with me."

"I love this," he said. Which was not exactly the same as *I love you*. Which she'd said to him just a few hours ago. *I love you, but you are going to hammer me emotionally, so I can't do this.* Which was stupid. She'd found *that* out a few hours ago, too, when she'd thought Jimmy was dead. You couldn't attach a *but* to *I love you*. You could only attach an *and. I love you, and you are going to hammer me emotionally and that's just the way it's going to go.*

But wasn't it better to be hammered now than later? Wouldn't it hurt less just to get the hammering over and done with?

No. Yes. Maybe. She couldn't make up her mind.

Tess told Jimmy how she'd gotten out of her cell. The narrow walls, the high ceiling, the climb up, the clothes on the floor. The guard's expression of disbelief when he'd stared into what looked to be an empty cell. She didn't speak the language, but she understood his tone.

The door opened, he came inside, she dropped. A kick to the 'nads, a kick to the head, she'd grabbed his weapon, and locked him, unconscious, in the cell.

No biggie.

Except it was. She was proud of herself.

And completely in awe of Sophia when Jimmy, in turn, told how they'd walked in through the front gate.

"I can't believe she would do that." Tess shook her head. "I met Bashir. He's . . . frighteningly normal. He scared me to death."

He put his arms around her and held her close again. "I was . . ." He took a deep breath, blew it out hard. "Scared, too. When I found out where you were. All I could think was that I'd made you stay behind, because the thought of anything happening to you makes me . . . so freaking crazy. And here you were, in this awful danger that you wouldn't have been in if you'd come with us and . . . it was all my fault. I don't think I've ever hated myself as much as I did right then."

She pulled back, astonished at all he'd copped to. But now he wouldn't look at her.

"We need to get moving." He stood up, opened his phone, and dialed a number. "Tom must've hit a snafu," he said, phone to his ear. "Deck's not picking up—he must still be in the lobby." Where Bashir's guards would look at him hard if he—supposedly from a tiny mountain village—pulled out a phone and took a call. Jimmy shut his own phone. "Let's get that sat-dish and go."

"It's been only a few minutes," Tess said, squeezing the words past her heart, which was securely in her throat. "Let's give it a couple more." God, she wanted Tom to call. She wanted that chopper to swoop in and take them out of here. And she wanted Jimmy to tell her that he loved her.

"If we get separated," Jimmy said, still all business, "for whatever reason, work your way down to the garage. Do you know where that is?"

Tess shook her head.

"Other side of the palace," he said. "As far east as you can go. It's a separate building. You know how to fire a grenade launcher?"

"No," she said, blinking at the sudden change of subject. "I haven't ever—"

"That's okay. Take this then." He handed her a generic-looking 9mm semiautomatic and a couple of extra clips.

"Jimmy."

He stopped rearranging his equipment and looked at her, his face only dimly lit from the light in the hall.

"Thanks for . . . being so honest," she said.

He laughed, but it was without humor, and his words came back to her in a rush. *I don't think I've ever hated myself as much as I did right then.*

"What if I told you that about five years ago, I had the opportunity to rid the world of Padsha Bashir?" he asked. "But I didn't, because that part of my mission was optional. So I packed up and went home instead."

She was silent, hoping he'd tell her more.

"Sometimes the assignment is not optional. Sometimes the deletion order comes down and . . . Deletion—nice word, huh? 'Delete as many of the terrorists as possible.' I've been performing deletions a long time, Tess."

Now he was looking at her as if he expected . . . what? That she would faint? Scream? Turn away in disgust?

Was he serious? He was.

"I know that," she said. "Jimmy, do you really think I don't know that? Hello, I worked in support." She'd read all of his reports. All of Decker's, too.

Now he was the one who didn't seem to know what to say.

"You might want to check in with people every now and then," Tess told him, "before you decide—for them—how and what they should feel. Like Decker. Have you actually talked to Deck about the fact that this is your last mission with him?"

She answered her own question. "Of course not. Why talk to him and risk finding out how he really feels about losing your invaluable skills as a team member, your experience and expertise as an operator, and, oh yeah, your love and friendship. But hey. You already know how he *should* feel, so don't talk to him.

"And me, I guess I'm supposed to be, what? Repelled by

you? Horrified because you're so *bad*?" She laughed in disgust. "You're the one who hates yourself—I happen to like you. But you're so wrapped up in who you think you are and what you think you deserve. You enjoy being dark and tortured and . . . and . . . running away to Mexico, don't you? Because God forbid you ever let yourself be too happy—everyone knows bad people shouldn't be happy. Frankly, I think you're full of crap, because I look at you, and what I see is mostly good. But okay, fine." She went up the stairs, past him. "Be bad and dark and miserable. But do it by yourself, Nash, because I don't need that."

He followed her. "I'm sorry," he said.

Of course he was. Miserable people were always sorry.

"I've read your Agency file, you know," she told him.

"I don't have a file."

"That's what you think."

He paused. "Are you serious?"

"Nash, Diego. Subject must be convinced without any doubt whatsoever of both necessity and moral justification of mission," she quoted.

"You're making that up."

"Nash, Diego. Formerly known as James Santucci, aka Jimmy the Kid. Subject would not fold under pressure to provide information that would lead to the arrest and conviction of . . . What was the name? Victor something. Subject's mother didn't visit once while subject was in juvenile detention from . . . When was it? Something like 1982 to 1986."

"You hacked into an unhackable file," Jimmy breathed.

"No such thing," Tess told him.

"When did you . . . ?"

"Shortly after I joined the Agency," she admitted. "A few weeks after we met."

The look on his face was one she'd remember for the rest of her life.

"Imagine that," Tess told him. "I read your file, all those years ago and I still fell in love with you."

His phone rang, ending this conversation.

It was Tom. Jimmy spoke to him briefly, then snapped his phone shut. "We've got a *go*," he told her. "Ten minutes, LZ right here on the roof. We need to go tell Decker. Lock and load and follow me."

Tess grabbed the 9mm and followed him down the stairs. *Follow me* instead of *Stay here*.

It wasn't quite as good as "I love you, too," but it was close enough.

Sophia was watching Decker pace when she heard it.

Angry voices down the hall, moving toward them.

Decker moved in front of her, and Dave stood up.

She knew they'd both counted the guards. There'd been little else to do while they'd sat here and waited . . . for what?

For Nash to return, with Tess in tow, at which point they'd . . . what?

Stand up and walk away, hoping nobody noticed.

Stranger things had happened.

But now that scenario was off the table.

Sophia stood, too, glancing again at the guards who were drowsing by the door.

There were only two soldiers in here, but twelve others right outside and somewhere between five and ten hanging out in a nearby room that looked like it might be a cafeteria.

It was just off a corridor to the left of the front gate. Another hall led right. Decker had told her with his eyes that that was the route they'd take when heading for the garage.

Sophia wanted to flee, despite knowing that no one could outrun bullets.

Except Padsha Bashir wasn't brandishing a gun as he limped around the corner and into view.

He held his sword, the sword that had killed Dimitri, the sword she'd used to try to kill Bashir. He held it high as he came at her, roaring his anger.

He had the strength in his arms to separate her head neatly from her shoulders—her worst nightmare come to life.

Except, in her dreams, Sophia hadn't clutched a weapon of her own in her hands. And, in her dreams, she'd always been alone.

With Decker on her right and Dave on her left, they opened up on him all at once, and Sophia knew that the shock and surprise on Bashir's face, and the blood that bloomed on his white shirt and vest would replace the visions of Dimitri that haunted her dreams.

One violent end for another.

And no guarantee she would sleep any easier at night, ever again.

Jimmy moved silently down the stairs. Tess followed several steps behind, serving tray in her hands, 9mm hidden beneath her robe.

She'd read his Agency file. Shit, she was good.

What was she doing, wasting her time with him? She had to be crazy, knowing what she knew, to fall in love with him.

You might want to check in with people every now and then before you decide how and what they should feel.

"I think you're crazy," he told her now, talking even though he knew he should keep his mouth glued shut. For many reasons.

She didn't say anything as they went down another flight of stairs. They were on the ground floor now. But then she laughed softly. "Is that really a problem for you?"

Jimmy didn't answer—it would have been hard to talk over the tearing sound of machine-gun fire.

Tess dropped her tray and followed as he ran for the lobby.

Decker grabbed Sophia and pulled her toward the corridor while Dave, running backward, created a wall of suppressing fire.

Shit, someone was running toward them. He raised his weapon and—

Nash. And Tess.

"Go!" Nash shouted, covering the lobby so Dave could move forward.

They'd leapfrog like this, running and shooting and running and shooting, all the way to the garage.

Tess came to help him with Sophia.

"Upstairs," she told Decker as they ran down the hall. "Tom's got a chopper coming—comm system's up."

"No way!"

"Yes, way. Should be here any minute, sir."

"I love you," Decker said. "Tell Dave!"

Dave loved her, too.

Tess watched as Decker and Dave tossed Sophia into the helicopter. The racket of the blades drowned out the sound of Jimmy's weapon firing, as he laid down what was called in the military "a field of covering fire."

Basically the theory was if you fired an automatic weapon in a general direction, everyone in that area would hit the deck. With their heads down, they were thus unable to fire their own weapons in return.

Tess squeaked as Decker grabbed one of her arms and Dave grabbed another and then she, too, was on board the chopper.

Her landing wasn't as rough as she'd imagined, since she

was caught and held quite securely in the strong arms of a very young man in a desert-print camouflage uniform, streaks of black and green on his otherwise freckled face.

"Excuse me, ma'am," he shouted politely, as if they'd bumped into each other by accident on the street.

SEALs.

There were four others on board. One, with some kind of medical insignia on his uniform, had helped Sophia into a seat and was checking to make sure she hadn't been hurt.

Her SEAL—it was hard not to think of him as hers, he was just too cute with that choirboy face—pulled her toward Sophia and out of the way of the door.

The others helped Dave, then Jimmy, then Decker on board.

"Go, go, go!" one of them—brawny, with blond hair and a face like a boxer—shouted to the pilot.

Tess had just sat down, but now she sprang to her feet. "Wait!" Oh, God.

She looked at Jimmy, who knew exactly what she was thinking. "Will Schroeder," he shouted.

She'd forgotten Will Schroeder.

The helicopter was already up and moving out of range of the guards and their weaponry.

They were safe. They were heading for home.

"They'll kill him," Tess shouted, and Decker spoke to the SEAL who'd given the order to go.

Whatever Deck said seemed pretty persuasive, because the SEAL spoke into the lip mike he was wearing, and the helicopter circled back.

Jimmy had made his way to her side. "Where is he?"

"Lowest level, east wing," she said. "There's a second row of cells that you might not see if— Look, it'll be easier just to show you."

"No," he said. "It won't. Deck and I are going. I'll see you in a couple weeks."

A couple of . . . ? "Jimmy! This is my mistake!"

"You told me you'd found Will," he argued. "I forgot him, too." He kissed her hard, a swift good-bye. "This isn't about me wanting to keep you safe. This is about me and Deck being unstoppable together. Isn't that what you said?"

Tess nodded.

"We'll go back inside, we'll get him, we'll vanish," Jimmy promised her. "And I'll see you in a few weeks."

Because it would take them that long to cross the mountains.

The helicopter came in for a brief landing on the east lawn of the palace.

And Decker and Jimmy were gone.

Sunrise lit the sky to the east as the helicopter raced away from Kazabek. Sophia watched as Tess sat and clenched her teeth, her back to the splendor of the pink and orange clouds.

She watched Tess watch the uniformed men—the SEALs— as they spoke to one another over their radio headsets. There was quite a discussion going on. She couldn't hear what they were saying over the roar of the chopper blades, but every now and then she could read their lips. "Decker." They kept saying, "Decker."

Dave had told her that Decker had once been one of them—a SEAL. Apparently they knew him and weren't any happier about leaving him and Nash behind than Tess was.

Tess was closer and apparently could hear what they were saying, because she sat up, leaning forward.

"We have to go back," she shouted. "I just realized— Decker's got the laptop!"

The SEALs all turned and looked at her, almost as one.

They looked at Sophia, and then at Dave, who was cradling his bag with its important cargo on his lap. He tried to hide it within the folds of his robe.

It was so obvious that Tess was lying that several of them laughed out loud.

Sophia couldn't read their stripes and pins—she didn't have a clue who was officer and who was enlisted—but one of them was older than the others. He was ripped, with an upper body that looked as if he could bench-press this entire chopper. His eyes reminded Sophia a little of Decker. Not so much the color or even the shape, but the calm that lay within them.

Tess spoke directly to him.

Good choice, Sophia wanted to tell her. She moved closer so she could hear, too.

"Look, Senior Chief," Tess shouted "Obviously Decker's not that stupid. You know it and I know it. But whoever's in command doesn't necessarily know it."

"That would be Admiral Crowley," the SEAL with the freckles said. "His nickname is God. And he does know Deck. He probably knows you, too, ma'am."

Tess ignored him, refusing to give up. "We can turn this thing around and create a diversion, and Decker and Nash'll be out of there in ten minutes. I can call them, let them know—"

"You have working phones?" The senior chief cut himself off and sighed. "We cannot leave this helo," he told her. "The risk of creating an international incident is already—" He swore. "As much as I would like to, ma'am, and I would . . ." He clearly felt Tess's pain. "We can't fire any weaponry. None at all. I don't know what kind of diversion we could—"

"I do," Sophia said. Deck had thrown his backpack onto the floor near her feet, and she picked it up now. She unzipped it, showing the contents—the stacks and stacks of money that Decker and Nash had taken from the safe in

Sayid's hotel room—to Tess. "It's counterfeit, but it would fool *me* at first glance."

Tess looked at the senior chief, who started to laugh.

He spoke into his microphone. "Turn this thing around."

Decker felt his phone buzz in his pocket, and he pulled it out.

It was Tess. Nash clearly knew it, too, even before Decker spoke to her. Like Deck, he'd heard the chopper coming back.

"She better not be calling to tell you she talked them into letting her onto the ground," Nash told Decker through gritted teeth.

"Where are you?" Tess said. He could hear the thrumming of the helo's blades through the phone.

"Almost at the garage. We've got Will."

"Thank you," she said. "Thank God. Come out toward the back of the building, north side. Give us a couple minutes to get into range—lay low till then. I'll buzz you when it's clear for you to move across the open area and back behind the garage. Again, north side. There are no guards positioned back there. We'll scoop you up as close to the building as possible."

"Will do." Decker pocketed his phone and got a better grip on Will Schroeder.

Jimmy couldn't believe his eyes when they carried Will Schroeder out across the driveway toward the free-standing garage.

This part of the palace was usually heavily guarded—all those vehicles—but everyone had abandoned their posts and run to the front of the palace.

Where thousands of twenty-dollar bills were fluttering down from the open door of the chopper.

The pilot had that thing way up high, out of semiautomatic range. He was using evasive maneuvers, too, in case anyone got the idea to take a shot at them with a longer-range rifle.

Not that any of the guards were paying any attention to their weapons. They were all dashing around, grabbing the cash.

Apparently, Padsha Bashir hadn't paid his men all that well.

The chopper zoomed overhead, coming in low. Jimmy and Deck ran out to meet it, carrying Will, who'd opened his eyes, seen Jimmy, and muttered, "You better not fucking try to kiss me again."

And there was Tess, helping him into the helicopter, holding him so tightly as they launched back into the sky.

Decker met his eyes across the chopper's crowded cabin, and smiled. Dave was laughing and joking with the SEALs from Team Sixteen. Even Sophia didn't seem quite so brittle. And Tess . . .

Tess loved him.

He looked down at her, still in his arms, as they sat down and buckled themselves in. She was exhausted, and she rested her head against his shoulder.

That was nice. It was very nice. A good fit.

Jimmy sat back, trying this odd feeling—was this actually happiness?—on for size.

CHAPTER
TWENTY-SIX

KAISERSLAUTERN, GERMANY

SOPHIA WENT into the hotel bar in Kaiserslautern, just outside of Ramstein Air Base.

"May I help you?" a young woman at the hostess station said in perfect, nearly accentless English.

Sophia hadn't heard more than a few words of German since she'd arrived just a few days ago. And it was James Nash she'd heard speaking it. He and Decker had referred to Kaiserslautern as "McGermany," and it wasn't until she went out shopping for new clothes that she'd understood why.

There were so many Americans living in this part of the country—military personnel and their families—that everyone working in the shops and restaurants spoke fluent English.

Across the room, Decker had been watching for her. He was already on his feet.

"I'm meeting a friend," Sophia told the hostess, who turned to glance at Decker.

Dressed in an oversized sports jacket and tie, he looked small and nondescript. Unremarkable. Not at all worthy of a second glance, which the hostess didn't bother to give him.

But he smiled as Sophia came toward him. The transformation was instant.

"How are you? Nice haircut." He didn't try to air kiss her, he didn't even reach out his hand for a shake. His no-contact rule was apparently still firmly in place.

"Thanks," she said, self-consciously touching her short hair, recently returned to her natural shade of blond. She also wore makeup, lots of it, to cover her bruises. She wasn't sure which was worse, looking battered or looking as if her face might crack. "May I?"

"Please." He'd gotten a small table in the corner, and they now both sat.

The waitress was upon them immediately. "What can I get you?" she asked. Her English was even better than the hostess's.

"I'll have a Coke," Decker said. He looked at Sophia. "Beer? Wine?"

"House wine, please."

When the waitress left, he smiled at Sophia again. "Thanks for meeting me on such short notice."

Like she was doing him some big favor. He'd only saved her life about two thousand times. And he'd been instrumental in expediting the paperwork for her new passport. Not to mention . . .

"Tom Paoletti called," Sophia told him. "I'm heading for San Diego next week for a job interview." She paused. "He told me you gave me a glowing recommendation."

"Yeah, I did. You deserved it." Deck took an envelope from his pocket, pushed it across the table. "That's for you."

She opened it. It was a check, made out to her. For fifty thousand dollars.

She pushed it away. "I know this is your money, and I don't want it."

"We made a deal," he said.

"I changed my mind."

"Change it back." He pushed the envelope back toward her, leaned forward, and lowered his voice. "The client should have paid you, Sophia. Forget about what you did to help us get Tess out. The information you provided was instrumental in finding the laptop."

"I don't want your money, Deck. It feels too much like you're paying me for . . ." Sophia took a deep breath and said it. "For going down on you."

She hadn't heard the waitress approach. The young woman put their drinks on the table and practically ran away. No doubt to tell her friends back in the kitchen what she'd overheard.

Decker sighed.

"Sorry," Sophia said.

He briefly closed his eyes. "I'm the one who's sorry. It never should have happened."

She took a sip of wine. Cleared her throat. "Are you absolutely sure you want us to work out of the same office?"

"Yes," he said, looking up at her. "I'm sure. Sophia, you're good. I mean . . ." He laughed, embarrassed. "Jesus, this is hard—" He put his hand up right in front of his face, palm outward, as if to say *Stop*, and he closed his eyes again. "I'll just stop talking now."

Sophia laughed, and he glanced at her, chagrin in his eyes.

"I'm sorry," she said. "I know you don't think it's funny, but . . ." She laughed again. She couldn't help it.

"It's nice to hear you laughing," he told her. "I mean, really laughing—not that fake thing you do."

She nodded. "I do that too much, I know." She looked at the envelope on the table. "Do you think I could . . . borrow that money? Take it as a loan, until I find a job—"

"Tom is going to hire you, I know it."

Sophia took another sip of wine. "I don't think I'm going

to have that interview. I think . . ." She shook her head. "It's a bad idea."

"No, it's not," he said. "Tom could use someone as . . . capable as you. There, see? That's a good word. I can do this."

Was it possible that he wanted to work with her, that he wanted her around?

Decker pushed the envelope with the check back over to her. "Take the interview, take the job, and take this as a loan. You can pay me back when you're able."

"With interest," she said.

"Fair enough." He pushed his chair out, opened his wallet, and put some bills on the table. "I'm sorry to run, but I have to catch a flight."

"Thank you again." Sophia held out her hand, and he only hesitated slightly before taking it. Fastest handshake in the West . . .

"I'll see you back in the States," Decker said. He gave her one last smile, and then he was gone.

Sophia sat and sipped her wine, thinking about how much Dimitri would have liked Lawrence Decker.

SAN DIEGO, CALIFORNIA

It was weird being back.

San Diego still looked like . . . San Diego. The land of eternal non-seasonal sameness.

And the office of Troubleshooters Inc. still looked like it needed a serious overhaul by Thom from *Queer Eye for the Straight Guy*.

Damn, what a dump.

Jimmy walked in, feeling exceptionally nervous.

He hadn't seen Tess since the flight home two days ago. And before that, there'd been no time to talk. In fact, because of all of the debriefings and meetings and official business, they hadn't said more than a few words in private since that last conversation in Bashir's palace.

She'd been mysteriously absent last night. He'd expected her to be on the flight into San Diego, but she wasn't. And she didn't—or wouldn't—answer her cell phone.

This morning, though, he was going to see her. She had to be here—they were having the very last of the debriefings.

There was a man who had the look of a Navy SEAL sitting at the front desk—tall and muscular, with a military-short haircut and pale eyes that made Jimmy think of a Siberian husky. He had one of those faces that looked as if it might crack if he smiled. And sure enough, he didn't smile as Jimmy approached. He just waited.

"I'm here for the meeting," Jimmy told him.

"Inside."

The door opened behind him, and he turned to see Tess coming in. She was carrying a tray of Starbucks coffees, and Dave was beside her. She was laughing at whatever he had said, and didn't see Jimmy. At first.

"James," Dave greeted him. It seemed the jeans and rock-and-roll T-shirts weren't just part of his disguise for travel to K-stan, but instead his whole new fashion statement. Today he was a walking advertisement for the Ramones.

Jimmy let himself look at Tess, and his heart actually skipped a beat as she met his gaze. "Hi."

Her smile dimmed a few watts. "Hey. I didn't expect to see *you* today."

She didn't? "Why not?"

She took the tray over to Dog-eye Man and gave him one of the coffees and a far sunnier smile than she'd given to Jimmy.

"Extra sugar, extra cream," she said.

"Thanks," Fido said, and smiled back at her.

His face didn't crack. Far from it, in fact. When he smiled, the fucker looked like he belonged in the pages of a magazine.

"Have you met Cosmo?" Tess asked Jimmy.

Cosmo. God *damn*. Her hand was on freaking Cosmo's freaking extra-broad shoulder.

"No, I haven't." Jimmy forced a smile. Held out his hand as Tess introduced them.

"Diego Nash, Cosmo Richter. Cosmo's a chief with SEAL Team Sixteen."

Of course he was.

Richter's grip was firm and dry. He nodded, because speaking more than a single word was obviously just too taxing.

"Nice to meet you," Jimmy lied. He turned his attention to Tess. "Why didn't you think I'd be here?"

"This is a planning meeting as well as a debrief. You said—"

With another big smile at Cosmo, Jimmy pulled Tess back down the hall. "Forget what I said. Where've you been?"

She blinked at him. "I came out here early, to see my mother in San Francisco, but . . . Forget *which* part of what you said?"

"It's crazy, I know," Jimmy said, "but when you didn't call me back, I got scared that you, I don't know, went to Mexico or something."

Tess didn't laugh. She was silent, just looking up at him. That was when he stopped being nervous and got good and scared. "You, um, planning any trips to Mexico?"

"Do you really want to keep seeing me?" she asked. "Because I was going to play our . . . time together like it was just a fling. You know, the assignment ended, so thanks, that was fun, see you around."

"So . . . what are you saying?" he said. "You're moving on to Cosmo Richter?"

She laughed. And then stopped, no doubt when she saw his face. "Are you actually jealous?"

"Shit, yeah."

Her eyes were wide. "Really?"

He couldn't bring himself to hold her gaze. "Yes." God, he was pathetic. "Is that so hard to believe?"

She just stood there looking at him, arms folded, one hand up over her mouth.

That was when Dave poked his head out of the conference room. "Excuse me, we, uh, need to start? We've got Murphy online from Germany, via digital cam. He's under doctor's orders not to talk too long, so . . ."

"Thanks," Tess said. "We better . . ." She gestured toward the door, forcing a smile that turned real as she went into the room and caught sight of Murphy on the video monitor. "Hey, Murphy, how's the leg?"

"Much better, thanks."

"I can't believe it's been only three days since we got back," Tess said, sitting at the big table between Decker and Tom Paoletti. She'd already set up her laptop, and her jacket was on the back of her chair. "It feels more like three months."

"That tends to happen," Dave told her.

There were people in the room that Jimmy didn't recognize. Still, it was clear from just the way they sat that they were more of Tom's operators—even before the former SEAL rattled off introductions.

Jimmy took a seat along the wall, near the door, even though there were still empty ones at the table. Decker gave him a nod but didn't ask him to move closer. He knew that meetings like this gave Jimmy a rash.

Even Cosmo Richter came in and sat down. Next to Jimmy. Of course.

They went through the entire mission, picking it apart. What worked. What didn't work.

"Sat-com radios," Tess kept saying. "Next time we need to make sure we pack enough sat-com radios."

Tom Paoletti finally turned to him. "You haven't said anything, Nash. Any suggestions for a smoother mission?"

"Yeah," Jimmy said. "Stay the hell out of Kazbekistan."

Everyone laughed. Except Cosmo Richter, who merely smiled. Obviously it took too much effort to laugh.

"I actually do have some questions," Jimmy told Tom. "For you, and for Deck, too. Maybe we can talk after the meeting's over."

"Good," Tom fired back at him. "Because I wanted to talk to you—about the possibility of your taking a team leader position." He turned to the video monitor. "You, too, Murph. After you're back, we'll talk, okay?"

"With utmost respect, sir," Dave said, "stay away from me. You can't pay me enough to make me a team leader."

Again, everyone laughed—everyone but Jimmy this time. He heard the words, the conversation continuing on around him as they all said their good-byes to Murphy, as the connection was cut.

Tom was talking to the entire group now about some kind of meeting next Wednesday morning—a chance to meet his second in command, a former Navy sharpshooter and FBI agent, Alyssa Locke.

Jimmy didn't listen. He couldn't listen. He'd been knocked out of his chair. Oh, he looked as if he were still sitting there, but in reality, he was on the floor with Tom Paoletti's almost casual invitation to be one of his team leaders lying like a cinder block on his chest.

Everyone was talking—there were lots of individual conversations now. Plans for the weekend, the best way to fill out the expense reports in order to be reimbursed for incidental items, hey, anyone want to go grab some lunch?

Jimmy was still speechless. Tess was silent, too. She was just sitting there, gazing at him, everything she was thinking and feeling right there in her eyes, for the entire world to see.

"You okay?"

Jimmy looked up to see that Decker had come to stand beside him.

"Yeah," he said, but then corrected himself. "No! I came here today to—" He laughed. "I didn't expect him—Tom—to . . ."

The head of Troubleshooters, Incorporated was getting ready to leave the room.

"Excuse me, sir." Jimmy stood up, blocking Tom's route to the door. "I'm honored that you would want me to, um . . ." He laughed. "Actually, I'm totally blown away. I'm—" He had to clear his throat. "Thank you, sir. Thank you, but no, thank you. I appreciate your confidence in me, honestly, I . . . It means a lot. It does, and thank you, but Decker and I are a team." He glanced at Deck. "And as long as he wants me, I'm going to be his XO. I, um, didn't want to let you think there was actually a chance I might become a team leader. I know you're actively recruiting, and . . . There's no chance of me . . . No. Thank you."

Tom nodded, looking from him to Decker and back. "I appreciate your letting me know." He held out his hand for Jimmy to shake.

Jimmy met Tess's gaze again. She'd misted up, and she wasn't even trying to hide it.

As Tom went out the door, Decker shook Jimmy's hand, too. "I'm glad you decided to stay," he said.

"Me, too," Jimmy admitted. Figures Deck would know that he'd been thinking about leaving. He pulled his gaze away from Tess and looked into his friend's eyes. "I hope I, um, never give you cause to regret that."

Decker hugged him. God, no, not in front of the Navy SEAL—

But Cosmo was gone—back to his job at the reception desk, which, come to think of it, was far more embarrassing than any manly embrace could ever be, especially one with plenty of backslapping.

"I just won you about a hundred extra bonus points with that hug," Decker whispered as he gave Jimmy one last slap on the back. He gestured to Tess with his head. "Look at how she looks at you. You'd have to be a real master to fuck this one up." He looked at Jimmy hard. "Don't fuck this up."

And with those words of comfort—at least Jimmy thought they were meant to be comforting—Deck left the room, closing the door tightly behind him.

Tess pushed her chair back from the table and stood, as if she'd just realized they were alone in this room together. She focused all of her attention on packing up her laptop and zipping the case closed. "Are you going to have lunch with Dave?" she asked without looking up.

"Marry me," Jimmy said.

She looked up. In fact, she stared at him, her mouth slightly open.

"This wasn't a fling," he told her. "What we had. What we *have*. If it was just a fling, you wouldn't care what I said to Tom or to Deck or . . . You wouldn't care. And you definitely care. I can see that you care."

She laughed. "There you go again, deciding what it is that I feel."

"You love me. I'm not deciding, I'm reporting what I see. I see you looking at me as if—"

"This isn't because of . . . Jimmy, I got my period yesterday."

"This has nothing to do with that."

"So you've just . . . randomly gone insane."

Jimmy laughed. "Yeah, I guess. It feels a little like that." He cleared his throat. "Love has often been compared to insanity."

She pretended to organize the pile of papers that was still on the table, putting them neatly into a stack. Finally she looked at him again. "You think you love me."

He met her gaze. "I know I do. And you love me, so . . ."

But Tess shook her head. "You're a player," she said. "I would have to be crazy to marry you. You don't know the meaning of the word fidelity."

"Yes," he said, refusing to be offended. He didn't blame her for thinking that. "I do. It's all about giving your word, about making promises and then keeping them. I don't break promises, Tess. I've just never given any like this before."

She was silent.

"There's a lot that's wrong with me. I'm a mess—I'm the first to admit that. But I promise to be faithful. I promise I'll never intentionally hurt you," he said. "I can't promise I'll ever be able to tell you much about"—he cleared his throat—"Jimmy Santucci, but, see, I was hoping it would be okay with you if we focused on the future instead of the past." He took her hand, needing to touch her. "I love you, and if you really are crazy enough to love me—"

"I do," she said. "I am." But then she pulled away. She took several steps away from him. Turned back. "I never expected this."

He answered her honestly. "I didn't either. I never thought . . ."

"What if you change your mind?"

"I won't," he said.

"But what if you do?"

Jimmy shook his head, unable to give her the answer she wanted. "Why would I change my mind," he asked instead, "when being with you is . . ." He cleared his throat again. "Rumor has it I'm a good person. When I'm with you, I can almost believe it."

Tears filled her eyes. "Oh, God, Jimmy, I can't just marry you. How can I just . . . ? I'm not that crazy." She covered her face with her hands. "Oh, my God, maybe I *am* that crazy."

Victory. The relief that filled him made his knees weak. Jimmy pushed himself to his feet, ready to move in for the kill.

But she held up her hands as if to keep him at arm's length. "Can't we start with dinner? Wouldn't it be smart to date for a while, to take it slowly, before—"

"Absolutely," he said.

That made her pause. "Really?"

"I want you in my life," Jimmy told her. "You want to take this slowly, well, okay. We'll take it nice and slow."

He smiled then, and Tess laughed, because she surely knew exactly what he was thinking.

"You think all you have to do is kiss me," she accused him, "and—"

Jimmy kissed her.

And she didn't stand a chance.

<u>GONE TOO FAR'S</u> PARTNERS—AND LOVERS— SAM STARRETT AND ALYSSA LOCKE ARE BACK IN ACTION IN AN EXCLUSIVE SHORT STORY!

SAM WAS hovering.

He'd already made up a multitude of excuses to come into the bathroom while Alyssa was in the shower, and now, while she brushed her teeth, he lurked just outside the door.

She'd scared him tonight.

They took turns when out on assignment. Tonight Sam had been on lookout, hiding on the hillside, watching for headlights that would announce an approaching car, as Alyssa jimmied the cheap lock on the door to Steve Hathaway's ramshackle cabin.

The place had been deserted. In fact, this entire part of the county was deserted—they were at least forty miles west of the booming metropolis of New Hope, in northern New Hampshire, population 473 at the height of ski season.

Getting inside that cabin undetected had been laughably easy.

Alyssa now dried her face on the plush resort towel as

Sam checked up on her for the twenty-seventh time since they'd returned to their suite here in the ski lodge.

"I'm really okay," she told him.

"I know," he said.

Sam bent over backward to make sure he never said anything that might make her think he doubted her ability to take care of herself.

Earlier tonight, when she'd pushed open that cabin door, switched on her penlight and gone inside, Sam had spoken into his radio from his perch on the hill.

"Lys, I can't see you." He'd worked hard to keep his voice sounding calm, relaxed. Filled with Texas. Because he knew that *she* knew he dropped his honeyed drawl when he was stressed. "Talk to me."

She'd flashed her little light across the walls and floors, giving him a running commentary. "I'm in a room with a bed, no other furniture. Just piles of trash—classic love shack. It smells like old socks and mildew, with a dash of overflowing septic tank."

"Yum."

"Yeah." She'd sifted through one of the garbage piles with her foot. It was mostly paper—newspapers, empty food boxes, stacks of junk mail. "Honestly, Sam, I can't imagine Amanda Timberman being caught dead here. Even for some of Stevie Hathaway's golden-tan pretty-boy ski-hero booty."

"What's in the other room?" Sam had asked.

"Looks like a combination living area and kitchen," she'd reported, opening up the kitchen cabinets, looking for . . . what? She wasn't even sure. "Sink, stove, refrigerator . . ."

Alyssa pulled herself back to the pristine warmth of the bathroom. "I wish they made some kind of nostril brush—you know, like a toothbrush only smaller," she told Sam now. "I can't get that awful smell out of my nose."

He leapt into action. "Whiskey'll take care of that."

She followed him into the other room. She didn't particularly want a drink, but he seemed so glad to have found a way to help, she didn't want to stop him.

As Sam opened the minibar, she wandered toward the balcony window, where the pink of dawn was lighting the sky to the east. Glasses clinked, ice tinkled.

"Here." He handed her a glass. "It'll make you stop smelling it." He corrected himself. "Her." He tried again. "Death."

Just a few hours ago, during dinner, this had felt more like a vacation than a paid job. It was, at the very least, a silver bullet assignment. She and Sam had been forced to stay in this four-star ski lodge with room service, balcony views of gorgeous autumn sunsets, and chocolates on the pillows.

They'd been assigned to find twenty-five-year-old Amanda Timberman, who'd vacationed at the New Hope Ski Lodge a few short weeks before her disappearance.

Lucas Timberman, the young woman's father, was a total pit bull when it came to placing the blame on Randy Shahar—Amanda's ex-fiancé. He claimed Shahar, born in Saudi Arabia, had killed his daughter after she'd discovered he was part of an al-Qaeda terrorist cell.

Shahar—who had moved to the U.S. when he was four months old—had come to Troubleshooters Incorporated, hoping they could locate Amanda. A former lieutenant in the U.S. Navy Special Boat Squadrons, he now ran a fleet of whale-watching vessels out of Provincetown, Massachusetts.

Timberman's accusations were bad for business.

As if it weren't hard enough to be an Arab American business owner after 9/11.

Finding a missing person wasn't the sort of job that Troubleshooters Inc. usually took on. The company specialized in security—personal and corporate—with a leaning toward counterterrorism. But Tom Paoletti, the former commanding officer of SEAL Team Sixteen who owned and ran TS, Inc., was friends with Shahar. Tom had not only taken the assignment, but he'd given it to Alyssa Locke, his second in command.

Formerly an FBI agent, and before that an officer in the Navy herself, when Alyssa had taken this job with Tom Paoletti, she'd permanently partnered up with Navy SEAL Sam Starrett.

In more ways than one.

A few months ago, she'd married the man—a fact that still seemed surreal.

That she was married at all was odd enough. But that she'd married a textbook alpha male . . .

Sam—her husband—was standing in front of her now, looking hopefully at her empty glass. A man of action, he liked having something to do. "You want another?"

"No," she said. "Thanks, but . . ."

"Didn't help, huh?"

She shook her head.

He pushed a strand of hair back behind her ear. It always amazed her that someone with such big hands—and an ability to put his fist through a wall when provoked—could have such a light touch. "Another might help you sleep."

Again, she shook her head. "Tom said he'd call after he spoke to Randy. I want to be coherent."

"I could talk to him," Sam volunteered.

"I know," Alyssa said. "Thanks. But . . ." Sam hadn't looked inside that refrigerator.

Her cell phone rang, and she opened it. "Locke."

"What time is it there?"

That wasn't Tom Paoletti's voice. It was . . . "Jules?"

"It's nearly three a.m. here, which means it's not quite

six there. Aren't you allowed to answer your phone with 'Alyssa' at least from, say, two to six a.m.?"

"It's Jules," Alyssa told Sam. She and Jules Cassidy had been playing phone tag for weeks now. It was exactly her former FBI partner and best friend's MO to call in the middle of the night after being frustrated by voice mail.

"Are you—honest to God—in a town called No Hope?" Jules asked. "Because I got this weird message from Sponge Bob and it sure as hell sounded like he said you were in No Hope, New Hampshire, and all I could think was, *shit*. No Hope High School . . ."

"You called Jules?" Alyssa asked Sam.

"No Hope Hospital," Jules continued.

Sam lifted a shoulder. "It's been a rough night. I thought you might want to talk to him."

"I'm really okay," she said again.

"I know."

"No Hope Hair Salon . . ."

"It's *New* Hope," she told Jules as she sank down onto the leather sofa, one leg tucked up beneath her.

"New Hope Hair Salon—that's almost as good." His voice changed. "You okay, sweetie?"

Sam sat down on the other end of the couch and put his feet up on the coffee table, his long legs stretched out in front of him. He was trying hard not to look worried.

"We've been looking for this woman, Amanda, and we found her today. In the refrigerator of an abandoned cabin. She'd been there for six months and . . . Whoever killed her had . . ." Alyssa had to stop, take a deep breath.

Sam reached over and put his hand on her foot.

"He mutilated her," she said. "It was . . . gruesome and surprising, and . . ." Sam's gaze was as warm and solid as his hand. She was, in truth, talking to him. "I think I'm embarrassed. My reaction to seeing her was . . ."

She'd actually screamed. Only her years of training had

kept her from running from the cabin after opening that refrigerator door. Or maybe it had been the light-headedness and suddenly blurred vision that kept her glued to the spot.

"I almost lost it," she said. "I actually had to put my head between my knees." All the while unable to say anything more than, "Oh, shit, oh, shit . . ."

Which had sent Sam running down the mountain, racing to her unnecessary rescue.

Or maybe it had been necessary. She'd been beyond glad to see him, to feel his arms around her. She'd done everything but burst into girlish tears.

"I mean, come on," Alyssa told Jules. "What's that about? I've seen murder victims before. This is nothing new."

But Sam shook his head. "You were caught off guard. We both were. We were sure she was still alive."

They'd spent dinner trying to guess where Hathaway and Amanda had gone.

Such optimism was new for Alyssa. In the past, she'd always been a worst-case scenario thinker. Anyone who'd been missing for six whole months *had* to be dead. But this time, she was positive that they'd find Amanda by finding Hathaway. Instead . . .

The FBI agents heloed in from the Boston office were convinced that Amanda was the latest victim of a serial killer they'd been tracking for years. The Bureau was excited because, even though Steve Hathaway was an alias, for the first time, thanks to Randy Shahar, they had a photo of the man they were after.

"I liked her—Amanda," Alyssa told both Sam and Jules. Although she'd never met the woman, she'd read her diaries and talked with her friends. "I thought she'd found true love. I thought she was hiding from her father because she knew he'd be mad that she'd married the ski bum instead of the businessman. I actually pictured her with Hathaway in some little house with a white picket fence, living happily ever after." Instead, he'd probably made a necklace with her teeth. "God."

She looked up at Sam and told Jules, "Two months of marriage to Pollyanna here, and I've already moved into Sunnybrook Farm."

Jules didn't laugh. Instead, he sounded wistful. "That must be nice."

"Yeah, it is," Alyssa said. Sam was shaking his head over his new nickname. "It's scary, though. The potential for disappointment can be pretty high." As opposed to always expecting to be disappointed . . . "Look, Jules, I have to go. Thanks for calling."

"Anytime, sweets. Give Pollyanna a big, wet, sloppy kiss for me."

"I will." She hung up the phone.

"You know he's going to call me that, from now on," Sam said. "For the rest of my life. And, by the way, it's Rebecca who lives at Sunnybrook Farm. As opposed to Laura Wilder, who lives in that little house on the prairie. Pollyanna lives . . . Shit, I have no idea where Pollyanna lives."

"Come here," Alyssa said, moving toward him, meeting him halfway, in the middle of the couch. He put his arms around her, so that she was leaning back against him, her head beneath his chin.

Outside the window, dawn was putting on quite a show.

"Are you going to be able to sleep?" he asked. "Ever?"

She laughed, except it came out sounding like a sob, and his arms tightened around her. "I keep thinking, if only . . ."

"Don't," he said. He kissed the top of her head. "Just don't."

"I can't help it," she said. "I hate it when the bad guy wins."

"I know. But they're going to catch this one now," Sam said.

"I hope so."

"They will." He kissed her again. The way he put it, it was a *when*, not an *if*. He had no doubts whatsoever. For Sam, the future was filled with possibilities, not possible disappointments.

"Nice, huh?" he said as, outside the window, the brilliant colors of dawn—a new day—streaked the sky.

"Yeah," Alyssa said, loving the feeling of his arms around her. It was very nice, indeed.

For a sneak peek
at Suzanne Brockmann's

HOT TARGET,

please read on.

Available in bookstores everywhere
Published by Ballantine Books

COSMO'S MOTHER was driving him crazy.

Well, okay, to be fair, it wasn't his mom, but rather her choice of music that had pushed him out of her condo, into his truck, and back down the 5 to San Diego.

He parked in the lot next to the squat, ugly building that held the offices of Troubleshooters Incorporated. The sun was warm on the back of his neck, as he crossed to the entrance door. As usual, it was locked—apparently Tommy Paoletti had had no luck yet finding a receptionist for his personal security company. But he *had* installed a system that would allow him to let people in without having to run all the way to the door, twenty times a day.

A surveillance camera hung overhead, and Cosmo looked up at it, making sure Tommy would be able to see his face as he hit the bell.

The lock clicked open as a buzzer sounded, and Cosmo went inside.

"Grab some coffee, I'll be right out," Tom shouted from one of the back offices. "How's your mom?"

"Much better, thanks," Cosmo called back.

And she was. Right after the accident, when Cosmo had first gone to see her, she'd been in a lot of pain. Her face had been almost gray, and she'd looked old and frail, lying in that hospital bed.

But she'd been home a few days now and was feeling far more like her old self.

Which was great.

But, dear sweet Jesus, if he had to listen to the soundtrack from *Jekyll & Hyde* one more time, he was going to scream.

Cos took his coffee and sank down into one of the new leather sofas in the Troubleshooters waiting room. Buttery soft and a light shade of honey brown, they replaced the former mismatched collection of overstuffed chairs—thrift-shop rejects—that had cluttered the area in front of the receptionist's desk.

Whoa, the walls had been repainted, too.

Tom's wife, Kelly, had been threatening to redecorate for months, insisting that the image Tom was trying to establish for his new company shouldn't be "piss poor and tasteless to boot."

"Are you here for the meeting?"

Cosmo looked up. The woman coming down the hall toward him was a stranger. She was wearing a pinstriped suit that had been tailored to accentuate her feminine shape. Petite, with blond short-cut hair and delicate features in a launch-a-thousand-ships face, her blue eyes were coolly polite. Professional. Ivy-league intelligent.

Her hands were ring free. Both of them. Her fingernails were short, bitten down almost to the quick—a direct and intriguing contrast to the career-woman persona.

She took a few steps closer and tried again. "May I help you?"

"No, ma'am," he finally answered her, then mentally kicked himself. *Talk, asshole.* She mostly certainly could help him. He would love for her to help him. And at least be polite. "Thanks." More. Explain. "I'm waiting for Commander Paoletti."

She finally smiled, and it transformed her from breathtakingly beautiful to full-power-defibrilator gorgeous. He wanted to drop to his knees, and beg her to bear his children.

"You must be one of his SEALs," she said.

"Yes, ma'am." *Stand up, fool. But, Christ, don't spill the coffee. . . .* Too late. It splashed over the edge of the cup and onto his fingers. Gahhhhd, it was hot.

She pretended not to notice as he pretended that he hadn't just been scalded. She even held out her hand to shake. "I'm Sophia Ghaffari."

Sophia. It was a beautiful name, and by all rights, violins should have started playing when she said it. She looked like a Sophia, she dressed like a Sophia, she even smelled like a Sophia.

He tried to wipe his fingers dry on his pants, but it was hopeless. "Cosmo Richter. Sorry, I'm . . ."

. . . A freakin' idiot.

He crossed to the coffee setup, where he found some napkins, thank the Lord.

But Sophia didn't run out of the room screaming *Save me from cretins!*, as he wiped his hands. "You must be here to help out with the Mercedes Chadwick job."

"I'm not sure," he admitted, turning back to her. "Tommy said something about an easy op in L.A."

"That's the one." She was holding the files she was carrying against her chest with both arms. "She's a movie producer—and I guess a screenwriter, too. She's been getting death threats."

His chance to touch Sophia, to shake her hand, now that his hands were clean, had apparently passed. What a crying shame.

"Hey, Cos." Tom Paoletti came out from the back, smiling his welcome. He looked at Sophia. "Soph, you better get going if you're intending to catch that flight."

"Yeah. It was nice meeting you," Sophia told Cosmo.

As she hurried down the hall, Tom led Cosmo back toward his office. "You've got . . . how many weeks of leave left?"

"Three weeks, two days, seventeen hours."

His former SEAL CO smiled. "Well, at least you're not counting the minutes."

Cosmo glanced at his watch. And fourteen minutes.

"And you're sure you don't want to use this time as a vacation?" Tom asked.

"I'm quite sure, sir." Like many SEALs in Team Sixteen, Cosmo wasn't good at taking vacations. After just a few days, he got bored. Restless. "I just want to be able to check in on my mother once or twice a day." He got down to business. "So tell me about this Hollywood producer. What'd she do to piss people off enough to make them want to kill her?"

"I don't need personal protection—a team of bodyguards? God! This is absolutely ridiculous." Jane Chadwick told Patty, her new college intern.

Patty didn't seem convinced, so she turned to Robin, hoping for just a teensy bit of brotherly support.

But Robin wasn't paying attention. He was giving Patty one of his "hey there" smiles. The girl, naturally, was dazzled. Of course, she was impossibly young and didn't yet have the mileage that would enable her to see past Rob's gorgeous face to the lowlife womanizing scum within.

"Yo," Jane said, clapping her hands sharply. Half-brother. At times like this, it helped to remind herself that they shared only a fraction of their genetic makeup. "Robin. Focus. Patty, go call the studio back and tell them no. Thank you, but no. I'm perfectly safe. Be firm."

Unlike many young movie-loving girls who made the pilgrimage to Hollywood, Patty's freckled-face cuteness wasn't an act. She wore kneesocks and actually meant it. Jane didn't know her that well yet, but, unfortunately, being firm didn't seem to be high on Patty's skill list.

But at least she was out of Jane's office, closing the door behind her and releasing Rob from her captivating spell.

"If you touch her," Jane told him, "I will kill you and I will make it hurt."

"What?" Rob said. Mr. Innocent. He made that sound that was half laugh, half indignation. "Come on. I was just smiling at her."

One thing was certain, her too-handsome half-brother was a brilliant actor. If they could get this movie made, and—most important—if they could get it distributed and seen, he was going to be a star.

"Besides," he added, "you of all people shouldn't be making idle death threats."

That was supposed to be funny. Jane didn't crack a smile.

"That wasn't a threat," she said. "It was a promise. Let me put this in terms you'll understand, Sleazoid. If you sleep with her, she'll think she's your girlfriend. And when she finds out that she was merely your Friday night distraction, she'll be badly hurt. Now, maybe you don't give a rat's ass about Patty's feelings, but I do. And I also know what you do care about, so listen closely. If you break her heart, she will quit. And if she quits, you will become my personal assistant, and you won't have a single minute to yourself from that moment until we are done making *American Hero.* Which means, in sleazoid-speak, that it will be two months before you have sex again. Two. Months."

Her little brother laughed. "Relax, Janey. I'm not going to sleep with her."

Jane just looked at him. She liked Patty. A lot. The girl was smart, she was sweet, she was way overqualified for this glorified gofer position. The lack of backbone could be worked on—besides, Jane had plenty of that to go around.

Best of all, though, despite being paid only a stipend, Patty also liked Jane. It was a win/win situation.

As long as Robin kept his *own* little win zipped up tight inside his pants and out of the equation.

Problem was, Patty had a serious crush on Rob. Which meant that it was going to fall on him to keep his distance.

God help them all.

"You need to lighten up," her brother told her now. "What is it *Variety* calls you?" He reached for a copy of the trade magazine that was out and open on her desk, and started to read the latest section that Patty had highlighted. " 'Never too serious, party-girl producer and screenwriter Mercedes Chadwick heats things up at the Paradise. . . .' " He looked at her over the top of the oversized page. "Who are you, you too serious she-bitch, and what have you done with my real sister, the party-girl producer?"

Jane gave him the evil eye that she'd perfected back when she was six and he was four.

It didn't scare him as much anymore. "Look," he said, "I know you're freaked out by these e-mails—"

"But I'm not," Jane said. "I'm freaked out by the fact that the studio's freaked out. I don't need a bodyguard. Robbie, come on, it's just a few Internet crazies who—"

"Patty told me you got three hundred messages just today."

"No," she scoffed. "Well, yeah, but it's, like, three crazies, each sending a hundred e-mails."

"You're certain of that?"

"Yes," she told him.

Robin was silent, obviously not believing her.

"Really," she insisted. "How could this possibly be real?"

More silence. "Who's paying?" Robin finally asked.

"For my lifetime of sin?" Jane responded. "I am, apparently."

He gave her a get-serious look—which was vaguely oxymoronic. Robin, telling someone else to get serious. "For this added security that HeartSong Studios wants to set up," he clarified.

"They are," Jane said. Her budget for this film was already stretched thin. She was using her personal credit cards to pay for craft services. No way could she afford around-the-clock guards.

"Then I don't see what the big deal is," Rob said.

"You don't understand," Jane said. And he didn't. Her brother, while not exactly simple, presented his true self to the world at all times. Well, except for lying to her about Patty. . . .

Robin was a player and he didn't try to hide it. *Too many women, too little time*—he'd said as much in his first interview with *Entertainment Weekly*. Consummate actor that he was, he came across as charming. The reporter—a woman, natch—portrayed him as boyishly honest about his inability to resist temptation, rather than selfish and spoiled.

To be sure, his being spoiled was partly Jane's fault. As his older sister—well, after she'd ended that phase where her every waking moment was devoted to tormenting her wimpy little freak of a half-brother—she'd bent over backwards to try to make life as easy as possible for him.

It had been difficult growing up with their parents. Most weekends it was just Jane and Robin and their father's housekeeper, who was replaced with an even higher frequency than the stepmom of the moment, and rarely spoke English.

It was during one of those weekends that Jane first discovered that Robin's entire life reeked of neglect. His mother was referred to by her own mother as "that drunken bitch," so she probably shouldn't have been too surprised.

Somewhere down the line, just a few years before Robin's mother died and he moved in full-time with their father, she stopped being his chief tormentor and became his champion. His protector. His ally.

"What's not to understand?" he asked her now. "HeartBeat wants to hire a couple of bodyguards for you. Use it. Spin it into something that'll get us two, maybe three stories in the trades. If you do it right, maybe AP'll pick it up."

"I don't want a bodyguard following me around day and night." Jane's public persona, "Party Girl Producer Mercedes Chadwick," was as much a fictional character as any she'd ever created for one of her screenplays.

For the first time in her career—a crazy, seven-year ride that had started with a freak hit when she was still in film school—Jane was making a movie based on fact.

And was getting death threats because of it.

"I don't want to have to be the 'Party Girl Producer' here in my home," she told her brother. Her feet hurt just from the idea of wearing J. Mercedes Chadwick's dangerously high heels 24/7. Which she would have to do. Because her bodyguards would be watching her—that was the whole point of them being there, right?

And no way would she risk one of them giving an interview after the threat was over and done, saying, "Jane Chadwick? Yeah, the Mercedes thing is just BS. No really calls her that. She's actually very normal. Plain Jane, you know? Nothing special to look at without the trashy clothes and makeup. She works eighteen-hour days—which is deadly dull and boring, if you want to know the truth. All those guys she allegedly dates? It's all for show. The Party Girl Producer hasn't had a private party in her bedroom for close to two years."

Patty knocked on the door, opening it a crack to peek in. "I'm sorry," she reported. "They've set up a meeting here for four o'clock with the security firm they've hired—Troubleshooters Incorporated."

Jane closed her eyes at Patty's verb tense. *Hired.* "No," she said. "Tell them no. Leave off the thank you this time and—"

"I'm sorry,"—Patty looked as if she were going to cry,—"but the studio apparently called the FBI—"

"What?"

"And the authorities are taking the threats seriously. They're involved now—"

"The FBI?" Jane was on her feet.

Patty nodded. "Some important agent from DC is going to be here at four, too. He's already on his way."

It was very clear to Cosmo that J. Mercedes Chadwick couldn't believe what she was hearing.

"You're telling me," she repeated, making sure that she got it right, "that there are thousands of people—tens of thousands—who consider Chester Lord, a little-known Alabama District Court judge who's been dead since 1959, to be their personal hero?"

FBI Agent Jules Cassidy nodded. "Yes, ma'am. They call themselves the Freedom Network. Chester Lord wrote a number of books and—"

"This is a man who was über-conservative even for his time," she pointed out. "There are rumors that Judge Lord looked the other way and allowed lynchings—"

"I believe they refer to him as honest and old-fashioned," Jules told her. "And his son, Hal, was a highly decorated war hero—you surely know more about that part of it than I do. But I can tell you one thing. Apparently these people are very protective of the memories of both father and son, and they're not at all happy at the idea of you outing Hal in your movie."

Mercedes's assistant had put a copy of the *American Hero*

script onto the table in front of them, along with the warning that they could not take it out of this building.

Like . . . what? They were going to sell it on e-bay? Or give a copy of the most provocative scenes to a tabloid like the *National Voice*?

Cosmo flipped through it. It was the story of Jack Shelton and Harold "Hal" Lord—two young American soldiers who met in Paris in early 1945, toward the end of World War Two.

Hal was a highly decorated war hero, and because he spoke fluent German, he volunteered to be part of an Allied team determined to find out whether Hitler's scientists had succeeded in creating an atomic bomb. The movie alleged that Hal Lord was gay, but in total denial. He was not just in the closet, he was sitting so far in the back with his eyes shut, he couldn't even see the door.

Until Jack Shelton made the scene.

"Hal's own granddaughter has given our movie her blessing," Mercedes pointed out. "If you're looking for the sex, the first gay love scene isn't until page seventy-two."

Cos looked up, directly into her eyes, which were a remarkably pretty color. She was talking to him. She thought he was looking for . . .

"The hetero couple doesn't get it on until close to the end of the movie either—page seventy-nine," she continued. "I think you'll find it's all tastefully done. We fade to black in both of the romantic subplots. We've been very up-front about that, so I'm not sure why all those Internet crazies have their panties in a twist."

"I wasn't . . ." he started to say, but her attention was already back on Cassidy. Fine. Let her think whatever she wanted to think.

"Can we back up a bit?" Mercedes asked. "You said earlier that these Freedom people—all megathousands of them—have these weekend get-togethers up in, in . . . Monkey-Fuck, Idaho, where they sit around a campfire, doing what? Reciting eighty-seven-verse epic poems lauding the glory that was Chester 'Baby-Lyncher' Lord?"

"Well, we're not exactly sure what they do during their retreats," Jules told her. He was trying to keep this serious, but Cosmo could tell that "Monkey-Fuck" had him biting the insides of his cheeks. "They're pretty adamant about not letting outsiders into their inner circle. Still, whatever they do up there, we think it's probably more likely that it has to do with firearms rather than poetry."

"But whatever they're doing, they're doing it in Idaho, right?" she asked. "So I should be okay as long as I stay in California." She looked over at her assistant. "Patty, call Steve Spielberg with my regrets. I won't be able to attend his potato-picking party in Boise next week, gosh darn it."

Jules was hanging in. "Ms. Chadwick. With all due respect, yesterday this was a joke. But today the Freedom Network's involved. There have been several e-mails that have raised a red flag. I don't have the details yet, but my boss, Max Bhagat, is concerned. And believe me, when he becomes concerned, you should take it seriously."

Mercedes looked again at the computer documents Jules had given her—pages upon pages, printed directly from the Freedom Network's website. They included a sheet which had a picture of her face in the center of a bull's-eye target.

She laughed, but to Cosmo's ears it sounded a little forced. "This is priceless, you know. I couldn't buy this kind of publicity."

Her brother spoke, his voice sharp. "I think we've all agreed this has gone too far, Jane."

Mercedes—or Jane, as her brother called her—looked up at Cosmo, as if she'd somehow decided that she trusted him above everyone else in the room. "Am I really in danger?" she asked.

He put down the script. Not from him. Nothing moved him less than a woman like J. Mercedes Chadwick. Yes, she was beautiful, with a perfect oval of a face that hinted at a Middle Eastern ancestry. And that body . . .

He cleared his throat. "Lotta crazy people out there," he told her. She seemed to want more, so he kept going. "Seems like a no-brainer to me—letting us come in and provide security, letting HeartSong pay for it."

She looked down at that picture again, frowning slightly. And Cosmo suspected that it scared her more than she was willing to admit.

But she kept up her act. "They spelled my name wrong," she said.

"Yeah, but they got our address right," her brother pointed out.

There was silence then, as that bit of info sank in.

J. Mercedes finally sighed, swearing under her breath. Then she looked up again, directly at Cosmo. "How do we do this?" she asked. "How exactly is this going to work?"

Pillow Talk